PRAISE FOR
CITADEL OF THE SKY

"Make room, GRRM: Chrysoula Tzavelas knows how to bring on the pain.... This is a rare book that I have every intention of re-reading before I read its sequel, which, frankly, I would like to get my grabby little hands on right now."

— C. E. Murphy,
author of *The Walker Papers*

AND
INFINITY KEY

"Fast-paced.... In a genre that tends to emphasize young women's romances with male supernatural beings, this focus on female friendship and solidarity is deeply refreshing."

— *Publisher's Weekly*

BY CHRYSOULA TZAVELAS

THRONES OF THE FIRSTBORN

CITADEL OF THE SKY
GREEN WILD
SHRINE OF SUMMER

SENYAZA

MATCHBOX GIRLS
INFINITY KEY
WOLF INTERVAL
DIVINITY CIRCUIT

NIGHTLIGHTS

CHRYSOULA TZAVELAS

CITADEL OF THE SKY

THRONES OF THE FIRSTBORN
BOOK 1

DREAMFARMER PRESS
DREAMFARMER.NET

Dreamfarmer Press
www.dreamfarmer.net

CITADEL OF THE SKY
ISBN: 978-1-943197-00-2

This is a work of fiction. Names, characters, places, and
incidents either are the product of the author's imagination, and any resemblance to actual persons, living or dead,
events, or locales is entirely coincidental.

Cover art by Ravven Kitsune
www.ravven.com

Author's Note

There is a list of important members of the Regency and Justiciar's Courts, along with a family tree, at the back of the book. These can be referred to at will and may be useful if names get confusing. (Like many royal families, the Royal Family of Ceria tends to reuse name elements. I am only grateful I convinced them to not actually duplicate entire names.)

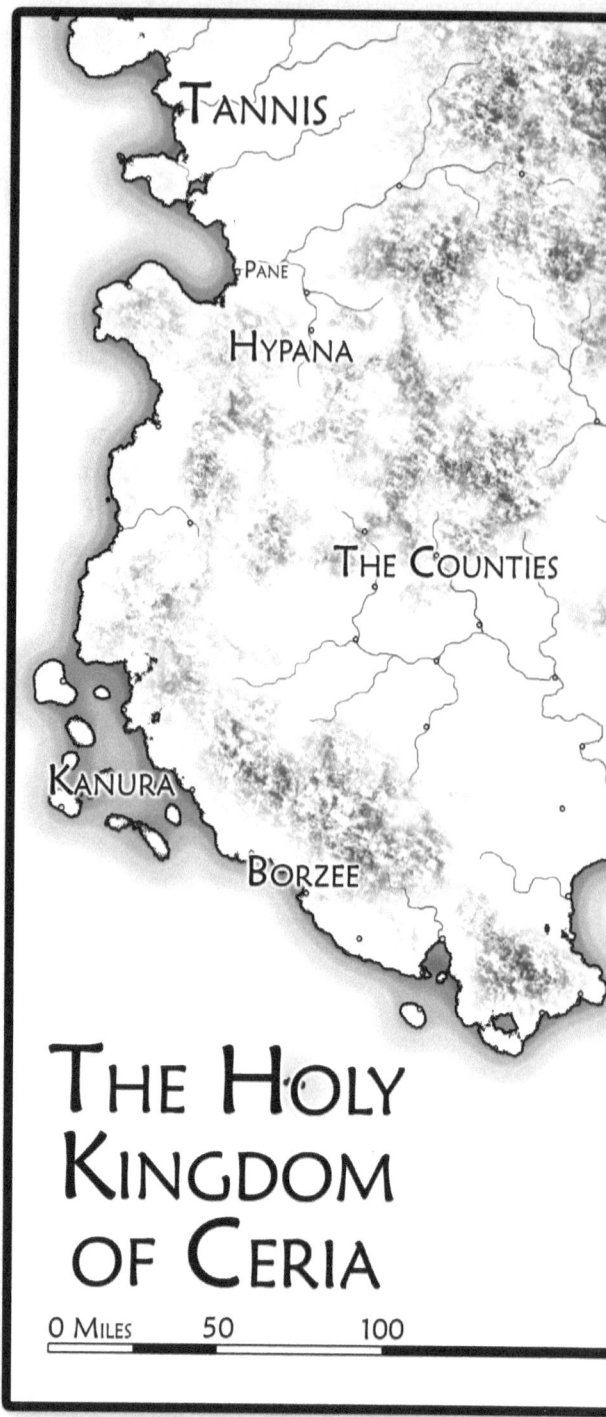

TANNIS

PANE

HYPANA

THE COUNTIES

KANURA

BORZEE

THE HOLY
KINGDOM
OF CERIA

0 MILES   50   100

VASSAY

LEIN

SEL SEVANTH

CITADEL
OF THE SKY

LOR SELENI

ARDOZA

LACHAN

MWATCH

EIRCEDE

SHELL COAST

HESEVIC

A

URA

CITADEL
OF THE SKY

For those who can't tie their own shoes: you can still manage to save the world.

CHAPTER ONE

TASTELESS

Great-Uncle Jant's Regent died of old age, and Cousin Cathay's Regent was thrown from his horse, and Uncle Yithiere's Regent had a heart attack, but it was all just bad luck until the King's Regent died. It took more than bad luck to tear somebody's arm off. It took a fiend, or a team of horses, or somebody really spiteful.

"Perhaps an eidolon," Princess Jerya observed to her companions. It was a rainy early morning two days after the tragedy, and the daughters of the King were waiting for the funeral procession to begin.

"What a horrible thought," Tiana, her younger sister, said. She looked critically at her lace gloves. "Do you think these are the proper gloves? The milliner swore they were ash-grey, but in this light, they look silver."

"Other people have suggested it already," said Jerya. "You'll hear it eventually. Best to be prepared." The wind gusted rain under the umbrellas held by their Regents, and Jerya clapped a hand on her hat.

Tiana frowned at her hand. "But eidolons are part of our magic. That's ridiculous. We all loved Tomas." As she considered, her expression grew more shocked, and she added, "How can you make accusations like that?"

Lisette, her Regent, touched her arm soothingly. "It's not an accusation."

Jerya said, "It's a problem, though. The Court won't let it go." She paused, reflective. "And they shouldn't. Look at Cathay." She nodded at their cousin, a handsome young man their own age, as he walked into the yard.

He was alone and soaked to the skin, oblivious to the rain. His hands were clenched into fists, and one of his cat eidolons prowled beside him, only half-real. "His Regent Sennic was an excellent rider, after all. Do you really believe his horse just threw him?"

Tiana pulled off a glove and crumpled it. "No one talked about murder at Sennic's funeral." She shook her head. "It's so tasteless, Jerya."

Jerya shrugged. "I'm just warning you. Others will bring it up. But as you wish. Look, here comes Father with Tomas now. Put your glove back on, it's fine."

The cavernous funeral carriage was pulled by six grey horses. When the footman opened the door, the Niyhani priest emerged first and then the Chancellor. He gave the princesses a grim nod of greeting and turned to steady the King as he stepped down. The King's six eidolons, all in his likeness, descended the stairs after him, more adroitly than their creator.

"I'm glad the Chancellor made sure he dressed appropriately," said Tiana, "but he should have a real escort. Poor Father. It breaks my heart." She looked away, at her hands again.

"He insisted," Jerya said. The Chancellor guided the King around to the back of the carriage, where the coffin was mounted under twin lanterns. The King looked startled, as if he'd forgotten why he was there. Then his eidolons flowed past him to lift the polished box.

He turned and looked at the three monolithic Royal mausoleums. His shoulders slumped. Then a seventh eidolon stepped out of him, and his face emptied of pain. The Chancellor took his arm again, and together they led the eidolons and their burden into the cemetery. Tiana and Jerya, along with their own human entourage, fell in behind him. Their other relatives followed after, and so Lord Tomas Ferya, King's Regent, was escorted to his final rest.

It wasn't like Sennic's funeral at all. Tiana disapproved. For one thing, it was raining, and it was hot. It was far too hot for a proper autumn rain. People had grieved at Sennic's funeral, not whispered and stared at the Royal Blood. She'd put a jade falcon into Sennic's basket, and she hadn't cared who watched her cry. But today, it was as if the sky was crying everyone's tears, and there were only nervous rustles from under the umbrellas as the Niyhani priest performed the rituals that accompanied the closure of a life.

As she passed by the casket, she put a painted porcelain mask into the funeral basket, next to Jerya's golden chain and her father's rosewood violin bow. Tomas had shared her affection for the theater, though he hadn't the time to lavish on it as she did. When they had been at dinner together, she told him the gossip of the Small-light District. Not anymore, though. It was an obvious little thought, with a shocking punch she pushed away.

She watched the crowd; better wandering eyes than looking at her father's distant gaze and his empty face. Her extended family was spread among the mourners, most of them absorbed in their own grief. Her uncle Yithiere was reserved and distant. Her cousin Shanasee seemed more concerned about the state of the sky. But little Gisen, the youngest of the Royal Blood and her Regent Yevonne hugged each other, and behind them, Cathay looked angry.

Other than the Blood, she only knew a small portion of those who gathered to bid the Crown Regent farewell: the Justiciars, her music teacher, a few of the nobles. The rest were strangers: nobles and bureaucrats, the less prominent members of the Regency and the Justiciar's Court, all turned out for a full state funeral. They whispered to each other. She caught herself scowling at them and straightened her expression carefully. It was no concern of hers if they were there to see and be seen, instead of to say goodbye.

Beyond the crowd, though, was someone she thought she should recognize: a woman with the distinctive dark coloring of the Blood. Although she resembled Tiana's family, Tiana had no idea who she was. Her hair was very long, nearly to her feet, and her face was as empty of emotion as the King's.

Tiana moved her head to catch the eye of Lisette, her Regent and best friend, but as she stared at the woman, the woman faded away, like spots on her eyes after she looked at the sun. Unease prickled at Tiana's neck, and she was suddenly uncertain the woman had ever existed. Was she staring at empty space? She averted her gaze and realized she was rubbing her thumbs together. She smoothed her dress instead and took a deep breath.

It was just the phantasmagory, another component

of her family's ancestral magic. If she wasn't strong, the phantasmagory could pull her mind away, leave her standing there senseless, or worse, half-aware and very dangerous. That was why each member of the Royal Blood had a Regent to help them.

The dreamlike phantasmagory offered unparalleled magical focus, private communication, and even escape from boredom and physical torment, but entry was not invisible. When a member of the Blood sent her soul to the phantasmagory, her eyes glowed with a pearly white sheen. She had to resist it; people were watching.

Under her wrap, she fumbled for Lisette's hand and Lisette squeezed her hand back reassuringly. She turned to her father at the foot of the bier. His eyes were black, not white. She had to be strong for him. Again, she rearranged her frown into something more pleasing. She was rewarded by her father's gaze focusing. He gave her a faint, worried smile.

The priest paced around the bier, waving an amber-tipped wand at the heavens and the earth, to the east and the west, invoking the Firstborn to carry Tomas's soul home. His assistant lit the incense, and the rising scents of sandalwood and jasmine overpowered the smell of the rain.

"Why is everyone so tolerant?" a man cried out. It was a tall man in a pleated grey coat, with wild chestnut hair tied with an ornate black ribbon. He looked like he hadn't slept in days. Tiana only knew his face, not his name.

"Lord Brehain, drinking companion to the Justiciar Lord Warrane," Lisette whispered to Tiana.

Lord Brehain's outburst continued. "Where are the honors due a Regent who died in execution of his highest duty? That was no peaceful death in bed, and yet he stands there unashamed." An unsteady finger pointed at King Shonathan.

Lord Warrane, nearby, snapped, "Be silent, you fool."

The Chancellor, maintaining his grip on the King, said, "We don't know what happened. We're investigating. At the moment, it looks like a terrible accident."

"An accident!" But Lord Warrane clapped a heavy hand on his shoulder and Brehain's speech stumbled to a halt.

The King spoke into the sudden silence, despite the Chancellor's hold. "I don't know myself," he said thoughtfully. "It almost seemed like an eidolon. Almost like one of mine. I counted mine, though. And that doesn't make any sense."

"Daddy, no!" said Tiana. Lisette held her hand tightly.

"What's the use of covering it up? There's never any punishment, never consequences." It was Lord Brehain again, apparently drunk or suicidal. "Bring it out, so everybody can grieve for everything properly, for this mad world—" This time Lord Warrane pulled him away, into the crowd.

Tiana called after him, "You don't deserve to be here."

Sharply, Jerya said, "Tiana, enough. I'll deal with this later."

The crowd murmured, but slowly settled back toward silence as the Niyhani priest gazed around expectantly. But just as quiet returned, and he raised his wand to provide the final benediction, someone shouted in alarm.

Something formed in the sky. In one distinct area, the path of the rainfall changed, spiraling like a tiny storm. Shadows rushed together, and borrowed color from the mourning clothes and the graveyard. In a final splash of magic that Tiana could feel in the back of her head, a creature, blurred and ragged, unfolded colorful taloned wings.

It descended, hovering over the bier. The strange, many-legged form had the washed-out unreality of an eidolon, but it was no shape Tiana was familiar with. It cried out, as if in response to the priest, a perfect clear note, and dived at the center of the crowd. Mourners scattered.

Tiana stared at it, not even bothering to duck. The tingling at the back of her head grew stronger, and she shook her head in irritation. "It's not ours," she complained. "We wouldn't do this!" She stomped her foot, staring at the creature. It couldn't be from her family. She refused to believe it. "Who made you?"

It dove a second time. Everyone was screaming and running. Rain fell through it, but its talons shredded umbrellas. The Chancellor and her uncle were urging the King under the cover of the Dawn Age mausoleum.

"Tiana!" called Jerya. "Get over here, under—"

A sparkling at the edge of her vision joined the tingling. She didn't care enough to hear the rest of what Jerya had to say. She focused on the alien eidolon. "I don't want you to exist."

It spiraled up into the sky again, and she was sure a rainbow eye was fixed on her, just as she was sure her own eyes were turning pearly white. Eidolons and the phantasmagory weren't the only magic of the Blood.

"Go away!" she shouted. She pushed her hand out, curved it into talons of her own, and slashed downwards. Gashes opened up within the shape, and she pulled her hand back, pushed it out again, then shook it like she was shaking rain off. The shape of the eidolon shook apart, until it was nothing but colors washing away in the rain.

Sullenly, she said, "Why do things like this happen? I try so hard." Then she sighed and let the phantasmagory take her before the embarrassment could.

CHAPTER TWO

WALK UNDER THE WORLD

The retreat into the phantasmagory was a slow, familiar descent. Detachment came first. Tiana watched incuriously as her Regent Lisette shoved the umbrella at her cousin Kiar and took her hand. *Let's walk,* she said. *Let's move our feet. That'll help.*

Tiana moved her feet. The colors of the world were melting around her, but that was hardly a bother. The rain against the umbrella was the sound of a heartbeat, until that faded away as well, and she was cocooned in a comfortable world of silent, grey cotton, only perceiving the phantasmagory.

Somewhere far away, her feet were moving. That was all right. Somewhere out there was Lisette, too. She trusted Lisette, just like Father trusted Tomas. That was what Regents were for. But Father didn't have Tomas anymore, so who was helping him walk?

One step after another, Tiana. We'll sit here, shh, shh, it's just me now. Lisette. Can I join you?

The soothing murmur continued as the grey veil parted, and pink hills under a yellow sky appeared. Her place. She was walking in a storm of blue and orange flowers. Somewhere far away, her feet weren't moving, but here, a butterfly floated beside her and she caught the petals in her hand. *Pretty, don't you think?*

A silver fish swam by, familiar and far away — a cousin. *Don't worry about her*, the butterfly said. *She's calm, too. There are no threats now.*

The grass became paving stones, became the tiles of the Palace. The storm of flowers became a salty rain. Who would Father trust? Who would kill Father's Regent? Was Father here, all alone, lost? But Lisette was the one she could trust, and the butterfly flapped its wings and flowers drifted out. *Let's go see*, the butterfly said. *If you're worried, let's see. I'm here.*

She could smell the flowers as she drifted down stone corridors, up stone steps, to where they'd found Tomas. It was near Father's rooms, very near. But no one could say Father hurt Tomas. That was ridiculous. Yet there Tomas was, his eyes wide and staring as they'd never been in life, and his body was so terrible, so twisted. She tried to pull the greyness back, tried to wash the colors away, but the phantasmagory was not kind.

The disappearing woman from the funeral, the woman Tiana thought she should know but didn't, knelt beside Tomas and closed his eyes. There were white flowers woven into her endless midnight hair, and her eyelids and lips were painted silver. Her gaze blank, she spread her hands, and a white lamb stumbled out of her. Then she and her lamb were no more, lost in the walls closing around Tiana.

She heard a heartbeat. Was it Tomas, alive again? But no, his body was twisted and broken. What had happened to his screams? Did they echo still in the walls, trapped by the mystery?

A heartbeat. It came from under her feet, loud and insistent.

The walls closing around her slid apart to reveal a staircase down. She descended, but the butterfly could not follow. It called after her, the perfume from its wings lingering in her nose, but there was a heartbeat and it called louder. She descended past the place where the kitchens stored the meat, past the old catacombs, into the ancient tunnels where only the foolhardy went. At each landing on the calling stair, a door closed behind her.

That was scary. There were stories of ancestors lost in the phantasmagory, their bodies left behind to die slowly. Would that be her? Further down she went, into dungeons she didn't know existed and a prison where nightmares writhed in stone.

She missed the butterfly, then.

She could no longer sense the faraway place where her body dwelled. Under the forgotten dungeon, the stairs ended at a door that was already closed. Behind it, something lived; something breathed and longed for escape. She reached out to open it.

But behind it was nothing at all.

Tiana opened her eyes. She was lying on the chaise longue beside the fireplace in her parlor. Someone had kindled a small fire and her cousin Kiar was adjusting a lamp on the west wall. The wan, grey light streaming in from the diamond-paned window told her it was past midday. A light blanket had been arranged over her, and she was still in the gown she'd worn to the funeral, though it had been loosened.

She sat up, kicking off the blanket. "What happened? Where's Lisette? I need her. And you."

Kiar stepped away from the lamp, brushing her hands off. "You went further into the phantasmagory than she could follow, she said. I couldn't find you either. Then you fell asleep. What happened?"

Tiana pushed herself to her feet. "Where is she?"

Kiar assessed Tiana until Tiana fidgeted under her stare. Kiar was a Royal bastard, but two years her elder and far more sensible. That was annoying, sometimes. "The Chancellor wanted to talk to her. He sent guards as an escort. About an hour ago, right after we got you back here. What's going on? Why so intense?"

Tiana went to her dressing room, leaving the door open, and twisted around to finish unbuttoning her dress. Her maid was nowhere to be seen. "Help me with this, won't you? There's some kind of sub-basement under the catacombs. There's a fiend down there! I think it's the one that killed Tomas. We should go find out."

Kiar stopped mid-reach. "Tiana…."

Tiana fumbled. "I'm serious! I saw it. Something is down there. Something that caused that *disaster* at the funeral. I need to deal with it." She yanked on the dress in frustration, and Kiar reached over to work the back buttons.

"If there is, *you* don't have to deal with it, especially when you're so… upset. Despite what the Regency is telling people, I'm almost certain there isn't a fiend in the castle. There would be signs."

"You mean, more than Tomas being murdered?" Tiana shrugged out of the formal dress and dug through baskets for an old, comfortable sundress.

"Yes, actually!" Kiar said. "Fiends leave impressions in the Logos. I looked around a little, right after Tomas was found. All I found was us."

"Shut up! It's not us!" Tiana's composure cracked. Then she muttered, "I'm sorry." She sought for distraction, the sundress almost over her head. "Did you talk to Twist, too?" Twist was the Royal Wizard and nominally Kiar's tutor in the ways of the Logos. Students of the Logos could do all sorts of things, from enchanting orbs to glow at a touch, to diagnosing obscure structural problems in buildings and people. Sometimes they could change the world just by speaking sternly to it.

At least, that's what happened in the stories and plays. In Tiana's experience, Twist mostly appeared places he couldn't possibly be and gave obscure advice, and Kiar spent a lot of time staring at things and muttering.

Kiar bit her lip, then said, "I'm sure he checked around on his own. He would have said something if he'd seen anything like that."

"Maybe he did, to the Chancellor."

Kiar worked on reassembling the formal dress on a hanger, rather than meeting Tiana's eyes or answering her. She did that a lot these days, whenever anyone brought up Twist.

Tiana sighed. "Well, that's why I need you, anyway. I *know* there's something down there, Kiar. Something alive. I could feel its heart beating."

Kiar said, "Tiana, you were really deep in the phantasmagory. Your eyes were glowing. You stopped talking, or moving. Lisette was terrified. And no one's sure what happened at the funeral, either. It scared Shanasee into the phantasmagory too, and that eidolon...."

"It couldn't have actually been an eidolon. Who would disrupt the funeral like that?" Tiana said firmly.

Kiar shook her head. "It wasn't a familiar one, but it was definitely an eidolon. Maybe whoever spawned that eidolon also spawned something that killed Tomas. No fiend necessary. Just another undiscovered bastard, screwing up." The hint of bitterness in Kiar's voice was old and familiar.

"Why is everyone so happy to believe we're murderers? No, don't answer that." Tiana could feel the undertow of the phantasmagory, closer than usual. She thought she could hear the heartbeat within, calling her. Taunting her. She wouldn't let it drive her mad. Pushing her feet into a pair of sturdy slippers, she said, "Come on, let's go find Lisette. I need her. Do you know if there are any maps of the catacombs in the library?"

In horrified fascination, Kiar said, "You really want to go down there, right now? You, me, and Lisette?"

"It doesn't have to be you, me, and Lisette. I could go by myself, without a map!" She stopped, modulated her voice. "And if there isn't a fiend, what is there to worry about?" She narrowed her eyes at the taller girl.

Acidly, Kiar said, "Falling rocks. Getting lost. Us." She paused and then said quietly, "I do know what it's like. To feel totally driven by a desire, out of nowhere. And I know what it's like to act on that desire. And I know what it's like to regret it, afterwards." She hesitated and then sighed. "And I know no wisdom in the world would have stopped me. No falling rocks, no locked doors, no hungry animals."

Tiana stopped dressing again. "Kiar...."

Kiar shook her head in a rejection of sympathy and opened the suite door. "Oh, hello, Lisette. Tiana has been asking for you."

Lisette was walking down the hall towards the suite, flanked by four men in Knights of the Regency tabards. She looked tired and irritated, and her chestnut hair had been plucked out of the elaborate braid she'd put it in for the funeral. But when she saw Tiana in the doorway, a smile lit up her face.

"You're awake! I'm so glad." She ran the last few steps to Tiana and embraced her. Then she held her by the shoulders, looking at her carefully. "What happened? What pulled you away?"

Tiana looked at the guards behind Lisette. Normally they guarded the entrances to the Palace and accompanied the Blood or Regents on expeditions. They looked uncomfortable this deep in the residential area of the Palace. "Why did the Chancellor want to see you?"

Lisette's breath hissed between her teeth. "He doesn't want any of the active Regents alone, ever again. If I'm not with you, I'm to have a Regency guard. And they're to escort me everywhere. He was very firm. Also, he rescheduled tomorrow's reception to next week, so no one has an excuse not to attend. And Pell's old Regent has agreed to come out of retirement to assist the King." Pell, one of the King's brothers, had been dead a decade now.

Tiana chewed her lip and considered the rescheduled reception. Then she blinked at the guards. "What, all four of them? That seems… crowded." Tiana frowned at the guards. She recognized faces, but only recalled one name.

That one, Lieutenant Slater, a tall, dark-haired man, cleared his throat. "Your Highness, only two of us will be escorting her Ladyship. The others are on their way to Lady Iriss. We'll try to be inconspicuous. Oh, and…." He cleared his throat and recited, sing-song, "The Chancellor has all faith in your ability to protect your lady companion when she is with you. Our presence is merely a precaution against an opportunistic assassin."

Then his eyebrows drew together, and he added in his own voice, "The King's tragedy is already too much for the Regency to bear." He nodded at two of the guards, and they bowed and continued down the hall. "This is Guardsman Berrin. He just transferred from Stormwatch. An old friend."

Berrin, who was almost as tall as Slater and far broader, said, "We *don't* want to get in the way of your usual pursuits, Your Highness." Then he grinned. "I'd be lying if I said I wasn't looking forward to attending some of those Small-light shows, though. We'll just be in the background. Lurking."

Slater said sharply, "Guardsman!" and Berrin ducked his head, still grinning.

Tiana was taken aback. "Oh. Well… now we're going to the library. Right, Kiar? The library?"

Kiar sighed. "It seems as good a place to start as any, Tiana."

"Right," said Tiana. She slipped past the guards and walked down the hall.

Lisette fell into step at Tiana's side. "Why are we going to the library?"

Tiana glanced at the guards trailing them and shrugged. "I want to look something up. I need Kiar to translate Aunt Rinta's catalog." Lisette responded to her vague answer with silence and a sympathetic smile.

The library was on the first and ground floors of the Palace. On the first floor, the paneled double doors opened to a lofty space encircled by galleries. Four fluted columns rose from the ground floor to the frescoed ceiling. Long, narrow windows along the west wall spilled dreary light across the tables and chairs dotting the worn carpet, while Logos-inscribed, flameless lights illuminated the shelves. Rolling ladders allowed access to the hardest to reach volumes. The reconstruction and organization of the library had been a family project for the previous generation, and now, with most of them dead, it was a lovely, pleasant, rarely visited space.

Tiana pulled her companions away from the entrance where the guards had stationed themselves, down one of the curving staircases to the ground floor. "I need to find maps of the catacombs. There's a level underneath it, with something down there. If I find it, I can prove no one killed Tomas."

Lisette asked, "You saw this in the phantasmagory?" Tiana nodded, and Lisette looked thoughtful. "If you wandered into an ancestor's construct, that could have pulled you away from me. That's very interesting."

Tiana flashed a smug look at Kiar, who shrugged. "I'm not a Regent and I don't have access to Regency journals like Lisette does, so don't give me that look. I have to base my opinions on my own experiences. The crazy, distracted, weird stuff."

"I'm not weird!" said Tiana, looking offended.

Lisette said, "Kiar, the Chancellor would still like to provide you a Regent, you know. He worries."

Kiar flinched from Lisette's words. "No, thank you. As long as the Regency agrees I don't require one, I don't want one. I don't get lost in the phantasmagory. I don't forget to eat. I can dress myself. And Yithiere will never legitimatize me. I like things the way they are."

Tiana looked back and forth between them and wondered

what the fiend below the Palace was doing. Kiar and Lisette were standing around talking about unimportant things while Tomas's murderer lurked somewhere. "Maps!" she said. "We need maps."

Aunt Rinta catalogued everything in the library before she died. Yithiere, her older brother, then convinced her it was a good idea to let him encrypt her work. After her death, he wasn't inclined to share the key, but Kiar had cracked it on her own. That was the sort of thing she did for fun.

Kiar led the way over to the catalog table, where a giant book sat open. "Any idea who to look for? Any ancestral names in the phantasmagory?"

Tiana shook her head, choosing to believe that was a serious question. "No names. There was a woman, but… there was something strange about her. I don't think she was real."

Lisette suggested, "Pell's journals? He did rebuild most of the Palace." Most of the Blood kept journals, although sometimes about very peculiar subjects or in peculiar forms. "Are they here, or did Yithiere remove them for safekeeping?"

Tiana thought that was a very diplomatic way to refer to obsessive theft. "Yes, find those. Jerya says he used to roam all over the old Palace. We went exploring with him once. Just before he found you, Kiar."

Kiar began to thumb through the catalog. "He was building Starset then. The kitchens hated it. The maids had to deliver lunch to him and his building crew every day, and it was always freezing up that high." She paused her turning of pages and said reflectively, "He almost claimed me as his own daughter, you know. He said, 'But I don't know if it will be easier for you, and I don't know if Yithiere would ever forgive me.' They came to look at me sometimes in the scullery. Two tall men, one nice, one scary." She shook her head and resumed paging through the catalog. "I'm not seeing the adult Pell in here, though."

"Yithiere or Cathay have them, then," said Lisette. Cathay was Pell's son.

Tiana said gloomily, "I'd rather not ask either of them." Yithiere was prickly, and Cathay would want something particular in return.

Lisette gave her another sympathetic look. "Cathay's very persistent, isn't he? But I doubt he'd be much of a bother today." She sighed. "He must be thinking about Sennic's death again."

Tiana scowled. "He wouldn't let anyone get near me at the last reception. He made fun of all my suitors."

Lisette said gravely, "And yet, you seemed to enjoy yourself."

Tiana's face warmed. "Well, it's Cathay."

With a little smile, Lisette said, "Yes, I know."

Tiana made a mournful face. "Do you miss him? I didn't mind, honest. I'd rather have things back the way they were." Regents couldn't marry, but chastity was neither expected, nor valued, in their service to Ceria.

Lisette shook her head. "You know it couldn't have lasted. It's his way. I expected him to move on to you or Kiar. I wish he wasn't so fickle, but I don't think he can help himself."

Tiana grumbled, "Well, Kiar doesn't even enjoy the receptions, so he couldn't ruin them for her. And she's taller. Why couldn't he have fixated on her instead?"

"Too blonde. He prefers brunettes," said Kiar absently. "Here, this is a list of topics. Let's look around in the library some more before involving anyone else."

"Architecture?" Lisette asked.

"Maps?" Tiana suggested, patiently.

"No such topic. 'Maps' refers to Geography." Staring at the book, Kiar muttered, "Rinta, what was the Palace to you? The Royal Library? Pell rebuilt that as well." She looked around the room and then back at the designation. "Over here." She led the way to the shelf. "Up there."

Tiana pushed the rolling ladder over and climbed up, pulling out a thick folio. It was loosely packed with documents and folded diagrams, and half its contents slipped out of the folio to flutter to the ground. On the floor above, Slater leaned against the railing, watching casually, until she glared at him. Then he raised his hands, lowered his eyes, and turned his back.

She handed the rest of the folio to Lisette and climbed down. "They're not going to like us taking you to the catacombs, off the usual strolls. After all, we could be planning to murder you. I've read that in Cylisse, Royal guards protect the royalty, they don't protect people *from* the royalty."

Not looking up from gathering the scattered documents, Lisette said, "No one thinks you're going to hurt me. Well, no one you should listen to, anyway."

"Yes, Tiana," Kiar added. "It's just another missed bastard. You know how much trouble they cause."

Tiana frowned at Kiar. Was she *trying* to pick a fight? Lisette handed the sheaf of papers to Kiar to sort, looking exasperated. "The two of you are quite the pair today. Kiar, no one thinks it's you, either. The Chancellor thinks that it's a bastard of the King who recently discovered his powers and is angry at being overlooked for so long."

Tiana was shocked. "There's no such thing. Father's never been with anyone else since Mama left." But Lisette just smiled in her soothing way.

Kiar, however, said, "That doesn't explain what happened to the other Regents. Or provide a motive for killing them, either."

Tiana sighed and took the book from Kiar. She went to the nearest table to spread out the contents, trying to pay no attention to the conversation.

Lisette said, "They were very different deaths! The Chancellor is assuming those were still natural." She glanced up at the guards. "He's just being careful."

Tiana unfolded a thick sheaf of paper and announced loudly, "Maps of the castle. With…" she peered closer, "notes on the construction. And dates. Old dates. When it was built, I suppose." She shuffled through the stack, tossing useless maps aside. Kiar grimaced and gathered them up again.

"Here! The catacombs!" Tiana sat down and smoothed the paper, focusing. Lisette read over her shoulder, and Kiar leaned across the table on the other side, reading upside down. "He says people used to *live* down there. Hundreds of years ago." She ran her finger across the fading penciled lines, tracing the common strolls.

Kiar flicked at her fingers. "Don't touch, Tiana. You'll make them fade faster. I'll get a scribe to recopy them in ink."

Tiana flipped through several pages of the catacombs and then back to higher levels of the castle, poring over the diagrams. Finally, she sat back, running her hands through her hair. "There should be a down staircase. I don't see that symbol, though." She fought against the rising tide of frustration that brought the *thump-thump* of the beating phantasmagory with it.

"Here, let me look." Kiar pulled the map away. "Well,

this is a down staircase symbol." She flipped quickly through the catacombs maps. "And no, there aren't any marked on the catacombs."

"Always so fast, Kiar," complimented Lisette.

Kiar's cheeks turned pink. "No, I'm not," she muttered, and flipped through the pages again. "Here, there's a door marked on the edge of the map. And here's another one." She leaned in to read the writing. "One's locked. The other leads to a collapsed stairway. He thinks there's a flooded sub-basement. The masonry there dates from… at least six hundred years ago. He's got a note to return and investigate further, but I guess he never got around to it." She looked up and her smile was brief and pleased.

"Locked doors are not a problem," said Tiana happily. "Come on. Let's get some lights and go see. If you can memorize it, we can leave the map here, Kiar."

Kiar's smile flashed again. "I don't have your father's gift for memorization. But I can recopy it. Hold on."

CHAPTER THREE

AND THROUGH THE STONE

Parts of the catacombs were clean and well-lit, with lamps maintained by the housekeeping staff. The main promenade was popular for strolling, and past generations had left a wealth of art on the walls to admire. Someone was employed to take care of those. Most days there was always somebody down here, cleaning or doing a restoration. Not today, though. Today was a day of mourning, even for the staff.

Both ancient frescoes and contemporary murals lined the wide corridors, illustrating the great victories of the Blood. The lamps occupied niches in the wall. Old sculpture and dusty crockery were casually displayed in some of the rooms that opened off the main promenade, alongside damaged carvings and wall segments rescued from one renovation or another. Tiana paused alongside one, looking through the archway at the broken mural someone was painstakingly reassembling.

It was old, showing an interpretation of the events surrounding the founding of Tiana's family. Shin Savanyel, seven feet tall and bearded, wielded a white sword against a shadowy figure that dominated half the fragment. The white sword was painted with the curls that indicated eidolons and emanations in older works; it was just a symbol for the family magic.

The shadow clearly represented the first Blighter, whom Shin had destroyed when it had risen up after the Firstborn's removal from the world. That part of the mural had been mostly reassembled, but the flecks and cracks made it seem like something hidden lurked under the shadow of faded paint.

Tiana shook her head and kept moving. Somewhere in the library she knew there were nearly-contemporary accounts of her ancestor's days. But they were written in an old dialect and hard to follow, and very often boring. Or so she'd read, in the forward of a novelization of a play commissioned in her great-grandmother's day, *The Chosen King*.

The play and novel made dusty history very exciting, and while Tiana was technically *aware* that probably Shin hadn't quite done those things that way and said those things and romanced those ladies, she had never seen how it mattered very much what had actually happened. It was all a very long time ago, and even the more recent histories always seemed to examine the older histories through the lens of *The Chosen King*.

It had all happened a long time ago, just like these murals had broken long ago. But someone was restoring them, and something was calling her from the depths of the phantasmagory. Something that *had* to be old. Maybe something even older than *The Chosen King*. It was disturbing.

Tiana, Kiar, Lisette, and the lurking bodyguards walked down the promenade, past other gallery rooms that Tiana ignored. Other corridors opened off the promenade too, untended depths only rarely explored by wanderers. They could be dangerous. Even the gallery curators preferred some kind of backup when looking for treasures.

Kiar led them down one of them, lifting up her lamp. "This way." She paused and looked at the floor. "I'm not sure if anyone's been here since Pell. Look, you can see a little vermin trail in the dust. Charming."

Tiana closed her fingers around the inscribed lightstone she'd taken from the library. They didn't need that much light, just to see vermin tracks.

Slater cleared his throat. "My Ladies, Your Highness... where are we going?" He raised his hands again as Tiana glanced at him. "Just curious."

"Exploring," she said. "You can stay behind, if you'd like."

"No, we can't," he said. He hesitated. "I'll get a lamp."

Kiar started walking again. After a while, she passed her lamp to Lisette so she could study her map. She led them into a room with a square door frame, which led to a sequence of rooms, each one perfectly square and completely empty. The plaster had long ago chipped from the stone walls, and there was no sign of the chambers' purpose. Their footsteps were odd, loud clicks. Tiana thought the ceilings were getting lower in each room.

Kiar paused at a doorway ornamented with carved vines. "Do you think Pell was so used to this he didn't bother to label it?" Her voice echoed.

Tiana opened her hand to let the lightstone illuminate a broad staircase and a sunken hall, far larger than could be lit by a single stone. Stacked columns supported a ceiling that definitely seemed too low. Kiar continued, "The door we're looking for is on the other side of this hall, down several more corridors." She descended the steps. "I suppose this was some kind of banquet hall, eight hundred years ago."

"Eight hundred years ago... that was when Shin brought the Blood into Ceria," Lisette said, and lifted the lamp higher. "I wonder if they danced here."

Tiana pointed ahead. "It's an Antecession chamber." There was a broad, shallow basin with a broken fountain in the stone floor. On the far side, a spillway opened into a deep, narrow pool, now dry and dusty. It looked like the channel stretched the rest of the hall; Tiana could just see the shadowy corners and the darkness of doorways.

She shuddered. "It's lonely down here. I'm glad we celebrate Antecession in the city now. Though I guess you'd like it more here, Kiar." The ritual holiday of Antecession involved a public performance, and Kiar hated public anything.

The corridor on the other side was narrower than the corridors they'd traversed thus far, and it had a mild downward slope. It took them past a room that Kiar guessed was an ancient kitchen, and past two intersections, until finally there were four steps down and a real door, rather than just an opening.

"Here we are. Metal, not wood," said Kiar. "It won't be easy to open." She gave Tiana an expectant look.

Tiana said, "Will you try the Logos?"

Kiar shook her head vigorously. "Absolutely not. Not down here. If I made a mistake, I could bring the whole ceiling down."

Tiana said, "You wouldn't make a mistake. You hardly ever make mistakes." When an encouraging smile only met with another head shake, Tiana sighed and went down the steps. That sort of cajolery always worked for Lisette.

She pressed her hands against the black door. It was cool and rough, and she could feel the ornamentation of the cast bronze, with shallow divots that might have once held gold. There was a ring in the center of the door, and she tugged on it, pushed on it, with as much effect as pushing on a wall. She slid her fingers to the edge of the door, where it fit against the jamb. It wasn't a tight fit, but it was close enough that she couldn't get her fingers around it. Then she stepped back and sat on the steps.

"First, I'll need to see what I can learn with an emanation." She thought that was more responsible than just knocking the door down.

"Don't *you* make the ceiling collapse," Kiar warned.

"This is the sort of magic I'm supposed to be good at, remember?" Eidolons were avatars of the Blood's will, but emanations were a far more direct manifestation of their power. She preferred to do things the normal, human way when she could, but this just wasn't the day for that.

Tiana narrowed her eyes at the door and stretched out one finger. A slender ribbon of phantasmal force emanated from the tip, glimmering like a prism in the lamplight. She swept the ribbon of pressure around the door, noting where it encountered resistance. Finally, she let her breath out and curled her hand up again.

"I think I can just cut through the connections linking it to the rest of the wall. Then I should be able to push it over. I wish I could see what was on the other side first." She looked hopefully at Kiar. Kiar only frowned in response. "Well, it doesn't matter. I have to go through, or all this murder business will get worse."

She extended her hand like a blade, and this time the emanation that she sent out was not pressure, but an edge, sharp and fast, biting through ancient stone, the warped metal, and the clots of mortar. By the time she was on the final side, eating through one of the hinges, she could tell that the door was sagging towards her, though it wasn't yet visible to the eye. "Back up, back up," she muttered, trying not to lose her focus. "Get out of the way!" The phantasmagory yawned beneath her, eager to pull her down and change her perspective.

She stumbled backwards, tripping over the stairs. She couldn't stop the magic. She hadn't prepared properly, she'd rushed, she was scared, and if she stopped now, she'd fall into the phantasmagory again. For the second time today. And then the door would fall on her.

A horrific metallic squealing twisted out from the door, rising in intensity as she tried to focus another emanation to press the door away from her. But the phantasmagory was still open, and the *thump-thump* of the presence she sought was getting louder. She couldn't hold on to two emanations without giving into the phantasmagory. Not today. Not now.

An arm hooked around her waist and lifted her over the stairs. Gasping, she released the door. It finished falling forward, smacking into the stone steps with a ringing clang. Beyond the door, the staircase continued down into darkness.

Berrin set Tiana on shaky legs. "Sorry about that, Your Highness."

Behind him, Slater removed his hands from Kiar and Lisette's arms. Kiar rubbed her arm, while Lisette favored him with a smile. Berrin coughed. "Didn't want you to get flattened, and it seemed like the door was leaning close."

"Thank you." Tiana took a deep breath. "I was careless. I should be more careful." Kiar nodded vigorously.

"Of course," said Berrin. He placed a boot experimentally on the fallen door and then pushed. The door vanished into the darkness. The noise was horrendous. The bottom edge thudded into a step and then screeched across the stone until it reached the edge, at which point it thudded again. The top edge rang like a poorly tuned bell on each step. The echoes grew louder and louder until the there was a final, ringing thud.

Slater found his voice. "Guardsman! Do you want to be transferred someplace even worse than Stormwatch?"

Berrin saluted. "Not possible, sir!" He bowed deeply to Tiana. "My apologies for not thinking things through!"

Kiar shook her head. "I wonder if that's why the other stair collapsed. If there is anything alive down here, it knows we're coming now." She peered down the narrow staircase. "It's really dark."

"I'll go first," said Berrin brightly.

Briskly, Tiana said, "Well, it's a good thing Shanasee isn't here, then." She raised the lightstone and marched down the stairs, pushing past Berrin.

The corridor at the bottom was narrow and lined with more open doorways. It was also far dirtier than the hall above, with dust thick on the floors and heavy, ancient cobwebs a shroud on the ceiling. Passing by the doorways, she saw that each one once had a metal door similar to the one at the top of the stairs, and in each chamber, the door had fallen inwards. The rooms beyond were painfully small. She remembered the vision in the phantasmagory and shuddered. "A prison."

"Or a cloister," Lisette said. "Before Shin came, the Niyhani Magisters lived here, after all." Tiana didn't realize she had stopped moving until Lisette squeezed her hand.

"There were... nightmares living here, in the phantasmagory. Somebody's very bad memories."

"Would you like to go back? Is this what you came for?"

Tiana shook her head. "No. Below...." She pointed into the darkness. The cobwebs seemed to catch the light, swallowing it, so that the darkness was more than simply a lack of illumination. It had depth to it, a murk that made Tiana suddenly understand a little of her cousin Shanasee's fear of the dark. But Shanasee was ruled by her fears, and Tiana couldn't let that happen to her.

She said, "We have to find it, for Tomas. We'll solve the mystery. We're..." She sought for the right word. "We're plucky." When Kiar rolled her eyes, she quoted, "'Pluck up your courage, my dears. We go forward.'"

Behind her, Kiar completed the quotation: "Into the heart of the maelstrom." She muttered, "Didn't some of them fail to come back?"

Tiana ignored this. She moved her feet forward. The dust muffled her footsteps, hid her feet in the clouds she kicked up. At the end of the long, crowded corridor, there was another staircase down. It was a half-spiral, so that the bottom was just out of sight of the top. Tiana hesitated. Then the others moved up behind her, and moving forward was easier than backing down.

There was another black, corroded door, but this time, a disc of bright gold was pressed into the door just above the ring. The seal of the Blood was pressed into the gold, as were the marks of Niyhan and the other three Firstborn. Inscribed above them, in heavy, ponderous lettering, it said

'Let The Shadow Sleep Forever.'

Tiana squeezed her eyes shut and passed her hand over the gold seal, feeling the texture of the impression. Then she pressed her ear against it, listening. She heard the low murmur of the guards above, Lisette's breath as she waited a few steps higher, and Kiar's lighter voice as she said something to the guards. From the metal and the stone, there was only silence.

"Will this door open?" asked Lisette. "What does the cartouche say?" Tiana moved her head out of the way. Lisette read it and then called, "Kiar…."

Kiar poked her head around the curve, blinked, and said, "That's distressing. Somebody wanted that door to remain closed."

"I'm sure it's locked, then." Tiana found that her hand was on the brass ring. Experimentally, she pushed.

With a creak, the door swung open.

A long silence followed, until Kiar said, "Is this it?"

The room beyond was uninhabited. Lamplight illuminated some stone furniture, but other than that, it was empty. There was no other way out. At first glance, it was beyond disappointing.

Then Lisette said, "There aren't any cobwebs. There's hardly any dust at all."

Tiana moved into the room, feeling warm and tingly. Was this it? Was this the source of the heartbeat? But there was nothing here. Just the *thump-thump, thump-thump, thump-thump, thump-thump, thump*—

"Just furniture," said Kiar from the door. "None of the other rooms above had furniture. If they left anything behind, it must have fallen to dust long ago. But this is made of stone."

Tiana tried to focus on something other than the throbbing heartbeat of the phantasmagory. There was a rounded stool and table of white stone situated in the center of the room. Somebody sitting at the table would have their back to the door. On the table was a plain casket of yellow bone.

She set the lightstone on the table and pulled the box closer. Agitated, Kiar said, "Tiana, there isn't a fiend down here. There's nothing alive. Maybe we should think about this again."

Tiana looked up, puzzled. "Can't you hear it here? How can you ignore the phantasmagory when it's so loud?"

Kiar stared at her, then inhaled through her teeth. Her eyes fluttered closed. When they opened, they were pale silver instead of Blood black, just as Tiana knew her own were. Lisette, standing between them, opened and then closed her mouth.

In a strained voice, Kiar said, "I hear it. Oh, Lord of Winter. There's something here! What—" she jerked, her gaze traveling up to the ceiling of the room. "There's— it's—" She whirled around, her eyes brightening to a cloud-white sheen.

Behind her, Lisette gathered herself together and moved beside Kiar, touching her arm and murmuring familiar phrases.

Kiar was not as comfortable with the phantasmagory as Tiana. Lisette could draw her out just as she could draw Tiana out, soothe her waking nightmares before they became manifest, just as she soothed Tiana's. But the panic of someone else lost in the phantasmagory created an undertow, treacherous and powerful, threatening to entangle Tiana within her own chaos. She closed her eyes to try and drown out the heartbeat and push the phantasmagory far away.

She could be normal if she tried. She was very proud of that. She had real friends, outside the court, outside her family. There were people who understood how much she wanted to be like them. The theater. At the theater, a special kind of magic happened. It was like the phantasmagory, but outside, where everyone could share it. She imagined the curtains closing on the phantasmagory.

"I'm here," said Kiar. "I'm better. I'm sorry. I saw… it doesn't matter. It wasn't useful, just my own bad memories. I'm sorry. But you're right. There's something here. I've never fallen so easily. Tiana?"

Tiana realized Kiar was talking to her. "Oh. Don't apologize. I understand. I'm going to open the box now."

Kiar nodded, moving closer. The surface of the box was cool and just barely uneven. The bone jewelry boxes Tiana had were all ornamented with carvings and wire and glass beads. But this one was smooth and darkened with age, the size of both her hands put side by side. There was a clasp. She opened it.

The heartbeat in the phantasmagory stopped.

The box slipped out of fingers suddenly nerveless with dread, spilling the large opal pendant inside onto the table. Tiana stared at it in silent horror. She recognized it.

Kiar stepped back. "That's the Royal Pendant. The King is supposed to be wearing it. How did it get down here?"

Tiana found her voice. "How did it *break*?" A deep, viridian flaw ran up one side of the opal and, within the flaw, the stone had shattered.

CHAPTER FOUR

LET IT SPIN

Tiana stared at the pendant. In a faraway voice, she asked, "Kiar, do you know what time it is?"

Kiar frowned and looked inward. "Almost six. What are you going to do with the pendant?"

"Oh, no, already?" Ordinary life reasserted itself. Tiana snatched up the jewel. "You take the box, Kiar. We can ask Father about it tomorrow. But I have to get to the theater!"

Kiar picked up the bone box. "What? How can you think of the theater after a find like this?"

"It's been here this long; it can wait until morning! I'm going to be late and I said I'd be there!"

Lisette said, "Tiana, nobody would blame you for staying home today."

Tiana looked sideways at Lisette. "After a day like today, I've got to go."

Lisette studied Tiana and then nodded. Kiar blew out her breath. "Well, let's get out of here, before something collapses."

On the catacombs level, Tiana started for the main gate of the Palace. Lisette said, "Tiana, you want to change clothes."

"Zenith!" Tiana swore. She looked down at her filthy sundress. "I do. Yuck. I don't have time!" But she ran up the wide, curving stone staircase all the same. She was out of breath by the time she made it to her rooms, but when Lisette showed up, she was wheezing. The guards, jogging behind her, were hardly winded.

"Take a rest, Lisette," Tiana called as she dropped the pendant on a table and hurried into the dressing closet. She pulled a dusky rose walking gown over her head, and washed her face and feet. Then she peered at herself in the mirror. Her morning's makeup was beyond salvaging, so she washed it off. She spread a drop of lavender oil through her hair with her fingers, followed it up with a comb. Then she sat down to lace up her city boots.

They were her favorite boots, made of tan calfskin with silken laces. There were nine pairs of eyelets up the front and six up the inside calf. She got her left front entirely laced before she realized that she'd missed an eyelet, which left the pairs askew. She took a deep breath and relaced. After a second time through, she paused and stared at the lacing, trying to decide if she'd done it correctly this time. She only counted eight pairs. Where had the ninth one gone?

It had to be close to seven. She didn't have time to get confused about how her boots went on. She laced up the inside left eyelets and realized she was using the wrong set of laces. It couldn't be helped. Right boot on.

She stared at her hands. They seemed like normal hands. Why couldn't she do normal tasks? She pulled her fingers away from the laces and wiggled them. Ribbons of emanation appeared, and she stared, fascinated, as the tendrils tied the laces into knots.

The clock in Starset tolled. Tiana jumped and realized she'd been staring at her hands for far too long. Lisette appeared at the dressing room door. "Did you change your mind?"

"No! It's these boots. They're complicated." Tiana put her hands over her face and then dropped them, steadfastly ignoring an old, familiar shame.

Lisette knelt in front of her. "Untie the knots." Obediently, Tiana wiggled her fingers again, and an emanation pulled the knots apart. Then, swiftly, Lisette laced up both boots.

"It's just been a long day," Tiana said, watching Lisette's hands fly.

Lisette stood up again when she was done. "You can run, if you'd like."

Tiana hesitated. "No. I don't want to leave you behind. Let's just walk. Very quickly."

They hurried through the Palace. There was an excellent sunset visible from the conservatory on the west wall, but the crimson rays streaking across the slopes of the mountain Sel Sevanth just made Tiana even more agitated. She was late, and she was very conscious of the two guards behind her. Her friends at the theater would not be comfortable. Maybe her escort could stay outside.

Emerging from the Palace, she was abruptly reminded that she hadn't eaten since breakfast. A cart nearby was selling stuffed pastries to some pilgrims, and they smelled heavenly. "Did you have lunch while I was sleeping, Lisette?"

Lisette shook her head. "Just a snack."

Tiana revised her earlier decision. "That won't do. Here, pick up some pastries for us, and meet me at the theater. I'll go on ahead, so I'm not even later."

Lisette looked grateful. "Yes, of course."

Tiana was pleased she didn't argue. "Make sure to get some bean sauce!" Then she held up her skirt and ran. There was a reason she loved her city boots, even if they were complicated to lace up.

Alone, she hurried down Brief Street and through the remnants of the Silk Market as it closed for the day. Grey bunting hung from many of the shops to honor the passing of the Crown Regent, but business carried on as usual. Many city folk recognized her and called out greetings, pulling their children and carts out of her way when they realized she was in a hurry. She smiled at them as she passed. A group of mounted nobles pulled their mounts to a halt, and their greetings were far cooler. She smiled at them as well. Lisette said it always helped to smile.

The Small-light District, south of the Silk Market and west of the Spice Market, was home to half a dozen theaters, but Tiana's favorite was the Let It Spin. It was a new building, constructed in Tiana's lifetime, and she'd watched every show put on its oval stage. The jointed dancer of bronze spun on its roof in the hot evening.

She'd been invited on backstage tours, and even once held a party for the luminaries of the Small-light District, but it was only this year that she'd actually been invited to help make the magic happen. Her favorite director was putting on a new show by a popular playwright, and the owner of the theater had invited Tiana to be a producer.

She was still learning what was involved with being a producer, so the owner of the theater handled most of the details. But she was having a grand time sharing her opinions on costumes and sets, and she was pleased to help offset the costs of a first-rate production.

She pushed open one of the double doors and slipped through the lobby into the theater. There was a rehearsal in progress. The director, Maidre, was standing before the stage, watching. Deneris, the playwright, and Baxer, the theater's owner, were sitting halfway back, on the tier with the comfortable seats. She seated herself in the row behind them.

"Your Highness," said Baxer, leaning back to greet her. He was younger than her uncle Yithiere, with thinning, dirty blond hair. "We didn't expect to see you here today. And without your lady? However did you escape her?"

"Oh, no," she said. "I had to come today. I've missed so much." She shook her head. "Lisette will be along."

Deneris tapped a finger against his mustache and said, "We're all bereft by the loss of the Crown Regent. We've had no shows at all since the news, so that our players could honor him. Maidre insisted on today's rehearsal."

Tiana looked down, uncomfortable. "That's perfectly understandable. How is the show going?" She tried to focus on the stage. It was lit by both a chandelier and a row of small lamps along its base, partially hidden behind a dark veil. "That's not our star, is it?"

Deneris sounded tired. "No. That's someone new. One of the little dramas you missed. Our girl Chenye has gone off to visit a sick sister in the hinterlands. Maidre was not pleased."

Baxer chuckled. "Told Chenye she'd never star in a show again." He always seemed to find the interactions between the luminaries of the Small-light District amusing.

Tiana watched the rehearsal for a few minutes. "She's not very good, is she? I don't know her."

"Just fell off the vegetable cart last week," said Baxer

cheerfully. "In the right place at the right time. Maidre aims to show Chenye a thing or two." Judging from her tone of voice, Maidre was just as unhappy with the new actress's performance.

Tiana leaned back again, wondering if there'd need to be a costume change. The new actress had a farm girl tan that wouldn't go with the ivory gown Tiana had paid for. She tapped her thumbs together, considering. Leaf-green, perhaps?

Someone sat down next to her. It wasn't Lisette. After a moment, Tiana realized it was the vanishing woman from the phantasmagory. Her arms rested on the wooden panels that divided the comfortable seats, and she sat back, but her head was turned towards Tiana. Her eyes were black from rim to rim, and she had no expression.

Tiana squeezed her eyes shut and shook her head. The woman sat there still when she opened her eyes. Her astonishingly long hair fell over the back of the seat and pooled on the floor behind her, and she was wearing a high-necked, plum-colored gown. Tiana leaned forward, and the woman's head turned to follow her.

It was just stress. Sometimes, when the Blood was overstressed, they saw things that weren't really there. Everyone knew it. She couldn't control it, but she could control her reaction. She wanted to be different, and if she could make other people think she was different, that was practically the same thing.

So she set her jaw and said, "How are the theater modifications coming along?"

Baxer gave her a sidelong glance. "Reasonably well, although—" he shook his head.

"What? Please, tell me."

He crooked a smile. "The lights are always a problem. Blaine talks about what we could do with some inscribed lights, the ones that don't use fire. Like those at the Palace."

Tiana sat back again. "Oh, is that all? The Magister of Niyhani brings us a new supply every year when he visits for Antecession. I'm sure I can get a few then. They wear out, you know."

Baxer looked surprised. "Well… that's very kind of you, Your Highness."

Deneris frowned and said, "We don't need them, Baxer. You shouldn't—"

The door to the lobby opened and closed, and she heard the soft voice of Lisette telling the guards to wait there.

"No, no, it's fine," said Tiana hastily. "I can see the advantage. It'll be splendid."

Then Lisette sat down beside Tiana, in the seat occupied by the phantasmagory woman. "What will be splendid?" She passed Tiana a wrapped pastry.

It was still warm, but Tiana's appetite fled at the sight of Lisette overlapping the ghost. There was the glint of bone at the intersection of flesh and ghost.

Baxer said, "The show, Your Ladyship. Her Highness's assistance guarantees it will be like nothing the District has seen before."

Suspiciously, Lisette said, "Do I need to sign another letter of credit? Producing a play is far more *expensive* than I expected."

"No, no," said Deneris, giving Baxer another frown. "No, we're doing just fine."

Tiana risked a look up. The ghost was still overlapping Lisette. She couldn't bear it. She pushed the pastry back into Lisette's hands. Then she extended a single finger of emanation and poked the ghost, trying to scrape the hallucination off Lisette. After a moment, a spark of white flared in the ghost's eyes, and she vanished entirely.

Tiana released the emanation and blew out her breath. Only then did she realize that Baxer was carefully looking away, while Deneris was staring in open concern. Horror flooded through her as she realized what she'd done. She opened and closed her mouth, unable to even imagine any reasonable explanation other than what they'd seen with their own eyes: Tiana using her magic to poke Lisette. She lowered her gaze as tears filled her eyes, blinking rapidly to keep them from falling.

Lisette put her hand on Tiana's own, a silent, comforting gesture. Deneris said kindly, "You've had a terrible week. I imagine the Crown Regent must have been like a second father to you."

"Everybody's very frightened 'round these parts. Wondering where a fiend might appear next," said Baxer.

"I assume by 'round these parts,' you mean in the taverns," said Lisette, her voice cool.

Why does she disapprove of them so? But the thought drowned under the ocean of grief that Deneris's words had unveiled. Not her second father, but half her father, and he was gone, in a burst of strange and horrific violence. He would not be there tomorrow to hear about the fight between Maidre and her star. He was *gone*.

The phantasmagory called her to go and weep among her memories, but she had never, *never*, gone into the phantasmagory while at the theater. But if she didn't— The lump in her throat was growing larger. Lisette and the others were talking, but their words were just a buzz. The sobs were going to escape, no matter what she did. There was just no way to stop them and why should she? Tomas was gone. How could a play compete with that? How could an entire theater district?

She stood up. Lisette was standing, as well. "I have to leave," Tiana explained, blinking rapidly, holding a hand in front of her mouth. "I do miss him, very much. I have to go." Then she was running out of the theater.

No matter what, she had embarrassed herself. But Tomas mattered more. She'd find his killer, and maybe that would let the show go on.

CHAPTER FIVE

THE GEOMETRY OF TRUTH

Kiar wasn't surprised when Tiana didn't knock on her door until late in the morning. Her cousin was not traditionally a morning person. She much preferred to stay up late indulging her taste for fairy tales and melodramatic plays.

Still, Kiar was surprised to see the dark circles under Tiana's eyes. Lisette, beside her, looked ragged. It wasn't that Kiar expected Tiana to have slept well after the day before. It was that both princess and Regent were far more concerned with appearances than Kiar could ever manage to be. That they'd emerged in any kind of disarray was unsettling.

Tiana silently held up the Royal Pendant.

Kiar observed, "You look exhausted."

Tiana only said, "It was a long night," and tucked the pendant into the sash around her waist.

Kiar reached out and took Tiana's hand, letting a sympathetic squeeze say what she couldn't quite put into words. *Yesterday was so very hard.* Tiana was a dreamer who refused to face reality unless forced to, but they'd grown up together, and Kiar cared for her more than she could say.

Then she turned away. "Here, I'll get the box. I've been studying it. I think it's been worn smooth through use, somebody touching it over and over." She folded a crimson piece of silk around the bone box and picked it up.

She considered inquiring after Tiana's show, but she always took her cues on social encounters from Lisette, and Lisette was very quiet this morning as well. All she said was, "Jerya, Iriss, and the King are in the Southern Solar this morning."

Violin music drifted out of the ajar doors of the solar. It was a small room, crowded with far more chairs and tables and music stands than Kiar preferred. She did enjoy the three large windows overlooking the Justiciar's Courtyard, though. At the moment, one of them was blocked by several of the King's eidolons, and the second was hidden behind the bulk of the Royal Music Master. The guards assigned to Iriss, the Crown Princess's Regent, were sitting on the edge of chairs, but sprang to their feet when Kiar opened the doors.

Iriss played a viola, while Jerya and King Shonathan played violins. Kiar recognized the remembrance hymn "Memory Moon." It was traditionally performed at the Mymoria celebration at the end of the year.

The Royal Music Master turned around as "Memory Moon" completed and immediately focused on Tiana. "It's Her Serene Highness! My dear, have you been practicing? How is your voice?"

Taken aback, Tiana said "Practicing? For what?"

The Music Master was astonished. "Why, for Antecession. It's quite soon. Her Royal Highness insisted on a lesson today, despite...." He closed his mouth and shook his head.

Bewildered, Tiana said, "What, already? What happened to Kiprin?"

Lisette said, "You spent it hiding from Cathay, remember? You thought he might try to ask you for a Kiprin Favor."

"Oh, yes," said Tiana gloomily. Kiar hid a smile. It was easy for her to be amused; as a bastard of the Blood, she wasn't required to publicly participate in the yearly cycle of holy day rituals the Royal Blood led.

"My dear, the voice is an instrument just as the violin is. You cannot simply expect to," the Music Master grimaced, "belt out a tune for Antecession."

Hastily, Tiana said, "Yes, of course. I'm ready! Lisette and I sing every week." Then, more formally, she said, "Master, I apologize for interrupting your lesson, but I need to speak with my father privately. Perhaps you could visit my cousins while you're here?"

"Oh?" the Master rumbled. "Yes, I was planning to look in on Her Little Highness while I was here." He looked between Kiar and Tiana, and then shook his head again. "Of course, of course. I'll just gather up my notes, shall I?" He perambulated around the room, picking up papers and muttering to himself.

Finally he heaved himself over to the door, which the guards had opened wide. "Yes, well. Watch that fingering, Iriss. I'll just go see Princess Gisen, shall I? Yes."

After the Music Master passed through, Slater bowed and closed the door with all four guards outside, leaving the Blood and their Regents in relative privacy.

"He's a good fellow," said the King fondly. "Always has the most delightful little stories. But good morning, Tiana, Kiar, Lisette." He sounded cheerful, but he had the same shadows under his eyes that Tiana had. Jerya, on the other hand, looked flawless. Kiar avoided make-up herself, but she could appreciate Jerya's mastery of the art of appearance.

Jerya said, "We've been playing for an hour. It's good to have a break. And I think Father is feeling better. Aren't you, Daddy?" To the others, she explained, "Father had an argument with the Chancellor about a new Regent. He's quite happy with his manservant for now."

"Yes, thank you, Jerya. You and Iriss have been very comforting." A third eidolon drifted out of him and joined the first two by the window. "I miss Tomas but I understand that sometimes these things happen. And I'm not lonely, of course." He gestured at his eidolons.

Tiana bit her lip. "We went exploring down in the catacombs yesterday. Down to places I don't think anybody has walked in centuries. And we found... something odd." She hesitated a long moment and then said, "Daddy, do you know where the Royal Pendant is?"

He frowned and looked around uncertainly, patting the table beside him. The three eidolons all turned to stare at Tiana. Then he looked down his shirt. "I'm wearing it."

Tiana said, "Are you sure?"

He smiled in a way that was becoming less and less common. "Yes, Tiana. I look at it every day." He pulled out a twin to the pendant they had found. One of his eidolon companions reached for the pendant, but he lifted it away.

Silently, Tiana let her own pendant dangle from the chain wrapped around her fist. The King cocked his head. "Is that real?" Another of his eidolons drifted forward and Tiana allowed it to brush spectral fingers over the pendant. The King's eyes flashed to white and then to black again. "How... amazing. You found this in the catacombs?"

Kiar turned her head, comparing the pendants. "They're the same, Tiana. Look. His is cracked as well."

The King looked down at the amulet resting on his chest and covered it with his hand. Then he sighed and lifted the pendant over his head. "Yes."

"Daddy!" said Jerya, surprised. "Has it always been cracked? It hasn't, has it?" She wrinkled her brow. "You used to wear it on the outside, right after Math died." Kiar was impressed Jerya remembered that; she couldn't have been more than three when King Math died. Maybe she'd inherited a touch of King Shonathan's famously perfect memory.

The King looked ashamed. "It hasn't. But it cracked many years ago. We didn't... we didn't ever tell anyone. Because it was our fault. An artifact from the time of Shin, a symbol of the Blood, and we allowed it to be cracked! I only ever wore it out at the big ceremonies, and, well, everybody was looking at Tomas then, not me. I always meant to tell... someone, but... these things slip away, you see. And then suddenly it's a confession, and there's hardly ever a good time for a confession. I thought perhaps I'd tell you, at least, Jerya, someday. If only because how it cracked was interesting. To the monarchs, you understand. That's what Hook said."

Jerya shook her head. "It's just jewelry, it's not even magically inscribed. But tell us the story, Daddy."

One of the eidolons snapped, "Let him gather his thoughts, you wretched girl," while the others grumbled.

The King waved his hand soothingly at his companions. "It's an ancient family heirloom, they have every right to know the story. To call me to task like an errant child." His mouth thinned. Then he murmured, "But I do need to gather my thoughts, as it were."

Iriss ran her fingers lightly over her viola's strings and

said, "Your Majesty, I know a jeweler who might be able to repair the fracture, so please don't worry about that. He says opals have some unique properties." She added, "You shouldn't have to bear such a burden alone. We're here to help."

The King drew in a deep breath. "A month after Tiana's first birthday, Hook—that was the previous Royal Wizard, Tiana—came to me and asked to borrow the Royal Pendant. He thought that it had some kind of connection to, well... the fate of our family, especially the monarchs." He paused. "Hook was always so polite. He meant our madness. I suppose at another time, I might have needed more convincing, but... I thought that if I could understand our problems, I could please the Queen. So I gave it to him. He had it for five months. I didn't actually reclaim it from his workshop until after he died. When I found it, it was cracked."

Jerya said, "Oh, Daddy!" and reached over to squeeze his hand.

"Did he discover anything?" Tiana asked.

Kiar said, "Hook died insane, according to Twist. Very insane." She tried to remember more.

The King wove the chain between his fingers. "He behaved erratically near the end, it's true. No, Tiana, if he found anything, he never informed me."

Tiana said, "Weren't you afraid to wear it after that?"

A fourth eidolon spawned from the King and drifted to stand in a corner by itself, face to the wall. The King said, "Well, he hadn't been wearing it. We discussed that part very carefully before I gave it to him. And I wasn't quite sure what else to do with it. Wearing it seemed to... be the least trouble. Tomas said it was probably just a coincidence and if it wasn't, well, most monarchs fared much better than poor Hook."

Tiana said, "What about the one I found? It looks identical, even down to the crack! That's very mysterious."

Jerya smiled, "Or just geology. We're none of us experts. Perhaps they were cut from the same rock."

Tiana asked, "You don't think it's strange? I found it through the phantasmagory."

Jerya raised her eyebrows. "Not just exploring, then?"

Tiana flushed. "I was looking for the fiend that killed Tomas. I wanted to find it so you'd stop talking about one of us having done it. None of us are Benjen. Ooh, maybe the fiend cracked it?" She frowned. "But I still don't know how they connect."

Kiar ground her teeth. Benjen. He had plagued two generations of the Blood, stolen and killed King Math's son. When most people referred to the Bastard, they still meant him. If people ever talked about her, they thought of him.

She focused on the pendants again. It was a better use of her time. "They don't look completely identical, although the cracks and the flaw that surrounds them are very similar. The stones are brothers, not twins."

Tiana said, "Perhaps there are hidden clues. Can you look for traces of the fiend through the Logos?"

Kiar sighed. "And find whatever made Hook die insane?"

"You're of the Blood, Kiar! Just looking can't hurt!"

Kiar looked away. "It can. I have to be careful, Tiana. I can't… I'm not you." *I can't just push away bad thoughts,* she couldn't say.

There was silence, until finally Tiana said, "You really think I should find somebody else?"

She'd find Twist. He was probably reckless enough to experiment, despite the way Hook had died. Kiar rubbed her hands across her face. Then she said, "I hate working under pressure. It's harder to focus. It takes me forever to get my concentration together when I'm not alone. But I'll try."

Kiar sat on a chair and stared at her hands, letting her eyes lose focus as she tried to bring about the frame of mind that made the Logos comprehensible. The others made it hard—the sound of their breathing, their eyes on her. Her mind kept freezing. She couldn't do it.

She breathed. She tried to block out sound, block out their presence. Her eidolons naturally manifested as shields. She could keep people out, so she could do this.

Slowly, she pulled the special Logos-vision over her eyes, being careful not to go too far. It was usually easy to get halfway there, to start perceiving the basic component nature of the universe. The problem was resisting going further than halfway. If she didn't hold it back, it would dominate her vision, turning everything she looked at into an incomprehensible jumble of passive linguistic noise.

She looked at the Logos of her hands and tried to sort the jumble into meaning, into something she could interact with and describe in a way the uninitiated would understand. But she wasn't ready and comprehension came too easily, moving beyond interpreting into active vocalization. Looking *could* hurt. She clapped her hands over her mouth, her face burning.

They shouldn't have expected better, she was terrible with the Logos, she was terrible at showing off. Nervousness once again froze her mind, and she felt her mouth stop moving under her hands.

She tried again. This time she progressed slowly, bringing comprehension just into focus. She missed the fine, complex details at this level, but she knew she would not do better in front of her cousins. Her control was inconsistent these days, even when she was alone.

She turned her hands over, staring at the way her dark skin absorbed warmth from the window, and how moving her fingers pushed air aside. She could see the shadow of the phantasmagory just under the flesh and the nacreous glimmer of her life-force that marked her as a member of the Blood and possessor of the Blood's family magic.

It wasn't as strong as Tiana's or the King's, but through the Logos, there was no denying it was there. Tiana blazed like a fire and the King like coals, while Jerya was the stars' glow, just like her. Once, she'd looked at Shanasee and turned away, dazzled by the gift her older cousin kept hidden.

Tiana moved beside her and put her hand on Kiar's shoulder. "It's all right, we can ask Twist…."

Kiar flinched. "No, I'm there." She looked up at her cousin. To mundane vision, Tiana was a perfect specimen of traditional Royal Blood, with cinnamon skin and long, black hair. Through the Logos, though, Kiar could see Tiana's recent use of magic as a smear of darkness obscuring the components that defined her. Jerya, on the other hand, had touched magic much less recently. The King was hardly anything but darkness and glow, with his near-constant use of magic.

Lisette and Iriss had healthy human patterns, without the nacreous glow, although they were marked by their proximity to others' use of magic. They were comforting to look at. The Blood always made Kiar feel sick if she gazed too long. It was the way they blotted out parts of the fundamental structure of the world.

Tiana said eagerly, "Wonderful. I knew you could do it. What do you see?"

Kiar dragged her gaze away from watching Iriss strum her viola and peered at the smears across Tiana and the King. Her eyes stung, and she said, "Can you put the necklaces down? It's hard to see them under your own markings…." She heard the gentle clinks as the necklaces were placed on a table. But all she saw were the smears, a darkness across the Logos where she thought they must be.

"Lord of Winter," she breathed. Fear rushed through her, and she wondered if Hook had seen this. She turned towards the window and brought herself into focus with the King's eidolons. Their outlines were distinct, their features invisible, and as they moved, they left a fading visual echo behind them that didn't quite match their movements. Then she looked at the opal necklaces again. In comparison to the eidolons, the darkness of the pendants was as vast and deep as the Logos itself.

"How can that be? What am I missing?" she muttered and picked up one of the necklaces, trying to recalibrate her sight.

"How can what be?" asked Tiana. "What did you see? What's going on?" Jerya shushed her, and Kiar was grateful.

She squeezed her eyes closed, opened them, and promptly over-focused. A horrible buzzing attempt to describe the smear emerged from her throat. Panic overwhelmed her and she flung the necklace away from her. Stuffing her fist in her mouth, she stumbled to the window.

The eidolons scattered away from her as she fumbled open the latch and pushed the window open. Then she spat out a mouthful of blood and vomit, and leaned out, gasping for breath. Her natural vision blinded by tears, she still registered the Logos of the outdoors, and it was a balm on her sight.

In the courtyard far below, a line of supplicants waited for admittance to the Court of the Justiciars, to beg for judgement or rewards. The detailing of their life-forces was sharp and beautiful, for the most part. Too sharp; it would cut her if she couldn't ease back out of focus again.

"Kiar?" Tiana said behind her. Her voice was high. "Are—are you all right? I didn't think…."

Kiar dragged in a deep breath. "I've been better."

Tiana said, "What was that… sound?"

"That's what happens when you have a half-trained idiot look too hard at eidolons." She stared at the line outside. There was something odd about it, but she couldn't identify what it was.

"What… can you explain?" Tiana's voice was timid, and Kiar felt even worse for worrying her.

"Everything around us is just information, Tiana. It's just words. The difference between an ordinary person and somebody who's taken plepanin is that plepanin tears away the gift of interpreting the world as a coherent whole. Surviving the plepanin means relearning how to do that. But our Blood magic isn't part of the Logos and it obscures it. If you're properly trained, like Twist, you learn how to work around the marring. If you're me, you try to put words to what can't be described."

She turned around and looked at the necklaces again. The one she had flung away was still on the ground, and the other one was on the table. No matter how carefully she looked at them, she couldn't see anything underneath the eidolon shadow.

"Well, they're the same in at least one way. They're eidolons or so deeply touched by them that the taint obscures anything I could see. I'm sorry."

Jerya frowned. "Both of them?"

Kiar nodded. "Yes. I know they look... real. But they smear the Logos exactly the same way eidolons and emanations do. I don't know what Hook saw that made him think they might be connected to... to the Blood's madness. Honestly, I have no idea how he hoped to interact with them, now that I see them with the Logos." She paused and added bitterly, "I'm sure Twist would know."

Tiana sounded puzzled. "No matter how I approach it, either someone with the family magic has to be involved, or there's some new kind of fiend."

Kiar frowned. "What makes you say that?"

Tiana looked up from her fingers. "I know they're connected, Tomas and the pendant. I just can't see how."

Kiar frowned and turned to lean back out the window to look at the line again. Normally, she'd believe Tiana's certainty was self-delusion. But because the phantasmagory was involved, because Tiana had led them unerringly to the second pendant, that certainty could be significant. Or it might just be her fantasy. There was simply no way to tell.

She finally identified what had she had noticed staring out the window before. "There's someone in the plaintiff line marked by family magic. Why is that?"

Iriss stopped her melodic strumming and Jerya rose to her feet. "Who?"

Kiar pointed out two peasant men standing together, near where the line vanished into the court, at the second guard checkpoint.

Jerya stared at them for a long moment and then turned

and marched to the sitting room door. She opened it and said, "You, come here."

Berrin followed her back to the window, where she pointed out the same men. "Bring those men up here. Tell them they've been granted the honor of a personal audience with the King."

Berrin looked taken aback, almost as if he was going to argue. But then he gave a quick smile and bowed. "As you say, Your Highness." Then he left.

Jerya said, unsmiling, "Let's find out. Maybe there's a simple explanation."

Tiana moved her hands in agitation. "More bastard theories."

Iriss spoke up, "Parts of the Regency Court have been talking about Benjen again."

Lisette said, "The courts like to see Benjen in every shadow, despite the more recent Blights."

The King said flatly, "Benjen is dead." Everyone looked at him. Kiar thought he would know, since he'd been there.

But Jerya said, "We shall see." She returned to the window and watched.

Kiar closed her eyes until Berrin returned and announced the visitors. "Presenting Wallis Jacoby and his brother Clary, from the village of Rushing Fork."

He herded in two men. One was clearly frightened, holding his hat in his hands with his eyes on the floor: a typical peasant pulled aside to meet people high above his station. The other's form rippled with unformed eidolons, cascading and dancing within him. His behavior was extraordinary as well; his head was high, wild eyes staring around the room, his mouth moving constantly. His brother maintained a tight grip on him, even as he bowed deeply.

"Thank you, Berrin," Jerya said, turning from the window. She smiled at the visitors.

Iriss murmured, "Gentlemen, you are in the presence of His Majesty King Shonathan, Her Royal Highness the Crown Princess Jerya, and Her Serene Highness Princess Tiana." She gestured fluidly at each princess as she identified them. Kiar had long ago convinced the Regents to leave her out of any introductions.

Tiana touched the King's hand, and he jerked. "Ah, yes. Always good to meet new people. Why are we meeting these fine men, Iriss dear?"

Wallis Jacoby looked up from his bow, saw the King's eidolons, and fell to his knees. "Honored... we're honored, Your Majesty."

He didn't sound honored. He sounded terrified. His brother, free of Wallis's restraining hand, took two steps forward before tripping over his feet and sprawling across the carpet.

Jerya seated herself, still smiling. "Why did you come to court today, Wallis?" Clary pulled himself to his knees and sat there, his mouth moving in silent speech.

The man stared silently at the ground for so long that Kiar had to look elsewhere. Looking at the liquid movement of the substance of Clary's form was making her stomach turn again. Tiana had her eyes closed, and Kiar was more than willing to believe the younger princess had slipped into the phantasmagory. But Jerya just sat there, her smile fading into a patient, reserved expression. Iriss was equally still, her pale shadow, although her gaze was focused on the afflicted man.

Finally, the man Wallis risked a glance up. "The taxes, Your Highness. Half our village has been afflicted by the plague, and we're having difficulty with the crops." Clary's eyes darted around the room, and he pushed himself to his feet. Wallis pulled him down again.

Jerya said, "The plague… tell me about the plague, if you please." Her brow furrowed.

The man said, "Oh, Your Highness, it's a terrible thing. My brother Clary survived it, and as you see, he's only fit for the simplest tasks now, even with supervision. You see? You see how his mouth moves? Once he spoke and he described the nightmares the fever brought him, but his voice died and all his stupid jokes with it."

He swallowed and continued. "Half the village has been touched by the screams, and it kills at least half those it touches. My daughter and wife are gone as well." Sorrow and rage threaded through his voice.

"I see. My sympathies for your loss," said Jerya. She paused and he lowered his gaze again. "But you say you came about your taxes? Surely, even if you reside within this county, you wouldn't need to come all the way to the Justiciar's Court to renegotiate your tax obligation. Has the count's magistrate failed you in some way?"

"The magistrate died, Your Highness, and the replacement selected by the count has chosen not to inspect the territories, in light of the troubles we've been having."

Jerya said, "Ah, the troubles." She paused, then said, "Tell me about the troubles?" There was an expression Kiar didn't recognize on the elder princess's face: a strange sort of intensity.

The man looked up again, doubt and confusion on his face. "Which ones, Your Highness?"

It was Jerya's turn to be silent, gazing at the man. He ducked his head and pulled his brother closer. Finally, she said, "Let's start with the one that caused the death of your magistrate."

"A fiend," he said promptly. "There are a terrible number of fiends about these days, spoiling crops and stealing children and preying on the lonely."

"And?"

"My granddaddy always said that fiends bring out the bandits. But everyone's pretty sure a fiend took this one, on account of the tax money being left behind, and all the blood."

"And the other troubles?" Jerya laced her fingers together.

"The weather. It's been so… wrong." The sour rage under his terror leaked through his voice. His brother tried to stand again and was jerked down. "It's hurt the harvest the last three years running."

Jerya said, "Your count is not sympathetic? There has been peace for almost a decade."

"We're farmers, Your Highness. The failure of the harvest is our own fault, or so our lords claim."

Jerya frowned for the first time. "I see. And does your count protect you from the bandits?"

The man looked down and chose his words with care. "I'm sure he tries very hard, Your Highness." Then he turned to look silently at the King, who was tapping his fingers together in sequence and watching in bemusement.

Jerya said, "Very well, Wallis Jacoby. I will investigate the situation. I would like you and your brother to be our guests for the next few days, in case I need any clarification." He slumped, looking beaten.

He's expecting a prison, realized Kiar.

But Jerya went on, "Berrin. Escort these men to the

Palace housekeeper and see that she finds them appropriate quarters. Comfortable ones, please."

The man blinked and then rose to his feet, bowing and pulling his brother after him. "You're very kind, Your Highness." His hunched shoulders smoothed out as he bowed.

After Berrin shepherded the men out, the King said, "Yithiere stopped the last Blighter at the border. It had almost no impact on the common folk. What they remember is Benjen." He sighed. "What they fear is us."

Jerya glanced at her father and then said, "Kiar? What did you see?"

Kiar said, "The simple one was touched by eidolons. Not like the pendants, but like Lisette or Iriss."

Iriss said suddenly, "I could read his lips. At least, I think so. The brother. Clary." She said his name like she was tasting it. "He was saying the same thing over and over, mostly. Like he had a song in his head." She absently began strumming her viola again.

"Well, what was it?" Tiana asked.

Iriss said, "Oh! Um. Let me see. Dead, dead, dead star, between midnight and dawn. Dream, dream, dream, night drags on. Monster, monster, monster, it's not real. Never, never, never, nightmares don't heal." She fell silent, and as the silence dragged out, she turned pink. "I didn't say it made sense. But I did see it. I practice!"

Kiar blew out her breath. "Very cheerful. So. Eidolon pendant. Eidolon-touched plague victim. Unfamiliar eidolon at the funeral. I think there *must* be an unknown member of the Blood."

Tiana said, "Are you sure it was eidolons? Our magic?"

Kiar's patience snapped. "Benjen the Bastard gets not

one, but two, entries in the history of Blighters. Why are you so set against the idea that any of the Blood could do something bad?"

Tiana looked frightened. "I'm not. I just don't think it—I don't want another Blood Blight. I—" she glanced at Jerya. "I know how bad they are. This isn't anything like Benjen. A plague? Is it, Daddy? Tell them. Whoever it was would have to be *here,* and you can't make people sick with eidolons or emanations."

Kiar took a deep breath. Then, begrudging the words, she said, "You're probably right. Without seeing more survivors of the plague, I can't prove a supernatural influence. Depending on where his village is, Clary may have run afoul of Cathay or Yithiere on one of their rides, or something even more arcane. The pendants date from long ago. And one stray eidolon does not, strictly speaking, make a Blight." *Even if it killed Tomas.* "But it *was* an eidolon, Tiana."

Tiana lowered her gaze and sat, chewing her lip. Iriss asked, "Will they ever forget, Your Majesty?"

Kiar said, "Not as long as bastards of the Blood go Blighter."

Lisette said sharply, "It's not limited to bastards, Kiar."

The King said to Iriss, "I don't know. You know me and memory. Rinta and Yithiere didn't think they would. But Tomas... Tomas had a plan for easing some of the nightmares."

Jerya said, "What was it?"

The King scratched his chin. "I'm not really sure. He didn't want to burden me with it. Something to do with the Justiciars. I don't attend council meetings much, you know." Another eidolon stepped out of the King. "Tomas did that for me."

Kiar announced, "I'm dropping the Logos-vision now." No one protested immediately, so she did so.

Jerya bit her thumbnail. "I wonder what it was. I don't think it's working." She shook her head. "I'm concerned that he didn't bring these troubles to our attention."

Tiana said, "Maybe it was just politics making things bad. Politics aren't our job."

"But fiends are," said Jerya. "And Tomas hated politics. Something's going on. I think the only way we'll find out is by going to Court."

CHAPTER SIX

LOVE ME NOT

Kiar slouched down the Palace hall that evening, deliberately taking the longest possible route to Twist's chambers. It wasn't where she wanted to be, but Jerya had insisted.

"And you," she'd said. "You keep saying Twist would know these answers. You're his apprentice, go ask him. Today. I know you've been skipping lessons with him." Kiar had argued for procrastination, tried to forget, tried to ignore the request, but Jerya was indomitable.

She took the long route. She skirted the Crystal Room, where some reception of the Regency Court went on and on. The Blood attended a few of those, but the Regency Court had a great deal of work to do managing relationships with the nobles, and it seemed to require many parties. She avoided as many as she could.

She wandered through the kitchens, stealing warm bread before Min Baker chased her out. Her earliest memories were of carefully shelling beans by the kitchen fire. Her mother had been a Palace maid who won her father's rarely-given trust for a short time, before war had come again. But she'd died just after Kiar had been weaned and Kiar didn't remember her enough to miss her. The kitchen had been her nursery, the kitchen maids her nurses.

There'd been reason, at the time, for all of Kiar's mother's friends to think her daughter would be safest if no one important knew her father's name. The Blood fought among itself, and children died. Even after she'd been taken away to join her cousins on the floors above, the kitchen was warmth and order and strength for her.

She walked along the Palace wall, until a strolling lordling tried to engage her in conversation. The greater nobles rarely courted her directly: her servant's blood and blond hair were a bit too base for them. But if a lesser noble could win her, it would be quite the stepping stone for their family. That wasn't going to happen, of course, but they were always so hopeful. She corrected his poetic description of the stars, then escaped back into the main Palace.

She stopped by the Scrivener's Office and asked them to recopy the maps Tiana had found. Then, she lingered to admire the Vassay hand press they were clustered around, until they closed the office. The scribes bid her a cheerful good evening and went off to their supper, taking away her last distraction.

And now she was standing outside of Twist's chambers. How had Jerya known? Had Twist told her? She hadn't attended a weekly lesson in months, but no one had seemed to notice.

She felt like she was standing before an executioner. Jerya, or Twist? She told herself Jerya was family and knocked at the door.

There was no answer. Relief rushed through her.

"Right!" Kiar said. "I came by, he was out, oh well, ask him yourself, Jerya."

But she didn't leave.

"I'm not good enough to be here," she said to the door. "I'm aware of my problem. Jerya should be talking to Twist directly; she's wasting her time with me. Just like Twist's wasting his time with me. I wasn't meant to work with the Logos. It was a mistake. I was confused."

She remembered standing before this door eight years earlier, scared and determined, tired of feeling small and powerless in a world of the powerful. She knocked, and there was no answer.

Then, as now, she pushed on the door.

It was unlocked. "Why doesn't he lock his door? Why?" she demanded. "What if another confused child wandered in here? Didn't he learn anything from my mistake?"

When the door opened wide enough to step through, she gasped in horror. Scholarly, wizardly, and personal possessions were scattered around the room indiscriminately. She started instinctively cataloging it all. A work shirt was draped over a chair, a collection of geometric wooden blocks in primary colors littered the floor, rice spilled from a bag in a corner, the fireplace overflowed with cinders, dozens of books had been removed from shelves and incorrectly replaced, six folded paper birds occupied the desk chair, and a pair of empty boots dominated the desk. A ripped pillow rested on a table, feathers spilling everywhere, and a crust of dried bread lay in front of it. Four empty wine bottles formed the arms of a cross on the floor, right next to the door, and a rag doll sat in the center of the cross. More dolls leaned against each other on a shelf. A stack of bowls teetered on another table, threatening a mug encrusted with a patina of old tea. There was a jar of mysterious, lumpy goo beside the mug.

At that point, Kiar squeezed her eyes shut in horror, but still couldn't block out the old, acrid smell in the air. "It's never been this messy in here before," she said, outraged. "It's a good thing I've been skipping class. How could he expect to have a lesson in here? It's intolerable!"

When she'd come here eight years ago, it had been untidy, but she'd hardly noticed. She'd been so intent on finding the plepanin. It was a powder, she'd read, dull red. It made things and people magical. Maybe it could make her more like her cousins: braver and stronger and more talented. He'd had a shelf full of jars then, each one carefully labeled: spices, teas, poisons, plepanin. There was only a little, but it only took a little. He'd never notice.

Kiar looked around until she spotted the nearly-empty jar of red powder, high atop one of the bookshelves. He'd peeled the label off long ago, but that didn't matter. She stepped over clutter on the floor and absently began to reshelf the books. She couldn't see it from here. It was out of sight, but she could practically feel it, all the same.

"A mistake," she muttered. "It made things worse. These stupid lessons, where I just get to see how bad I am at something else. Jerya and Tiana relying on me for answers I can't even see properly. It didn't help at all."

She moved to the next shelf of books, making a disapproving sound under her breath at the state of the shelving. "This never happened before. I wonder what's going on?" Then, she looked up at the jar she couldn't see.

Sometimes, she wondered if she just didn't have enough. If it didn't fully sensitize her to the Logos like it did to normal people. Inscribed objects need a refresh every once in a while, after all. Maybe the Blood did too.

She shook her head violently.

"You're so predictable," said a calm, familiar voice behind her. "I'm disappointed." She whirled around, spilling a stack of books across the floor. Twist stood in the door leading out of his chambers, a long dark coat dripping water on the floor. His dark hair was barely damp, which looked like a neat trick. She bit her tongue on asking him about it.

He chuckled, removing his coat and tossing it over the back of the nearest chair. "I thought you'd quit your studies. Or died of that sore throat. Three weeks claiming illness, and then you stopped even sending messages." He smiled at her and her cheeks flushed in embarrassment. "I was hurt."

"You saw me at Court meals," she protested. "You never said anything."

"Well, what if you'd died and the King had made an eidolon of you? If I'd spoken to you, I would have ruined it for him." He swept a pile of papers off an upholstered chair and sat down, looking her over. She dropped her eyes to the messy floor nervously, and then wrenched her gaze up again.

He sprawled back and continued, "But I thought that if you were still alive, I'd find you here someday, sneaking in when I wasn't home, reaching for the plepanin again." His blue eyes glittered. "More wouldn't help you, Kiar."

She narrowed her eyes. "I came here for Jerya. No other reason."

"For Jerya you came to my workroom and began to clean the case with the plepanin? Oh, yes. You climbed the shelves when you were nine, as I recall."

She took a deep breath, ignoring his final comment. "The door was open. How can you *exist* in this… travesty of a workroom? I thought I'd come in and wait for you. Jerya was very insistent. She wants answers, you see, to certain questions."

Twist waved a hand dismissively. "Perhaps we'll get to those tonight. At the moment, I want to hear your excuses for the last six months. Since you aren't dead."

She stared at him in horror. He stared back at her, apparently serious. Then he added, "Pick up the books while you're at it."

She looked down at the pile of books she had knocked off the shelf. That little mess was her fault. She knelt down and stacked the books again, unfolding bent pages and checking the spines. She would clean up her mess. She had always cleaned up her messes, from the very beginning. "Jerya wants answers, not me. I didn't want to come. She insisted. If you're not going to answer, I'll just go. Maybe she'll come herself."

"If she wants her information soon, that might be for the best," Twist agreed. "What happened, Kiar? For four years, you were the brightest student I could imagine. And then it all started… disintegrating." He sounded sad. She could imagine the disappointment on his face, and she couldn't bear it.

"The Blood just shouldn't use the Logos, that's all," she said. "The histories say so and we had proof as soon as I took the plepanin. Everything after was just salvage. I was always slow. Clumsy." She aligned the spines of the books carefully and then picked the stack up and put it on the shelf again. She managed to avoid looking at him even once. "You did what you could. Don't worry about me."

She risked a glance and discovered he was standing right behind her. He could do that, travel without crossing the intervening space. It was his special Logos trick, and it was always surprising. She recoiled into the bookshelf again, and he put a hand out to steady her. "I was proud of you. Did I push you too hard?" He turned her around, searched her face.

She flushed again, uncomfortably aware of how close he was. He hadn't aged a day since she'd met him. The plepanin did that sometimes, preserving those who survived it for an extended period of time. And he was still as shockingly attractive to her as he'd ever been.

Not noble born, oh no; he'd told her stories of his life as an urchin before his mentor Hook had collared and adopted him. His skin was city-folk pale, and his hair black as tar; he was her opposite, coloring-wise, which made them the same, somehow. It was irrational, but she felt it all the same. And while he was handsome enough, it was the way he practically buzzed with energy and strength and humor that made her want to simultaneously throw herself at him and run away.

Then he sighed, pulled his hand away, and stepped back. "Don't lie to me. It won't do you any good. I've been planning on bringing you back to lessons for a while now. I was just... busy." He frowned and scratched his chin, his eyes going distant.

"It's a waste of time," Kiar said wretchedly.

"I'll be the judge of that," he said, his gaze snapping back to her. "I won't allow you to wander around, barely functional."

Her lips tightened. "I have other things I'm doing now. And they're none of your business."

Pleasantly, Twist said, "I'll find you at them and remove such distractions. There are those who will help me."

Kiar flinched. He leaned close again. "You can't hide

from me, Kiar. I will find you and I will not let you lock me out." His words were harsh, his voice gentle. She fought a tremble at his nearness and swallowed hard. He smelled like old leather and apples. He'd always smelled like apples, even then....

She was nine, and the red powder had changed her. She saw the inherent order of the world around her and where it was out of place, and she couldn't fix it. No matter how she organized and sorted, she couldn't order things to her satisfaction. It overwhelmed her. She panicked, as she had once before, three years earlier, and an eidolon crowded around her, an unbreakable shield against a world of madness. Except that after the red powder, the eidolons and emanations of family magic were... nothingness, nothing she could see, nothing she could manipulate. She was trapped inside a shell she couldn't control, and she was screaming....

His eyes, such a deep blue, widened as he stared down at her, and his mouth parted, as if to speak more. Then he shook his head, twisted the Logos around himself, and was once again back at his chair. "Tuesday," he said calmly. "Come at the usual time and we will have a lesson."

She sagged against the bookcase, trying to find a line of reason, a purpose within the buzzing in her mind. But all she could find was *Tuesday, Tuesday,* and the memory of a tall man wrapping a long coat around the shoulders of a sobbing nine year old. She bowed her head and said, "Yes."

Then she trudged out of Twist's chambers, aware of his gaze on her every step of the way.

Halfway back to the residential hall Kiar realized she'd let Twist drive her from his chambers without gathering the information Jerya was expecting. For a heartbeat, she wanted to go back. But she knew she was too much a coward to face Twist again tonight, and too tired besides. Better to face Jerya's disappointment after all.

The Logos-vision flickered; her exhaustion made it hard to keep it suppressed after activating it earlier. When she'd been attending lessons, she had spent half her time with the Logos-vision active. She knew that as a master wizard, Twist had it active almost all the time. She looked at her hands, at the darkness within them, and shuddered. She could never understand how he could teach her, how he could function so close to the Blood, without going mad.

He could always choose to avoid the Blood, but she could not. Both the Logos and the family magic would always be with her. Shanasee, her older cousin, refused to use her magic, but the mark of it was still under her skin, and she was still called to the phantasmagory. And once the plepanin woke someone to an awareness of the Logos, the awareness could only be suppressed, not sent away again. Death was the only escape, and the path most of the previous Blood Logos-workers had chosen. But half of those normal human initiates died too, and she was still glad she'd survived the first few minutes.

As she entered the ladies' residence hall, movement against the wall caught her attention. Down the hall was Jerya and Iriss's quarters. A Regency guard was staring straight ahead outside the door. But on the wall she passed swirled the fading taint of an eidolon. It looked as if something had pressed against the wall until it passed through, invading the suite.

Kiar's stomach twisted in a sudden rush of anxiety. The wall bordered Iriss's bedchamber.

If it's just a remnant of something Jerya did, there's no harm done by the asking. She darted to the suite door, and the nearly-dozing guard jerked his head up and held out his hand. "The Princess has retired for the evening."

Her anxiety exploded into hot worry. "Actually retired or just shut you out?" she snapped.

He yawned. "It's the same thing as far as guests are concerned."

A vision of Tomas's brutalized body rose in front of her and she put her hand on the door handle. The guard looked alarmed. "What are you doing, Your Ladyship? I can't let you—" He grabbed her wrist as she pushed the latch down and opened the door.

The sitting room on the other side of the door was dark, lit only by the faint light from the cloudy night visible through the large windows. But to the Logos-vision, light was just another piece of information, rather than a means of illumination. She lunged forward, twisting her wrist out of the guard's grasp. He shouted, but she ran across the room to Iriss's door.

She flung the door open and shrieked at the eidolons writing around Iriss's form. The young woman was drifting in midair, limp in the arms of one of them, a terrifying parody of a lover's embrace. Other dark shapes swirled around her, twisting away at Kiar's cry. One of them immediately faded away, but the one holding Iriss remained, as did another smaller one.

Her shout turned into a sob and she flung out her own eidolons, swords to stab, shields to interpose themselves between the monster and Iriss. The smaller eidolon caught one of her swords and reversed it to point at her. It looked at her, saw her, with intelligent eyes no eidolon had.

She gasped, and a dark tide of fear rose over her vision. The larger one lowered its top portion to engulf Iriss's head. Desperation overwhelmed fear and she launched herself at the monster, trying to twist the Logos around her as she'd seen Twist do so many times before. There was a horrible wrenching sense of disjuncture and—

She felt the Logos reject her request as impossible, more than impossible: indescribable. Something vast and alien opened around her. For the space of a missing heartbeat, she was painfully cold. Then she gasped for breath, standing with Iriss in her arms, the eidolon monster she'd replaced draining inside of her, swallowed down to the place where her own eidolons came from, just as if she was putting away one of her own weapons.

The other monster leveled the sword at her and readied a thrust. She stared, her limbs and mind stiff with shock and confusion. Then Jerya's eidolon, an iridescent falcon, soared out of the darkness, silent talons tearing at the monster, ripping its essence to shreds.

Still fighting to pull breath into frozen lungs, Kiar stared at Iriss in terror. She could see through the Logos that Iriss was dying, her life leaking away through injuries inside her. There were words she could say—words that would at least slow the leakage and bind her life more strongly to her flesh. But her mind was so cold, and the words that spilled out of her were simple, no more than animal cries to the Logos.

Then the Logos twisted on itself, and the Royal Wizard appeared beside her. His glance seared her as he reached for Iriss. Hot tears burned her face as she released the Regent. She watched as he whispered to the Logos and the words merged with Iriss's form. The leak slowed and stopped, though the strange hidden injuries remained, perverting her essential structure.

The inscribed orb in a sconce on the wall flickered to life, shedding a warm yellow glow. Somebody's cold hand took her own. She wrenched her gaze away from the still form of Iriss. Jerya stood next to her, eyes wide, face white. Helplessly, Kiar squeezed the princess's hand.

Jerya said, "Is she…?" She closed her teeth over her lip and looked between Kiar and Twist.

Twist placed Iriss on her bed and said. "She's alive, but not by much. There's something wrong with her. I've stopped it from getting worse, but I don't know how to repair it." He looked at Iriss one more time and then turned his attention to Kiar. "What in the name of Night did you do? I felt it. The Citadel probably felt it. Whatever it was, never, ever do it again."

Kiar said, "There was a monster attacking her. I tried to do your trick, to move to inside it. But it was an eidolon, not of the Logos. The Logos got confused."

He closed his fingers around her arm and shook her gently. "For an instant, you stopped existing. Never again. Tuesday."

Jerya released Kiar's hand and moved to her Regent's bed. Light and noise filled the sitting room as other people arrived to see what the commotion was. The guard was pointing fingers and Kiar stared at Twist, wanting nothing so much as to hide and sob. But Jerya was the one who needed to be allowed to hide and weep. It was up to Kiar to answer the questions.

She tilted her head back, blinking rapidly. There was a fresco of the Firstborn Atalya in her guise as Spring on the ceiling, and she concentrated on the greens and blues until the tears were under control. Then she shrugged out of Twist's grip and said, "I have to go explain. Stay here, see if you can do anything else." And without letting herself look at him, she went out and closed the door behind her.

CHAPTER SEVEN

COURTROOM DRAMA

Tiana sprawled on her bed, every coverlet kicked to the floor, pressing her hands to her eyes. "How can it almost be Antecession? It's *so hot.*"

"I've picked out something cool for you to wear, Your Highness," said Misa, her maid. She held up a white frock that was barely more than a shift.

Tiana said, "I refuse to believe that Jerya actually means to get up and go to the Justiciar's Court after last night. It's unthinkable! She can't have had any sleep. I didn't, anyhow."

From the entrance, Lisette said, "All the same, she's expecting us to meet her at the door in half an hour." Tiana looked at her. Lisette had made an effort to appear respectable, but even with Misa's help, she looked pale and fragile. Two eidolons flanked her in the doorway, a wolf from Yithiere and a hunting cat from Cathay.

Last night, right after Iriss was attacked, the Chancellor had decreed that not only would the Regency guards continue their watch, but each Regent needed two eidolon guardians who would *always* be with them: one from their own charge, one from another member of the Blood.

Tiana pressed her fists into her eyes again. She couldn't make eidolons. She was oh-so-talented with emanations, as long as she could map the action onto her own body's movement. But eidolons? They were the most basic magic. Children of the Blood invented them when ordinary children invented imaginary friends. She'd never even managed a firefly.

It hadn't ever bothered her much, either. Until now. After they'd finally gone to bed, it was that, and not the heat, which had kept her awake until the sun rose.

"Come on, Tiana. I'm tired, too. But today will be a distraction," Lisette said. Tiana could tell she was trying to sound cheerful, and guilt stabbed at her. She rolled to her feet and let Misa dress her, staring anxiously at Lisette the entire time. Lisette hardly seemed to notice; when she wasn't talking to Tiana, her gaze was far away.

When Misa was done, Tiana said, "That's one way of looking at it. Lisette—" and she stopped. How could she say, *I'm sorry I chose you, so long ago, and put you here, now, in the path of a monster?* She didn't know who she'd be without Lisette. She really didn't want to find out.

Lisette's blue eyes met her own. "I'm worried about Iriss, too, but I'm sure everything will be fine. We'd better hurry if we want some food before Court starts, though." Tiana took a deep breath. *Everything would be fine.* She'd just have to believe that. Anything else was a short walk to madness.

By the time Tiana and Lisette made their way down to the back entrance to the Hall of the Justiciars, it was as hot as high summer, despite being deep autumn. Their light clothing was already beginning to stick to them.

Tiana groaned and pulled her frock away from her skin. "Today is going to be miserable." She flapped her hand at her face.

"That's right, keep your spirits up," said Kiar, standing at the open double doors. "I looked inside and there's hardly anyone there today. But Jerya's already in the Royal Box, so we'd better go in."

A guard in a Justiciar tabard, standing at attention beside the double doors, had been watching them with undisguised curiosity. Finally he said, "If I may ask, what is Her Highness here for today?"

Lisette smiled at him. "The princess wishes to observe the Court in action."

The guard chuckled. "It'll be an oven in there today. You might want to come back on a cooler morning. Though I don't think the work of the Justiciars will ever be the kind of entertainment a princess would enjoy."

Still smiling, Lisette said, "Nonetheless, today they will start observing the court. But your consideration is appreciated."

As she passed him, Tiana told the guardsman, "Believe me, we're not here for our own entertainment."

Inside the Hall, it was cooler than the outdoors; the stones and dark wood absorbed heat slowly. At the back of the hall, where the princesses entered, there was a raised dais with six chairs arranged around a crescent table. There was another, higher dais behind it, but it was empty. Close to the dais were raised boxes with cushioned seats, one for the Royal family and another for various honored guests across the Hall. Closer to the front entrance were three rows of benches on each side. There were also desks lining the walls between the boxes and the dais, out of casual sight of the plaintiffs and petitioners.

It was only partially populated. The front doors of the Hall were still closed, and clerks and other officials were at their desks at the back of the Hall. The dais was empty, though Tiana did identify the door she thought the Justiciars must arrive through. There were only a few people on the benches. Jerya was in the Royal Box, all alone.

Tiana climbed the steps to the Box and settled into one of the plush seats. "Who uses the benches? I thought petitioners stood in line."

Jerya said, "People who don't want to stand in line can have a servant stand in line for them. The servant introduces them when they get their turn to present before the Justiciars. And other observers are permitted."

Tiana leaned back in the seat and then leaned forward on the railing. "I'll try not to fall asleep," she said doubtfully. It was quite a comfortable seat, and it was already getting warm. "Are we early?"

Jerya said, "I don't know. I thought this was when the Justiciars arrived." She chewed her lower lip, staring at the door.

Kiar yawned. "It used to be. I don't know why it would have changed."

Jerya turned to look at Kiar, sitting behind her. "What did you learn from Twist yesterday?"

Kiar ducked her head. "Nothing. Except that he's been investigating something and thus been busy." Her mouth twisted as if she'd eaten something sour. "You're probably better off asking him yourself, Jer. Or writing a letter. Questions from me he'll just treat as lessons."

Tiana said, "Iriss hasn't woken up?"

Jerya looked away. "No. She hasn't. Thank you for your concern."

Lisette touched Tiana's shoulder. "Tiana, let's change places so I can sit beside Jerya. I can take notes for her."

Jerya lowered her voice. "Yesterday, I had a theory. I didn't expect the theory was completely accurate, but it was proven wrong when Iriss was attacked. Whoever it is, whatever it is, it wants to kill our Regents. They want to provoke us into misbehaving and use that against us. So please, no matter what happens today, we must keep our tempers."

Tiana, next to Kiar now, on the second tier of seats, noticed a guard opening one of the two front doors to look down the Hall before closing it again. "The Justiciars are late."

"Yes," said Jerya, settling back in her chair.

Lisette said, "What did you find in Tomas's notes?"

Jerya squeezed her eyes shut and shook her head. "He wasn't worried about the troubles. He was very interested in Vassay. He admired their recent achievements. That Collegium...."

Kiar said, "Who wouldn't? They can work the weather with the Logos. They don't have our recent heat problems." She sounded impressed.

Jerya said, "Yes. They do amazing things. But Vassay replaced their nobles with scholars, and their King with the Collegium. And Tomas was working on a plan for relieving the Blood of its exclusive burden." She fell silent, and Kiar and Lisette both frowned.

Minutes crawled by. Tiana watched Kiar rub her eyes, pinch the bridge of her nose, watched how perfectly still Lisette sat, looked at how Jerya's eyes closed. Finally, the door at the front of the Hall opened at an unseen signal and a line of servants and peasants were allowed to shuffle in, stopping at a line of white tile on the otherwise dark floor.

Through the far door flowed in observers, half-filling the rows of benches, more nobles in light, fine clothing. The

Only then did the door near the dais open and the six Justiciars pace in. Each seat on the Council was appointed by one of the Great Dukes of Ceria. Tiana knew all of the Justiciars by face and name, though they impacted her social circle only indirectly.

Leading the procession was Lord Terence Aubin of Borzee. He was the eldest on the Council, a grizzled old man with a neatly trimmed, snow-white beard. He'd observed at her Regent auditions when she was seven.

After him was Lord Donatien Wichard of Kanura. His hair was still dark, and Tiana had attended his third wedding two years previously. In the middle of the procession was the only woman on the Justiciar's Council, Lady Rosalyn Scott of Ardoza. She was an attractive, older woman with blond hair tied back, and was a particular friend of Tiana's old tutor.

Walking close behind her was Lord Warrane Dunstan of Dalein. Of him, Tiana only knew that he was some kind of radical and that he had terrible taste in friends. Second to last, there was Lord Millard Bellamont of Ingae. He was a thin, middle-aged man with a bald pate. Tiana had encountered him at the theater occasionally. Finally, there was young Lord Jasper Gueran of Hypana. He'd only been appointed two years ago and Tiana had visited him when he first came to the Court, seeking stories of her mother, who made her home at the Court of Hypana.

Of the Justiciars, only Lord Jasper glanced at the occupied Royal Box as they took their seats, and his expression was concerned. A guardsman with the insignia of a captain appeared at Jerya's elbow then, and said quietly, "The Justiciar's Council welcomes you to their audience hall, but we wonder which case brings you here today?"

Jerya said, "No specific case, Captain. I'm here in response to the Crown Regent's death, to observe the Council." She offered the captain a charming smile, which he did not return.

He lowered his voice. "Lord Ferya left much of the day-to-day work to the Council, Your Royal Highness."

Jerya said, "I believe that is traditional, yes. However, I should still like to acquaint myself with the current situation in my country, as presented by her people."

His eyes narrowed. "I see. May I inquire how long you plan on making your observations?"

Jerya's chin tilted up imperiously. "As long as I feel like it. Your name, Captain…?"

The soldier inclined his head in a scant bow. "Captain Urhal, Your Highness." He turned and vanished into the dimness of the hall as the first of the petitioners addressed the table.

Jerya and the other young women turned their attention to the court, but Tiana observed the path of Captain Urhal instead. He made his way to the work desks at the back of the Hall and spoke with a red tabarded clerk. The clerk wrote something down and discreetly delivered the message to Lord Donatien. Lord Donatien read it, glanced up, met Tiana's gaze, and then looked down again. He scribbled a response and passed the note back to the clerk, who went back to his desk. And that seemed to be the end of that.

Then there was nothing to do but watch the petitioners. The first petition of the day was a pair of minor nobles who wanted their offspring to inherit both of their estates, despite the fact that they were in different duchies. Lady Rosalyn assigned a clerk to research their request and instructed them to come back when the clerk was done with his signed and sealed testimony. Meanwhile, Lord Donatien and Lord Warrane had a whispered conversation.

The next petitioner was the formal presentation of a report by the army quartermaster on the disposition of uniforms. Tiana amused herself by whispering comments to Kiar on *his* uniform, until Jerya turned around and glared at her. This report was lauded by Lord Jasper, who sounded as bored by it as Tiana had been. It too was passed off to a clerk.

Then it was an irate complaint of highway banditry. Lord Terence assigned a clerk to this one, looking tired already. After that was a return petitioner, with a clerk's testimony on his request to allow splitting his lands between his daughter and his son. He shuffled to the line and passed a scroll to a waiting clerk, who read it aloud: a short description of the tax and military history of the estate, a description of its crops, and a note that the family didn't have any distinguishments from the past three generations. Lord Millard and Lord Donatien consulted on this and then Lord Donatien denied the request.

Tiana watched as the disappointed petitioner strode off, a clerk catching at his arm and turning him towards the right exit from the Hall. She wondered if the clerks ever briefed the Justiciars on secret details before a session. There were certainly a lot of red tabards circulating. Then she yawned. It was getting warmer and warmer. The people in the benches moved restlessly, trying to catch every breeze that stirred in the hall. Tiana leaned back in her padded seat and observed with slitted eyes that if she did doze off, Jerya would hardly notice, unless she spent time looking over her shoulder.

The person at the white line was talking about maps.

Some sort of gift was made. Somebody asked about taxes. Jerya whispered to Lisette. The heat was making Tiana's head hurt, and she wanted desperately to lose herself in the phantasmagory, where she would no longer sense her body's discomfort. But while sleeping might be overlooked, everyone would notice her eyes glowing white. So, she tried to resist. She knew she looked sulky and miserable, slouched back as she was, but *that* Jerya would just have to accept. This was incredible weather. It was *autumn*. Last autumn the snows had come too early, and now this?

Her eyes drifted closed. Kiar touched her arm, and she sighed and shook herself awake again. Kiar whispered to Lisette, who whispered to Jerya. There was somebody at the line talking about taxes again. The next petitioner made a nervous comment about the heat, and Lady Rosalyn observed tartly that the Council would not be reopening after the luncheon break unless the muggy heat relented. That almost made Tiana smile, but even smiling seemed like too much movement for this heat. She remembered how cold it had been down in the catacombs. The sun hadn't warmed those rocks in centuries, and right now that sounded like bliss.

She yawned again and let her eyes close, wondering if the phantasmagory would still take her down through a phantom version of the prison. Sweat rolled down her forehead, stinging her eyes, and she sighed, sat up, blotted at her face with her sleeve. Jerya was whispering furiously to Lisette, and she tried to make out what the subject now being petitioned was. More taxes, it sounded like, two men and a woman. Lord Donatien was refusing their request.

Suddenly, Jerya raised her voice. "My lords, wouldn't a deeper investigation of their request be in order? This is the third report of plague today. I'm certain there are means of investigation that have not been pursued."

The crowd murmured, and someone called, "It's the damn weather! Benjen's curse!"

Lord Donatien stiffened at the interruption. Then he smiled and said, "Their Highnesses deign to join us today. How pleasant. We do not, however, think an investigation of this case is warranted. Previous investigations have found that adequate preparations can stave off an outbreak of the plague; villages that still suffer from it have simply failed to prepare." The lord's eyes were hard and angry, and Lady Rosalyn was shaking her head at Jerya in a warning.

Jerya hesitated and then said, "But you don't know all the facts. We should gather—"

Sharply, Lord Terence said, "Your opinion is appreciated, Your Royal Highness!"

Tiana looked at the Hall full of petitioners, who were growing loud again. Somebody shouted, "Let her speak!"

A man called, "What does she know?"

The crowd started arguing with itself. "It's probably her family's fault! Her father—"

"No, no, you've got it all wrong. It's Vassay stealing our weather. Everyone knows there's more sickness in unnatural weather."

Jerya stood up. "There is more going on than you know!" she cried. "I am a Princess of the Blood and I—" Lord Warrane also stood up and began to speak at this point, but Jerya just raised her voice, "WILL BE HEARD!"

Lord Warrane thundered, "You are a sheltered young woman playing a game. You must stop disrupting this court and pretending an authority you do not have."

Jerya stared at him. "I'm the Crown Princess!"

Lord Warrane said, "It is a time of peace. I see neither

your father nor your Regent here. In fact, I understand your Regent was attacked by an eidolon last night. And now here you are, unsupervised and causing trouble. It is clear the Regency is ineffective. Perhaps we should open our own investigation into what took the Crown Regent from us."

Tiana was astonished by Lord Warrane's behavior, but not so astonished that she didn't notice the expressions on the faces of the other Justiciars. They weren't astonished at all, and she wondered again what Tomas had been involved in.

Jerya was silent so long that Lord Warrane sat back down. Just as he opened his mouth to address the line, she spoke again, her voice quiet and controlled. "There are signs that dark forces may be at work in the plague, my lords. I hope that it is not true. But it is the duty of the Blood and the Regency to protect Ceria, and your opinion on our effectiveness is irrelevant.

"Lady Kiar will travel to a plaguestruck village of some petitioners tomorrow to investigate, and she will report her findings to me. Good day." And then Jerya swept out of the Royal Box, her head held high.

Chapter Eight

Stage Blood

Jerya was as calm as a frozen river until all four women had entered her chamber and Kiar had closed the door. Then, she turned from the wall she'd been staring at and her hands were fists, her eyes fire. "How dare they! We are the *Blood*! We are not dogs to leash and unleash at the Council's whim! The Firstborn themselves placed Ceria in Shin Savanyel's care!"

Uneasily, Tiana said, "They were probably just surprised. You know how Father is." Jerya's eyes were pale and Tiana could feel the first rush of the undertow of the phantasmagory.

"That man all but accused me of attacking Iriss. You always cover your eyes and pretend all is well, Tiana. I've sheltered you, but there is something seriously wrong happening! I don't know exactly what Tomas planned, but I know what I saw today. They are not our allies. Tomas was a dear man, but he was blinding himself to that."

Jerya drew in a ragged breath, turning her own blinded eyes towards Tiana, and Tiana felt another wash of the undertow, inviting her into the deepness. She was amazed Jerya was even still talking; if Tiana was as upset as Jerya seemed to be, she would have already abandoned herself to the phantasmagory.

As it was, she nodded weakly in response to an enquiring look from Lisette; she would be strong. Lisette could only help one of them at a time. The Regent moved to Jerya's side and touched her hand gently. Jerya shook herself and said, her voice small, "This is why, you know. We have Regents, who are our keepers, and we need them, because we can't control ourselves, because we are mad, lost, cursed."

"Gifted," said Lisette lightly, turning Jerya's hand over and putting her thumb in Jerya's palm, then peering closely at her eyes. Tiana lowered her gaze. *Cursed.*

Jerya laughed, a hollow sound. "I'm still here, Lisette. Not far, now. I have a house with all the bad dreams I had after Mama left us. I was bad enough; she didn't stay long enough to learn what a good little girl Tiana was, and look how Tiana's grown up. And Iriss! Iriss is dying, Lisette! That was my nightmare when I was eight and now it is coming true. She's dying. This madness is seeping through our skin and into the air of the castle, taking on a life of its own. It lives all around us, and it wants what we have."

Tiana squeezed her eyes shut, drew in a careful, painful breath, listening to Lisette's calm murmuring. A fish swam across her mind's eye and a red stag bounded and she gently sank down. *No!* She forced her eyes open, tried to clear her vision of the fog and phantasmagory. Were there new eidolons? It was so hard to tell what was the phantasmagory and what was being generated by Jerya, by Kiar, by herself.

A bird spread great wings over the top of the door and keened a mourning cry, and a beautiful, familiar-looking woman passed through the door to glide right through Lisette and Jerya. Then the crimson stag rushed into the room and Seandri, Jerya's favorite cousin, followed, his eyes wild.

"What's wrong?" Seandri demanded. "What's happened?" He didn't quite look at Iriss's room, but Jerya began sobbing all the same. Cursing, Seandri advanced on her, folded an arm around her.

Tiana exerted all her will in an epic effort and pushed the phantasmagory down, cleared her sight. Jerya was manifesting her bird eidolons, wild and angry creatures, though the glow in her eyes was still dim. Kiar held herself tightly under control, watching Lisette carefully. She always managed control over the vortex of the phantasmagory, because she was so frightened of what she could do to herself if she lost her sight.

Tiana, though, could not bear it. She left Jerya to the care of Lisette and Seandri, and fled the room.

Somehow, she ended up outside again. She hardly noticed Slater following her at a discreet distance as she wandered through muggy courtyards and darkened cloisters. The exterior halls were nearly abandoned to the heat, and the sky was darkening with storm clouds that would not, if this were a summer day, ever rain. She stepped out of her shoes, spread her toes on warm tile. She couldn't stop thinking about her sister's tears.

She'd never seen Jerya cry before. Her sister was four

years her elder, and Tiana remembered the day their mother left, eleven years ago. Jerya had watched from the front drawing room, dry-eyed. She'd steadied Tiana against a paned window as the carriage bearing the Queen Consort drove away, forever. Tiana had sobbed and begged, bewildered and confused and betrayed by the beautiful lady she'd always wanted to please.

She'd cried many times since, at funerals, at weddings, at the theater, but Jerya was brave and calm and focused in a way that Tiana could not emulate. Tiana thought it was a gift inherited from their mother, and sometimes she wondered if it was her own crying that had driven their mother away. It was a silly, irrational thought; she understood perfectly why the Queen had abandoned her children and her husband. *Mad. Cursed.*

As Slater appeared in the doorframe behind her, she put her shoes back on. She needed to get out of the Palace, away from all the reminders of everything she failed to be. If she didn't, she'd end up in the phantasmagory, and the more upset Blood there at once, the worse it was. That was why she liked the theater. Somehow, they had the same passion as the Blood, but they managed to turn it into art.

She hoped that she'd be able to take a hand in directing one of the shows someday. Her ancestors had contributed to Lor Seleni's culture in all sorts of ways—art, architecture, music. Deneris had talked to her of writing plays, but she wasn't sure her talents lay in that direction. It seemed like a difficult task. But turning someone else's story into something real and breathing? That sounded wonderful.

Distracted by such thoughts, Tiana wandered out of the Palace. Another Palace guard called to Slater as she left, but she didn't pause. He wasn't *her* bodyguard, after all.

As she drifted down familiar streets, she barely noticed the greetings of the city folk, few that there were. Anyone who could afford to be inside thick cool walls, was.

At the front door of the Let It Spin, she woke up from her reverie. There was a padlock on the double doors, which she'd never seen before. Frowning, she looked around and then up at the sky. It was only noon, and theater folk were notorious night owls. She'd never been here so early in the day.

She went around the side of the building, down the alley that led to the stage door. It was very narrow; there were corridors in the Palace significantly wider. Trash had been swept into it. Something smelled sour and rotten.

She'd only ever looked out the stage door from the inside, and at night, when shadows obscured the dirty details. The paint on the red door was chipping, and there was an unused lantern hook beside it. The far end of the alley was a brick wall, the back of some tall building; the only reason the alley existed was to provide a back entrance to the theater.

She pulled on the handle, but it didn't move. Wasn't there supposed to be a caretaker? Was it locked from the inside?

Voices interrupted the frustrated disappointment bubbling up. "Look, it's Her Most Generous Highness." The entrance to the alley was suddenly blocked by young men. "So early in the day too. Rann favors us!" The speaker sounded strange, his words a little too fast, bumping into each other in their hurry to escape his mouth. "Perfect opportunity, just like I said."

"Hey, Princess," a different man called. "Out without your lady friend today? That's too bad." There was laughter and jostling. The first speaker unwrapped a piece of candy and put it in his mouth before taking a step forward.

Tiana looked around vaguely and realized she'd left Lisette back at the Palace. It'd been years since she'd gone out into Lor Seleni without Lisette nearby.

"Good afternoon," she said. "Have we met?" She supposed they were probably actors. There were six of them, half dressed in casual quality, half wearing worn hand-me-downs. None of them looked familiar, but that didn't mean anything.

A woman's voice called out from the street, her words incomprehensible. One of the young men called something back and pushed the first speaker. "Treyl, it's the laundry woman."

Treyl stared at Tiana as he said, "Tell her to mind her own business, Ivor." Tiana twisted her fingers together before putting her hands behind her back, uncomfortable.

The woman in the street didn't seem inclined to move along, and two of the young men moved away from the alley to help her along. Tiana said, "Have you seen Baxer?"

Ivor said, "Nice dress. Looking for a morning tumble, Princess?"

Tiana looked down at the lightweight white shift she'd worn to the Court session. The fabric clung to her body. She tried to ignore the snickering, her head spinning. "I'm looking for Baxer," she repeated.

Was he not hearing her? Somebody else said, "Where does she like it?" Another voice crowed, "Haven't you heard? She likes everything!"

Treyl advanced another step. "Don't get caught by the glamour, boys. That's just one of their tricks." He sucked on his candy, his eyes wider than anybody's should be. "I've heard about this one, though. She's all take and no give. She barks and barks, but she's afraid to bite." He smiled. "We can bite."

Tiana stared at Treyl blankly and then decided it was time to go. "I'm afraid I don't understand you," she said politely, and moved forward. Then she had to ask. "Are you actors? Did I hire you for the play? I can't quite remember."

Treyl watched as she walked towards him. "Oh, no, Princess. We're not your theater whores. You can't buy us with our own money. I think Evrent's right. Time for us to be having our say. Leave a loud message." He smelled like alcohol and something spicy.

She walked in the muck rather than brush against him, and he turned, staring as she passed. There were three young men at the mouth of the alley now, not quite blocking it, but she could see the other two returning from their conversation with the laundry woman. She moved faster.

Treyl said, "Don't you want to spend some time with the people, Princess? We have some complaints. Don't you want to hear them?" And as she got close enough, one of the men grabbed her. He was dressed in ragged canvas pants and a stained, blue silk shirt, with dirty blond hair, and stubble and scabs on his hands. He smelled like alcohol, too.

But she was a spring wound tight, and when his fingers closed around her arm, she lashed out. Her backhand became an emanation that thrust him away from her violently. His head cracked against the corner of the alley.

Already, more hands held her, and she realized that steel glinted in Treyl's hand. She thought, *Oh! This is some kind of crime.*

She thought, *I should be scared.*

She thought, *A normal girl would scream now.*

She tried to scream, but nothing happened. The phantasmagory opened beneath her and she balanced on the very brink, looking at her attackers. Six again. Steel edges. Finely dressed and not. Men. Criminals. Threats. She was a Princess of the Blood.

Carefully, distantly, she said, "You'd better run, because I'm not going to."

One of the men holding her said, "We aren't going anywhere, sweetheart." Other voices buzzed around her, made meaningless as she let the detachment of the phantasmagory fill her.

Stinking flesh crowded close. She spread her arms wide and pushed it away. Men tumbled down. "Run," she said again.

Instead, they advanced on her. What was wrong with them? Did alcohol do this? They caught her arms so she couldn't move. Her uncle and teacher had both warned her about this, warned her about her dependence on her body's movements. What had they said? She couldn't remember. She couldn't think. She shook them off, like a dog shaking off rain.

"Run," she said, more urgently. Were they stupid? Metal lunged towards her and she swerved, ducked. Her shoulder burned, and the man with the metal flipped over her head.

And they still kept coming. They kept coming back. Why? She didn't want this. She swept them away again, but that didn't include the two behind her. Somebody pushed her and she stumbled, fell. Laughter, curses, the smell of blood, and that strange, spicy scent. Somebody put their foot on her back and she turned and broke his knee, flinging him into a wall.

"Run!" she shouted. "Run, go, go away!" She lifted herself upright, trying not to fall further into the phantasmagory, where she would not be able to stop what they'd started, not until it was done, ended in the most final of ways. From the brink, the faces that stared at her seemed strange, alien. The laughter and jeers were gone and they shifted uneasily, suddenly desperate men, yet unwilling to flee.

Except for the leader. Treyl. His eyes were still wide, and his mouth was twitching in a kind of grin. "She's ours, boys."

Tiana's shoulders slumped. "Run," she whispered. Treyl tossed his knife in the air and caught it again. The others shifted their weight to move towards her.

When it came down to the truth, she was a Princess of the Blood, nothing more, nothing less. She hated Treyl for making her see that, even as she snatched him into the air and *twisted*, like she was wringing water from her hair.

"Run!" she screamed at the rest of them, as Treyl died. "Leave me alone!" Bone popped. Four men fled. Beyond them, in the street, a woman with a basket and a small child stared at her, met her gaze, and hurried out of sight.

She dropped the wrecked remains of Treyl to the ground and realized the sixth man, the one whose knee she'd broken, was still on the ground. Blood smeared down the wall to where he lay crumpled. The detachment of the phantasmagory vanished.

Her shoulder screamed in pain, and the smell of blood and shit was overwhelming. She gagged, touched her wound, brought her bloody fingers to her mouth. Footsteps pounded up and she looked up fearfully. Slater and two other Regency guards appeared, a stocky laundress behind them. The laundress said, "Right here, sir, right—oh no."

"Blood have mercy," Slater swore. It wasn't an oath used around the Blood much, for it tended to offend.

"I tried," Tiana said bleakly. She watched as the two

guards went to check on the bodies. She distantly wondered if Jerya was still upset. This wouldn't help.

Slater said, "Is that your blood? Forgive my language, Your Highness, but to hell with them." He glanced at his men. "Clean up. Find out who these creatures were and where their friends might be. I'm taking Her Highness home." Then he looked at Tiana again. "If you don't mind?"

The laundress said, "Her wound...? I can wrap it."

Tiana said, "There's no point in staining anything else." She walked past them, out of the alley, down the street.

At the Palace, she went directly to her rooms. She dropped the bloodstained white dress on the floor and changed into a lightweight sleeping chemise that provided easy access to her shoulder. Then she huddled in her window seat, waiting for the consequences.

People arrived soon enough, a stream of faces and voices. She had trouble connecting them to comings and goings, and sometimes statements people made didn't register until much later.

The doctor cleaned and bandaged her wound. "Straightforward enough for a knife wound. It'll leave a scar, though." He patted her other shoulder. "The Blood heals faster than most people. You might not even notice it after a few days. I'll give Lady Lisette instructions on changing the dressing."

"That's true?" She'd heard about the Blood's accelerated healing, but she'd never had an opportunity to see it in action. *Hurrah.* But the doctor was gone. The Chancellor was there instead.

He stroked his neat beard. "That man, Treyl. You didn't know him? The great-nephew of the mayor of Lor Seleni." He patted her hand. "We'll smooth this over. They shouldn't have touched you." Thoughtfully, he said, "We've only found one of his friends, though. The rest have run away."

"Not soon enough. I killed him," she said. "I wanted them to run away before."

Jerya was there, holding her hand. "Yes," she said. Tiana could tell she was angry. She carried silence a certain way when she was angry.

"I don't know why I didn't run away myself. I couldn't."

"I'm glad you didn't," said Jerya. Then she was gone.

Lisette was there, and Kiar. Lisette stroked Tiana's hair and said to Kiar, "The Mayor tried to suggest the city courts review the attack. What was he thinking?"

Tiana said, "Never any consequences." A dry sob escaped. "But *he* attacked *me.*"

Kiar said, "He was using a drug. Something new, they called it 'clarity.' I wonder where it comes from. The merchant who sold it is foreign."

Lisette said, "Jerya thinks whoever was manipulating Tomas was put off-balance by his death. These weren't just some bad men. It was an assassination attempt. If they'd killed you… or if you'd killed all of them…."

Tiana started crying in earnest. "Treyl looked like Tomas when I was done."

Lisette hugged her, rocked her back and forth. She slept.

She woke and Yithiere was there. His black eyes bored into her even when she looked away. "You forgot your lessons. And now you have killed."

She wanted to cover her ears. She was the first of the younger generation to take a human life, but Yithiere and her father had been to war, fought against Blighters, both kin and foreign.

"It's a hard thing," Yithiere said. "Most of the others won't understand. You carry a piece of them inside you now."

"I don't want it."

He lowered his head, reminding Tiana of his wolf eidolon. "This is what it means to defend Ceria. Shanasee is primus since Viani died, but she would have died there." Primus, the old term for the most powerful living user of family magic. Her great-aunt Viani, Seandri's mother, had held it until her suicide. Now, technically, it belonged to her cousin Shanasee, though she never used her magic anymore.

"Shanasee wouldn't have been in that situation, or all alone," Tiana said.

"Yes," Yithiere said. She closed her eyes.

Her father sat beside her, holding her hand as Cathay stalked around the room. Cathay was angry, but pleased. "The fools got what they deserved."

Sadly, King Shonathan said, "Fools usually do."

"I wish they'd set upon me instead, though." Cathay crouched by Tiana's side. "You did very well, stormy, but look at you now. So sad and withdrawn." He brushed hair away from her face. "Where's my lightning and thunder?"

She looked into Cathay's dark eyes and knew Yithiere was right. He wouldn't understand until he'd been there.

She slept again, through the night. Then Kiar was there. "I have to go. Jerya's right; I'd rather face mysteries and peasants than Twist and the reception tomorrow night." She hesitated and then kissed Tiana's forehead.

"Find answers," Tiana said. Kiar smiled as she left.

Lisette said, "Baxer sent a message and a gift. Do you want to read it?"

Tiana said, "Read it for me." She wondered what would

have happened if the door hadn't been locked, if she hadn't been in that alley. Perhaps they would have found Cathay somewhere else in town, instead. He trained with weapons. She didn't know if that would have been better or worse.

Lisette scanned the letter. "He's horrified you were assaulted right outside his theater." She paused, eyes on the letter. "He doesn't come out and say it, but he's worried you'll never come back to the Small-light District again. And he's sent a new dress." She lifted the lid on the box and the scent of yellow roses emerged. A bouquet was pressed against a lightweight black and white dress.

Tiana looked at it for a moment, unsure how to respond. Lisette sat down beside her. "The Chancellor is resigned to losing Kiar tomorrow, but he's hoping you'll still come to the reception. There're some young men he'd like you to meet."

"Of course," said Tiana absently.

"That's what I told him," Lisette squeezed Tiana's hand. "These things happen, these complications or attacks or whatever, but life has to go on."

Still looking at the dress, Tiana asked, "What's going to happen with the Mayor?"

"The Regency is handling it." Lisette's voice was cool; she disapproved of whatever the Regency was doing. She hesitated, then added, "Everybody's going end up pretending it didn't happen, Tiana. The Chancellor is worried about how the city will react otherwise. The Mayor is powerful." She squeezed Tiana's hand again. "But dealing with this is our job. All you need to do is recover. And come to the reception."

Tiana dragged her eyes away from the dress Baxer had sent and stopped holding onto her fear. It was so easy to let it drift away, to let herself think instead on the party ahead. The Regency receptions were organized in an attempt to find mates for the Blood of marriageable age. Tiana was the only member of the family actually enthusiastic about them. It was true, she was picky: whoever she chose had to be just right. But she and Lisette and Iriss had a good time, even if the Chancellor's selections were all lacking so far.

"It's going to be a quiet, little affair without Iriss," Tiana said. Lisette broke into a radiant smile and Tiana blinked at her, surprised.

"I thought the same thing. We'll tell her stories when she's feeling better." And then she hugged Tiana. "I'm so glad you're you again."

Tiana tilted her head. "I just… I'm fine. For now. There's the scent of blood in the phantasmagory, though."

Lisette nodded. "I know. Nothing is ever left entirely behind. You have to move on, but things move with you."

Tiana chewed on her lip. "Tell Baxer 'thank you' for the dress, and reassure him that I'll be back at the theater eventually. Right now, I've got to decide on outfits for tomorrow."

CHAPTER NINE

THE SCREAMING PLAGUE

Lisette and Tiana never had any trouble talking to strangers, but for Kiar, it was always difficult. So she said no more to the guards and villagers than was utterly necessary to get the party on the road, and pointed in the right direction. Somebody had sent Berrin along, for which she was grateful; he was no longer a stranger after their walk through the depths of the Palace. He was happy to take charge of maintaining the pace.

Jerya was right, though. Better this than a lesson with Twist. Better this than the reception tomorrow night. Better to be useful, she told herself, but she couldn't help worrying that her traveling party expected to talk to her, expected to her to make polite, social conversation like the Princesses. She thought she could feel them staring at her. She wished it would rain so she could put her hood up. She wondered if Twist would notice when she didn't show up for the lesson. Would he shake his head and sigh?

It was better once they were out of the city, on the Royal

Highway. In Lor Seleni, anyone who cared to could recognize her, but on the road, her lineage was unclear. Her peasant's blood bleached the dark Royal hair a dirty blond, and while her skin was dark, some farmers turned quite dark in the sun.

Of course, no peasant rode a horse like Spooky. He was a liver-colored Altas stallion, a racehorse, taller even than the soldiers' mounts and looming over the Varyan riding horses that were popular with most nobles. He stood out everywhere. But Yithiere had found her at the horse fair three years ago and pointed him out to her, as the horse worked on a lead with his trainer for an admiring audience.

"The Ganying have been refining the Altas for a thousand years. They control the bloodline strictly. You will only see geldings of the pure line in Ceria." And then, just as abruptly as he appeared, he'd vanished. She hadn't noticed at first, she'd been so absorbed by watching the horse. But Yithiere's Regent, Zavien, stayed behind.

"Do you like him? The horse?"

"He's beautiful. I suppose they're the Blood of horses, and he's a prince." She couldn't keep the wistfulness from her voice.

"Very astute," Zavien said. He sounded irritated, and when she looked at him, he was looking at her, not the horse. He opened his mouth, as if to say more, and then shook his head. "Yithiere is an idiot sometimes," he said, by way of explanation, and walked away.

The next day, the Royal stable master found her. "The bloody Ganying have, haha, decided to give you a present. That stallion. They even found a justification for it, too, bless his soul." The stable master seemed at once both horrified and delighted. "They say it's on account of you being Blood and having survived five years after taking the magic powder. But I suppose if there hadn't been that, they might have suddenly fallen in love with that mop of hair."

There'd been a ceremony and everything. And nothing seemed hastily improvised, and Yithiere hadn't even been present. It all seemed to be exactly as they claimed. Except it was totally without precedent. So, they said, was she. But that was ridiculous.

She still hadn't worked out what exactly Yithiere had *done*. But the attention Spooky got made her feel the same way she used to feel in the kitchens when she was three years old: safe and warm and totally unnoticed. It helped that he was perfectly mannered, far easier to handle than the rest of the stallions in the stables. And he could, of course, outrun anything. Nothing but the Hanna messenger horses could even wind him.

It was like he could read her thoughts; he frisked and bounced, and as she calmed him, she relaxed herself. No racing today. But she let herself drift off into the rhythm of the ride.

At midday, they left the Highway for a smaller road. It curved around bedraggled fields of winter wheat, and pastures for goats and cattle. She passed a pear orchard, and the wind brought her the scent of the fruit harvest. The homes in this area were stout, with thick, white walls and pale yellow shingles, and they were often in the midst of large beds of flowers. That wasn't something she'd seen before. When she summoned up the courage to ask about it, the farmer she was escorting explained that the flowers responded favorably to recent weather conditions, so everyone had planted more of them. It was a small brightness in an otherwise awful season.

It took about two hours for the travelers to arrive at Rushing Fork. As Kiar waited outside the inn for the village elder to arrive and greet her, she concentrated on activating the Logos-vision. It was easier today, and the vision more stable; no one was staring at her expectantly this time. The mind-ravaged victim she'd traveled with was crouched down in the mud next to the pump, drawing endless circles with his finger. She could see the shadow of the magical taint lying over him, like the mud still clinging to his finger even after he'd wiped it on the ground.

There was a crossroads in the center of the village, where a farmer's track intersected with the county road. A stream just south of the crossroads was lined with unhealthy apple trees. Across the track from the inn was a blacksmith's shed, and three children were playing a game with metal studs. The fourth, watching, had the magical taint of a plague victim. Kiar dismounted and passed the reins to Berrin. "I'm going to talk to the children."

The children didn't notice her at first, which was fine with Kiar. Children made her nervous. The magic-tainted one watched instead of played, but her eyes weren't empty like the previous survivors Kiar had observed. When the children did notice her, they began picking up their game. The survivor transferred an intense stare to Kiar, chewing on her lip.

"Hi," Kiar managed. She was bigger than they were, after all. The little girl looked to be nine or so, and she didn't respond at all. One of her companions pushed her gently.

"C'mon, Mere, get out of the lady's way."

Mere pulled herself away from her companion. "She's not a lady. She started staring at me first."

The other child, a boy of about the same age, looked

embarrassed. He met Kiar's gaze briefly and mumbled, "Sorry, Lady." Then he took Mere's hand and tugged at her.

Kiar lowered her gaze. "She's right, I was staring. Was she ill recently?"

The boy said, "Yes, ma'am, she had the plague. She doesn't anymore, though, see? All better. Mere, stop staring."

Kiar said awkwardly, "I'm glad you're feeling better, Mere. Can I talk to you later about when you got sick?"

Mere finally dropped her gaze and shrugged. "I don't care. I don't remember anything from then, though. Just bad dreams. I can't think about those."

"Why is that?"

That penetrating, unblinking stare rose again. "I might get sick again."

Berrin called to her from the inn, and Kiar said, "I see. Well, goodbye." She didn't see. She hoped she could learn to see.

Berrin stood on the inn porch with who was presumably the village elder, a thin, stooped, older man who would have been quite tall and powerful in his prime. His nose was crooked and his hair was iron-grey. Berrin said, "Ah, Your Ladyship. This is Elder Whitestaff. Elder Whitestaff, this is Kiar Suan, Lady of the Blood. The Crown Princess has sent her to investigate the sickness here."

Kiar endured his scrutiny as stoically as she could. She wanted to run away, of course, but that was normal. She distracted herself by wondering what impact the last bastard Lord of the Blood had on the village. That worry always put everything else into perspective.

Then the Elder nodded. "Your ladyship. Are you a physician?"

She shook her head. "I'm a student of the Logos. I've

come to see if there is something wrong with the Logos around the victims of the illness." She wasn't going to tell anybody but Twist about the taint of the family magic until she had a better idea of what was causing it.

Whitestaff's sleepy gaze sharpened. "That's wizardry, not the Royal magic?"

Kiar nodded. "I'm not very good at the Royal magic." That always reassured people. "Have you had any wizards pass through recently? Or anybody strange?"

The Elder's bushy eyebrows lowered. "Traders pass through every month, Your Ladyship. Some are stranger than others. Wizardry isn't something I know how to recognize, unless things are changing in front of me or there's chanting going on. No obvious Blighters, though."

"That would be too convenient, I suppose. How many people are sick in your village now?"

"Twelve, Lady. There're nine that've died and two that have recovered recently."

"Are the recovered still functional?" She looked down the porch stairs at the man still playing in the mud like a child.

The bushy brows twitched like a snowy caterpillar. "Some are handier than others, Your Ladyship. The children that do not succumb entirely survive the best, but that's the way of children. They all change, though." He shook his head. "Before this illness came, I'd only seen that kind of change once before. Fellow's skull got crushed by a bull. A killing blow, but he survived another twenty years. His whole manner was different, though."

Kiar tried to steer him back on topic. "And it has struck men, women, children, all equally?"

"Aye, Your Ladyship. I've been more concerned with

keeping my village alive, so I can't say for other places afflicted, though I know they exist. The traders bring word, and sometimes they've left their own victims with us. I've seen it in the young and old, male and female: the fever, the vomiting, the hallucinations, head pain and seizures. It doesn't spread like other illnesses. Usually, if one person gets something bad—and it ain't the flux—the whole family gets it. That just isn't true for this. A mercy, I suppose. Given how it kills."

Kiar asked, "How long does it take? Is there someone I can observe directly?"

The old man hobbled down the stairs of the porch and Kiar followed him, Berrin trailing behind her. "Once we know they have the screams—that's what we call it around here, Lady—they last anywhere from three days to two weeks. Usually at least a week, though. The fever rises and falls and rises again, and there's the seizures and the delusions. They get worse throughout the week and then, well, the victim either lives or dies.

"If they survive the peak of the illness, like young Mere, there's another week of a cool fever, and weakness, and lots of sleeping. Then, well, they're either like Mere, or like Paul, who you came in with." He fell silent.

Sickness was rare in the Palace, where everything was kept scrupulously clean, and everybody was well-fed. The Blood themselves hardly ever contracted physical illnesses. But Kiar knew the poorer districts of Lor Seleni had outbreaks of worrying illness, the generic 'plague.' And she knew that city officials responded to such outbreaks by strictly controlling traffic in and out of those districts, as well as taking other steps, depending on the illness. Three years ago, they'd fought an outbreak with imported beer, and Twist had showed her the contaminants in the water.

Elder Whitestaff had a long, if uneven, stride once he found his rhythm, and Kiar had to quicken her usual pace to keep up as he led them out of the village proper. "Mae Parker's husband died to the screams late last year, at the beginning of the outbreak. She didn't catch it until just recently. She and her family culture our silk." He nodded as they passed a large stand of mulberry trees on the west side of the road. Just south of the stand of trees was a fenced yard full of chickens and attached to a house.

Kiar's pace slowed. She could see the taint of the family magic on the house, a moving, morphing darkness much like the mark left on the wall outside Iriss's quarters the other night. She stared at the mark, watching as it faded and shimmered and grew again. Then she jumped as the Elder rapped on the door and called, "Good day, Parkers." He opened the door, and Kiar hastened to catch up with him.

The main room of the cottage was dominated by a large and ancient loom, where a very young woman had half-turned to greet the Elder. A door led off to the left, while a staircase led up to a loft, but Kiar hardly registered those details, her gaze glued to the bed made up against the right wall. That was the wall she'd seen from the outside, marked by magic. Something moved there, something dark and alien to the Logos-vision. It whimpered and turned towards the sound of voices.

"Good morning, Ilsa. This Lady's come from the capital to study the screaming plague. She wanted to meet your mother." The Elder's voice was soothing, and Kiar tore her gaze away from the mother to look at the daughter. She was touched only by her nearness to the thing on the bed, but her alarmed look and deep breathing bespoke a deeper disturbance. "Ilsa had the screams when her father did, last year, aye Ilsa? Your family's a strong one; your mum will pull through just like you did."

Ilsa nodded slowly, ducked her head shyly at Kiar, and turned to fuss at her loom. The Elder sighed and explained quietly, "Before the screams, Ilsa was as outgoing and sociable a girl as you could imagine. Afterwards... shy as a fox. Even the ones who survive... they don't survive the same." He shook his head. "But I'm going on. Here, why don't you take a look at Mae and see if there's any wizardry about."

He led her across the room, to the magic-tainted shape on the bed. Kiar took a deep breath, made sure she wouldn't start babbling gibberish, and forced herself to stare down into the taint. This time, it wasn't as if the woman beneath the taint were being attacked by eidolons, not like Iriss. Instead, it was as if she was *becoming* an eidolon, like the magic was crawling inside her, being absorbed under her skin.

With a rush of horror, Kiar wondered if that was what she'd looked like when she had absorbed the eidolon attacking Iriss. She looked down at her hands, saw the taint that was always there, and repressed a whimper. Panic made the phantasmagory surge up, and she struggled to untangle herself from it before she lost control.

The woman on the bed started screaming, broken cries from a tortured throat. The eidolon within her *reacted* to Kiar, its essence swirling and moving towards her, and then away. She saw the endless smooth wall of her rising shield overlaid behind it and she pushed it away, frightened of being enclosed with the plague eidolon.

The sick woman and her plague eidolon sat upright, cowering against the wall, away from Kiar, still screaming. Ilsa rushed over to the bed, passing right through Kiar's phantasmagory-expanded sense of self and tried to calm her mother, while the Elder said something, only words with no meaning. Ilsa was clean and untainted in the Logos-sight, with what looked like new patterns creating a fortification against the screams of the woman. There was something horrifying in the sound, a living madness that assaulted them all. But the Elder wasn't sensitive enough to Mae's nature to absorb the madness, and Ilsa had found a way of rejecting it, like white rejected light.

Kiar buried the phantasmagory deep inside and the woman's screams stopped. *Coincidence?* The daughter stroked her mother's hair, murmuring to her about nightmares. Kiar hesitated. She could see the Elder's concern warring with tired cynicism, emphasized in his Logos. Then, under her hand, she shaped a tiny eidolon probe, a dart of rainbow frailty. She felt it against her palm, and no sooner did she feel its half-real substance did Mae begin whimpering and crying out.

Kiar banished the emanation and stumbled from the cottage, past Berrin, past the chicken yard, and crouched down in the dirt of the road. *She reacted to the Blood magic. She felt it.* It made no sense, it was impossible, but she displayed a sensitivity even users of Blood magic lacked.

She heard Berrin's footsteps behind her. "Your Ladyship?"

"I need answers, Berrin. In the two weeks before the illness appeared, did the mother go to other farms? The village center? Did she meet anybody new? What does she do normally?'

Berrin hesitated and then said, "Yes, Your Ladyship." His footsteps moved away.

Kiar longed to banish the Logos-sight and go back to being just prickly Kiar. But she'd barely started. There were more people to interview, more victims to meet. More nightmares to see. She could conclude nothing from just one. But she couldn't let herself fall into phantasmagory while seeing through the Logos.

It was dangerous enough for her normally. But the Logos combined with the phantasmagory would leave her both blind and beyond anybody's reach. She had to resist panicking, even though she was seeing impossible things, frightening things.

She looked at the chickens, their simple patterns and complex, distinctive traits. She murmured a description of the closest one, a white hen with a red splotch on her back. It was like her in only the most basic ways: a living, mobile thing that ate and slept. It was unable to control its reactions or choose what it feared. It was unable to have courage, only blind stupidity. She was Kiar, half servant, half princess, and she had to have courage.

Two sets of footsteps returned, Berrin and the uneven rhythm of the Elder. The Elder spoke. "Mae mostly stayed on the farm. She didn't meet anyone new that Ilsa or I know about. She works on the weaving and takes care of the trees when it's not silkworm season."

"No changes in behavior? No new interests?" She turned around to face the Elder.

He looked disturbed. "You one of those who thinks sickness is a punishment for misbehaving, Your Ladyship? I suppose it's easy for castle-born to think that, but it just isn't so. Maybe you have to be old to understand that." He scratched his face.

Kiar shook her head. "Not a punishment, just a consequence. I'm sorry." She turned and looked at the grove of mulberry trees. "I suppose I might as well look around in the stand first. Then I'll want to see the others who are sick."

"As you wish," the Elder said.

Though the day was bright, the grove was cool and shadowed. The mulberry trees in the Royal Garden were small, pruned things, barely more than bushes, and widely spaced. These trees were large and old, with wide-spreading branches and long weeping twigs full of leaves. There were ladders lying here and there on the ground, and large wicker baskets were piled under trees, barely visible beneath the drapery of leaves.

The trees were evenly spaced here as well, she realized. They'd been planted by someone who had anticipated just how big they could get. Under one drapery of leaves, she saw some children's toys, and she realized what a wonderful hiding place this would be. She stopped, pushed through the drape of leaves and then turned to look out, her back against the broad trunk. It was a little, living version of her phantasmagory world, and she could just barely see outside the strands of leaves. They rustled together pleasantly. There was an old rag doll and two rough clay cups nestled in the roots of the tree.

"Lady?" queried Berrin.

"Just looking," she said, and pushed her way out of the hiding space again. She walked along the wide rows, concentrating on the Logos-vision, looking for any sign that someone with the family magic had been there recently.

And much to her surprise, that was what she saw.

First, she saw the markings along the ground, as if someone had a drawn a path that blotted out the real path beneath it. She swerved from her route and followed it, walking alongside it down the narrower way. Where she had found it, it was fading, but as she tracked it, the mark grew stronger. It was more like an eidolon than typical magic taint, a stable darkness interrupting the patterns of the Logos. Eventually, it led under the veil of a tree's canopy.

Kiar stopped and tilted her head. "Do you hear that?" she asked the two men following her.

Elder Whitestaff listened. "Some animal den in the roots, perhaps." The rustling behind the canopy stopped, and then a low, bestial moan emerged.

Kiar pushed some of the branches aside and peered in. "Lord of Winter," she whispered.

To her human vision, the creature in the den among the mulberry roots was a monstrosity, a horned mastiff with a mane of spikes and three tails. To her Logos-vision, it was something new, something she only recognized from other wizards' written descriptions: a sky fiend. Earth fiends were children of the Logos, just as animals were: infused with it, defined by it, controlled by it.

Sky fiends, she'd read, were not part of the Logos, but they affected it and were affected by it in turn. And they were capable of using it directly, just as wizards did, which made them a rare and frightening monster.

She saw the horned mastiff, and she saw the hole in the Logos that it occupied: not a blind spot as the eidolons were, but a place where the Logos curved around *something else*, embracing it. It looked at her with mad, red eyes and roared, pressing itself against the tree trunk and then falling on its side in a violent seizure. The Logos twitched and flowed, and Kiar could feel strands of power grasping at her. She muttered her own words of defense, rejecting the Logos strands, and started to back away.

Then she saw the iridescent shimmer of an eidolon

around the torso of the sky fiend, and she froze. It was not a taint on the Logos, for there was no Logos there to taint. But she was just as familiar with the look of family magic in the normal world. Somehow, there was an eidolon inside this fiend.

The spray of pale color shifted and moved, and then swelled out from the thrashing creature's side. The eidolon within emerged. It had a head and arms, and it moved like one of the King's companions, almost like a person. It pulled itself free of the sky fiend, and slowly its color darkened to the color of shadow. Kiar stumbled backwards, reached for her own magic, and faltered, remembering the screams of the woman in the house. She didn't know how the magic was related to the illness yet—

Berrin grabbed her around the waist and lifted her out of the way, pushing her towards Elder Whitestaff. Then he drew his sword. "Not one of yours, Your Ladyship?" He backed away as the shadow-colored eidolon emerged from the veil of leaves. The bellowing of the sky fiend faded away to a sobbing.

"N-no," Kiar said. "If you can drive it away, please do! But I don't know what it's capable of. I don't know if the sky fiend spawned it or if it was… an illness." She wondered why she'd said that.

The shadow eidolon twitched and tilted its head, then sidled to one side. Berrin sliced his sword at it. "Feels kind of backwards. Usually it's the other side cutting at 'em, hey?" His blade penetrated the eidolon and slid through, and the eidolon stopped, wavering. Then it glided towards Berrin, extending an elongated arm that sprouted claws.

"Lady, we must flee and gather your other guards!" Elder Whitestaff tugged at her hand. She resisted and he released her, planting his feet. She shook her head.

"No, this is my responsibility; this is why I'm here. You go!" He stared at her and then began hobbling out of the grove.

Berrin slashed at the arm reaching for him, and the eidolon recoiled. Kiar ducked under the veil of leaves again and began to describe traits to the Logos, assigning them to the empty space in the Logos where the sky fiend was. It cried out and twisted, clawing at the mulberry tree with thick, heavy claws. The shimmering began around the sky fiend's torso again.

Changing the Logos was a lot harder than just describing it, but describing it was where change started. Then she had to find the words to make the changes within her imagination, and if she couldn't imagine it completely enough, it would fail. Kiar clenched her fists and let the Logos flow through her, taking her desires and tumbling out of her mouth faster than she could consciously shape the sounds. Mist was simple, mist was easy. It could fill the space, push the monster out. The eidolon magic blooming against the creature's side was a problem and as she realized this, her speech faltered.

Then she lunged forward and pressed her hand against the writhing creature's side. Her fingers sank into the eidolon, past a barrier of warmth and life, into something terrible and far away. She reached for the memory of what she'd done in Iriss's room. It had been a terrifying accident then, but now she realized it was a discovery. She opened herself and pulled the burgeoning eidolon into herself, stuffing it into her own magic source.

Something inside her stretched painfully. She was choking, like she'd tried to swallow dry bread. There was a tearing sensation and then alien memories of a place without light opened up inside her head. The Logos-vision vanished. Darkness moved against her skin. There was screaming—

She opened her eyes. Her cheek was pressed against dirt; she lay flat on the ground. The sky fiend was still thrashing, half-banished. She was so tired.

She pushed herself to her knees and shook her head. Then she opened herself to the Logos again, not the gradual raising of the vision she preferred to practice, but a full embrace of the power.

Once again, she let herself become a channel for the Logos as she concentrated fully on her vision of mist, in that place right there, right now. The sounds tore themselves from her throat. The Logos around the sky fiend slammed into it, reclaiming the space it had occupied, forcing the entity back to the place that had spawned it, outside the world.

She fell onto her side again, rolled over, and stared up at the branches overhead. The leaves were still swaying, and a sunbeam flickered through the dissipating mist. She didn't hear anything other than her own labored breathing. Then the leaves rustled, and Berrin called, "Ladyship? Kiar?" He sounded healthy.

She said, "I'm alive," and pushed herself to her feet. "Did you dissolve the eidolon?" She emerged from the veil of leaves.

Berrin said, "Yes. More like fighting a shadow than a real man, but it didn't like being cut."

"They don't. Well, ours don't. They take their reality from us and we don't like being cut either." She shrugged.

Berrin lifted a tail of leaves with his sword. "What happened to the other thing?"

Suddenly self-conscious, Kiar said, "I banished it. I don't know how or why it was doing what it was doing, but sky fiends can be kicked out of the world, just like the books said."

Berrin grinned. "Lady Wizard." He bowed and sheathed his sword.

Kiar blushed. "Twist would have been much faster about it."

He still grinned. "Of course. Here, you'll want to brush that dirt off before the old man brings back the militia." He pointed a knuckle at her face and side.

Her blush deepened as she rubbed at her face, and shook soil and dead leaves from her clothes. "I'm sorry I left you to fight the eidolon alone. I wanted to see if I could deal with what created it." *I don't understand what sky fiends have to do with rogue eidolons and a screaming plague....*

"Lady, I'm your guard. If you didn't trust me to handle that kind of thing, I'd be ashamed of myself." He pulled his grin back to a solemn expression.

"Well, thank you." She walked out of the grove and looked up at the sky. "I really hope there aren't any more of those around. More sick people to inspect is bad enough...."

CHAPTER TEN

A MEASURE OF NIGHT

Jerya and Lisette went to the Justiciar's Court again the next morning, and Tiana thought she'd start the day on a positive note by keeping her sister company. The reception was in the evening, so she could easily spare the morning. This time, however, she brought her long-neglected basket of lace crochet with her.

The Hall was full this morning, with a crowd of finely dressed people brightening the audience. More than once, as she let her gaze rove the Hall, she met the stare of someone watching the Royal Box. She smiled the first time it happened, out of habit, but then she realized why they looked away. Her smile took on a feral edge she couldn't control.

Jerya said, "What a frightening expression," and Tiana wilted. Jerya patted her hand. "It's all right."

The clerk went to the Justiciar's table and passed a message to Lord Warrane. He read it, covered his eyes and then glanced at the box, meeting Tiana's stare. This time, he smiled. Then he scribbled something and passed the note back.

After the third case, a request for arbitration on who was responsible for fixing a washed out bridge, Jerya and Lisette consulted. Then, Jerya announced her approval of the decision, her voice firm. The Justiciars muttered, except for Lord Warrane and Lord Donatien, who both frowned at the Royal Box.

The audience, however, murmured and moved in response to Jerya's approval. A bearded man called to the favored plaintiff, "Bad luck, getting the Blood's attention."

Tiana transferred her gaze from Jerya to the audience, and the neighbors of the unwise speaker moved several steps away from him. It was funny, she told herself, and tried to bring her best glare to the surface. *The monsters are back.* And the murmuring stilled. Hysterical laughter bubbled to the surface, and she giggled before she managed to calm herself. She was the perfect patron princess, everything Jerya would be proud of.

As the morning wore on, she amused herself by trying to guess what each group or individual standing in line was there for. The servants were almost always dressed in some kind of livery, with the absent-minded attentiveness she'd come to recognize. The peasants were far more aware of their position in line. Some of them huddled close together, while others were rivals and shared a case, but no amiability. The scholars occupied a third category of petitioner; their clothing varied wildly, but they almost always had documents, or even portfolios, with them.

An example of the third set was next in line. There were two men and a woman. The woman was wearing the sigil and stole of an astrologer, and she held a case. One of the men was dressed like a well-to-do merchant, the kind who would ordinarily have a servant stand in line for him. He was holding a chain with a number of small clocks attached to it.

The other, bearded, was dressed in the simple homespun robes of a monk. Tiana leaned forward, and around his neck she could see the wooden torc of the Firstborn Keldera, plowman's patron, with a blue and yellow bead on each side. She couldn't remember what the colors of the Keldaran beads signified, but she knew that only two meant he wasn't highly placed in Keldaran hierarchy.

The center of Keldaran power was far to the east, at Lachan and Lake Morning. The priests appeared at Sangwys to welcome the summer and at Nomenflor, Keldera's high holy day, but otherwise, she had little experience with them. She wondered if they'd come to report on the harvest.

The trio moved to the white line. The merchant introduced himself. "I am Gregori Yale. I make fine clocks. This is Mistress Vanelle Petring, a customer of mine. Several years ago, she expressed a complaint about my craftsmanship and, in doing so, brought something very disturbing to my attention. She said that over the past seven years or so, my attention to detail had slipped and that my clocks were no longer as precise as they used to be. I take pride in my work, so I investigated."

Tiana glanced at the Justiciar's table and saw members frowning, several shifting impatiently. Perhaps this wasn't a scholarly report, as she'd thought. Perhaps this was some sort of dispute they needed settled instead.

"Her specific complaint was that my clocks were losing time much faster than they used to. She produced records of certain astrological events which happen reliably, at the same time, on the same day, every year. She brings those with her today."

He gestured at the woman and her case. "I checked my mathematics and they were sound. The materials were not degrading more quickly. We could find nothing that would account for it.

"Eventually, I invited her to my shop, which has hundreds of clocks of my own and others' craftsmanship. There we observed and timed the display of a certain stellar phenomenon known as the Winterdark Companion. Its passage, two days before Pyrvalis, is very predictable."

The man paused and took a deep breath. "It was late. By every clock, by every calculation of dusk and dawn, it was late." He looked around, at dozens of puzzled faces, and nodded. "I was confused. I turned to another correspondent of mine, Brother Jan Black, of the Keldaran Canticlars.

"Once I explained what concerned us, he was able to corroborate our findings. But what we concluded was so… disturbing that we decided to spend several years seeking opinions from others before we decided that it was worth reporting to the Court."

Lord Aubin, eldest of the Council, said, "What were your conclusions, Master Yale? That the astrologer's art is less precise than previously thought?'

Gregori Yale shook his head and glanced at his companions. The monk raised his voice. "My Lords, My Ladies, honored Justiciars, today will be approximately ten minutes shorter than this day three years ago. The night will be that much longer." He paused and added, "That is what I tracked, you see. The dawn. It comes later and the sun sets earlier, each year. Once, this was not so."

Jerya spoke abruptly, "Do you know when this changed?"

The astrologer worried her lip with her teeth and stepped closer to her companions. "We are not sure, Your Highness. The change seems to have... accelerated in the past few years. I first began noticing irregularities a decade ago. At first, it was a change of less than a minute from year to year." When Mistress Vanelle fell silent, the Hall was so quiet nobody seemed to be breathing. Then it exploded with the clamor of voices.

Jerya looked at Lisette and then across the crowd, chewing on a finger. Lisette was doing math on her ledger. Tiana stared at her sister, trying to understand the meaning of what the scholars were claiming. The days were getting shorter and the nights were getting longer. "Some kind of eclipse?" she called. The crowd quieted.

Mistress Vanelle lowered her gaze. "That is one way of understanding it. It is not a phenomenon documented in any of my art's tomes. But we may hope it comes and goes with no more import than an eclipse."

Jerya said, "Brother Jan Black, has your order no thoughts on this? Keldera is the mother of dawn, is she not?"

The monk bowed deeply. "Your Highness. While she does look with affection on the dawn, Keldera is the mistress of summer and agriculture. The movements of the celestial bodies are the province of all the Firstborn. My order is concerned by this, but we believe it to be a consequence of a greater ill, just as the disrupted weather patterns are."

"Which is?" Jerya demanded. The audience caught its breath, anticipating the answer.

The monk shifted his weight and looked at his feet. "Opinions vary on the source. Some blame Vassay's recent activities. Some call it a Blight—" The crowd rippled.

Lord Warrane interrupted, "And what do the Niyhani

and the Logos-workers say, sir?"

The monk weighed his answer carefully. "The Logos does not seem to directly indicate anything has changed. However—"

Lord Aubin said, "Ever since Benjen, it has been popular to blame any ill on a Blight. But history tells us that there is perhaps one a generation. Doesn't it seem far more probable that some sort of new phenomena is distorting your figures? Perhaps you should reanalyze the basic tenets of your discipline. Or redo your math. In any case, leave your charts with a clerk, and we will consult experts in the field and decide what is going on."

Silence pooled around the three scholars. Then a clerk took their documents and the audience came back to life, rustling and murmuring as if nothing very interesting had happened. Jerya stretched, elaborately casual, and then leaned her chin on her palm. She held up the back of her other hand to the Justiciars, unfolding her fingers, one, two. Tiana realized she was keeping count of each major problem the Court was ignoring, and that somehow, just by moving her fingers, she was making a threat. She wondered if they were as intimidated as she was.

Jerya's voice was light as she said, "It's not a universal conspiracy to suppress information, whatever our Uncle Yithiere tells me. I spoke to him yesterday and—" She shook her head. "Well. That isn't happening here. The guards screen the petitioners. Those they deem inappropriate or dangerous are turned away, without recourse. Somebody decided their story needed to be publicly heard."

Tiana leaned forward. "What's the worst way to interpret it?"

Lisette looked up at Tiana, pushing her chestnut hair

aside. "If the days keep getting shorter? Between that and
the weather, there will be a famine. Life is already hard for
the farmers and peasants. If their discovery is true…."
Lisette shook her head. "It would be very bad. I've never
even heard stories of anything like this, have you? But even
if it's a cycle that will peak and end, like the year itself, the
Court can encourage people to start planning for it."

Tiana pushed her own hair back behind her shoulders.
"Isn't that good? I thought stores were how one survived
famines."

Lisette shrugged. "Maybe. Maybe not. I don't know. Ask
Yithiere."

Tiana frowned and sat back again. It was disheartening.
Something was going on. Somebody was trying to keep
them out. She wasn't sure about getting involved in ordinary
politics, but it *was* the ancestral duty of the Blood to protect
Ceria from supernatural threats. She worried that this was
both politics and a supernatural threat, though. And who did
you kill to keep the sun in the sky longer? She closed her
mouth over another burst of shocked laughter. What would
they do in the theater?

She entertained herself in this way for a while. Then she
noticed that another homespun-garbed monk was in line. This
one carried a bundle wrapped in burlap, which prevented her
from seeing which of the Firstborn he was associated with.
He was alone, and he kept looking at the Royal Box, his eyes
feverishly bright. She met his gaze, and he smiled and nodded
to her jerkily. His smile was a frightening, gap-toothed thing,
with no sense behind it. She lowered her eyes and watched
him more furtively, braiding a loose lock of her hair.

When he approached the white line, Lord Donatien
smiled grimly. "Brother Helliac," he said. "We've heard so

much about you."

The monk nodded eagerly, trying to bow around his bundle. "I've come and come and waited and thank you so much for allowing me in today. It's been so important. I'm glad you finally agree. I spoke with a young man about the night, is that why? No matter, but now you understand."

Lord Donatien said generously, "Oh, of course we do. You had a gift for the Blood and they've been so unavailable. But today, we have two members with us, observing."

Brother Helliac turned his bright gaze to the Royal Box. "I know."

Jerya tilted her head and called, "What is this about, my lord?"

Lord Donatien said, "Brother Helliac here has been petitioning the gatekeeper for access to the Blood. He has a mysterious gift that he resists identifying, Your Highness. Normally, we strive to protect the Blood from dangerous wastes of their time, but since you're here anyhow, I thought perhaps you'd like to meet him and accept his gift." The monk nodded throughout Lord Donatien's words, the absent smile never changing.

Once again the Hall was silent. Encouragingly, Lord Donatien added, "It doesn't seem to be a poisonous snake, but if it were, I'm sure you could handle it." The silence rolled back across the room.

You'd better run, because I'm not going to. Tiana rose to her feet. Lord Donatien closed his mouth abruptly, and Lord Warrane scowled. She looked down at Jerya's impassive face and said loftily, "I'll accept his gift in the name of our family, if you don't mind, my darling sister." *The monsters are back.* But laughing was inappropriate. So was crying.

Jerya nodded once, and Tiana approached the white line

and the monk standing before it. Slater shadowed her, two steps behind. The monk held his bundle close, staring at her. His smile faded, and he rasped in a voice suddenly rough, "You're of the Blood? You've the hair and the eyes, but show me your power."

Tiana resisted rolling her eyes and looked around at her observers. The Justiciars wore a mixture of amused and concerned expressions. Lisette shook her head almost imperceptibly, while Jerya nodded approval. This was probably an attempt to humiliate them, but she felt supremely unconcerned about the possibility.

She rose up on her toes and then hoisted herself into the air, floating on an emanation. She folded her legs beneath her into a dignified sitting position, for all that her skirt remained hanging down. Murmurs rippled across the audience.

The mad smile returned and the monk said, "Oh, wonderful, wonderful, you're real this time. The games they play…." He shook his head and clicked his tongue. "Come down, come down." He fumbled under his bundle and pulled out a small pot. From her vantage point, Tiana could see that he wore no church insignia at all.

He laid the bundle on the ground; it was almost as big as he was. Then he waved her closer, within easy reach. She heard Slater hiss a warning behind her, but she ignored him and drifted closer, letting her feet touch the ground just a step away from the monk and his bundle. He was barely taller than she was, a shriveled old man with a bald pate and big, bushy eyebrows. In his pot was what appeared to be some kind of blue salve or cosmetic. He dabbed his fingers into the substance and then held them out to Tiana, as if to put the substance on her face.

There was a chuckle from the Justiciar's Table behind her,

though she wasn't sure who it was from. She'd have to find out from Lisette later. She studied the monk, if monk he was. The substance in his pot didn't have much of an odor. She looked at the color on his fingers and then at the man's vivid blue eyes, his crazed smile. But a crazed smile didn't mean much; if she avoided crazed smiles, she'd be avoiding half her family. She had to trust her instincts and to her instincts, he just didn't feel dangerous.

She lowered her head and let him dab some of it on her forehead. It was cold. He was drawing a shape. She tried to look like she was being generous and kind to a mad, old man, rather than embarrassed, even if she wasn't sure what was going on. After he was done, he picked up his bundle and stroked his hand along the coverings. Then, still crouched down, presented it to Tiana, lifting it higher than his bowed head.

Tiana lifted the bundle from his hands. It was lighter than she expected and she found, as she pulled the wrappings away, that the weight was mostly from the fabric. She pulled away two layers of cloth, found a third layer and glanced up uneasily to see the monk's intent smile. She repressed a nervous laugh. Whatever it was, it was long and slender—a cane or a staff?

The fourth covering, of silk, slipped away, and she stared at gleaming, razor-sharp metal peeking out from beneath the fifth and final hide wrapping. Then, carefully, she adjusted her grip downward until she found the bulge of the quillon and below that, the handle. Then, gripping that with both hands, she let the rest of the wrapping fall away from the sword.

The blade was wider than the swords used by the Guard, but it was heavily etched and engraved with short lines and swirling designs. A deep groove paralleled the edge of the blade. Closer to the hilt, the blade widened even further, with frightening, fang-like protrusions. The rough interior of the lower part of the blade was stained a reddish black and an ebony stone was set directly in the metal above the handle.

The marking on her forehead tingled. Then, it burned. She clapped one hand over it, turning an embarrassing shriek into a less embarrassing whimper. Her forehead was cool to the touch, and she couldn't feel the paint at all.

As she traced her fingers over the place where the mark had been drawn, the monk rose to his feet and lightly touched the blade with his hands, directing it down on the level, so it pointed at him. He smiled at Tiana, holding the blade down as she frowned at him. This time the smile wasn't mad at all, but calm and encouraging.

Softly, he said, "He will be cruel, but you are strong."

Then he stepped forward and pushed himself onto the point of the sword, pulling himself forward with bleeding hands until the blade emerged from his back. Falling to his knees, he reached up to brush Tiana's shocked face with crimson fingers.

The stained interior of the blade turned from black to scarlet. This time, she failed to control her scream.

Chapter Eleven

Cookie Reception

Lisette tried to suggest, in her delicate Regent way, that Tiana miss the reception that evening. She'd had quite a shock, after all. But Tiana wasn't having any of that, not after her first day at court, not after today. She'd *earned* the reception. Twice in one week, her hands were covered in blood, but so what? She was the Blood; did they expect something else?

The Chancellor tried to suggest, in his gruff Chancellor way, that he take the sword and put it someplace safe. It would only further disturb her if it was around. Tiana wasn't having any of that, either. She put it on the mantle over her fireplace, where some people put trophies.

Then she went to write a letter to her mother, detailing all the pleasant parts of her week. It was very short, but it was traditional. When she was done, she put the letter into the same box she'd been putting letters to her mother in for the last eight years. It was a big box, with three neat stacks of paper. But it didn't bring her the usual release from anxiety when she was done.

She drifted around her rooms, frowning over Lisette's shoulder at the notes she was copying. She picked up the copy of the Royal Pendant she'd found in the catacombs, toyed with it, dropped it again. Kiar said it was nothing but an eidolon shadow, and Tiana needed something real to distract her. Something real and decidedly unmysterious. She scowled at the gown she'd picked out yesterday. It displeased her.

"I want something red, Lisette," she announced. "A red dress."

Lisette looked at her. "Red."

"That's what I said!"

Lisette said, "I'll see what I can find." She blotted her writing and went to the dressing room.

Tiana called, "I'm fine, you know. And everybody needs to know I'm fine. The Chancellor works so hard on these receptions and nobody ever appreciates them." She worked on unbraiding her hair. "We should do something nice with my hair. Something that shows I take the receptions very seriously."

Lisette emerged with a crimson dress Tiana had never worn before. It flared at the hips and had long, tight sleeves. "Did you outgrow this?"

She stood up and let Lisette measure her. "I'm quite looking forward to being engaged, actually. And married. Do you think anyone will want to marry me now?" Before Lisette could answer, she laughed. "I'm being silly."

"I understand it's quite nice for the right people, but not for everyone." Lisette observed, and helped her put the dress on. The vows of a Regent forbade her to marry and have a family of her own.

"Yes, but the Blood has to reproduce," Tiana protested. The Chancellor was very concerned by the subject. "Everyone's been so stubborn about it lately." She shook her head sadly. "It's so unfair. I can't carry on the line alone, Lisette!"

Lisette patted her shoulder and then pushed her to a chair, so she could begin working on Tiana's hair.

"Do you think we have to find a husband for Shanasee before anybody else can wed?" Shanasee had been engaged once long ago, when Tiana was still in the nursery. Tiana had never quite worked out what had gone wrong; the suitor had run away, Shanasee had changed her mind, or one of her uncles had meddled.

"Lord of Love! Or do you think it's Yithiere? He's got a grown daughter! And no one would want him!"

Lisette laughed. "It's not a curse. Seandri was engaged once, after all."

"Yes, but he never got *married*. That was a mess." Right after Tiana started attending the receptions, Seandri liked a Kaximon girl enough that the Chancellor felt comfortable moving forward with an engagement.

Seandri didn't mind but unflappable Jerya *did*. She found the Kaximon girl utterly repulsive, and overnight she became moody and snappish. Iriss provided no explanations, and Lisette and Tiana both worried Jerya would lash out at the next reception. And then, one day, it was all over. The engagement was called off, the Kaximon girl was never again seen at court, and Jerya returned to her old self.

"We all meddle too much," she said. "With each other. Jerya meddled with Seandri's engagement, and Uncle Pell or whoever with Shanasee's. Why do we do that?"

Lisette said, "You know the saying: 'Only the Blood can

understand the Blood.' In the phantasmagory, you've got a connection to each other that nobody else can share. And who, but the Blood, understands the eidolons?"

"Yes, but that doesn't *go away* if we get married. We don't lose that connection. Look at Jant." Jant was Shanasee's father and Tiana's great-uncle. "He's been married for forty years, and he's still closer to us than his wife. There's no *reason* to meddle."

Lisette shrugged, smiling faintly, and adjusted a ribbon. "People are complicated in ways that don't always make sense. Would you like to go for a walk before the reception?"

Tiana said, "Something terrible would happen to ruin my hair. I'll just look out the window while you get ready."

There was a five sided table in the center of the Gala Room, where the reception was held. On the table were four platters of cookies, in four different colors. Against the wall was another table, with four matching bowls filled with tiny wrapped packages. Inside each cookie was a tiny scroll containing instructions. It was traditional that if you ate a cookie, you followed the instructions it contained.

Lisette insisted they arrive late, as she always did, so that the reception was already in progress. There was the usual mix of strangers and familiar faces; the Chancellor had perennial favorites he liked to invite, and any member of a Regent's immediate family had a standing invitation. A string ensemble was in the corner, playing atmospheric music.

Jerya was standing in front of the cookie table, staring at it, chewing on her lip. Her dress was silver with gold accents, and nicer than what she usually wore to the receptions. When

Tiana and Lisette joined her at the table, she said, "What color should I pick?"

Tiana said, "Iriss is going to kill you when she wakes up and sees what you've done to your lips the last few days."

Lisette said, "It depends on what you're looking for. Red's the most dramatic. Yellow is fun. Blue is subdued. Green is a mix."

"Which one has the duets?"

Tiana said promptly, "Green."

Jerya picked up a blue cookie and tentatively took a bite. The pastry crumbled against her lips, and she pulled out a scroll with her teeth. Then she ate the rest of the cookie and read the scroll aloud. "'Turn a quarter-turn to your left, and ask for a childhood memory of the person you find there.'" She turned her head.

"Oh, it's Yevonne's mother. That's a good start." Yevonne, Regent to their youngest cousin, was born a commoner, and her mother often took advantage of the receptions to work on furthering connections for her family. It wasn't at all *usual* for the Blood to choose a commoner child as a Regent. But Gisen had firmly rejected all the noble children presented to her and found Yevonne instead. It was the Regency's policy to work with what they had, rather than what they wished they had.

Before she could walk away, Tiana said, "Jerya, why are you suddenly interested in the cookie game?"

Jerya paused and turned back. "We wed for political gains as well as children, Tiana. We all grew up here, together, because of Benjen, but in previous generations, some of our cousins would have grown up in other noble houses, with other family names. Nearly strangers, meeting again at a reception like this and our Blood drawing us together. We should be keeping the country together, not hiding in a fortress. If I'm to be a good Queen, I can't avoid parties forever." She smiled absently and went to speak with Yevonne's mother.

The Chancellor joined them, while Tiana wondered if Jerya was prepared to let Seandri wed as well. "Ah, Your Highness. I see Cathay hasn't joined us yet. Would you mind eating this cookie, while facing in this direction?" He proffered a yellow cookie. "It's lemon, your favorite."

Tiana rolled her eyes. "That's cheating, Your Excellency."

"Cathay cheats shamelessly, my dear. The vermin thank him, but he makes my job much harder." He waggled his eyebrows.

Tiana took the cookie and opened it expertly, rescuing the scroll before popping the two halves in her mouth. "'To your right is a lady or gentleman dreaming of a dance to the gentle strains of Ja Nei Terrel. Grant their wish.'"

Tiana looked to her right. A few yards away, a young man and a young woman stood together. Siblings, Tiana thought. He was reasonably attractive, with thick chestnut hair, striking green eyes, and a lovely embroidered green shirt. "Who is it?"

"His name is Brandon Lanadon, from Hypana. He has excellent court manners and a strong sense of family."

Tiana felt a brush of irritation at what the Chancellor considered valuable in her future husband and then wondered what *she* considered valuable. Didn't she cherish a strong sense of family, after the decision her mother made?

She strolled over to the string ensemble and asked them to play Ja Nei Terrel, the Candy Waltz, then wandered over to Brandon and his sister and smiled at them. "May I borrow your brother, Your Ladyship? I've instructions here to dance with him." She offered Brandon the scroll.

The sister curtseyed, even as her eyes widened. Brandon took her hand, smiling broadly, and they began the simple steps of the dance.

"I've been looking forward to meeting you, Your Serene Highness. I didn't anticipate it would be quite so soon. I only arrived in Lor Seleni last week."

He must be nervous, Tiana decided. "Was your journey pleasant?" she inquired.

They twirled in unison, and when they came together again, he said, "It was wretchedly hot, actually." And then he fell silent, staring at her. Tiana found she was little motivated to do the work to encourage him.

After another twirl, he said, "You do resemble your mother. I see it in the nose and the set of your eyes."

Tiana missed a step. "You know my mother?"

He sounded more assured as he said, "Yes, of course. She's a cousin. The Queen's Court is quite elegant."

Tiana back stepped, as the dance dictated, and stopped. "How pleasant for you. Unfortunately, I've just realized we're not accepting new friends from Hypana at this time." Suddenly shaking with nerves, she curtsied to end the dance and fled back to Lisette and the Chancellor.

"I hate you," she said to the Chancellor.

He was surprised. "Whatever for? You've enjoyed conversation with those connected to the Queen before. Was he rude?"

Tiana frowned. It was true, she had. But they were just daydreams of another life. Today, those daydreams felt shallow and cheap. And she was angry at her mother, without quite knowing why. The realization made her dizzy, made her ache for the comfort of the phantasmagory.

She squeezed her eyes shut and blindly reached for a cookie. It was a red one. She broke it open. "Give a RED TREASURE to the person who arrived after you." She scowled. "That's you, Lisette."

"Do over?" Lisette suggested.

Tiana shook her head and marched over to the treasure table, snatched a red package from its bowl, and returned to hand it to Lisette. "This isn't as much fun without Kiar and Iriss," she complained.

Lisette opened the box. Inside was a tiny, iron brooch, wrought like a gauntlet. She made a face and pinned it carefully to her sleeve. "I hate the iron prizes."

Yevonne and Gisen appeared at Lisette's elbow, both grinning. Among the family, they were known as the 'little girls,' but recently they'd encountered puberty and puberty was winning. They were still smaller than Tiana, though, and she hoped that would remain true.

Yevonne said, "You have to sing a duet with me, Tiana. It says "Mirian Riding," but Gisen wants us to sing "Elohin's Younger Sister" instead. Do you remember it?"

Tiana embraced the chance to lift her plummeting mood. "Of course I do, but what's the point if you're not going to follow the instructions?"

Gisen poked Tiana, and Yevonne's smile became her 'I'm a stupid commoner brat' grin. "'Cause it's music and Gisen said so, obviously."

Tiana resisted a smile. "Oh, very well then." She and Yevonne moved to the head of the room to serenade the reception, Gisen trailing behind them. Gisen didn't talk much, but she had a phenomenal gift for music, and Yevonne's voice was one of her pet projects. And it was true that "Elohin's Younger Sister" sounded better with their voices than "Mirian

Riding." It was pure joy singing with Yevonne in public; suddenly Tiana felt a rush of anticipation for Antecession and the musical performance that came with it.

She felt so good when they were done that even seeing the Chancellor pass a cookie to a young man didn't ruin her mood. He was slender, not very tall, with dark hair and an expressive mouth. When he approached her, she even remembered his name from previous receptions.

"Perre, right? From the Shell Coast?" He had a slip of paper and a blue package.

"That I am, Your Highness. I'm to deliver this prize to a lady who shares an interest with me."

Tiana smiled, looking up at him. "And what interest is that?"

He smiled back. "Do you know Tel-Lor-Moon?" He had a beautiful smile.

"It's one of my favorite plays." Tiana watched Jerya stroll past with an older man.

"Well then, it sounds like you win." He offered her the package. "I played Kestrel for a fortnight, in a performance back home. Have you seen any other of Jennet Damarcy's plays?"

Delighted, Tiana said, "You act? On stage? That's wonderful." She opened the package. Inside was a smoky quartz charm, shaped like a closed book. She beamed and added it to her reception bracelet. When she looked up, Perre was watching her in some amusement, and she recalled he'd asked her a question. "Oh, no, I haven't. I've read them, but they're didn't engage me as much."

"They're dense," he said agreeably. "I've heard tales that you're involved with a show in the Small-light district. Is it true? Which one?"

"Yes, I am! But I'm not on stage. It's new, it's by—"

"I hate to interrupt," said Cathay, her cousin, from behind Tiana, "but I have an instruction here that requires Her Highness." Irritation surged through Tiana again, and her head started to distantly ache. But Perre just smiled.

"Another time then, Your Highness. Enjoy the charm." He bowed and slipped away as Cathay took Tiana's hand.

"Give me that," she snapped and plucked the scroll from Cathay's other hand. "'Stroll around the room with the loveliest person present.'" She stared suspiciously at the calligraphy. "Do you write these yourself?"

"Stormy weather! You wound me." He tucked her hand into his arm and grinned at her, his black eyes dancing. Her irritation ebbed away. "Each scroll is written by the Royal Calligrapher himself. Though I must admit, I do lie sometimes."

"Yes? Only sometimes?" She tucked the scroll into her wristlet.

He tweaked the tip of her nose. "You make it hard to confess, you know. I was actually quite happy to interrupt. I've heard he's a terrible actor, stormy."

"Mm-hmm," she said. She couldn't help herself. It was like his voice wove a spell. He'd only started flirting with her recently. Before the last year or so, he'd just been her handsome older cousin, more interested in swords and horses than her, more involved with his Regent and his uncles and even Jerya, who was his own age, than with his younger cousins. But she'd watched him focus his interest on Jerya, on Iriss, on a noble girl or two, then on Lisette, all with a single-minded intensity.

So, she hadn't been surprised exactly, when he turned his attention to her. Not surprised, but definitely unprepared.

His attention was as genuine and as warming as the summer sun. She knew it wouldn't last, but the temptation to bask in it was so strong. And here, compared to all the other boys— well, he was her own kind. He knew the phantasmagory; he practiced the family magic. He was intimately aware of the fate that seemed to await them all, and he wouldn't reject her because of it, the way Tiana's mother had rejected her husband and children.

No. He'll just find something else that interests him more. She wished her head would stop hurting, though. Each time he smiled it jarred her, and she knew that made no sense.

Cathay continued abusing her previous suitor. "Oh, yes. He botches his lines. Dozes when he's offstage." Sudden inspiration seemed to strike Cathay. "And he can't sing." He shook his head. "It's very depressing. I've also heard that he's a coward…."

"But you lie sometimes," Tiana reminded him sweetly.

He spun her around to face him. "Truth of the mountain, I swear!"

She looked at him skeptically. His face was empty of all guile, as sweet and honest as a monk's, and he held the earnest expression for a long moment.

"You should be an actor yourself!" she said, laughing, and pushed him away.

He caught her hands as she pushed and pulled her close to him. "Would you like that? I'll do it, but only if you direct me." Tiana's stomach flip-flopped.

"Hey, Cathay. Hey, time to let Tiana go, Cathay," It was Yevonne. "Gisen has an instruction for you. Come see."

Cathay made a face and said, "Little girls should go to bed early, don't you think, Tiana?"

Tiana looked to the wall, where Lisette and Gisen were

standing. Gisen waved a piece of paper imperiously.

Yevonne bumped her little hip against him. "Come tell Gisen that. Come on. Look at that face. You don't want to break her heart, do you?"

Cathay said, "Oh, all right." He pointed a finger at Tiana. "You be good," and then followed Yevonne over to Gisen.

Tiana looked around. Jerya was nowhere to be seen, and the Chancellor was talking to one of the ambassadors. She spotted Seandri loitering in a corner with his Regent and had just started that direction when Twist stepped into existence beside her. He had a slip of paper.

"Delicious," he said. "I love macaroons."

Tiana blinked. "They're pastry, not macaroons!"

Twist said cheerfully, "Oops! Here." He passed her the scroll. There was nothing on it.

"It's blank! Apparently because you found it in a macaroon!" Her head pounded. She shook her head and looked over her shoulder. "Is somebody calling for me? I thought I heard my name." But nobody seemed to be looking for her. Nervously, she scanned the room, wondering if the phantasmagory was leaking again.

The Royal Wizard shook his head. "Forget my own name next." He touched a manicured fingernail to the scrap of paper, muttered something, and words bloomed across it.

"Why does *everybody* cheat at the cookie game?" She stared at Twist fiercely, rather than reading the slip.

Twist smiled at her. "Because you make it so much fun." She blushed, and again her irritation melted away. Her head hurt. She ignored it.

She read the scroll. "'Advise somebody consorting with fiends.' What? I am *not* consorting with fiends!" But she wondered again about the pendant she'd found.

Suddenly serious, Twist said, "I inspected the monk's sword before, and it seemed quite ordinary. But I think I should inspect it again."

Tiana did *not* want to think about the sword, of all things. "Why?"

"Because it seems to be leaving—" Twist paused to pluck invisible cobwebs out of her hair, "—sticky fingerprints—" he brushed his finger under her left eye, "—all over you." Her headache magnified. "Or something is."

"Well, fine," she muttered, moving away. "Later." Her head was down, so inevitably, she collided with somebody.

"My apologies," said an intense, low voice. It was another vaguely familiar face, high cheekbones and beautiful eyes, a neatly trimmed goatee. This time she didn't recall his name.

"Should have looked where I was going," she said. "Did I hurt you?"

"'The Blood walks where it pleases,'" quoted the young man, and Tiana started.

"Most people don't say that to us. Not to our faces, anyhow."

"I search for truth, Princess Tiana." He didn't smile, and his gaze was intense.

"How can you recognize it when you see it?" she asked, with more than a touch of irritation. He fell into step beside her.

"It's in the moments." She could feel his eyes on her. "You've had several moments recently, I think."

"What are you talking about?"

"You were attacked in the city. That was a moment; what you felt then was truth. And today, with the monk and the sword. How did that feel?" He was too close, leaning in with an avid curiosity. She recoiled.

"Have you no manners at all? How did you get in here?"

He stood quietly. "I was invited, Your Highness. I am Rayle Orthoza, from Dalein. And as I said, I seek truth. Manners are a veil that often hide it."

Tiana remembered him now. He was a poet. Suddenly, poetry seemed like the worst form of obscenity.

She fought down a snarl. "Go away. Don't come back." He paled, but bowed and retreated.

Tiana pressed her fingers against her temples. The room felt too crowded. She had the hysterical desire to sweep everyone away from her. It was ludicrous.

Lisette appeared at her elbow. "You're not having a good time. Would you like to go outside and get some fresh air?"

Tiana bit her knuckle hard, and it still didn't cut through the pain in her head. She was certain someone was whispering her name. "No," she said. "No. This isn't fun. I want to go to bed. Things will be better tomorrow."

Chapter Twelve

Enter Fiend

Eventually, Tiana fell into a restless, painful sleep.

After a time of darkness, Treyl and his companions emerged from the shadows, but the sword was in her hand. She swung at her attackers and they fell away, shattered by the power of the sword. She knew its name: Jinriki the Darkener. More shadowy enemies rose to threaten her, and the sword Jinriki hungered to slay them, thirsted to take vengeance on those who had wronged her.

She opened her hand, let the sword tumble out of it and turned to gather the shadows to herself with her own power: phantasmagory dreams. She didn't like swords. They weren't hers, pointed pieces of metal, shining, dangerous things. She didn't need them to be dangerous. Only Shanasee had the capacity to be more dangerous than she. Tiana was gifted. She was special. But she was the one who wasn't going to go crazy. She was the one who was going to escape.

From darkness, walls rose around her and Jinriki the

Darkener was in her hand again, slicing through walls of metal and stone and betrayal. She was caged and the sword could free her, the sword could bring her out of the darkness, to freedom and vengeance on those who had imprisoned her.

Phantasmagory dreams, but walls were Kiar's quirk, Kiar's fear. The cage was in herself, in her own blood. A woman watched her curiously, her hair a river, her eyes the night. Tiana opened her hand, let the sword tumble out of it, but it didn't fall away. The quillon and the guard curved around her hand, clasping itself to her palm. She swung her hand and the blade cut an arc from the darkness. A crescent of crimson, a scarlet tear, and she panicked, shaking her hand, pushing at the guard with her other hand. Part of the quillon twisted to catch her other hand, holding them together, curling her fingers around the handle. She was trapped, imprisoned by a sword in her hand. She shrieked. "No! I don't want the sword! I don't want it! That isn't me! I won't use it!"

An unfamiliar voice said, "You will *learn*."

Fear spiked down her spine and she reached out with her emanation, her third hand, and ripped herself free of the weapon. Her hands ran red with her own blood now, as the sword bit down rather than release her. But it could not hold on to something that dissolved when caught, and the sword flew away from her. It vanished into a darkness that opened silver eyes. The silver eyes grew larger, larger, and became the morning light streaming through her window.

Tiana woke up ravenous. She sat up, an echo of the earlier headache still lingering, and looked at her hands. They were uninjured. Her shoulder was still sore and stiff from two days ago, though. She thought about how nice it was to have physical reminders of what was real and what wasn't.

She stood up and immediately sat down again, feeling dizzy and uncoordinated. Deep breaths made her head spin and her headache intensify and her palms hurt. She checked her hands again to make sure they weren't injured. *Maybe I was clenching my nails into my palms.* But there were no marks at all.

She heard sounds in the parlor, and a moment of listening identified the sounds of Lisette, Cathay, and dishes. *Breakfast.* She ignored the dizziness and headache, and went to find clothing that wouldn't distract Cathay while she devoured the food.

When she emerged from her bedroom, Lisette looked up and smiled. "Hungry? I had breakfast brought in this morning."

Tiana said, "Starving. Not just breakfast, I see." She made a face at Cathay. She picked up the hem of her dressing gown as she stalked across the sitting room, until the dizziness overwhelmed her and she stumbled. Cathay sprang to his feet and caught her arm and waist.

"Let me help you, stormy. Are you feeling better? I was worried when you left so suddenly. Chancellor Hayle and I both had stern words with that fellow who drove you off. Tasteless bastard."

Decorously, Cathay placed her in the seat he'd just vacated and whisked the plate of bread crumbs there away. Lisette put a new plate in front of her and Tiana helped herself from the tray of fruit and bread and ham in the center of the table.

"Thank you," she remembered to say, after a moment. She wondered if he'd actually chastised the poet.

Cathay laughed and watched her eat, a smile lingering on his face. She wondered what he and Lisette had been talking about before she woke up.

"I dreamt about the sword," Tiana said, waving a spoon at the shelf where Jinriki rested. It had split the scabbard the Chancellor found for her when she insisted on keeping it; the flanges near the handle were too wide.

Cathay considered and then said, "I have to say that if you were going to dream about recent events, that's almost the best of the options." He smirked. "Almost."

Tiana frowned. "Not really. Well, maybe for you."

Cathay stole a covetous glance at the sword. "It's a magnificent thing. I can see that from here."

Tiana narrowed her eyes, suddenly not certain Cathay was there to visit *her*. His fixation on swords was almost as renowned as his womanizing. She jabbed her spoon into her melon half. "It's a horrible thing. It even looks evil. It has these spiky bits that look like they're just as likely to cut me as anyone on the other end. I can't imagine who would use it or why that old man was carrying it around.

Foolish child.

Cathay stood up. "May I look at it?" Tiana waved her spoon at the shelf again, her mouth full, and Cathay went to pick it up. He pulled the ruined scabbard off and held the quillons up to eye level. Tiana watched anxiously, but the crosspieces did not curve around to embrace Cathay's hand.

He may look.

"Very ornamental. Some kind of lord's or general's weapon, probably. Maybe from the Soosing Coast. It's very old." He extended his arm and moved the blade in a tight maneuver. "Nicer to handle than I expected." Cathay gave her a bright smile. "What will you do with it?"

Tiana shrugged again. "It'll give me nightmares. Do you want it?"

I am not his.

Cathay said, "I'd be honored, stormy." He swished it again, looking smug.

No.

Cathay grunted suddenly, his eyes widening. Blood welled from the spaces between his fingers on the hand holding the sword. Then, his eyes turned pale as his attention focused inward. He lifted his other hand to grip higher on the handle.

"Cathay!" Tiana sprang to his side, food forgotten. Cathay's knuckles were white under the blood and his teeth were gritted. His eyes flickered between black and white, and Tiana felt the jolt of his dance around the phantasmagory.

"Cathay," she cried again and wrapped her own hands around his, trying to pull the sword from his grip. The red stain on the blade flared and pulsed, and Tiana felt warmth on her own hands again. She remembered the quillon of the sword moving in her dream and she slid her own hands up to the guard, tugging at the sword. Cathay groaned and a small cat eidolon scratched at Tiana's leg, clawing its way up her. The guard moved in her hand, curving ever so slightly around her fingers.

Mine.

"Let go of him!" Tiana shrieked and sent her emanations through her hands, a breaking force to snap the quillons, the hilt, even the blade. And yet, nothing broke. There was a dull boom around them. Cathay's eidolon, eyes glowing white, leapt to the top of her head and raked at her face. She howled and flung it away.

Lisette put her hand on Cathay's shoulder and said, "Yield," right in his ear.

And suddenly, the tension holding the sword away

from Tiana was released. It flipped around, into her hands, the curving guard snaking around her wrists to guide its movement. Once it was firmly nestled against her palms, the guard released her, becoming stiff metal once again. She stared at it and then flung it away from her. She sent the emanations after it, pinning it against the wall, holding it there with one hand. Then she clapped a hand to her scratched face and stared at Cathay.

He was on his knees, his hands hanging loosely at his side, his eyes blank and pale. Lisette transferred her hand from his back to his neck and glanced up at Tiana. Droplets of blood dripped from his hands to pool on the floor and Lisette called, "Misa, we need bandages."

From the corner of her eye, Tiana saw Slater look in and then vanish again. She dropped to her knees before Cathay and turned over one of his hands. The bloody palm and fingers were raggedly torn, as if he'd been bitten repeatedly by a savage animal. Lisette leaned over and began whispering in Cathay's ear. His head turned towards her and he said, "Pain, pulling me apart. It's only a sword?"

"No," Tiana whispered. "I'm sorry. I thought it was just a nightmare."

Foolish, dreaming child. You were given to me. My vengeance.

Tiana clutched her aching head and shouted, "Shut up! I'm not going to listen to voices in my head! So just shut up." She looked down at Lisette's concerned face and shook her head. "I'm not going to listen. Don't worry."

"Look at his hands, Tiana," Lisette said. "What happened? What did you dream?"

Misa appeared with a basket of linen strips, and Tiana moved so that her maid could bandage Cathay's hands. "That it could move. That it could talk."

Lisette said, "I've never seen Cathay go into the phantasmagory so quickly." She stroked his hair.

He turned his head blindly towards Lisette and muttered, "Knives in my head."

He was significantly easier to penetrate than you were. Mewling little kitten. Do you know what he wants to do to you? The voice she wasn't listening to sounded smug.

"I remember now. It's a cursed sword," said Tiana blithely. "Twist said something about fiends last night. I forgot. We should take it to Kiar and see what she can see." She crouched down in front of Cathay and placed her palms on his face. "Come out, Cathay. Your hands will heal. We must deal with the curse on this blade."

Cathay groaned and pulled a bandaged hand away from the maid, raising it to Tiana's face. The maid began to bandage the other one, and Lisette went to change out of another set of bloodstained clothes. Cathay said, "Why are you so hard to reach, Tiana?" His fingers touched the scratch on her face. "What happened?"

His eyes were still pale; he was partially in the phantasmagory. From the feel of the undertow, he was close to the surface. As he was, he'd be almost normal, almost predictable. Almost a man. Most of the Blood wore the shape of their eidolons in the phantasmagory. Kiar and Jerya told Tiana she was a flame, but she always seemed like herself to her.

"Come on, Cathay. You'll see, just a scratch. Stupid, cursed sword. Come up. Look at me." His eyes darkened as he returned to himself, and he looked at her. Suddenly, the same nearness she'd been using to coax him out of the phantasmagory sent a rush of warmth through her belly. She stood up. His dark gaze followed her as he waited for the maid to finish wrapping bandages around his other hand.

Him? Oh, come now. There's no substance to him.

Tiana muttered, "It's a Blood thing," and then shook her head. She was ignoring the sardonic voice that came with the sword. She wished it out of her head.

"It's a 'you' thing," said Cathay, standing up at last, his eyes still intense.

Tiana backed away. "I have to go get dressed." She felt his eyes on her until she closed her dressing room door. She wondered if doors would keep the voice out, too.

No.

Tiana kicked over her chair. "Shut up! Get out! Go away! Good Lord! I wish he wouldn't look at me like that."

Dispassionately, the voice said, **I see through your eyes.**

She wondered what Cathay saw when he looked at her, and in wondering, went to the mirror. Her hair badly needed brushing, and a spot was developing on her left cheekbone.

Very pretty. Frail. Why you? This power you hold me with? It is very strange. It tastes… familiar.

Tiana yanked away the emanation she'd been pinning the sword to the wall with and heard it clatter in the other room. Then she turned her back on the mirror and pulled on some clothes, something good enough to get her to Kiar's door, but not much further than that.

Then she took a deep breath, realized her headache was gone, and returned to the parlor. Lisette had already emerged, rather better attired. Cathay was sitting in a chair again, staring at his bandaged hands.

Tiana said, "Kiar did return yesterday, as expected, yes?" She went to the tray of food, not looking at Cathay, and picked up a roll. Lisette always knew everything.

Lisette said, "Yes, very late. She met with Jerya and Twist and then went straight to bed."

Tiana said, "Oops. Wasn't she trying to avoid Twist?"

Lisette seemed amused. "Yes. He ambushed her in Jerya's sitting room and told her it was lesson time."

Tiana was horrified. "In the middle of the night?"

Lisette just shrugged and smiled, and Tiana shook her head. After she swallowed the last of the roll, she went to the wall where the sword lay and pushed it with her foot.

I'm much more useful in your hand. She thought she could see it quivering.

"You bite," she told it. "I'm not holding you in my hand." She flexed her fingers over the sword and hoisted it magically again, carrying it sideways in front of her.

Down the hall, Kiar opened her door at Tiana's knock. She stared at the sword floating in front of Tiana and took a step back into her room. "Oh, no, not another sky fiend."

CHAPTER THIRTEEN

OPENING DOORS

" Sky fiends are the rare ones? Twist didn't say 'sky fiend.'" Tiana asked Kiar, after everybody had made themselves comfortable in Kiar's parlor. The sword was left to float near the door. Kiar catalogued Tiana's too-bright eyes, the scratch on her face, the bandages on Cathay's hands. She hadn't had nearly enough sleep, but this was a better distraction than sleep.

"That's what it is," she told Tiana. "I banished one yesterday. They aren't formed from the Logos. It's easy to see, if you can see the Logos at all. I'm amazed Twist didn't notice."

"Ooh, banishment, that's exciting," Tiana said. "I want to hear all about it. Could you banish *this* sky fiend, too?" She turned to give the sword a particularly annoyed look.

"Is the sword what happened to you and Cathay?"

"Yes," said Tiana, and she did not elaborate, even when Kiar waited expectantly.

Kiar covered a yawn. She'd made sure to return late last

night, after the reception. There hadn't been any more sky fiends to deal with, but she'd ridden around all of Rushing Fork, searching vainly for answers. And then she'd returned to report to Jerya, and Twist had been with the princess, apparently idly discussing the weather.

She'd tried to make the situation clear to Jerya even though he was there, distracting her. She described the mystery of the link between the family magic and the sky fiend and the illness, the way even her magic caused reactions. The way an eidolon had climbed *through* the sky fiend, into the world. But Jerya had wanted answers, or at least theories, and Kiar didn't have anything she was ready to share.

And then Twist, displeased, had insisted on a lesson. Jerya had been no help. *"It seems I must share you,"* he'd said, and, *"Missed lessons must be made up."*

She didn't want to think about Twist. She turned up the Logos-vision and examined the sword instead. That it was a sky fiend, she had no doubt. But it was different from the one she'd seen the day before. This one didn't have an eidolon growing out of it, true, but it also puckered the Logos around it. There was something….

"I don't know if this is normal," she said dubiously. "It's very… dense, and there are lines…. It's *connected*, somehow. To the world. And to you, Tiana." She muttered a shaping of the Logos under her breath and smoothed out one of the lines. The Logos itself resisted at first, then once she'd convinced it to comply, the sky fiend did something to reestablish the line. She de-anchored another line, and the same thing happened.

"Very odd," she said, at last. "No, I can't banish it. I think it would take a number of initiates working together to banish it. And even then, it could be… unpredictable. But I don't know very much, after all. Um, Tiana, can you put it on the ground? I discovered something yesterday that makes me think we should be careful using our magic for a while."

Tiana stared at her like she'd grown another head. "I'm not carrying that thing in my hand," she said flatly. "It's clingy and it bites."

Kiar tried to sound like a Regent. "Fine, fine. But just put it on the rug for now?"

"Fine," Tiana snapped, and the emanation holding the sword aloft vanished. It thudded to the rug.

Kiar resisted rolling her eyes. Tiana was still such a child sometimes. She supposed it was the result of having an older sister.

Tiana snapped, "I am not a child!" Kiar jumped and stared at her.

Lisette coughed delicately and said, "The sword has been talking to Tiana."

It was Tiana's turn to stare at Lisette. "How did you know?"

Lisette gave a little smile. "I'm a Regent."

"What has it been saying?" asked Kiar. She reassessed the shape on her carpet. It had sounded like a sword when it fell, but there it was, distinctly something other than Logos.

Tiana blushed. "Nothing. Other than the obvious. Criticizing my age, mocking me."

Kiar turned pink herself.

Cathay cleared his throat and spoke for the first time. "It talked to me as well. It's nasty. Vicious. Cruel." He winced and shook his head.

Tiana said, "Don't talk to him! Are you still talking to him? Stop it! Kiar, what should I do with it? If it requires lots of wizards, maybe I should send it to the Citadel?"

Cathay's breath hissed through his teeth. "Unless you take it there yourself, that won't work."

Tiana shrieked and stomped her foot, which Kiar thought was rather extreme. The sword must have said something as well. Carefully, she asked, "What does it want? Most fiends are in a more monstrous form."

Tiana hesitated. "Death. Shut up! Vengeance. It wants me to take it and go kill things."

Kiar said, "You seem to be resisting it so far. It hasn't hurt you yet?" She studied those lines connecting the blade to Tiana again.

"Well—no. Not—that was you? You stupid piece of scrap. I had a headache yesterday, but that's gone now."

Lisette had her hands to her mouth, and Kiar realized she was hiding a smile. If Lisette wasn't worried, that made Kiar feel better about what she was going to say next. "The Blood is supposed to protect Ceria from fiends, so I think you're the best qualified to take care of it. Protect the world from it. At least for now?"

Tiana said, "Don't say that! You don't want me to use the emanations! How am I better qualified than anybody else?"

"The connection lines… and it hasn't hurt you. You said so yourself!" The Logos shivered, seemingly in response to her words, and she fervently hoped she was right.

Tiana nudged the sword with her slippered toe and then yanked her foot back as if burned. The shivering of the Logos became more pronounced, an almost audible buzz. Kiar felt as sleepy as she had late last night. But she wasn't thinking about Twist. Was she?

She suddenly remembered the lesson, rather than the teacher. *How can we teach the Logos to recognize the signature eidolons of your family?* And *How might the Logos speak back to an initiate?*

They'd constructed more protections for the Regents.

"An attack!" Everyone stared at her. "One of the unfamiliar eidolons—an attack! Somebody!" She shook her head, her drowsiness gone, and ran out of the room, following the tremors in the Logos.

She ran down the hall, past closed suite doors, and around the corner, her feet thudding against the carpet. Cathay, far more athletic, caught up with her and jogged easily beside her, one of his eidolons beside him. "Where?"

The Logos was rippling so much she was astonished that it wasn't making everybody dizzy. Where was Twist? Then Yevonne ran straight into her as they both tried to round the same corner in opposite directions. Beyond, there were shouts and animal growls. Cathay barely paused before speeding past, but Kiar caught the younger girl in her arms. "Is it you? Are those your guards?"

Yevonne's face was hard and determined, but as Tiana and Lisette tumbled into Kiar's back, she blinked and stopped struggling. "Y-yes. I was in the garderobe. I ran. My guards…." She looked over her shoulder.

Kiar peeked around the corner in time to see Cathay wading into a tangle of eidolons and two wounded guards. A single shape detached itself from the swarm and lunged down the hall, towards them. Kiar scooped Yevonne up and whirled out of the way. The eidolon, squat and the color of glass, bounded around the corner, into Tiana's outstretched hand. The princess's expression was savage as she slashed at the creature with fingernails like knives.

Kiar backed up, letting Yevonne out of her arms. She watched intently as the Logos quavered around each of the four enemy eidolons, breathing out as two of the three fighting Cathay and the guards dissolved. A voice breathed in her ear, "I'm pleased to see it worked."

She jerked and then ducked her head. "Twist!" she said, but she didn't look at him. Intently, she continued watching the trembling. Tiana's victim popped like a soap bubble, and she saw the ripples of the final eidolon fade away, until only the shadows of Tiana's emanation and the friendly eidolons marred the Logos.

Only then did Kiar look over her shoulder at Twist, who was lounging against the wall, studying her instead of the scene of the attack. "I was out of the Palace," he said. "Looking at some of these plague victims. Good thing you were here! Though, I'd like to change places tomorrow."

She tried not to feel too relieved that his anger had passed as he went on. "I can see the Logos monitoring plan will need some adjustments if it's to work when no wizards are around to get the message. Busy, busy." He raised an eyebrow at her, right before something tore a wound in the universe.

A perplexed expression, unusual on Twist, found its way onto his face. "Wha—"

The Logos screamed. The world wept as something terrible and enormous clawed a hole in it. It couldn't be real; only in nightmares did the world bleed words through Kiar's mouth.

She blindly tried to staunch the wound, tried to listen to the blood, but the words were the buzzing, meaningless syllables of books in dreams. They left the taste of ash and tears on her tongue. Then she could try no more, because the phantasmagory reared up and wrapped her in a demanding, stifling embrace.

She stumbled, pushing away spider webs. There were always spider webs in her phantasmagory: webs, and the walls. The webs were in her hair and her mouth, in between her fingers. Sticky things, dusty, and woven whenever you weren't looking. You could kill the spiders but there would always be new webs.

They crowded around her, tangling up her arms and her feet and she fell. A long-haired woman she didn't know watched her and then turned away. She saw a dazzling sunfish writhing frantically, caught by the webs, panicking. *Shanasee.* A hawk screamed, and a cat tore violently at the webs, and a wind like knives with blades of fire blew through the night, and the yellow eyes of her father surrounded her and the mirrors of the King, the white horse, the red stag, the fox, the swan, the snake, the—

They were all in the phantasmagory, all at once, all the Blood, every last one of her family. The undertow threw them into each other, scraped them against the bloody coral of each others' egos. She couldn't help it; the walls shimmered into existence around her. She could still feel them fighting, tangling into each other in an uncontrolled frenzy of hallucination and power, but they were outside, against the walls.

Inside, it was her, just her, nothing but herself and the pearlescent grey shimmer of the walls. There wasn't even her. All that she was, was walls. *Nothing there!* There was nothing inside the walls and only chaos outside. Despair swept over her as she searched frantically for something, anything within the walls. And then she lost herself in all that there was to find: the walls contained her scream.

She felt hands holding her shoulders. But who would look for her? She'd been afraid of all the eyes and wished herself out of existence. There was only an empty shell. What was there to want inside a shell? They wanted her to be them, but she couldn't, she wasn't, she disappointed. They turned away. She was not enough to fill the spaces inside her, but the red powder didn't fill her either. It showed her that she didn't exist.

No. He whispered to her. She was nine years old, trapped and screaming inside what she'd conjured, and no one could reach her but him. He'd come to her, out of darkness and terror, out of desperation and growing madness, and he'd held her, wrapped warmth around her.

He was touching her, and she felt it through the thickest walls of the phantasmagory. She opened her eyes. With some surprise, she remembered color. Blue. The walls of the world still clung to its foundations. He hadn't shaved. He hadn't slept. She could smell sweat.

She worked a jaw clenched with suppressed screams, tasted blood. Twist's hands were on her shoulders, his fingers brushing the bare skin of her collarbone, his head close to hers. His eyes were dark and hollow, but she tore herself away from him, stumbling backwards.

"Everybody...." she murmured, and felt her lip, swollen and bleeding, where she'd bitten it. Tiana and Lisette were nowhere to be seen, Yevonne had fled, and Cathay had flung his sword down the hall and was walking in a small circle. One of the guards had died, eidolon-torn. She tried to recall if he'd died from the enemy eidolons. She hoped so.

"Tiana ran off. Lisette went with her. Yevonne went to Gisen when she understood what happened." Twist stepped back, brushing lint from his coat. "Are you free of it?"

Kiar shook her head to clear it. "Cobwebs. I hate them. Yes, free enough. What happened to the Logos? Was it backlash from the working?" Recklessly, she opened her vision again. But the Logos was placid, as if it really had been a dream.

Twist shook his head. "No. That was to backlash as an earthquake is to a house fire. And now it's smooth again." He put his hands in his pockets. "And it touched the phantasmagory. Double-sighted Kiar. Did you see the connection?"

Kiar looked away. "No." She tried to determine if she could have caused it, as a bridge from the phantasmagory to the Logos. The cobwebs threatened to return.

He sighed and when he spoke again, last night's winter had returned to his voice. "Spend today as you need to, but come see me before nightfall. I've mapped the local plague outbreaks, and tomorrow you can ride that path and see what there is to see." And then he was gone.

Kiar stared at the place he'd been and wondered why his coldness made her sensitive, instead of numb. Then she turned away. There were messes to clean up.

Chapter Fourteen

Wildfire

Tiana hated that she had to waste another day recovering from something unfair and ridiculous. Great-Uncle Jant, phantasmagory expert and eldest of the family, said that he'd never experienced something like the day before. No one knew what to make of it, but he was going to find out.

Meanwhile, Tiana dreaded returning to the theater. No matter what reassuring notes and gifts they sent, she didn't think anybody would perform their best on a stage she was directing now. Would all her hard work keeping everything under control be ruined in less than a week? It couldn't be true. She had to find some way to fix it.

Mummers? You want to direct mummers? When you could be directing armies? Well, you will never see more obedient mummers than with me in your hand.

But first, she had to get rid of the sword.

The sword was in her hand, wrapped tightly in a blanket,

as she walked through Palace halls. She'd sent Lisette to Jerya's court today, with her regrets. They were going to watch for clues explaining what had happened the day before, anything that could help them understand the Logos shuddering and the phantasmagory's spasm.

She was going to deal with the sword. She had a plan. It wasn't a clever plan, but she'd come up with it herself. It would work until Antecession, when the Magister of the Citadel of the Sky visited.

It couldn't hear her, she'd found, if she kept her thoughts deep inside, as if she was looking for the phantasmagory. But it wasn't a natural skill, to surf the edge of secrets that way.

"Yes," she said aloud. "That's exactly what we're going to do. Dominate actors. That's even better than killing people. That'll solve my problems admirably. You stupid piece of metal." She pushed open the door to the catacombs.

You're lying to me. What are we doing? She felt a spike of headache and resisted dropping the blade right there. It would be found too quickly if she did that. ***Found? Foolish little child. Are you really going to hide me away like the prize in some scavenger hunt?***

"Well, yes," Tiana said. "Except without the scavenger hunt part. I said I didn't want a sword. Especially a fiendish, talking sword. I suppose you can't help being murderous, but I don't need you for that. Unfortunately. Still, we've got to do something with you."

How very distressing. It didn't sound the least bit distressed. It sounded amused. ***I am certain that my keepers intended for us to work in partnership. It's much more satisfying than the other option. Are you sure you won't reconsider?***

Tiana said, "Pfah." But her pace slowed as she walked familiar paths. "You said you wanted vengeance."

Yes, the sword practically purred.

Tiana compressed her lips. "On me? On my family?"

On that which destroyed my master, my maker. I had thought you to be the method of my vengeance, but your magic is very strange…. The headache spiked again, fingers of pain that crawled up her skull.

Tiana pulled the curtain of the phantasmagory up, and said, her voice flat, "Stop it, or I will go beyond your reach again."

I must know. The pain became sharper, and she could feel it dancing among her memories, slicing pathways to forgotten things like a scalpel. She dropped the sword and pulled the phantasmagory over her mind, slipping away from the questing tendrils.

Yesterday, tangled in the phantasmagory, Jinriki the Darkener had not been able to find her. When Lisette had finally coaxed her back to reality, the voice of the sword had been unmodulated thunder in her head. There'd been nothing of her left, it had claimed, just the mark it was bound to, buried in her senseless flesh.

Once again, there was escape from the whispers of Jinriki the Darkener, and escape, too, from the pain of its searching for answers. Instead, there was the woman, the ghost with the long hair. She touched her lips, her heart, her brow, and her mouth curved in a mysterious smile. Her eyes were no longer empty. Then she spread both her hands and faded away.

Tiana drifted in silence for a time. The phantasmagory had been a nightmare the day before, but today it was serene and unoccupied. Yesterday, it had been impossible to resist being yanked in, but today she could hardly maintain herself in it. She itched with curiosity about the sword's reaction to her psychic departure. As soon as she thought it, the itch became literal, little monsters crawling over her.

She concentrated, bringing herself into a stronger alignment with the phantasmagory. If she really focused, she could see the impressions of where the ghost with the long hair had drifted. Tiana still couldn't tell if she was part of the phantasmagory or something else; only the Blood created ripples in the space. But sometimes the Blood left behind impressions so strong they took on a life of their own: memories and dreams permanently engraved.

Her great-uncle Jant had dedicated his life to studying the contents of the phantasmagory. She'd have to ask him about the woman sometime. Later. After she'd dealt with the sword.

No, she wasn't going to think about the sword, wasn't going to give into the crawling curiosity. She followed the impressions of the ghost instead. They were so hard to see that if the phantasmagory had been roiled by even one other of her family, she was sure they'd be imperceptible. Only now, in this quiet, could she do this.

Down she went, through layers of the phantasmagory. It was like before, like after Tomas's funeral: she was descending through history. Its strata passed her by, each one made of layered memories and dreams. Sometimes they could merge into something new and cohesive, something almost alive. Maybe that's what the ghost was?

Her feet touched something hard and unyielding. Bedrock. There was no more down to drift through. Barely had she realized that when a fragment of somebody else's memory swept over her.

A young man she didn't know worked at a workbench beside a small forge and anvil. Her point of view was strange, as if she was crouched on the workbench beyond his tools. She could best see his hands and what he held. It was the Royal Pendant.

Somebody nearby said, "Will it hold? The first one cracked."

"I think so," said the young man absently. "I didn't really understand what I was doing, the first time." He turned the pendant over in his hands, smoothing the opal with his fingers. An eidolon shadow fell across the workbench, as iridescent as the stone.

"It will hold long enough," said a third voice, old and grim. "If we are careful, it may hold forever."

The crafter sighed and set the pendant down. "The hard part will be getting a chance to use it. We have to beat him back first."

Somebody said, "We'll have a chance, at least. You've given us what we need."

The crafter looked at the speaker, his eyes dark and troubled. "That's what I'm afraid of." His hand came down on Tiana, closing around her as he said, "She wants this, to play with. I'm going to give it to her."

Muffled, far away, the old man's voice said, "That's fine. Cracked, it's useless."

Then the memory became only iridescent darkness. Tiana waited hopefully for another story, looking for new ripples to follow. But all she could see were the curiosity monsters, swarming around her. She wondered what Jinriki was doing. She wondered if he was angry. Had he turned on her? Had he sprouted spikes in a futile attempt to bite her? Was he ranting at her? Not knowing was impossible to bear.

She gave up and fled back to her body, straightening from where she'd slumped against a wall. The sharp headache was gone and the sword was just a wrinkle under the blanket wrapper. She waited for a moment, then nudged it with her toe.

I am paying attention, foolish child.

Tiana said, "Oh. Well, I'll leave again, if I have to. I can protect myself, you know." She picked up the bundle again.

Sounding bored, the sword said, **Not enough. In any case, I am certain now that you've never had contact with any of the Firstborn.**

Tiana was startled. "Well, no. No one has, for hundreds of years. Not for real. They left this kingdom to us, you know," she added, proudly. "To our family, after Shin Savanyel came. He was a great hero." She pointed the bundle at a mural she was passing. "There's him and his son Kir, defeating Balath the Arch-Inscriptor. One of many enemies he defeated."

Heroic for a human, I'm sure. But of the Firstborn, my master was the greatest.

Tiana bit her lip, thinking about the Citadel of the Sky on top of the mountain Sel Sevanth. It was sacred to Niyhan and the source of the powder that enabled Logos-working and Logos inscriptions. Its priests were her primary source of religious education, but it was a token sort of education, mostly concerned with holy days the Blood were required to participate in. The Magister of the Citadel visited annually for the three weeks it took to celebrate Antecession and the triple holiday.

But it was basic theology that Niyhan was foremost among the Firstborn. He was also the patron of civilization and the search for knowledge. Swords were not something associated with him. Perhaps the sword meant Rann, who was much more warlike.

Secondborn to my lord Innis, both of them. I do not know what happened to him, only that he died in a moment, without warning. I

*too would have been destroyed or taken by the wild madness that swept through all his children when he died. But his mortal servants, who were my caretakers, dedicated themselves to preserving me. They bound me to stillness and silence with promises of vengeance later, when the world was stronger.***

There was no Innis in any story Tiana knew. She said, "This must have been very long ago. At least, I've never heard of him."

A century or ten thousand years, it does not matter. Everything changed when he died.*

"Oh." Tiana shook herself out of listening and drifted down the catacombs hall, choosing her path almost at random. It was tempting to take the sword back to where she'd found the amulet, but that place made her uneasy. So instead, one of her play spots as a child would suffice. But as she walked, the story the sword had hinted at called her back again. "How could a Firstborn die? I've read stories of Secondborn pining away for love…."

He was murdered, of course. Foolish child. Do you think the Firstborn fall prey to grief or illness like a lesser creature does?*

Tiana sighed. "Of course. But you don't know who killed him? Which is why you attacked me?"

Hardly an attack, simply an investigation. Here, little one. Do you still insist on leaving me somewhere? Let me show you how I would attack you. The sword struck.

A great and dazzling geometric shape unfolded in Tiana's mind, infinitely complex. No sooner did she recognize its vastness than she was screaming, trying to deny it. She was drowning in its shallows. Its deepness could swallow worlds. She hid away from it, reaching for blindness or the phantasmagory. Instead she found a monstrous labyrinth of frosted glass.

She could feel the vastness shifting around her, and she understood immediately that she was a prisoner, snatched and caged so quickly that she'd had no time to flee. **Why?** she demanded of the labyrinth, of the geometry.

Only her own thoughts returned to her, distorted and blurred by the translucent glass. **Why? Why? Why?**

Why was this maze, this mental prison, possible when the phantasmagory challenged Jinriki the Darkener to find her? How was this not-place different from the phantasmagory? *Was* it different from the phantasmagory?

The phantasmagory was moldable; the emanations obeyed her in both that place and the real world, when she called them. She moved her hand to slice through the glass walls. Nothing happened. She had no hand to move. She had no breath to exhale. She was a thought ricocheting in a diamond.

Something else was missing.

She wasn't real.

New horror seized her. She wasn't real. She wasn't Tiana. Tiana was somewhere else; she was just a daydream, a stray thought, exiled, sent to hell. Was this where bad thoughts went when they died? This piece of crystal insanity?

That's exactly what it was. She was Tiana's insanity. This was where it lived when Tiana pushed it down, kept it from nibbling away the edges of her self. She'd spent so long resisting it. She cared about appropriate behavior. She'd taught herself to ignore things that upset her. She'd taught Lisette to distract her when she needed distraction, and she'd stayed so *good*. Jerya thought her shallow, Jerya thought her frivolous, but Tiana wasn't going to lose her husband the way her father had lost her mother.

But now she and her insanity had changed places. Was

that it? Was her madness out there, freed from the leash and chain? Was Tiana running through the halls, ranting about last year's fashions? She'd had to suppress the dreadful urge to giggle inappropriately, over and over, as the men attending the theater had pranced past in their feathered flounces.

Was she stalking down the halls, shedding her clothing? It had been so hot the other day. Was she looking for the nearest bottle of whiskey, was she climbing to the highest tower to see if she could really fly? Was she sawing off her hair?

Was she walking out of the catacombs with Jinriki the Darkener held in her hand?

Was that all that had happened? Had she lost her self, not to her insanity, but to the sword?

She was a thought, just a thought, but she was oh-so-quick. Her thoughts existed. She was glee. She'd lost her self, that's all, and this vastness, this glittering labyrinth, it only served to trick her that she was actually there. If she was a thought, it was a dream. But it was less than a dream, because dreams came from within. Dreams could hold you down because they were you. She was far too straightforward to be an infinitely complicated, crystal labyrinth. It could not hold her.

First, she stopped thinking about the labyrinth.

Then, she stopped thinking.

She felt her body walking along. It was her stride, careful and fast. Her body knew how to walk, even if it didn't know who was driving it. She hid in her toes, because it was the farthest she could get from the sword she was sure she held in her hand. Her toes flexed and shifted in their slippers. She itched, but her body did not scratch. Would the sword be so unkind to her? Her family would notice if there was a Tiana who did not fidget. Somebody would wonder. Cathay would guess.

She wondered how Cathay would fight Tiana for Tiana against an evil sword. She imagined him threatening the sword with another sword. It was tempting to encourage it to happen, just to laugh about it. She could wiggle her toes whenever Cathay got close, tap out a code against the floor. Uncle Yithiere was always making up codes. He'd understand what had happened, too. But the plan couldn't go very far, because toes didn't have very much in the way of imagination.

Foolish, foolish sword. It called her foolish child, but it would be lucky if it wasn't tossed into a furnace instead of just hidden in the dark for another generation to find. She itched more, twitching and convulsing. She extended herself throughout her feet, and then she cramped up and stopped walking. She was the feet, and she was in charge!

The hand not holding the sword touched her feet, and she stole it. Now she had one hand, and two feet. She took the knees, too, since they were hardly useful without the feet. And the sword knew she was there now.

It had the right hand, the head, the chest. It was a good chest, but she was standing tight as a soldier, and she always thought that must be painful. It did display her cleavage nicely, she realized, as she stole her left arm, her left shoulder, and felt the downward slope.

A mighty presence, not her, sank into the parts of Tiana she'd reclaimed, reaching out from the high places it occupied to reclaim what it had lost. But she was in the low places, the valleys, the far reaches, the depths and extremities. And it was not, she found, very familiar with how female bodies operated. The presence moved across her skin like the wind over a wildfire, trying to recapture that which had burned the prison down. She took back her mouth and laughed at Jinriki the Darkener, and then surged, roared, danced into the heart of her self.

Tiana opened her hand and let the sword fall, clattering, onto the flagstones of the small hallway. Then she wiggled her fingers, let an emanation buoy it up, and cocked her head to look at it floating in front of her. She was content to let it speak first, and she was quite certain that it wouldn't find a thing in her head to eavesdrop on. She knew it in her fingers. She knew it in her toes.

Finally, it said **I see you have returned again, yes.**

Tiana stuck out her lip and said, "That's no fun. I bet you've done that before, on other people, eh?"

Yes.

"But you didn't expect me to get out so quickly, I'd wager!" She bounced up on and down on her toes and made the sword spin in a circle.

It didn't respond, so she dropped it again and tapped her foot on the blade. "I've been thinking. Do you want to know what I've been thinking?" Still no response, but she fancied she was being annoying all the same. "I know you do. So I'll tell you. I've been thinking, rather than hiding you away, I should find the hottest furnace in the Palace and stick you in there until you're just a lump of metal. Maybe you'd still talk, maybe not. We could find out."

You'd be wasting your time. She thought it sounded tired. **No heat in this world could destroy me.**

Tiana scowled. "Well, we could at least test that." She waved the blade aloft a second time. "But I'm not that knowledgeable about furnaces, and I do know about my hiding spot, so I don't mind taking your word." She stumped down the hall, back into the catacombs.

After a time, she heard, **Do not banish me from your hand. It would not help you. You will hear my voice, no matter how far you go.**

Now the sword sounded desperate, and she felt the barest twinge of pity. But she said, "Cathay is drawn to swords, and when I'm lost in the phantasmagory, I'm unpredictable." She considered, and added, "Besides, you just stole my body. I don't want you near me.

"As for voices, that's nothing new. I've learned to ignore so many others." She did not share with the sword that its voice was different from the whispers of the phantasmagory, that it had a strength and vividness, an intimacy that she could not imagine shutting out. She'd learn to cope.

The sword was silent. So she padded through the halls, taking a lantern from one of the junctures before she left the lit area, until she reached the spot where she and Lisette used to play, back before they were even ten years old. It was down some age-roughened steps, around a corner. Perhaps it had been a larder, long ago. It had stone shelves, and under the lowest shelf there was a depression, where two little girls could hide and giggle.

When she was six and it was her turn to pick a Regent from the crop of noble daughters her own age, she'd led the flock of girls down to the catacombs. Three girls abandoned the quest for her favor there, at the entrance to the old halls, frightened by nursery tales of ghosts.

"Of course there are ghosts; it's where the Blood walks," had said Lisette, and walked down the stairs, completely unafraid. They'd played hide and seek there. The third time through, when Seandri was the seeker, Lisette had found the larder and led Tiana there, around the corner, under the shelf. They'd never been found, not when all the other girls were found, not when the adult searchers came with lanterns and shouts, not until Uncle Yithiere and his eidolon wolves had sniffed her out.

There was still the blanket she'd brought down another time, and the porcelain teacups, the old metal teapot she'd stolen from the kitchen, and a gold-rimmed plate. Tiana put her lantern on a hook in the wall. She took the hilt of the sword in her hand and rolled under the shelf, into the depression. Then she laid the blade beside her, on its edge. It made a disturbing companion. In the light that seeped under the shelf, she thought she could just see the colors of her reflection in the blade, wobbling in the uneven light.

She would leave it here, rolled up in the blankets. If the Magister could deal with it, she would come back for it. There was no reason she shouldn't. It was hers to deal with. Kiar might not think it was the responsible choice, and yet it had always worked before. But she held it loosely by the hilt, and she saw that it wasn't bending itself to wrap around her hand, as she knew it could.

"Why were you so cruel to Cathay? He'd appreciate you much more than I can. Even now. He's like that."

He isn't mine. You are.

Tiana shivered, but she said, "It's the other way around, if anything. I'm a princess. I don't belong to anybody."

When the monk—Helliac? When he woke me, he'd invoked you as the one who would carry me to the vengeance I was promised. You have the mark. You are the one. I can manipulate any mortal to fulfill my basic desires, but the mark is the only channel for my power. If you do not do this, there will be no one else who can.

Tiana laid the sword on its flat, arranged the blanket around it, and tucked her arm under her head. Cathay would never find it here, would never even consider looking. He was disturbed by small, enclosed spaces, and he'd never liked the catacombs. Neither did Shanasee, who disliked the shadows and the memories.

She ran a finger up the center of the blade. It looked like it belonged here somehow, like it was the bone of some forgotten creature. Even more than here, it belonged below, in the dungeons, with their thick dust and strange doors. But that place frightened her. The shadows, the memories. Even now, she felt that something lived down there, something that did not know how to die. She imagined something walking the long corridor of cells, touching doors, sitting in the chair with its back to the door. But where was it when they had gone looking? Had it emerged into the catacombs above? Was it walking these halls now, soft footsteps echoing in the halls, murmuring to itself, looking for something taken from it?

She inhaled sharply. She could hear it, really hear it. Footsteps in the corridor, the soft murmur of a voice. Then the murmur of a different voice. Coming closer.

Walkers. Are you afraid? If you hold me close and trust me, I promise you will never have anything to fear. Your curse, your madness is strange, but I am learning to understand it. We can conquer it, together.

"Hsst," she said to the blade, squirming further under the shelf. She snaked out a hand and took the blade's handle, sliding it deeper into the shadow. She tried not to hyperventilate, but she could hear the walker coming close, hear the uneven shuffle of the footsteps and the strange multi-layered way it murmured. She flicked her fingers and the candle within the lantern was snuffed.

The darkness was absolute; she couldn't tell if her eyes

were open or closed. She ran her fingers lightly up the blade again, feeling the cold metal, the sharp edge, the roughness of the blanket. In and out, she practiced even, quiet breaths. Would it be able to find her by the warmth of her body? Would it see the taint of her power through the Logos?

The voice was close enough that she could make out words. "—amenable. Just because she's suddenly taking an interest doesn't mean she's trying to get in our way. Maybe she'll be as cooperative as the other one."

Two people, talking. Just mortals. Something eased inside and the panic surging through her started to fade.

Only for a surge of adrenalin to replace it, as a second, familiar voice spoke. "She believes in the old ways. And she is stubborn, she and her uncle. They are the two who would fight us, no matter what. For tradition's sake, for history, for themselves. Lost in dreams of centuries past… They can't begin to understand."

"It's good that our crowd of one yet lives, then. Best keep him that way. Have your investigators made progress?"

She *knew* that voice.

"It's a tilting game, seeing what we can find out without someone calling Blight and activating them. And honestly, he's likely to bend his head to her. A family squabble that wipes out the top three and leaves us with the younger girl would be ideal. She'd be overjoyed to give you free access in exchange for a pat on the head."

The stranger said, "Judging from the past, the collateral damage would be tremendous. We don't want that. But this plague is a lever. The workers are very interested. I wish we could get the wizard to provide us with his insights. They're close to a way to neutralize their magic." The voices were moving further away.

"I think that's risky. Better to steal some of his notes. He's got the bastard as his apprentice and he's fond of her, to all appearances. I know someone…." It faded into indistinct murmuring again.

You see? I am trying to accustom myself to your needs. I do not suggest we go cut off their traitorous heads. But I do suggest that if you keep me near you, I may be able to nullify whatever their wizards might try as a neutralization tactic. I am a sky fiend, after all.

Tiana stared into the darkness. "What are you talking about?" She paused. "Were they talking about the *Blood?*" She gripped the blanket with her fists, thinking over the scraps she'd heard. Of course they were, even if she wished they weren't. Then she said, "Why did you attack Cathay?" she whispered. "Why did you take over my body? How can I trust you?"

He was unsuitable, the sword said pleasantly. ***Does it matter? You won that struggle. I promise not to bite your companions, as long as you don't try to give me to them.***

"You have to stop calling me a 'foolish child.'"

Yes, Tiana. Goosebumps raised on her skin as the voice said her name. Was that really any better?

"I'll test this nullification thing, you know," she warned.

Of course you will.

Tiana scowled into the darkness and then crawled out of the depression, pulling her sword Jinriki after her.

CHAPTER FIFTEEN

PLAGUESTRUCK

Kiar stood in front of Twist's workroom door, confused. She was often confused around Twist, but it was different, this time. She had something to ask him about, but she couldn't remember what it was. If only she could stop shivering, maybe she could remember why she was here. It was important, she was sure. If she didn't tell him, it would be very bad. But for some reason, she'd forgotten. That was bad, too.

She concentrated, trying to retrace her path here.

It was time to follow the path of the plague, inspecting the lines of contagion for any hints to the puzzle. Twist needed her help. She'd spend the day following the roads he'd outlined. Or had she gone on the circuit already?

She thought she must have. Her clothes were stiff with sweat and her muscles ached. She smelled more like horse than human, too. But it was hard to think. The last thing she could remember was riding her horse home. And now she was here.

Where was Spooky, her beautiful horse? Had she skipped through space like Twist? Wouldn't he be impressed if she had? But she remembered she'd already tried that and he hadn't been impressed, he'd been angry. So that couldn't be it. That wasn't *important,* and she knew she had something important to tell him.

She stared into the dizzy blankness that blanketed most of her mind. There were shapes hidden under there. Shapes and time. She *had* gone out this morning. But— there'd been something in the road. She'd seen something in the road, as she was riding.

Her teeth chattered together, which was annoying. She leaned her head on the door and tried again to remember how she'd gotten here from the road.

Her vision was dark. A herd of cows had broken out of their pasture and wandered into the beaten road. Spooky wouldn't move past them. He bucked and threw her. She got back on. But Spooky was strange now. He shied every other step. He wouldn't mind. He hated her. He threw her again. She didn't need him, anyhow. She walked. Voices followed her.

Was she coming or going? Was it the night before after all? Twist had given her the map and he hadn't smiled. She was to inspect the roads between the towns marked, looking for anything strange. She could do that. She and her beautiful horse, with his magical inscribed horseshoes.

Her feet hurt. She looked at her hands. They were dirty, scraped. She could see the eidolon pulsing inside her. A wave of nausea rocked her and she hugged her stomach. But she had her satchel with her notes in it. She wasn't walking now. Where were her guards?

She was standing outside Twist's door. That was where she needed to be. He'd want to know what she'd found. Did she already tell him? Jerya had asked her to work with him. Jerya relied on her. She was reliable.

Her head hurt. She whimpered and raised her hand to knock on the door. Twist opened it.

"Oh, no," he said. "That shouldn't have happened." He pulled her into the workroom. Her father was there. Prince Yithiere. He was a prince, but she was only a Lady, because he wouldn't admit she was his in public. But her mother was a housemaid, so surely she was grateful? She looked down. He gave her the best horse in the world, even though that horse threw her. He gave her puzzles to solve, even though he was a puzzle.

Everything was out of order. A candle's flame hurt her eyes, and an inscribed orb shed only darkness. A blue silk shirt was crumpled on the floor. Somebody could slip. It wasn't fair. She tried to keep things tidy. She bit her knuckles. It hurt.

"Kiar?" said Twist. She looked at the two men, and then let her satchel fall to the floor.

"I made notes," she said. "I talked to everyone who could talk. I knew what to look for. There were villages. Not isolated. Not patterned. Not a trail, not of a wandering you or me." She giggled and then stopped.

Twist's hand went to her brow, and she reached up, took it in both her hands and laid it against her cheek instead.

"Your hands are nice. So warm."

Yithiere said, "Is she sick?" He too moved closer to her, his eyes perfectly dark, his face expressionless.

Twist said, "Oh, yes. I can see the taint all through her." He patted her cheek. "Kiar, sweetheart, there was nothing?"

Yithiere's voice was very quiet. "You said this couldn't happen. You said it only happened to peasants. Farmers. On farms."

Twist took Kiar's hand again and drew her over to a wash basin. "Did you fall, Kiar?"

"Spooky doesn't like me anymore," Kiar explained. "I had to leave him behind. I'm sorry, Father. Sorry for Father. Don't you want to see my notes?"

Twist shook his head, looking at Kiar, with the Logos shimmering in his eyes. "So far progressed…." he muttered. He addressed Yithiere, "I've interviewed dozens of plague victims. It's a magical attack. I thought if anyone would be immune and forewarned, it would be her. But it's… growing faster in her."

"What does that mean?" Yithiere demanded. Kiar reached up to touch Twist's face. His cheek was much warmer than her hand, and he'd shaved today. She was so cold. She wanted to lean into him.

"You've got mortal eyes, Your Highness. Use them." He turned back to face Kiar, which she rather liked. "Kiar, why does your horse dislike you now? Where are your guards? Did something attack you again on the road?"

She shook her head. "Just the screams, the screaming people. They didn't attack me but it was—" she frowned. She couldn't remember. There were voices screaming, faces huddled over blankets, rocking back and forth, but it was scattered and broken, on the other side of the great chasm in her memories.

She peered into the chasm.

She was sitting down. Yithiere was standing behind Twist, who was kneeling in front of her, holding a bucket. Her father was angry. She could tell. It never touched his face but a white fire burned in his eyes and she could feel it in the phantasmagory. Twist said patiently, "Something happened on the road. What was it?"

She smelled something sour and unpleasant. She tried to remember the road. A shape flashed in front of her eyes.

She retched into the bucket and only then remembered having done it before. Was it a few minutes ago? A few days? Did she have too much wine? She was so *confused* and she *hated* it. Her mouth flooded with saliva. She bit down on a scream, but it emerged as a whimper.

Yithiere said, "Enough, wizard." There was a growl under his voice and a wolf paced out of him. "She is suffering while you play these foolish games. She is not a specimen to be studied."

He looked around the room and the lilt of his voice changed. "Isn't illness part of the Logos? We have only your word that this is family magic, and she's always trusted you too much." He tapped his fingers against his leg. He was counting. He always counted when he was nervous.

Twist wiped at Kiar's mouth with his sleeve and said, "I'm not lying to you, Yithiere. My words are clear. There is no hidden meaning."

"There's always a hidden meaning," her father muttered. "You may hear what I cannot, wizardling, but you understand it no better than I." He looked around again. "How do we cure this plague? You keep too many little secrets. Reveal this one, and I won't ruin your game."

The pain in her head spiked and once again a terrible blinding image flashed in front of her face. She brought her hands up to her mouth, willing herself not to vomit. Why couldn't she see inside her own mind? Was there a place within that was no longer hers? Was the plague a living thing? Could she describe it?

Her father was picking her up. She clutched at him, protesting feebly. She was getting his vest and tunic dirty.

He said, very coldly, "You either know nothing or you have turned against us. But, because of past services, I shall assume you've merely gone stark raving mad. I'm not leaving my daughter in your care. Good day, sir."

Yithiere called her his daughter! She hugged him as he carried her out of the workroom. But it was sad that Twist looked angry again.

Chapter Sixteen

Pretty Lies

Jinriki insisted Tiana find the leatherworker who supplied the soldiers so she could get a baldric and a special scabbard. But, just to show him who was in charge, she ate lunch in the Morning Room first. She laid the bundled sword on the ground beside her.

The kitchen was adjacent to the Morning Room. After a scullery girl had placed her plate before her, poured her wine, and left, Tiana said, "In the stories, magic swords are quite capable of resizing themselves from a needle to a... a really big sword. What's wrong with you?"

I'm exactly the right size.

Tiana opened her eyes wide and gazed at the sword. "I was thinking I could just carry you around, rolled up in a blanket. You said you see through my eyes; you don't need to be actually in my hand to do your nullification thing, do you?"

**Yes. I do. You will carry me properly, and when we decide it is appropriate, such as when someone is making unwanted advances, you

*will take me in your hand, slide me from my scabbard, and let me guide your hand in the proper motions.*** It paused and then added, ***A few practice sessions will make it less disturbing. Perhaps after you dine?***

Tiana choked down a swallow of wine and realized she was blushing. "That's—I don't think you had to protect monks from unwanted advances!"

No, the sword said. ***They were more likely to encounter thieves on the road and they were skilled in using me, as I recall. Much as your Cathay would be. But my memories are distant, and vague; I was never fully awake in their care. Perhaps I'm forgetting something that prompted that particular example. In any case, you are my bearer now, and pretty princesses are far more likely to encounter unwanted suitors, in many forms, than thieves.***

"What about wanted suitors?"

Do you desire suitors?

"Well, yes!"

Ah. That could be awkward.

"Hey!" Tiana paused and lowered her voice again. "Just because I said I'd let you help me doesn't give you the—" The Morning Room door opened and a servant peeked in. He met her eyes, puzzled.

"Are things well, Your Highness? You raised your voice," he explained.

Tiana snapped, "I'm fine." She made herself eat another bite of the chicken and rice, even though her appetite had vanished. The servant looked concerned but closed the door again. "Anyhow, carrying you around the way you want would completely mess up my dresses. And I'm not going to let you interfere with my suitors."

You already allow nursemaids and bureaucrats to control who may approach you and who may not. Why them and not me?

Tiana ate another bite and then pushed the plate away. "Are you trying to make me lose you again? Why are you provoking me?"

Do you consider honesty provocation? I was not made for pretty lies.

Tiana stared at the sword, thinking of the poet at the reception. Then she muttered, "You all think knowing the truth is so easy."

After a moment, it said, **You are far better at the pretty lies than I. See this: even your Lisette is a caretaker. I have seen inside you, and Cathay as well. All your kin require caretakers, or else havoc would sweep indiscriminately across the land. You should not hide from this. Havoc is part of my nature as well, but when I am sheathed, I do not cut freely.**

Tears stung the back of Tiana's eyes. "That's just it. I don't need you to kill people. I do that just fine on my own. The other day—"

I am aware of that event. Here is the difference: I would have killed them all. Only by your strength of will would fewer have died.

Tiana's breath quickened. That sounded almost heroic. It was a sky fiend, kept under control by her will, but sometimes, it might escape. When she was threatened or frightened, perhaps. The thought unrolled before her. She hadn't killed two, but saved four, from a disaster of their own making.

But would the mother and child who saw the bodies and the blood understand that? Would they still flee her gaze?

Her stomach curdled. Jinriki was offering her a story, and she liked stories very much. But a performance only worked if everybody knew the script. "Truth is not easy, no matter what that poet thinks. I could say that, you could claim that, but I couldn't make the audience believe it, because they already know what's true."

With time, and my assistance, you could teach them any script you wished. I am far more than an edge for cutting. I am the lens and the channel. I am the last voice of the secret knowledge. I am the sculptor of souls. This blanketed shape is but a small part of the whole of me. A world of power and knowledge has been lost while I was bound to sleep, with but time and your desire, much could be regained.

Tiana let the voice inside her head flow through her. It hinted at dazzling images of adventure, amusements, and accomplishments beyond anything the world now knew. It implied that she, Tiana, could be far greater than Shin Savanyel. She was more than capable of dreaming up details to match its words.

Twist said, "Oh, there it is. Still carrying it in a blanket?" The Royal Wizard was standing at the side of the room. Tiana fell out of her chair, jolted from her daydreaming.

"Well, it's useful for finding you in the Palace, no matter what you wrap it in. I hope it's behaving?" Twist's speech was more hurried than usual. "No blood, I see. Good. I need your help. Kiar is sick with this wretched plague, and Yithiere has taken her away, into the fortress." He frowned at the sword.

Tiana recovered herself and demanded, "What can I do?"

The wizard's gaze snapped back to Tiana and he said, "Your uncle would protect Kiar from the only treatment I can imagine. The plague is like an eidolon to the Logos-sight. Defeating it requires the family magic, not the Logos. Can you locate him?"

That was when the ghost woman stepped out of Twist, pulling herself out of his skin. Tiana felt sick and vehemently hoped she'd never see the bones beneath Twist's face again. The ghost's hair swirled around her, her bare toes just brushing the floor she drifted above. Tiana snatched up Jinriki and edged away.

Twist said, "What's the matter? Why—" He cut himself off, pressing his lips together.

The ghost's eyes were white. She stretched out her hand to Tiana. Tiana swallowed and said, "Nothing!"

She squeezed her eyes shut as a ghostly hand passed through her body and tried to focus. "Kiar's the one who knows all the locks, but I might be able to force my way in. Um. I don't know if he's prepared for that. He might be." She opened her eyes enough to peek. The ghost was standing right in front of her, tilting its head from one extreme to another as it stared at her. She closed her eyes again hastily, but not before she saw her own wrist bone.

Twist sighed. "I see that dealing with the fiend is taking up a lot of your attention. I shouldn't distract you from that. Keep up the good fight and so forth. Somebody else is sure to help." He vanished from the room before she could protest.

An interesting trick with the Logos. That wizard may become a problem. By the way, the woman that your eyes perceive is not real.

"I know that!" Tiana snapped. She backed up, eyes still closed, waving Jinriki in front of her. She was horrified that Twist thought she was mad, but she'd lose her lunch if she saw the ghost's passage.

Fascinating. There is nothing to see when your eyes are closed.

She opened her eyes. It was a mistake.

The ghost was still there. Tiana waved Jinriki and saw the glint of the glass labyrinth within the shape of the blade.

Then the ghost woman stepped forward, and Tiana could take no more. She fled the labyrinth and the ghost, into the phantasmagory.

It was moving around her, surging like water on a stormy day. She stood in the shallows and watched debris left by others bob to the surface. A decapitated head floated past, forever screaming. A book with half its pages ripped out, a bear's severed foot, a shield in which blood pooled, the torn wing of the Secondborn Ashadel, three iron nails floating in a black chalice. Nightmares. She pushed them away.

Then the ghost was there as well. It held her in a motherly embrace. Tiana wriggled, and the woman responded by pushing her shoulders and head down. The water became upsettingly real. Tiana was being drowned by the ghost woman.

A masculine voice spoke. "Madness." The water turned to clouds of hissing vapor. The woman pushing Tiana down looked up and frowned. It was a terrible, frightening expression, and Tiana squirmed away from her grip, pretending she was a fish like Shanasee. It didn't change her shape—nothing ever changed her self-perception in the phantasmagory—but the woman lifted her strong hands away and swept her arms through the rising billows of steam.

The man's voice said again, "Madness. This is where you hide?"

Her curiosity piqued, Tiana paused in her scramble backwards and asked, "What do you see? Do you still see through my eyes? How did you get here?"

"I followed you. I learn. It's my great strength. But this—this is… madness. Everything happens. At once. Now. How can you—but I suppose you're mad already."

Tiana rose to her feet, giggling. The giggle bloomed

around her, red and yellow, and drove the mist before it. "You're not made for pretty lies, silly sword. It's in our blood. I suppose you didn't taste enough of Cathay's to learn the knack."

"I could take some of yours…."

"That would be the opposite of protecting me, you understand," Tiana observed as her pink hills grew around her.

"It'd just be a nip. Can you really feel pain in here? You scarcely seem aware of anything."

Tiana stared at the windswept hills. A crimson rose danced before her, bowing like a suitor at a ball and she looked away. "Yes. There is pain here. Are you still trying to track the physical world? It takes decades of experience to master that; no wonder you're so lost. Stay or go, but don't try to straddle both worlds."

"That's exactly what I will do. Anything could happen, and you still have eyes for me to see through."

Tiana shuddered. Aviani the Blind, an ancestor, had clawed her eyes out while in the phantasmagory. She resisted the temptation to rub at her own eyes.

The phantom woman stalked past, flowers swirling and following her like a train. The landscape changed behind her. It was desolate and dusty, scattered with the skeletons of animals and monsters, most of which never existed outside the phantasmagory. The eidolon's graveyard.

"What do you see?" Tiana wondered. "Jinriki? Sword?"

"Did something change? I see the same. I am aware, as I am aware of blood on my blade, of you, mired within a morass of… memories. The memories of a thousand souls, all moving and flowing together, interacting and changing. Dreams?"

"A delusion so powerful it overwhelms every other sense. Influenced by the outside world, though, and by my worries and desires, and others of the Blood. It comes with the magic." That wasn't strictly true; long before she'd manifested emanations, she could access the phantasmagory and Shanasee used the phantasmagory while refusing the magic.

"I'm not personally familiar with dreams. Why do you stay? You seem coherent. Can you not control your return?" The man's voice was as close as her shadow.

"When I want to return, I do. If I don't want to return, I can't."

Jinriki demanded, "Well, come back, then."

She said, "But I don't want to." She set off walking across the eidolon's graveyard.

CHAPTER SEVENTEEN

THE SECRET VOICES

Once, the fortress had been just an old wing of the Palace. But when Benjen the Bastard announced his second Blight by kidnapping the baby son of King Math from his nursery, that old wing changed almost overnight. As Math, Shonathan, and the cousins hunted Benjen, Pell the builder and Yithiere the guardian turned a near-ruin into a twisty stronghold for the other children, for the spouses, and for the Regents.

When it was all over, when Math and Benjen were both dead, the family was happy to leave the fortress behind. But Yithiere kept the locks clean, the traps ready to arm. He rebuilt some of the corridor maze, and rememorized the routes. And after his Regent Zavien died, he moved back in.

Kiar laid her head on his shoulder as he carried her down grey halls. He moved quickly, silently. He was always silent unless there was something he needed to say. When Kiar was ten, he'd told her, "The less you say, the less those who listen can learn about you."

Then he was putting her on her feet again. "Can you stand? Can you walk?" he asked her, feeling her forehead. "I need a hand free to work the doors."

She smiled at him and tried to tell him about the words in her head. The road, the plague, the guardsmen. The cattle. He put his hand to her mouth. Then he touched the wall. It swung open silently and he pulled her through it. The floor beyond was bright and dark, like Logos and eidolon.

A moon-bright wolf emerged from Yithiere, shedding a dull glow. It led them across the floor. Then Yithiere slid another door open and drew her through into a dusty sitting room and bolted it behind him.

"What did he do?" she wondered. "Twist. Don't let him bother you. It's too much trouble, and once you start being bothered you just can't stop." For some reason, that was funny, so she snickered.

Her father looked around. "This will do. Rest on the sofa. Are you thirsty? I can fetch water." But he stood there, watching her. "I wish Zavien was still alive. I get tired...." He looked around the room and then up into a corner. "I can't quite...."

Then he stared at Kiar again, squeezed his eyes shut. "Zavien's gone. I'm stronger than this."

Kiar summoned a smile for her father. "I am very thirsty, yes. And cold." But of course, there were no windows in the fortress. Her head was stuffed with felt and parts of her skin prickled. "I can watch myself. See?" And suddenly she could see her body from the outside, as if she was standing beside herself. She watched as her mouth moved and words fell out. "Is this the Logos? But there are no shadows on my skin."

She watched as Yithiere put his hand on her face and head, and then set his jaw. "I'll be back. Sit down."

"Yes, sit down," she said to herself. Her knees bent and she sat. Yithiere looked at her a moment more and then strode to a bookcase and touched a volume. The bookcase slid aside and he vanished into the hall beyond. The entire room was dusty and untended, except for the bookcase, which gleamed.

It couldn't be the Logos she saw through, for there was no taint at all, not where she sat, not where Yithiere walked. That meant it was pure delusion, a half-step into the phantasmagory. The Kiar she saw was a ghost, an eidolon, just like one of poor Shonathan's twins.

The fuzziness in her head became a spike of pain. Time passed while she was lost in fire and misery. Where was the water? She was so thirsty. Then she became aware of a gentle knocking at the door Yithiere had bolted. A voice called through it, "Kiar?"

Kiar pushed herself to her feet and stumbled over to the door, where she slid open the bolt and fumbled at the latch. When she eased the door open, her older cousin, Shanasee, was standing beyond, with Cara, her Regent, peering over her shoulder. She looked like a more mature copy of Tiana, although she kept her hair as short as Kiar's.

Shanasee and Cara both had a glowing inscribed orb, and Cara had a bag with another inactive orb and a bundle of candles sticking out. Even so, Kiar was struck to unexpected tears by Shanasee's courage, coming this far into the unlit fortress, because she knew darkness upset Shanasee. "So little light. So brave," she croaked, then fell against a bookcase.

Briskly, Shanasee said, "If what the servants say is true, we'll be living by lamps alone in ten years. But for now, I've come to bring you out of here."

Kiar said, "Father—I mean, Yithiere—has already rescued me from Twist. I'm not sure what Twist was going to do, though. Would you like to come in?" She slipped down to the floor.

"She's really sick, Shan," said Cara, a tall woman whose hair had started greying when she and Shanasee were teenagers. "Let's get her back to the seat."

She and Shanasee crowded through the door and put Kiar on the couch. One of Yithiere's eidolons trotted in behind them and joined the moon-glow wolf. Jant's fox eidolon followed and scooted under a chair. Shanasee didn't have eidolons now either, though she'd manifested them before Benjen had died. Like Tiana, she was dependent on her relatives to protect her Regent from whatever stalked them.

Kiar wondered if a wolf eidolon was still protecting Lisette as well. How many eidolons was Yithiere maintaining? Again, she was struck to tears. He tried to be so tireless. But the more eidolons one projected, the less resources one had for one's self.

Shanasee said, "We're here to rescue you from Yithiere, actually. Where is he?" She looked around and Kiar pointed at the polished bookcase.

Cara sighed. "That man. Well, we can carry you between us."

Kiar hesitated and then said, "His eidolons are here. I don't want to make him angry. And he's trying so hard."

Shanasee said, "Is it true, people have died from the sickness you have?"

"Am I sick?" She tried to remember how she could have become sick. Had something happened? She was riding home. There was something—

The chaos in Kiar's mind overwhelmed her again.

She woke from dry heaves with Cara standing beside her, patting her back, and Shanasee saying, "—through the servant's hallways. They know you very well and they care about Kiar too."

Yithiere growled, "Kiar is not theirs, or yours, to be concerned over. Get out."

Kiar remembered freshly shaved skin under her fingers. "Where's Twist? Why isn't he here?"

Cara said, "Oh, sweetheart, he doesn't want to make things worse with your fool of a father." The moon-glow eidolon began growling at Cara. The two eidolons protecting Cara growled back.

"No, please, don't fight," Kiar begged. "I'm sorry I got sick. I'm not sure how—" She gasped and curled up into a ball, clutching her stomach as cramps seized through her.

Shanasee said, "Give her some of that water, Yithiere. Or let me." She reached out for the pitcher and goblet Yithiere still held.

Cara said, "The fortress can't protect the children from this." She stroked Kiar's hair.

"No!" he said. "I don't have to listen to you. I don't have to listen to any of you. None of you. You don't know what I know." He held the water away from Shanasee, narrowing his eyes at the inscribed orb in her other hand. "You have those. That's how you got here."

Shanasee flinched away. "Don't touch my lights." Something in her voice had changed, something crackled under her words. "If you have ever loved me, don't."

"Then go! Leave, or else…." The two wolf eidolons stopped growling at each other and turned as one to fix mad, yellow eyes on Shanasee.

Shanasee froze. Cara stood up hastily. "Neither of you want to hurt each other. Let's all agree that we want Kiar better and give her some of that water, hmm?" She reached across Yithiere for the pitcher. He jerked, looking around wildly. The water spilled on the floor.

Comprehension finally seeped through the fog in her brain. Kiar realized she was very sick, and her father was not just refusing to allow other people to care for her, but arguing with them and threatening them. Fear boiled through her. She moaned and began sobbing: dry, painful cries that threatened her ability to explain and calm matters. "People… have been dying. But… not fast. I was fine yesterday. Yesterday? Was it yesterday? I don't remember."

The wolf eidolons snarled in response.

Kiar stepped outside herself again and stared, horrified, at the tableau around her. Then, she fled. She left madness for the phantasmagory, but the wolves of Yithiere howled and hunted her into the dark.

Chapter Eighteen

Storm

Tiana walked in the eidolon graveyard. It had the dunes of a sand desert, but there was no wind, no sound, not even of her own footsteps. She passed through the shadow of a great skeletal beast and patted the ribcage as she passed under it. It felt like rough silk, not sand-etched bone. There had always been dragons in the phantasmagory, just as there were dragons in stories. "But nobody's ever seen one for real. I wonder why?" she asked it.

"What do you see?" demanded Jinriki.

"Why do you stay so close, if it doesn't help you understand? I won't translate for you." She looked up at the maw of the creature. Some memory or forgotten fantasy, left to the untender mercies of the phantasmagory. She turned away. There were walls of stone ahead, deeper in the wasteland, rising from the sand to the sky.

"I can see you. If I can't bring you out, I must stay with

you. That I am blind I lay at your feet." There was a new edge to the voice.

"Exactly why I'm in here, fiend." Then sound filled the world. Tiana's thoughts vanished as a set of howls spilled across the desert sky. A scream of anguish rose louder than the howls.

A wall of darkness rushed across the wasteland, unstoppable as the tide. After it came only a deep silence.

"Is this sleep?" Jinriki asked.

The darkness parted, and she was standing on a green hilltop, looking over a beautiful bay. In the center of the bay was an island, edged by high cliffs. Behind her was the desert wasteland she'd crossed. "That was Kiar," Tiana said. "And wolves." She shivered.

Something flashed, moving on the beach below the hill. As it came closer, Tiana recognized Shanasee's rainbow flying fish. At first a single creature, the shape shimmered and split into a school of smaller fish when it saw her on the top of the hill.

Tiana moved to intercept her. "What happened? Where is Kiar?"

The school spoke in a dozen high-pitched voices. "He has her—he holds her—Yithiere—she is ill—she is frightened—he is mad—no Regent—Cara—they are within—he drove me away."

Tiana stared at Shanasee and then looked at the island, remembering what Twist had said. "Sick? The plague?"

"Says Twist—are you lost—I was to bring her out—but he said there was a way—an idea—I cannot do it—where are you?"

Tiana shifted her weight, moved her hands in a restless pattern. "In the Morning Room, I think."

Jinriki whispered in her ear, "Yes."

The school of fish became agitated. "He is moving—he is here and there—Cara says he is moving—departing—how can he? So focused—such discipline—always—but he tried to break my lights."

Tiana closed her eyes. No one was better than Yithiere at walking in two worlds at once. He claimed it was a matter of survival. But how could he have even considered taking Shanasee's lights? It was unthinkable. And yet, he was less resilient without Zavien, and he was degenerating under the strain of maintaining multiple eidolons. She wondered what Twist had done to trigger this. "What was Twist's plan? He only said something about fighting an eidolon before he ran off."

The school scattered and then reformed. "To attack the eidolon in her—with our own—but I cannot—I cannot—I wished to convince Yithiere—I did not."

Jinriki's voice was acidic with amusement. "That was his idea? How very desperate. I could find a better solution myself."

"Don't even think about moving my body," Tiana snapped. Shanasee startled again, then reformed into the larger fish, murmuring to herself or her Regent.

His voice was silky. "Where would I go?"

"Nowhere," she muttered. "Stay where you are. Stop eavesdropping. No wonder Yithiere took her away. But she's got her own gifts; she did that thing with the enemy eidolon before. Absorbed it."

Lightning crawled across the sky and a foul stench drifted up from the place where the sea touched the shore. It was the smell of putrescence and bile, as if the sea was sour instead of salty, and all in it dead and rotting. Tiana looked at the lightning uneasily, then made a decision.

"I won't ever find him in the fortress alone. Shanasee... you're strong. You can do it. You can just step out."

The fish swished her fins fretfully. "I have no magic. Do not ask me."

Tiana said, "I've heard the stories, Shan! You were the tempest, you're the primus. Kiar needs you!"

"It doesn't matter! I did my part! I trapped Benjen, I held him while they pulled his secrets from him, I swallowed him down. Wasn't that enough? I *cannot* bring the darkness from myself again. You do it. You are wind and fire, to cleanse and burn. The darkness contains only... horror." Shanasee's voice trembled as a shadow crept across her form. "Cara, Cara, light the lamps. There isn't enough light anymore."

Tiana waved her hands. "I'm not there! I can't find him!"

Shanasee said, "Then it must be Yithiere, as I said. We must convince him. Come with me; we will return to his stronghold, across the sea."

The sky was low and ominous, crowded with charcoal clouds. There was a sound from the heavens as the clouds passed over and under each other: a slow ripping sound, like silken fabric, deliberately torn.

"What's happening?" Tiana looked behind her and the sand wasteland was gone, replaced by another shoreline, another cliff island.

"It's responding to Yithiere, becoming his stronghold. If he can, he will turn it against us." The fish turned and swam away, towards the island. Tiana drifted after her.

The stench of decay and vomit grew stronger at the waterline. Tiana put her hand to her nose and imagined rose petals. "Do you smell that? Is it me or the phantasmagory?"

"I taste it," said Shanasee. "And I see it, the color of rot and darkness across the water." She approached the water and then backed away. "I cannot cross that now. We need another way."

"You—" Tiana began, and stopped. She blew out her breath. "I will see if I can magic us across."

"It's better if you try than I. And… thank you."

It was more complicated than it would be in the real world. Using family magic in the phantasmagory was what made the phantasmagory so very dangerous. The Regents trained to assist the Blood in doing so. Without skill, what was done in one world was echoed in the other: to fly in the phantasmagory was to fly in the physical world. To strike at something in the phantasmagory risked striking someone in the physical world as well.

Usually, but not always. The Regents were hands and eyes, feedback on a world beyond reach but not beyond the ability to affect. But Lisette was not here. She would have to do it alone.

"I am here," said Jinriki, close to her skin.

She studied the island. A bridge would be convenient, but she wasn't sure she could make a bridge. That was like an eidolon. She decided if she had a rope, she could pull the island across the bay. She carefully tried to trickle out a ribbon emanation, one that would only affect the phantasmagory.

Nothing happened. The phantasmagory ignored her. It was like she was six years old again, and all magic was beyond her reach.

"I am here," Jinriki repeated.

"You are not a Regent," she muttered. "I do not trust you."

"I am aware of that, my lady. But I cannot let you bash your skull in, all the same." The sword's voice was curt.

Louder, Tiana said, "I can't do it. I don't have Lisette and I don't have the skill." *I'm the younger one*, she thought belligerently. *You're twice my age, you should have twice my experience.*

"Then we are useless here. I hope the Green Daughter looks fondly on Kiar." Shanasee backed further away from the shore. "I can't be here anymore. It's too dark. Cara, help me."

"No!" Tiana said. "No! Hiding and praying is not what we do, Shan!" She sounded like Jerya, which was irritating. "Lord of Winter!" she swore and cupped her hands around her mouth.

"Yithiere!" she shouted at the island, and she didn't care if she shouted in the physical world as well. When she shouted again, it was amplified a hundredfold by her magic. "Uncle! Come and talk to us! We are small and powerless, while you are wise and skilled! The two of us are hardly a threat!"

Shanasee finned backward in surprise. Lightning danced across the sky again and the rasping, tearing sound grew louder. A drop of rain plopped on Tiana's head and then skittered down her arm, now a glass spider.

She shuddered and stared as mist rose from the beach and the sea. "What is happening to the phantasmagory? This is... strange."

"I don't know," said Shanasee. "Not Yithiere after all. There's sand under my skin." The beach shifted underfoot, stable footing flowing away, and the mist thickened.

Tiana shouted again, "Uncle Yithiere! Please! Just talk to us!" She didn't try to disguise the desperation in her voice.

The mist swirled.

Then a tall, black wolf, elegant and lean, appeared through the drifting white, stopping a good distance away.

"Do you know what they want me to do, Tiana?" the wolf asked.

Tiana caught her breath. "What?"

Yithiere lowered his head, his yellow wolf's eyes narrow. "Attack her. Perhaps even slay her. But if I could just understand... I would know what to do. I can almost see the secrets, Tiana." He looked up at the sky, flattened his ears. "In the hidden corners of the world. I didn't want her to be a pawn. I didn't listen closely enough, so I couldn't protect Zavien. I knew this was coming. But not from Twist. How could he not know? I thought he saw into the corners."

Softly, Tiana said, "I have heard she is ill." Shanasee moved in agitated circles.

The wolf said, "She is strong, and there are many who survive. I will take care of her. Zavien wouldn't die a second time. If you want to help her, you should convince the others to leave us be. I can't concentrate with all these distractions." He pawed at his face. "I've almost got it."

Tiana felt like weeping. Had Rinta or Pell been like this, before their deaths? They were Yithiere's *younger* siblings, and there were such stories about them in the weeks before they'd died. Had Benjen been like this, before his Blights? Was this what lay before her, Shonathan's hollowness or this madness?

Jinriki whispered, "I can find them, with some time. Only a direct path, though."

Tiana shook her head and tried to focus. She remembered what Kiar had mentioned about the plague. "Many who survive the illness continue on only in body, not in spirit." She imagined Kiar with empty eyes and shuddered.

Yithiere took a deep breath and pawed at his nose again. "Is that so?" Wolf-ears swiveled to Tiana. "I have never seen an illness take hold so quickly, I admit. Save for the fever, I would imagine she's been poisoned."

"She has!" Shanasee burst out. Tiana made frantic shushing motions. "A poison, and you must leech it out. Like calls to like, Yithiere!"

The wolf's ears flattened. "Like calling to like is exactly the reason I will not use it. That is why Math died."

A trickle of cold went down Tiana's spine. "Oh, no," she said. She wasn't sure what he meant, but it invoked a powerful dread. Math had died in a final confrontation with Benjen, and Shanasee had never been the same. She glanced at her cousin, who had gone very still.

The mist roughened, brushing across her skin like sandpaper, then faded away. A road stretched across the sea from the shore. They all stared at it. Then Yithiere said, "I did not make that." He growled to himself. "This is a memory."

The breeze picked up, carrying the smell of grass and dust. Faded, green fields unrolled across gentle hills and in the distance, Yithiere's island wavered like a heat mirage. Beyond it rose the vast mountain of Sel Sevanth, whose shadow sheltered Lor Seleni and the Royal Palace. Astonished, Tiana said, "This is the Royal Highway. Why are we on the Royal Highway?"

Shanasee swirled a whirlwind of dust around herself and said uneasily, "It's just the tide of the phantasmagory. But look at the sky: something is wrong. Cara, please, help me!"

Tiana looked up. The sky was clear blue, but dread crept across it, a black wall. "Insects," she said. "Locusts? What's going on?" She reached out for her body, for any sense of the other world, and found only the current of the phantasmagory.

Panic rising, she said, "Jinriki?"

In her ear, the sword said, "I'm here."

"What's going on, Jinriki? Are you still... out there?"

Shan muttered to herself. Yithiere stared keenly at Tiana. She bit her lip and folded her hands behind her back.

There was silence. Then Jinriki said, "Yes. The place you are in becomes hostile, though. The dreams are sharp and jagged. If you would like to come out at last, I will protect you."

Tiana shook her head. "Are you all right?"

The sword said, "I'm sharp and jagged, too. It takes more than dreams to hurt me."

Irritation overwrote the panic. "Well, good for you."

Yithiere said, "Who are you addressing? Not Lisette, I think."

Tiana tossed her head. "Lisette is with Jerya. I'm talking to the fiend. My sword. Uncle, the phantasmagory's changed. I think it's because of Kiar's illness. I think if we don't cure her, we'll all be in trouble."

Yithiere bristled. "Do you see it too? You haven't the skill." He snapped his jaws in Tiana's direction and growled. "There is... you may be right. But Kiar... come and see." He trotted towards the island, down the road.

Tiana looked at Shanasee, who was swirling yet more dust around herself, her movements jerky and frantic. "Shanasee—" she began, then stopped. "I'm going to see Kiar. I'll come back for you if Cara can't help you. You'll be all right."

"Cara, Cara," the brilliant fish whispered. "Cara, the darkness is coming." Tiana clenched her fists and walked after Yithiere.

She walked, but the fields and the road did not move beneath her. Soon, Yithiere was walking beside her. "I'm tired of wondering what's going on," Tiana complained. The sunlit day darkened under the pestilent swarm that flowed across the sky, and black drops fell intermittently.

A fence beam broke with a sharp crack and cattle crowded over it. Mooing and chuffing, they wandered into the road. Yithiere said, "This is Kiar's memory."

Tiana was skeptical. "She's remembering cows? How do you know it's a memory?"

Yithiere said, "You never pay attention to lessons. Look how real it is. She was traveling this road, just today. The memory of this road, among others, has been emerging around her shell. Her horse threw her here."

"Spooky? Here? I don't believe it."

One of the cattle turned its brindled head to inspect them. Tiana's stomach lurched.

It wasn't a cow. It was a nightmare.

The world jumped and shuddered around her and she stumbled back, unable to tear her eyes from the horror. Small bulges writhed under the brown and white hide. The black crawling shapes found their exit at the monster's eyes and mouth, leaking like the black rain from the sky. A third eye, pale blue, shed black tears. Its front legs bent oddly, as if they had extra joints. Human hands dangled from the beast's udder, fingers wiggling.

Then she realized the large brown spots on the cow's hide were slowly changing shape. The cow-thing's horns seemed to grow and twist together without ever changing size, and its mouth was impossibly wide.

Her perception rebelled. She wasn't seeing hands hanging from an udder, or twisting horns, or an ever-growing mouth. It was something else entirely, but the only way she knew how to interpret it was as those things. It was all lies, she was telling herself, to try and put the impossible horror into a context she could understand. It was something deeply alien that had climbed inside Kiar's head through her eyes, then migrated from her mind to the phantasmagory.

A scream shattered the air around her, and she couldn't tell if it was coming from herself, from Kiar, or from the monster in front of her. She stopped up her mouth, gagging as her fingers turned to insects and crawled down her throat. Whimpering, she struggled to pull an emanation around her, but the memory remained stubbornly solid, the maw of the creature opening wider and wider, as if it would swallow her entirely. Then her horror turned to fury, and the road around her burst into flames.

She spread her arms and let the fire sweep through her, burning the blackness from her mouth, burning her vision with gold and red, taking away the nightmare. Higher and stronger she danced the fire, until the road was gone. But the flecks of moving black remained.

The wolf Yithiere stood untouched beside her, in the flames. He ran his tongue over his teeth and said, "Her illness has infected the phantasmagory. You're right. We cannot wait for her to recover on her own."

"That can't be true. I hope that can't be true. But that's not—I don't think that's a manifestation of the plague, Uncle." As she spoke, the flames faded away and they stood on a stone bridge over the sea.

"What, then?" He touched his lupine nose to the stones beneath him, testing the currents of the phantasmagory. A black drop from the clouds above fell in front of him, and he peeled his lips back from his teeth as he edged around it.

"I felt—I think if that had been more than a memory, I'd be sick now too. Didn't you feel it?"

His lips still curled away from his teeth, Yithiere said, "A misborn cow? Did it bite her? She would have said something. It was disgusting but so are fiends and nightmares. That was just more of the same." His ears flattened. "If it was a fiend, it might have cursed her. But she would have said."

Tiana didn't want to explain. It was hard. But she had to, so she tried.

"Kiar and Twist both said there was an eidolon marking the victims of the illness. Like a shadow. I think that horrible creature is casting the shadow and the shadow is making them sick."

Yithiere flattened his ears. "Eidolons do not make people sick. Neither do shadows."

"Maybe there's another word then, and I just don't know it," Tiana snapped fretfully. "Kiar is sick and the sickness is associated with the same kind of taint Logos-workers see as they look at family magic. And that thing—that monstrosity—you didn't see it clearly, Uncle. You couldn't have."

Her voice dropped to a whisper. "When I saw it, it was like it crawled inside my head and burrowed into all my worst nightmares. If I'd seen the real thing and not just Kiar's memory…." she trailed off, unable to wrap words around the horror.

He gave her a skeptical look, but his ears pricked up. "Well?"

She swallowed. "Don't you have things you don't want to think about, ever? I do. Things that hurt me. Sometimes I can't help it, and then I'm gasping and wishing I was dead. I'd do anything to stop thinking those things. There're times I think I'd bash in my own skull to stop thinking those things. Maybe Kiar's body is making her sick trying to burn that shadow out of her brain."

The wolf studied her. "Frightening. Enough." The sea and stone landscape vanished, and the two of them were inside a round room with a vaulted roof. Against one wall was an obsidian statue of Kiar.

Usually Kiar manifested as an all-encompassing, fantastic, elaborate suit of metal armor. But now she was still and only herself, no visor obscuring her face.

Dismayed, Tiana asked, "What's happened?"

"She's shielded herself in the real world." Yithiere paced over to the statue and pressed his face against it. "Inside her wall. She's lost, panicked."

Most of the Blood, when lost in phantasmagory, were dangerous to the people around them. Kiar's fugues had always been of the opposite sort, from the very beginning: opaque shields that kept everyone away from her and her away from everyone.

At age six, when she started service in the Banquet Hall and panicked at the number of people, her shield had expelled dozens of people from her immediate vicinity and lasted until Jerya had patiently soothed her. When Kiar had been nine and took plepanin, it had been worse. The Logos changed her perceptions, and only Twist had the understanding and ability to get close enough to calm her.

"I am speaking to her, but she does not respond." Yithiere had never sounded so frustrated before. Lisette or any of the other Regents would be more useful now. Or Jerya, or Twist—practically anybody but Tiana. Tiana, wind and fire, and nothing useful at all.

She stepped forward and put her hand on the statue's arm. "Kiar," she said quietly. "I'm not Jerya, but I'm here. I don't know what Yithiere has been telling you, but it's not good in here."

Roughly, Yithiere said, "The wall means she's still alive." It was a reassurance directed at himself, in the voice they all used for talking to their Regents.

Tiana said, "Uncle, you should go, if you can. Devote your energy to the real world."

"I'm fine," he snapped. "Better than you, little girl. Hone your own awareness of the real world and then lecture me."

Tiana pursed her lips and resolutely turned her attention to Kiar. She brushed her knuckles across the cool obsidian of Kiar's hair. The room became cold and long tendrils of mist stretched across the ceiling. Each arm of mist had a black shadow.

"Definitely not good in here, Kiar. I think we saw your nemesis. Something horrible, anyhow. And now bad things are happening. But, good news, we have ideas on how to cure the plague." She paused, scrutinizing the statue for any change, any reaction.

Yithiere said, "You tell her nothing I have not. This is useless." He darted over to a black blob oozing through the mortar of the stone wall and batted at it with his paw. "This is our place. Whatever this... invasion is, it crawls into our territory." He pulled his paw back, pulling black goo with it. Then he narrowed his eyes at the substance and folded an emanation into a knife that scraped the goo off the phantasmagory itself.

Tiana stared at him. Then she looked back at the perfect carving of Kiar. "Please, Kiar. There are bad things in here. I don't want to be alone, and I don't know where Lisette is, and to be totally honest, I'm afraid."

She didn't know what else to say, so she whispered the same thing a second time under her breath, and a third time. Then the statue opened its arms to her, and she fell into another place.

She was blind, but she never thought that blindness was a field of white. "Jinriki, what's going on?" she said uncertainly.

"Jagged dreams and hybrid magic. Nothing has changed outside."

"Oh," Tiana said. "Hybrid magic?" Slowly, the whiteness began to resolve. Flecks of black swirled around her. They made patterns. She realized abruptly they were characters, and they formed words. Hundreds of words, thousands of words. She was in a storm of words, more than she could count, more than she could imagine. They moved around her faster than she could process them.

"She is speaking as if to the Logos, but only nonsense."

That sounded like Kiar had somehow imagined her part of the phantasmagory was the Logos. Was that even possible? "Is that what all these words are? Can you understand them?"

He chuckled. She didn't know he could laugh. It was disturbing. "Analyzing...."

Tiana moved her hands around the storm of words while she waited, watching the way they grew denser as she focused.

Finally, he said, "Unexpected. What I sense feels like... a copy of the Logos. Can you even dream the Logos?"

"I have no idea. I barely know what the Logos is, but you can dream of anything," said Tiana firmly and then added, "Kiar says that when she looks at eidolons with the Logos, it's like a blind spot."

"Dreaming the Logos is dreaming everything. Her Logos makes no sense, though."

Tiana wondered, *where do I hide, if not the phantasmagory?* and then shook herself. "Is she trying to make an eidolon of the Logos? Trying to use the Logos while in the phantasmagory? I don't understand why *she's* not here anymore." She wished Great-Uncle Jant was there; he was the scholar of the phantasmagory and how it worked.

"She's not fully conscious, based on prior observations." The sword sounded far away.

"Of course not. If she were, she'd be talking and helping us out."

When she was eleven, she'd had a terrible sore throat and earache. While she'd mostly slept through the illness, she still recalled the vivid dreams of fighting off an endless swarm of enemies.

"So, let's go with 'She's trying to turn an eidolon into the Logos.'" She watched the storm of words for a few moments. There was something very worrying about all the movement, the flickering black on white. It was as if the words were forming patterns she could almost recognize.

A cow. One of them was a cow. The pattern shivered unpleasantly, then flew apart. The other, less recognizable patterns, flew apart as well and it returned to undifferentiated chaos for a time. Then the same patterns started coalescing again.

Tiana chewed on her lip as an idea surfaced. She hesitated, looking at the idea, and then words tumbled out. "The Logos... describes everything that's real, right? Even the words we say?"

"A child's simplification, but yes."

"No calling me a child!" she snapped and then took a deep breath. "What if she's trying to make the Logos describe the cow-monster, too? Or the shadows that come with the illness? What if she's trying to, well, make eidolons part of the Logos?"

"I have not yet found a way to apply the Logos to your magic." The sword's voice was flat.

Was it a stupid idea? She felt hot and flustered, and wished she'd caught the plague instead. Kiar was the clever one. "Our eidolons and emanations, they're copies of real things, so the Logos can understand them. But that abomination was horribly unnatural. I saw her memory and I thought 'cow-thing,' but it made me really, really unhappy. It's not the right word. I could talk forever and never describe it. There isn't a right word. It was like madness, made real." She paused and shook the nightmare out of her head, then continued.

"Even though the Logos can't touch our eidolons, they're not unnatural, because they come from us, and we're real. We have words. 'Yithiere's eidolon wolf.' That means something. And if I have the words, the Logos must as well. But if those plague shadows come from something that isn't real... the Logos wouldn't know how to interact with them." She paused. "And that's why the plague destroys people's minds—because they don't work properly in the place where the shadow is. The Logos doesn't know how to deal with it, so neither do people's minds."

Jinriki said, "You realize this idea presupposes a mysterious origin for this plague, beyond the Logos, from outside the world. Why do you have any reason to believe such a thing could exist?"

Tiana jerked and then shouted, "You! You're a sky fiend! From outside the world! And Kiar couldn't banish you! You're incredible. Do you think I'm stupid? Are you trying to hide something? Are you at fault? Lord of Winter, I—" She stopped. The sword was laughing at her.

"Clever girl. Your idea is troubling. I don't know if it's right or not. It seems like such an... engineered thing, to affect humans in such a way. But if so, it suggests that if a nearly-identical copy of the plague monster was added to the Logos, it would make the illness less a plague and more a bad day."

Tiana scowled. "That's what Kiar is trying to do, then. I should go tell Twist."

"That man? He can't possibly have the resources required."

"Then what?" Why was he laughing again?

He said, "Let us make this monster you saw, within the embrace of the Logos. Then the troubled mortal patterns will be able to accept it."

She gaped. "You can do that? Just like that? Just… make something? I thought Kiar was just trying to… teach."

"Oh, she can't. It requires some energy from outside the world. But, as you pointed out, I'm a sky fiend. I happen to have some left over, from before I was bound to sleep. I did say I was a channel." Why did he sound so happy? "I'll need your very close assistance, I'm afraid."

She growled, "How? Why?"

"Well, my pretty little princess, I can work the Logos in that way, and I have the energy source we need, but you're the one who saw the memory. You're the one who knows what to create."

Tiana knew it was useless, but she tried anyhow. "It was a cow. With three eyes. And… insects crawling out of its eye sockets. And the spots—they moved…." She shuddered convulsively.

Jinriki, though, was practically purring as he said, "Even now you try to pin it with mortal words, although you know you can't. That just won't do. You saw more than you ever could say. This phantasmagory is a wondrously useful thing,

I see. We must take the memory and go to the Logos. We must work as one."

Tiana's shoulders slumped. "Fine. I still don't know how to do that."

His voice seemed somehow closer as he murmured, "I do. Come out."

"But Kiar—"

"Will be helped, whether you are in the phantasmagory or not. You are hidden here. I am blind. Come." And somehow he pulled on her, quite unlike the gentle tugging of Lisette's touch and voice. Confused and curious, she didn't resist. The storm of words faded away but as it did, she heard a gasp and a sob, the whimper of a child. Then she opened her eyes. Her nose was pressed against the wall in the Morning Room, grey emanation char on the wall and floor, and the sword Jinriki in her hand.

"Didn't you get enough working-as-one when you stole my body?" She swallowed as she stared down at the blade. Somehow the voice in the phantasmagory seemed too real and complicated to originate from the sharp bit of metal.

Take a seat and continue holding me. You'd be unhappy if you broke anything. Once she was sitting at the table again, he continued. ***I am a weapon. When you hold me in your hand, I am the staff that lends reach to your arm, the emphasis that puts weight to your words. It is my task to focus and strengthen whatever you do. In this case, you will track down that memory of a memory, and I will create the words of the Logos that match it, put those into your head, and you will muster the will to present them.***

He paused. ***It will be hard, and it will be painful. If it is too hard, you can simply stop. Perhaps there will be a chance to try again later. Perhaps not.***

Tiana scowled and tightened her two-handed grip on the

sword. "Will you take over my body again?"

Suddenly the malevolent amusement and burning, violent hunger emanating from the blade was all around her. She choked and bent her shoulders against the onslaught of presence. She felt it scratching at her mind.

Only as necessary, I promise. I am not going to attack you. Fear will only distract us. Find the memory. Want it. Will it. Name it.

"But I don't want it," she whispered. "I've put it in the place I never look. There are other things there too."

Look anyhow.

My mother didn't love me. My father is insane.

My aunt and uncle killed themselves. I'm going to do the same thing someday, even if I don't want to.

I will never be normal.

She gasped for breath as her eyes flooded with tears. "Nemesis beast. Will it appear? Will it be real? Here? Not here, please. Somewhere else. Outside. Please. Not here."

A pause, and then he merely said, **Not here.**

She took another deep breath, pulling it in through her nose and sending it out through her mouth. Then she reached for her memory of the cow-monster again. Revulsion flooded through her, and sudden terror that what this sky fiend god-blade had convinced her to do was not a good idea. Then needles stabbed into her skull from all directions, and the memory dissolved into impossibly intricate symbols.

Her gorge rose, but it was words that spilled from her mouth. The sounds were spiky, many-edged things that clawed their way up her throat, scored her tongue, and made her teeth vibrate. She tasted blood, and the warm trickle in her throat gagged her, but the words kept coming.

The symbols were nearly incomprehensible, but she could dimly sense the physical nature of the creature in the word-shapes that chewed up her mouth. The smell of blood was thick when the words that described the physical nature stopped, but she wasn't done. There was still more.

She could barely imagine what she was describing now: the things that made it live and breathe, the things that gave it the nature of a monster. The words didn't just rip up her throat now, they hurt her ears, harsh, ugly sounds that she had trouble believing her throat was actually making.

Something else was flowing through her, too: it seemed as if lightning chained the words together, and she could feel the lightning stealing some of her own strength with each syllable. She wanted to sag, to relax, to forcibly close her mouth, but—

Twist stepped into existence before her, his eyes wide. "Lord of Winter—Tiana—" His gaze moved to Jinriki and Tiana felt herself pulled to her feet, the endless painful words still gagging everything else. Unbidden by her, the hand holding Jinriki moved him into an offensive position, pointed directly at Twist.

Twist stepped back, and she desperately hoped her own horror showed in her eyes, that everything that was Tiana wasn't obscured by blood and froth and the words.

His own word was as harsh as anything torn from her throat. "Enough." Two syllables followed, and he slashed his hand out. The words of the Logos vanished from Tiana's head, stolen by silence.

"A—Ah—," Tiana tried to say, and felt her knees fold under her, depositing her onto the floor. Her hand remained clenched around Jinriki's hilt. She swallowed a mouthful of blood and tears.

Enough, said Jinriki smugly. **We did enough. It is real, in a meadowed location very much not here. You did well, even though *it took more than I anticipated.*** The black stone on the sword's hilt was now clear, empty.

She realized her nose was bleeding too, but she couldn't summon the energy to do anything other than tilt her head back. She'd done well, the sky fiend sword said. And she had no idea what that meant, to the rest of the world.

Twist said, "Let the sword go, Tiana." And she tried. She tried to open her fingers, but they were white and tight.

"Jinriki!" she gurgled. "No!" Breathing hard hurt, but she couldn't help panting with panic.

Not me, little princess, but your own enthusiastic strength. He chuckled. ***But I will help. He is not dangerous, this time.*** Painfully, her fingers opened, and the blade dropped to the floor, the enveloping presence retreating with it.

Twist put his hands in his pockets and then pulled out a handkerchief to pass to her. "Do you know what you've been doing?"

She blotted at her lips and face, wincing. "Logos-working."

He wrinkled his nose. "Very unbecoming Logos-working, Princess. Fiend's magic is poisoning part of the Logos to make it pliable, ripping and shaping the Logos to your own ends. You created an abomination. I wonder why?"

Sudden anxiety spiked through her. "It's real, right? What I did? It's part of the Logos? The Logos is under it?"

Twist half-smiled, but his eyes were shadowed. "It's real now. What has the sword been telling you? You know it's not always a good idea to do what fiends suggest? There are consequences, as I'm sure you feel now." He rubbed his face.

"It was my idea. To help Kiar and the plague victims." Her voice sounded odd, liquid and husky. "I saw the illness.

It wasn't anything real. So we had to make it real. So it didn't hurt them as much." She realized her throat had been numb only when the feeling started coming back, and agony surged through her.

Twist stuck his hands in his pockets again, looking at the floor. Then he looked up and lightly said, "I think I'll go find Kiar. You get back to your room and rest." And then Tiana was alone.

Not alone. Jinriki was pleased. And she didn't know what to think about that.

Interlude

Blight

A stranger walked through the village of Tranning, north to south. He looked at the sky, turned in a circle in the center of the village, but he did not stop. No one spoke to him, though he was watched. He was garbed in elaborate layers, decorated with black jewels and wrought metals. That he went south made him less remarkable, not more. There were ruins to the south, and every season strangers walked through town on their way to find adventure and treasure. Mostly, they came back, disappointed. The old men of the town liked to tell stories of the ones who succeeded. The innkeeper liked to console the ones who failed.

The stranger walked across the fields, even though there was a road. Winter wheat was sprouting in the harsh, midseason sunlight, and so the watchers knew he was an aristocrat. The Highway wound through the hills close to the ruins, and the carters and the morning messengers saw him as he strolled down the biggest hill. They called it Little Sel, for its resemblance to Sel Sevanth far to the north. The oldest of the ruins in the valley was cradled along its western flank, where the remains of the old temple sprawled on the shattered tile plaza.

The stranger in his old black and iron stood out against the cream and pink stone of the ruins. Once there had been red in the heart of the mosaic, an eye or a bloody moon, but time and dust had washed the crimson to rose. The hunters and foragers kept the ruins clear of encroaching greenery. It was their history, even if nobody remembered quite what it was.

On the highway, a carter waved cheerfully at the figure and nudged his dozing companion. Then he stood up, letting the reins fall, shading his eyes against the late morning sun the better to see. A messenger, trotting by on his fine, tall steed, drew to a stop as well.

The stranger in his old black and iron had been starkly visible against the pale plaza. But now there was a puddle of blackness around him. It obscured the rose moon.

The messenger, whose name was Trace, wondered if the stranger was wounded. But the pool spread more quickly than any man could bleed, until the entire plaza was drowned in night. The visitor himself was just a shadow at the heart of the murk that he had awoken; his iron trinkets were dull and unreflective, coated with gloom.

A tremor shook the ground and on the road, men concerned themselves with settling mounts, checking cargo. When they turned their attention to the ruins again, the man was utterly lost among the darkness. It was now that the watching carters decided to tend to their calling and urged their frightened beasts on. Another solitary rider pulled rein beside Trace, and Trace said a single word to him before the second rider continued his journey.

Time passed. The sun reached its zenith and began a long, slow descent. Trace, in no hurry, continued to observe the ruins. A son of the Hathlanan family urged his horse off the road, down the slope, determined to investigate further. Halfway between the ruins and the road, his horse balked. The rider fought the animal for only a moment before dismounting and leaving the horse to wait.

Trace observed.

The Hathlanan walked only half the distance between the ruins and his horse before he paused. He took a few more uncertain steps. Then he turned to run. From his vantage point, Trace could see the expression on the explorer's face. It made him pull his bow from where it rested beside his saddle and send an arrow into the darkness.

The Hathlanan reached his horse and tried to mount, but the nervous animal shied and reared. Behind the explorer, the darkness was spreading, the puddle stretching after him. The explorer slapped his horse to send it fleeing and ran. And then he looked back.

The darkness swallowed him.

Trace lowered his bow, backed his horse up a few steps, absently reached out to catch the reins of the Hathlanan's mount as it fled past. Then he hailed the next rider to pass. Once again, words were exchanged. This rider wheeled his horse to stare at the ruins and then resumed his journey at a gallop.

Trace resumed his vigil. When other travelers slowed to gawk at the ruins, he waved them on, but otherwise he remained still. The darkness in the ruins was growing. The old temple was gone, as was the smooth marble facing on the Little Sel hillside.

When the darkness was over halfway to the road, Trace's agitation made his horse prance. He could see what the Hathlanan had seen.

The darkness was not a black storm cloud come to earth. It was not a localized patch of night. It was a hole, and on the other side was a place that had never known the kiss of the sun.

It expanded steadily, widened by the birthing struggles of something clawing itself from the ground. The newborn was already twice the height of a man, with a bell-shaped, obsidian head and a dozen spider-like legs.

Another earthquake shook the ground. Trace lost his hold on the explorer's horse and the animal fled down the road. He spent some time settling his own horse as he watched the strangeness at the ruins.

The newborn doubled in size and widened as well, pushing the hole of darkness before it, until it was climbing the slope to the road. The newborn—but it was no creature, no strange fiend. It was a stronghold, pulling itself into existence. It was unornamented, but the material that comprised it was slick and organic, with swelling buttresses and tooth-like crenellations. The curve of its highest dome was very like the curve of a skull. The first layer of spider legs had curled up and a second, larger, thicker set was pushing up the next level of the fortress.

On that level, there were doors.

Trace looked up and down the road, and bowed his head. Then he pointed his horse north, towards the distant bulk of Sel Sevanth and Lor Seleni, and let it run, crouched low over its neck.

An hour later, the first doors of the dark fortress were free of the earth that had encased them. The growth of the fortress did not stop, but the great doors opened. A swarm poured out. Black silhouettes moved like dancers with great gaping maws. Giants, carved from the same material as the fortress, galloped on four human legs, holding chains in each massive hand. Eight-legged, winged creatures, like dog-sized grasshoppers with fins, lifted into the skies.

The fields of Tranning were taken before the village was, but the road fell before fields or village. Even where it hadn't fallen into darkness, the road was torn and broken by the earthquakes. The creatures of the dark world roamed up and down the road looking for those unable to flee. When the fortress had swallowed the Little Sel, its growth seemed complete, but the dark world did not stop spreading until Tranning and its fields were just a memory, from the river to the far side of the road, fully twenty-four hours after the stranger in archaic clothing had walked south.

CHAPTER NINETEEN

THE CATALOG OF NIGHTMARES

Three days after the Blight was born, Tiana curled on a couch in the Blood's Hall and listened to Trace tell his story for the fourth time. The last time she'd been here, she'd been nine years old and snuggled up to Jerya while the adults discussed the enemy. Now, she was grown, and Jinriki was in her lap.

Then, as now, Yithiere stood over the map of Ceria marked with the approach of the Blight. It'd been to the north and outside the borders last time, an army raised by a Logos-worker who wanted the Citadel of the Sky. This time, it was inside Ceria, and she didn't know what it was.

Before, Rinta had overseen the Catalog of Nightmares, but she was gone now. Kiar stood at the table in Rinta's place, frowning and taking notes as Trace spoke. The Catalog itself was an enormous tome of fantastic creatures invented and compiled by one Amantha Savanyel. They were all quite imaginary, but it was a useful naming tool when a Blight brought a new kind of creature into Ceria.

This Blight brought at least six.

Kiar, still pale from her illness, finished marking down potential names and said, "I found this, and it seemed appropriate for the area around the stronghold. The Glooming?" She looked at Jerya for approval.

Jerya said briskly, "That sounds just like what was described." She nodded a dismissal at the messenger.

Tiana frowned. It seemed to her that Jerya was inappropriately pleased by this invasion. She was the one who had insisted on the full family gathering in the Blood Hall, even though the Blight hadn't been ratified in the Justiciar's Court yet. *They conspire against us,* she'd said. *You heard them yourself.*

Trace, who carried letters for Jant, had come straight to them, as fast as he could through the chaos. Tiana wasn't at all pleased by the Blight, but now that it had happened, she admitted to herself a certain, unexpected excitement at the thought of riding out.

"Is it just me, or did this happen awfully fast on the heels of Tomas…." Cathay's fists clenched as he paused. "On the heels of all the Regent deaths? Like it was planned?"

Yithiere said, "Of course it was planned. We must—"

Jerya's voice cut across her uncle's. "It may have been planned. Yithiere will investigate that angle further and present his findings to us. But for now…."

"Yes, now what?" Tiana asked. Her throat and mouth were almost healed, and she was glad she could talk again without too much pain. The day before had been unpleasant. Even Kiar had given her a bit of a lecture on foolhardiness, and Tiana couldn't defend herself at all without feeling the price she'd paid.

But Kiar had scolded her, and that was worth it. That very

morning, Twist had reported other people were recovering too, and that was worth a nemesis beast roaming the world. It had to be.

Jerya said, "Now we gather more intelligence." Yithiere nodded approvingly. He was better rested than the last time Tiana saw him. With a Blight on, that made no sense at all, she thought.

Tiana said, "That sounds interesting. Sneaking around in the dead of the night, that kind of thing?"

Jerya gave her that look she hated. "Not for you. You're busy keeping that fiend in check. I hope. So, you're not going anywhere."

Tiana protested, "It's in check! It can *help* us."

Jerya shook her head. "Perhaps later. There's too much we don't understand at this time and with the phantasmagory still plague-tainted, our communications are crippled. We'll use the Regency scouts."

"The Regency has scouts?" Tiana blinked and turned to look at the guards near the door. She'd forgotten.

Jerya just sighed and looked down at the map, which stung. She looked at her father, who was sitting at the old throne at the head of the table, fidgeting with his fingers. He had only four eidolons out today. He looked up and gave her a half-smile. "They're very useful, my dear."

"And loyal," said Cathay.

"We hope," said Yithiere.

Jant was huddled in another corner, holding an open umbrella. Shanasee and Cara flanked him protectively; he was a tiny old man. "About the phantasmagory," he said. "I think the taint is increasing, not decreasing. But it's not affecting our magic. It's hard to get out if the descent is uncontrolled, but we're not *crippled*."

"There are biters," said Gisen. "Avoidable." Everybody looked at her, and she blushed.

Jerya said, "The initial moments of the invasion map to when the phantasmagory pulled everybody in the other day. Great-Uncle, can you discover if that was a warning or something more ominous?"

There was a knock at the door, and then it opened. Lady Rosalyn of the Justiciar's Council peeked in, looking worried. "I'm not here to disrupt. I'd like to talk."

Jerya said, "Come in, Your Excellency. We were just discussing the Blight. You'll officially hear all about it at the next Council session." Her smile was hard.

Lady Rosalyn's mouth twitched. "Yes." Her gaze traveled around the room. "I've spent too much time with Etra to think their games are worth playing at this point." Etra had been Aunt Rinta's Regent and served as one of the younger generation's tutors. She was also Lady Rosalyn's particular friend.

Jerya raised her eyebrows. "Games?"

Lady Rosalyn coughed and said, "Your Royal Highness, your diplomacy is admirable, but there is trouble on the Justiciar's Council. I might even go so far as to say a rift is developing. We had news of the Blight yesterday from a private source." She paused to let that sink in. "There are those who will happily provide alternatives if the Blood is demonstrably unable to protect Ceria."

"Vassay," said Twist. He was leaning against a wall.

Lady Rosalyn glanced at him. "Vassay has a large population of Logos-workers. They've done some amazing things. Everybody's heard of the weather shield. They also have a much smaller fiend problem."

Dryly, Jerya said, "I was taught that was because they

were farther from the Holy Mountain, but the weather feat is certainly impressive. Are they offering to defend us from our fiends and solve our Blights as well?"

Lady Rosalyn said, "Not yet officially, Your Highness. But they're eager to have something to offer Ceria. Their Logos initiations require more plepanin than they can acquire, and that's not even considering inscriptions."

It only took a single dose of plepanin to awaken a person to the Logos, but plepanin also powered inscribed effects, Logos-working that anybody could activate. Because the Citadel only produced a very limited amount of plepanin each year, inscribed objects and tools were luxuries and treasures.

Jerya narrowed her eyes. "That motivation sounds very like a burgeoning Blight under a genteel façade. Are they offering this assistance or has someone solicited it?"

Lady Rosalyn shook her head. "I can't say, Your Highness. I haven't been communicating with them. But I know there are those in the Justiciar's Court who welcome them."

Tiana thought of the voices she'd heard in the Catacombs again. Had one of them been on the Council?

Lady Rosalyn went on. "There have even been those in the Regency Court who have sought to relieve the exclusive burden borne by the Blood." Her gaze drifted to the King, who was fidgeting with his fingers.

Jerya said, "A noble aim for the Regency Court. I'm sure nobody would misdirect such a pure ideal." Without transferring her gaze from the Justiciar, Jerya said, "Twist, why did the Council's private sources know about the Tranning situation before we did?"

Blithely, Twist said, "The Royal Courier service neglected to acquire inscribed horseshoes?"

Jerya glanced at him sharply. "You don't need inscribed horseshoes."

Twist half-smiled. "I know it may appear otherwise, but I must confess: I haven't yet worked out the trick to being multiple places at once."

Jerya had two spots of color high on her cheeks. "Tell me, are you in contact with the Vassay Logos-workers?"

Twist said, "Nope. They've rejected the teachings of the Citadel. They've thrown out the traditional master-apprentice relationship for a one-to-many approach. Lecture halls and a standard curriculum. Many annual initiation attempts."

Jerya raised her eyebrows. "I see. Innovators. And they are achieving great things with this approach?"

Twist waved away the Vassay great achievements. "They're able to manipulate large forces, but at the expense of the individual gifts fostered by the traditional methods of instruction. All of their Logos-workers have exactly the same capacities."

"They wrote you a letter," said Kiar suddenly. "I remember. Two years ago."

Twist laughed. "Yes. They've had a tiny amount of success incorporating some individual gifts into their curriculum. This encouraged them to write every Logos-worker of any renown, inviting them to share their secrets. I refused."

Jerya said, "Could they be spying on Ceria via the Logos? If not with your trick, with another?"

Twist considered. "I'll look into it."

Jerya transferred her gaze back to the Lady Rosalyn, her eyes hard and bright. "You did the right thing."

Lady Rosalyn smiled. "Others will disagree. The Council will not hesitate to use any out-of-order detail to postpone ratification of the Blight and ceding the resources. I hope

His Majesty will be able to observe all the formalities."

The King was walking his fingers under an arch made by the hands of two of his eidolons, but he looked up when he felt the stares on him. "Oh, I'm sure everything will be just fine. After all, they were always so nice to Tomas."

CHAPTER TWENTY

FIENDS AND BITERS

The next day, the Court was not in session, which gave them time to prepare. Well, it gave Jerya time to prepare. Lisette was helping her, doing research, discussing precedents and politics. And Tiana was kindly encouraged to quietly entertain herself in the Palace.

Without Lisette, she stayed in her suite, feeling neglected and irritable. She understood why Jerya needed Lisette's help, and she was so very glad Lisette hadn't been struck down like Iriss, who remained cold and pale and dreaming in her chamber.

Tiana was happy to make the sacrifice, but she wasn't used to being alone. Even Jinriki was relatively quiet. She told herself she was happy about that, but even she knew it was a lie.

She spent some time with the plays and fairy tales on her bookshelf, but those stories of things she wasn't doing just made her grumpier. She went from a sense of noble self-sacrifice to wishing Iriss was better for entirely selfish reasons. Jerya was so stodgy now and even if she insisted on being stodgy, Iriss would have kept company with Tiana while Lisette, more politically minded than Iriss, helped Jerya.

She drifted over to her desk and considered the letters she could write, but that didn't interest her either. While there, she noticed the wooden box where she'd tucked away the twin to the Royal Pendant.

They'd hardly had time to theorize on what it was. Connected, somehow, to Tomas's death, she knew. And perhaps to the plague, perhaps to the Blight? They all thought everything was about eidolons, but that made no sense.

Idly, she unlatched the box. The big opal necklace was still there, nestled on some crumpled satin scraps. Kiar had said it was made of eidolon stuff, but it looked real to Tiana. Kiar seemed to see eidolons everywhere these days. And if it was somehow an eidolon object, who was maintaining it? Eidolons didn't wander around independently, no matter what some of her relatives' crazy theories were.

She'd seen a phantasmagory memory of a pendant, down at the bedrock of dream. And if even the phantasmagory remembered the pendants, it couldn't be a simple eidolon. Could it? How could it have lasted?

You have never made an eidolon successfully, Princess. What would you know? Jinriki told her, with that undercurrent of laughter in his voice.

"Shut up! That just means I have a unique point of view on the subject. Maybe I can learn something from it that no one else could."

Oh, if it entertains you, by all means carry on. I'm curious myself.

She scooped the pendant up. Thorns bit into her hand

and she immediately flung it away from her. It thumped on the carpet, and she peered at her hand. She didn't seem to have any new injuries, and the sensation had faded as soon as the pendant left her hand.

She narrowed her eyes and muttered, "Why do all my new toys bite?" She picked up Jinriki and walked over to the pendant.

Whatever it is, it doesn't bite for the same reasons I do. Tiana inserted the point of the blade under the necklace chain and lifted it up.

"You said you'd protect me. So what is this thing? Father has one just like it. That one's been in the family for centuries. But this one was locked away in the catacombs."

What happened when you touched it?

"It bit me. Black thorns. It didn't bite last time I touched it." She deposited it on the bed but left Jinriki's tip touching it. "It's not biting you now?"

No. How did you know the thorns were black?

Tiana frowned. "I don't know. Wait, I do. It felt like the phantasmagory felt before." She plumped up a pillow and settled herself against it, still holding Jinriki. Then she opened herself to the other world just long enough. "Like it feels now."

My, how interesting. You haven't returned to the phantasmagory since the plague. Are you frightened?

"No! I'm just…." Tiana searched for an excuse that would still allow her to appear plucky, "…trying to be nice to you. Because you don't like it when I'm there."

How very kind. It must be hard on you.

Tiana smiled, pleased. "Oh, yes. But I can endure."

Very brave. But here, you should return to it, and I will endure for a while. It's only fair.

Tiana's smile turned to a scowl. "What are you up to?"

Go to the phantasmagory and perhaps you'll see.

She stared at the blade and then relaxed against the pillows.

The light floating of previous days seemed gone without hint of return; this time she fell like a rock. There were hooks on the surfaces she fell past, but they were small and easy to avoid. When the hooks ended, so did the fall, and she felt the wind of a nighttime city street blow through her, with the remembered scents of wine and jasmine. An indistinct shape beside her opened argent eyes.

"You see, the jewel is connected to your dream world somehow. I am not blind now." It was Jinriki's voice.

Tiana startled, remembering again the dream she'd seen deep in the phantasmagory days ago. Thorns—no, hooks—sunk into her in response. She concentrated, calmed herself, and the tiny biting things pulling at her loosened and drifted away. "This is our safe place. It shouldn't be unfriendly now." Her fierceness pooled around her as she attempted to impose her will on the space around her. In response, the hooks swarmed her again.

All over, she felt pricks of searing pain. She concentrated harder, and there was more pain in response. Then the city street rolled away, like a change of sets in the theater. The curtain of darkness fell and then rose on a river scene at dawn. The hooks were still biting her. But the rosy light of the sunrise radiated from her. The indistinct form of Jinriki drifted nearby, argent eyes in black smoke.

Encouraged by her success at changing the landscape, she concentrated again. "Mine!" she insisted again. "No biting. All you hooks, you biting fleas, you can just die." She spread her hands and pushed a wave of rose fire away from her. It was exhausting, but for a moment she thought she'd banished the hooks. Then agony swept over her.

"Stop. Stop it." The black smoke that was Jinriki moved over her, as another person might take her arm. "You fool, stop it. You can't fight it like that."

The hooks dug under her skin and pulled from every imaginable direction. She shifted, twisted, and was pulled ever harder. Panic rushed up from her gut. What if she couldn't escape? If she couldn't burn them away, if she couldn't fight, she would be caught here, pulled apart, lost, broken, dead.

No! She couldn't bear it! Fear made her strong again and again bloody fire exploded around her.

The moment of pain was endless.

She was being taken apart. She fought back! She would keep fighting—

Her volition vanished.

"If you struggle, you will die. That is unacceptable. Your strength is impressive. Conserve it, you mad little fool." There was some new emotion in Jinriki's final phrase. Was he angry? Tiana realized that the paralysis was fading and so was the pain.

"Calm yourself. Be peaceful. Be as the shadow. They are drawn to your fire and energy, so douse it." His voice was modulated, calm again.

Calm? How could she be calm? But she tried to dim her fire, open herself to the wind. More and more points of pain dissolved as she did so. As she released her will, the river sunrise reverted back to the night city, a gradual transformation. Finally, she stood in darkness again, breathing carefully, lightly, and it was as if the pain had never been.

"What are they?" she whispered.

"I don't know. I don't see them when you're calm. Is there anybody else here?"

Tiana shuddered. "Gisen said something about biters." She looked around, tried to ease her perceptions out. "I can't tell." Then she saw a figure moving down the abandoned night streets. She didn't recognize it, until she saw it drift through a cart abandoned in the middle of the road. Then she said, "Her." It was the ghost woman.

She moved closer to Jinriki's immaterial cloud, a little too fast, and felt the biters. She released her energy again and breathed, "She doesn't do much for my sanity."

The ghost woman moved closer, though she didn't seem to notice Tiana or Jinriki. Tiana stayed quite still, hoping that wouldn't change.

"Why do you fear her?" Jinriki asked.

"Shh. She's spooky. I've seen her in the real world, too. That's not the sort of thing that normally happens when somebody is sane."

The ghost woman was standing so close that she could have touched Tiana, but she was looking somewhere else. "What's she looking at?" she whispered to Jinriki, unwilling to change her focus.

"I cannot see anything meaningful. The stuff of the phantasmagory, the dreams and memories and such. I do not know if she is aware of the set in the same way you are. Ah, but now I see. The biters."

The woman tilted her head and cinders whirled around her, each one with a white speck at its core. They settled over her, flaring as they intercepted her shape. She spread her arms and the cinders flew away, coalescing into the blurry silhouette of a human. It glided toward the woman, who back stepped. It spread its arms as the woman had done previously and the woman blurred, then fuzzed into the general phantasmagory.

The silhouette's hazy head lifted like a hunting dog's, swiveling this way and that. It moved in Tiana's direction and her heart leapt into her throat. Biting motes swirled around her and if the creature hadn't seen her before, it certainly did now. A long, shadowy arm reached out, finger pointing at her. Tiana breathed out, pushing the motes away with her meditative wall and wondered if she could defend herself like that.

Before she had to find out, the ghost woman fuzzed into existence behind the silhouette again. The silhouette's head snapped around, and it flowed towards her, spreading its arms a second time. Again, the woman back stepped and then twirled like a dancer. She curtseyed to the silhouette, and it stopped its advance, its arms half-dropping.

The woman raised one hand to touch a biter, and the tip of her finger turned white. The biter flashed brightly and something glittering pulsed out from it. When it washed over Tiana, she tingled. And when the pulse was gone, so was the biter. There was, instead, a tiny tear in the night city, as if the backdrop had been damaged.

The silhouette tilted its head, looking at the tear. Then it exploded into motes, the little flecks streaming out of its form until the woman brought her hands together and the silhouette compressed back down to a figure again.

Jinriki moved between Tiana and the tableau. "Can you come out?"

"Now?" She couldn't tear her focus away from the mysterious scene unfolding.

"I'm starting to wonder if you're more trouble than you're worth. Yes, now. Your father's here."

Tiana said, "I wonder if anybody else has seen the ghost or that other thing. Oh! Daddy!" She concentrated, until she could feel the bed beneath her, smell the fireplace and the dried apples that scented her room. Jinriki was in her hand. She could hear voices in the sitting room, and an eidolon was peeking through her half-open bedroom door.

She opened the door fully and stuck her tongue out at the eidolon, which of course returned the sentiment. A guard—Tiana made an effort to remember his name and thought it was Saul—was arguing with her father in the middle of the sitting room, while his eidolons wandered around exploring, as if they'd never been there before.

"Daddy!" Tiana said. "Are you here alone?" Saul backed off, returning to the door, and the King frowned at his daughter.

"Of course not," the King said indignantly but then he tapped his nose and looked sly. "I did give that Chancellor fellow the slip, though. Have to keep him out of the way, or there's no telling what trouble he'd get into." He looked around, as if assessing the room.

He had five eidolon twins out now. Two of them were standing just behind him, staring at each other, while the other three continued to explore the room, picking up cushions, looking in drawers, ambling after each other around the breakfast table. But Tiana was good at ignoring them.

"How did you do it? Are you on the run, then?" Whether he was lucid or distracted, teasing him was always safe.

"Oh, I told him I'd turned one of the Blight fripperies into doll's clothes. That sent him right off." He looked around again. "Man's more taken with Jerya than I think a fellow of his age should be. I'm sure he's older than me."

"Jerya's rather taken with herself these days," Tiana said glumly. "She's gotten all bossy. Even of us. Was Mama so pushy?"

"She's a very determined lady. But so was your uncle Math. Jerya takes after him, I think. Somebody else I know is more like Annis." His eyes twinkled as he smiled at Tiana. Two of the eidolons rushed past, and the King batted at them.

Tiana looked down. She didn't know what to think about that anymore. She wished she hadn't said anything.

After a moment, the King said, "So you've been talking to a fiend, I've heard."

"Yes. But he's in check, truly. What happened to Cathay was a mistake." When he looked around again, she directed his attention to the sheathed blade that she'd laid on a low table near her bedroom. "I know he doesn't look like one." One of the eidolon twins wandered into her bedroom.

The King chuckled. "Fiends aren't always terrible monsters or scoundrel spirits. I've spoken to a few myself. One in particular, I remember very well. A beautiful creature, like a woman, but winged and feathered. That was in my first Blight. Caervyddin's Blight. She was an earth fiend, Caervyddin a sky fiend. Eyes like rubies." He stared off into space and then shook his head.

"What did she talk to you about? Why did she talk to you?" Tiana had never heard her father tell war stories before.

"We found ourselves with an opportunity to interrogate her about Caervyddin's forces. She was… chatty. She called herself the dream of the world and said the world offered safe harbor to the sky fiends. She chastised us for destroying them." He chuckled. "Said it was unkind. She also said there would never be an end to earth fiends and when we killed her body, she would move on. She scolded us for treating fiends in one way and Secondborn in another. Well, she scolded the

Regency commander who was with me.

"But she said I was the only one there with any right to challenge her or Caervyddin. She said we—the Blood, I mean—we have part of our soul lodged beyond the scope of the world." Two eidolons rushed past the King again and turned to pass right through him. It was so *odd* to see images of her father gamboling like children.

But the King didn't even seem to notice. "But she said a right to challenge is not the same as the right to win and, until that day, the earth fiends would rise to champion a sky fiend. She hummed a little tune whenever she wasn't speaking." The King hummed a sad little phrase that Tiana realized he often played on his violin.

"She kept telling us it was a terrible tragedy each time we destroyed a sky fiend, that they didn't have the possibility of reincarnation like everything else in the world and one day they would run out." He sighed. "She made it a hard, emotional Blight. Almost as hard as Benjen's. He had earth fiends, too. But I was wondering, has your fiend said any of that? Or was she deceiving us?"

Tiana paused to see if Jinriki had an answer, but he said nothing. He was paying attention, surely. He was always paying attention. She wondered if she could demand an answer and loosened the seal that kept him out of her most intimate thoughts.

No, he said. **You can't.** Then he added, *I am watching the eidolons. They are curious about your pendant.*

She dismissed his information about the eidolons; her father's creations were as distractible as he was. Jinriki's refusal was just the sort of thing that made her belligerent, but her father was looking at her with such a sad, hopeful expression. So instead, she invented wildly. "Oh, he's a very tragic figure. He doesn't want to die, that's why he's behaving so well. If he dies, pffft, that's it, and he… he likes the world. Wants to see more of it." She nodded, and then wondered if perhaps her father had wanted reassurance from the opposite direction.

Princess of pretty lies.

But her father's sad expression bloomed into a smile. "I'm glad. Not that we destroyed Caervyddin, no, not that, but that the earth fiend told me something true. And that she's moved on. Perhaps your sky fiend will find her someday and she'll remember me, eh? She called herself Liathan the Griever." He was so happy that two of his eidolons returned to merge with him again. "And now you're warned about that connection, eh? It's always important to know what you're getting into. That first Blight would have been so much easier for me if I'd known then…." He trailed off, his gaze sharpening as the energy expended on the eidolons returned to him.

Tiana stared at him, thinking about the Blight they currently faced. "I wish we knew more about this one. It's so close, so strange, and right behind all this other strangeness, and Jerya won't let us go investigate directly or anything."

"That's a shame," agreed the King amiably. "She does have quite a forceful personality. Someday she'll be the monarch my brother Math never had a chance to be."

"It's not fair, though, her forbidding me!" complained Tiana. "It's not like she's ever experienced a Blight herself. Not directly. She's never fought in one. She has *no idea*."

"That's true," the King admitted. "It's certainly a dilemma."

Tiana paused, suddenly thinking over the conversation she'd just had. "You're right. She may make a good Queen someday, but she's not the Queen yet. *You're* the monarch. *She's* just my sister."

The King's absent smile became a little bit fixed, as if he wasn't entirely following her line of thought. "Yes, yes I am. And yes, she is. And will be. It's not the burden you expect, you know. I was prepared for all the rituals and the war, but not… not other things. Dying for the land is just duty, but other things…."

"Don't think about them, Daddy," commanded Tiana. "Think about the current Blight. You think we should know what we're getting into?"

He sighed. "Yes. Yes, I do."

"And you're the King," said Tiana happily. "That's the word of a King, right there."

Yes. Do we go do something relevant now?

"Word of a King," Tiana repeated and kissed her father on the cheek.

CHAPTER TWENTY-ONE

A HILL WITH A VIEW

Kiar went to Court the next morning solely to fill out the Royal Box. Jerya wanted as many bodies as possible. "We have to look strong," she said. "They could try anything, and they might even try to stop Trace from speaking. They've got a lot of old rules in those books."

But the messenger Trace was the first petitioner into the Hall. He looked determined, but Kiar was still dubious that he'd ended up there on his own. He strode to the white line and in a strong voice said, "I call a Blight! The county of Tranninwyl has been swallowed by a vast darkness—"

Lord Aubin said, "Yes, yes, I'm sure we all know about it by now. My granddaughter rode off two days ago to sightsee."

Trace stopped, taken aback, and looked at the Royal Box. Lord Aubin followed his gaze and added, "I see His Majesty is decked out in ceremonial armor today. Did it take two days to put on?"

Jerya said, "So you do not dispute this call of Blight, Your Excellency?" Her voice only trembled a little.

Lord Warrane said, "There's a vast bloody hole where Tranning used to be. Nobody can dispute that."

Lord Aubin shot him a warning look and said to the Royal Box, "It's the Blood's role to stand against the supernatural enemies we call Blights, aye? Just as it's the Justiciar's Council's role to regulate the day-to-day affairs of Ceria. Do you think if you get your Blight, we can see eye-to-eye on that?"

Jerya looked thoroughly off-balance now. "I—no formalities, no strange old customs?"

"I've heard it's growing," said Lord Aubin simply.

Jerya said, "Ah." She studied the Justiciars. Then, almost helplessly, she said, "I agree with your allocation of responsibilities."

"Very good. Is there any on this Council who disagree that the destruction of Tranning constitutes a Blight?" Nobody moved. "Excellent. The Justiciar's Council agrees with the claim of this plaintiff: there is a Blight! The armies and moneys of the Court, and the lords of the six duchies are at your disposal." He called to the servant standing next in line, "Fetch your master while we sign the document." He gestured a clerk forward with a document to sign, and Kiar wondered why his little smile seemed so victorious.

But Tiana didn't. The whole hall heard her say, "Thank heavens that's over!" She climbed out of the Royal Box and Kiar joined her.

Jerya said, "Where are you two going? And you're taking Lisette? I'm not sure that's—"

Tiana smiled sweetly at Jerya and said, "We're going for a ride. Father said I needed to know what I was getting into." The King was staring vacantly at the doors. Jerya's gaze flicked over Kiar, and she felt a little rush of guilt that she was adding legitimacy to Tiana's little plan. Then Tiana was fleeing the Hall, and Kiar hurried after her, feeling a more than a little guilt. Not only was she adding legitimacy to the adventure, but she was hiding behind Tiana's brashness.

But the guilt only lasted until she was out in the sunshine on Spooky's back again. She patted his neck fondly. It wasn't that Spooky had been throwing Kiar when she was sick with the plague. It was that she'd kept falling off. And when at last she'd given up and walked, Spooky had followed her all the way home, his reins dangling. He would have followed her into the Palace proper, if the guards trailing her hadn't stopped him. The stable boys told the story every chance they had.

But even so, Kiar *remembered* the feelings of betrayal. She hadn't ridden since that day, even though she knew it was silly and childish, and when Tiana had bounced into the parlor late the night before, crowing, "Order a picnic, ladies—tomorrow, we're going to Mousame!" she'd agreed before she could come up with any reason not to.

Mousame. It was already a Court vacation spot, and someone in the Regency Court good with maps had discovered the little town and its great big hill offered an amazing view of the Glooming. It was said even the Stronghold of Glooming itself was visible. And it could be reached in only half a day by horses with inscribed horseshoes, which of course all their personal mounts had.

Lisette had said, "But we're not supposed to go near—"

Blithely, Tiana had interrupted, "Daddy said it's important to know what we're getting into."

When Lisette had realized Kiar wanted to travel as well, she gave up arguing. All she said was, "You can't sneak away.

And the eidolons will dissolve." Eidolons could only go so far from their maker before fading away and the will that powered them returning home.

Tiana shrugged. "Hey, Kiar, have you seen the phantasmagory tonight? It's different. The plague taint is gone. So is everything else. It's totally empty. Something Jant did, maybe?" And then she bit her lip, like she knew something she wasn't saying. Or, Kiar conceded to herself, like her damnable sword was whispering to her. Then Tiana added, "It's weird, but I think you might like it more now."

Kiar was forced into the phantasmagory to see what Tiana was talking about. And she was right. It was clean. All the residue of generations past was gone, like someone had scrubbed it out. It was like a blank sheet of paper. She thought that some of the Blood would be upset by that, but she couldn't help feeling more relaxed there. Maybe this time around they could implement a cataloguing system.

And when she confirmed that it was clean, Tiana said, "I don't know why. But if it's not dangerous, Kiar and I are better protection than those eidolons." And that was that.

A maid had told Kiar there were gangs of monsters roving the highway, so Kiar had conscientiously brought the list of possible names from the Catalog. It was important for things to have names. But all they saw on their journey south were other travelers.

A throng of people moved north, most of them with their lives in carts and on their backs. Twice, they passed noble parties returning from Mousame. The first party was subdued, and only nodded greetings as they passed. The second party was far more sociable. Taime Westerhoft laughed and encouraged Tiana to enjoy herself. The view, he said, was spectacular. 'Chilling,' voiced one of his female companions, and giggled.

"Oh, and don't miss the Mystery Spot," said Taime, as they parted ways. "East side of the town, near the edge. It's just… nothing. Absolutely fascinating and, of course, might be meaningful to the Blood." He saluted as he rode away.

As they approached the town, Tiana insisted they pick up the pace, and Lisette insisted they take their time. "What's the hurry? Are you *hoping* for a fight?" She looked at the sword strapped to Tiana's saddle.

"Oh, please. You too?" Tiana spread her arms. "I'm still me. The fiend is not dominating me. Yes, it talks. Yes, it likes fighting. It's a *sword*. And I'm the Blood. Fighting supernatural threats is what I was born to do. You know that!"

Lisette said, "I just wish I knew what was going on. You used to tell me everything."

Tiana said, "Well, you spend all your time around Jerya now. Maybe you should have just stayed behind. You saw how she wanted your help."

Before the argument could get worse, Kiar said, "We're here." It wasn't quite true, but it was close enough distract them.

The town buzzed with fevered activity. A few people were in the process of moving out. More were capitalizing on the town's sudden surge in popularity as a tourist attraction. As they rode through the town towards the great slope on the other side, it was clear that the town had many more inhabitants than usual. The inn was overflowing with the noble and wealthy, every vacation house was full, and there were many people camped out along the edge of the road. There was a holiday atmosphere.

"They're *selling* things!" Tiana said, shocked. She slid off her mare and crouched down to inspect the merchandise on an old woman's blanket.

The woman beamed toothlessly at the Princess, eyes lighting up in recognition. "Grandson's friend was noted bone-carver in Tranning. Gone now." She clicked her tongue sadly and then pushed a comb into Tiana's hand. "Made by Ajolo Rea, sold by Yatara Brighteyes. Take it. A gift, Your Ladyship."

Kiar surveyed the other camps. A wagon was dispensing the last shipment of doomed Tranning's fine wheat beer. Several other blankets sold accounts of watching the devastation happen. There were more trinket-sellers, but Tiana was walking slowly back to her horse, looking at the comb.

Lisette said, "Nobody likes to be afraid, Tiana, and this is more frightening than an army outside the borders. So they laugh instead."

"Are there always people selling things?" Tiana asked.

Lisette said, "Yes. Souvenirs from the front are worth a lot. Some people collect mementos from each Blight."

Kiar said, "They make stories of them." Tiana glanced at her, her eyes shadowed, and clicked her horse ahead.

Further down the road, a middle-aged woman with a covered wagon was selling spyglasses. She hailed Tiana with a brisk, "Your Highness!" proffering one of the brass tubes. Slowly, Tiana shook her head. Then she urged her horse to a gallop, sending dogs, chickens, and children scattering.

The vista from the lookout point was stunning. The river twisted along a panoramic sweep of green and brown, dotted with red tile roofs and grey stone castles. Here and there, the Niyhani peaks and Keldaran domes rose above the trees. It was beautiful, the stuff of paintings, until your gaze drifted to the east. There, half the vista was a shocking grey plain.

It cut off the river and the road as if they never existed and inside the boundaries, nothing grew. There were black shapes against the grey expanse that Kiar thought might be twisted trees. Hoped were twisted trees. And in the heart of the grey, the black stronghold loomed. It wasn't even the size of Kiar's thumbnail at this distance, but it hunched like a giant over the starkness of the cracked land.

Kiar realized she'd forgotten to breathe. She wondered what happened to the other side of the river. It didn't look like it was dammed by the land that had interrupted it. Then Tiana said, "That's what's going to kill us, Kiar."

"Yeah," said Kiar. Why did Tiana sound so enthusiastic? Then Tiana took her hand and squeezed it hard, white-knuckled and Kiar thought, *Nobody likes to be afraid.*

Lisette ran forward. "Don't *say* things like that! Don't be fools!" She held onto Tiana's arm.

Tiana wrenched herself out of Lisette's grip as she whirled around. "Would you rather I kill myself uselessly? Would you rather I grow old and mad, and hide myself away in my rooms because the world is too frightening?" She caught her breath. "I see that thing, that place, and I think maybe the reason the Blood is mad is because it takes a madman to fight against something like that."

Lisette shook her head, frantically. "This hasn't happened before. This is really bad. Really bad."

Kiar didn't want to listen to them argue. "I'm going to go see the Mystery Spot." She took her horse back from Berrin and started walking down the hill. After a moment, the other two caught up with her.

The road to the Mystery Spot was lined with more blankets, but this time, instead of merchants, there were priests and philosophers. Two itinerant priests of Niyhani argued philosophy with a laughing Knight of the Rose. A maiden of Atalya prayed on a blanket covered in silk flowers. A matron of Keldera, the Summer Goddess, comforted a man weeping into her bosom. A scholar of some sort worked furious figures on a chalkboard to an admiring audience of small boys and red-robed servants of Rann in his guise as Lord of Fire. A child with a dog instructed a pregnant woman. A woman sat on the edge of a wagon, staring at everyone who went by, carefully writing something down after each group.

By the time they reached the Mystery Spot though, the blankets and wagons were gone. No one wanted to be too close to it, whatever the mystery was.

"I feel strange," complained Tiana. She slowed, and Kiar moved ahead of her. The Mystery Spot beyond was encircled by rope twisted around some pegs and almost invisible to normal vision. But through the Logos-sight, it was a hole pulled open by eidolon hooks.

Tiana said, "Kiar, do you feel that? It's like a humming in the—" Kiar reached over the fence toward the nothing—

CHAPTER TWENTY-TWO

THE TIME FOR PRAYERS

Lisette's shriek as Kiar touched the Mystery Spot banished Tiana's curious disorientation. But Kiar fading away was enough to give her vertigo.

She took a wobbly step after Kiar. Maybe there was a trick to it…? Then she was borne to the ground by Lisette as Jinriki snapped, ****No!****

"Oof," said Lisette and lay there, gasping for breath.

Tiana complained, "What was that for?" and got back up again, moving over to the makeshift fence.

"No!" wheezed Lisette. "Don't go near it."

Annoyed, Tiana said, "I want to see what happened to Kiar."

"Please. No. Wait a moment." Lisette looked like a fish, mouth and eyes both round.

Tiana shook her head. "Why?" She shook her hair back and looked around the little street. Where could Kiar have gone? Any second now she'd probably saunter out of one of those buildings, looking smug about her trick.

Lisette rolled to her feet and took Tiana's hand in both of hers. "Because if something bad has happened to her, I don't want it to happen to you."

Tiana squeezed Lisette's hand. "Silly. Kiar's just playing a joke."

Lisette said, "Let's wait for her, then. Once she comes back, you can ask her what she did."

Tiana said, "Fine, fine." She looked around. Then she called, "Kiar! Come on out."

Only silence answered. An unpleasant feeling sprouted in the bottom of Tiana's stomach, and she promptly squashed it. "I wonder what else there is to do here. There's some kind of rural dancing, isn't there?"

Lisette said, "We could go ask someone." She pulled gently on Tiana, but Tiana resisted.

"We need to wait for Kiar. She *couldn't* have actually vanished. That makes no sense. If the Mystery Spot were eating people, there'd—well, there'd be a bigger fence!" The ache in the pit of her stomach surged up again.

Something happened to her.

"Shut up," Tiana snapped. She watched Slater and Berrin walking down the dusty street with the horses. Then she dragged Lisette over to them.

Berrin said, "Where'd Lady Kiar go?"

Tiana said, "When I find out, I'm going to shake her until her teeth clatter." She freed a hand and fumbled at Jinriki's scabbard.

Lisette said, "What are you doing? Don't do anything stupid, please." She looked on the verge of tears, but Tiana pushed that thought aside just as she pushed Lisette towards Slater.

"Take her off me." When Slater didn't obey quickly enough, she shouted, "Do it!"

Lisette jerked away, into Slater's chest, then lunged after Tiana again. Tiana ducked and stepped away. Lisette said, "Don't let her touch it!" But Slater's hand settled on her shoulder, and she slumped.

Tiana jerked the scabbard off her sword. Then she called, "Kiar, time to come out!" She scanned the street. People were staring. A small child ran away. Her shame mingled with a burning fury, and she ran over to the Mystery Spot. Emanations danced around her, lifting the dust in sheets.

She leveled Jinriki at the emptiness. "Tell me about it."

It is not a part of this world.

She pushed the tip of the blade into the space. "And?"

And what? It is not a sky fiend. I have not yet intersected it, though you think I have. I do not know how Kiar interacted with it.

One side of her head pounded and her vision flickered. "You're useless, then," Tiana said and sent the sword scything away from her. Then she kicked aside the makeshift fence and plunged her hand, and her emanations, toward the Mystery Spot.

Her hand never reached it, but the emanations did. While it seemed to drift just beyond her fingers, she could feel the broken-glass edges of it through her emanations. Blowing her breath out, she twisted and pushed against sharpness, staring at the spot until her eyes teared up. She couldn't tell if she was having any effect at all.

Blinking furiously, she released the emanations and turned away, rubbing at her eyes with the palms of her hands. What had Kiar done? Where had she gone? Lisette assumed the worst, but that didn't have to be true. It didn't *always* have to be the worst. Did it? No, it didn't. It didn't.

"Aunt Rinta," she whispered and bit her lip when she heard herself. Louder, she said, "No. I *will* find her." Aunt Rinta hadn't vanished, but Aunt Rinta had died. Just like Uncle Pell, just like Grandpa Anther, but Tiana *remembered* Aunt Rinta, remembered her face after she'd choked to death on her own blood. She remembered the yellow paper flowers at the funeral. She'd held Gisen's warmth in her arms, just as Jerya had held her when their own mother went away. Shonathan had wanted her to know what she was getting involved in, but he couldn't have meant this.

She sent her emanation probing into the Mystery Spot a second time, concentrating so hard that the pain in her skull faded away. Plumes of fire blazed across her vision, but she was precise and clean in her direction of the emanation. After a time, she thought she could manipulate the blurry emptiness, move its leading edge around, but what good did that do? She couldn't make it do whatever it had done to Kiar—

She realized that Berrin was standing patiently beside her and let the emanation drop again. The hollowness left her dizzy and swaying, and her headache surged back. "What?"

"What is it, Your Highness?" He seemed unperturbed, as solid and steady as a great ox.

"I don't know. Something unnatural." She felt stupid as soon as the words escaped her mouth. Of course it was unnatural, and of course he was asking her. "I'll figure it out." He ought to ride back to the city, tell Jerya, get Yithiere and Twist to come out. People who knew what they were doing. But she couldn't tell him that.

She realized that Jinriki was resting by her foot, placed neatly on his scabbard. "How did that get back over there?"

Berrin said, "Begging your pardon, Your Highness, but I

brought it back over."

She wrinkled her brow, staring up at Berrin's broad, bearded face. "You picked him up?" She glanced down at his hands, but he seemed fine.

"It asked me to. Wanted to be closer to you. Did I presume?" He moved his eyes from her shoulder to her face, and she twitched and turned away.

"It's *my* sword, not the other way around." She nudged the blade with her toe, but Jinriki apparently had nothing to say to *her*. Scowling, she added, "Go away. Go back to Lor Seleni if you must. Just let me be."

She raised her eyes to the blurred emptiness again and embraced the pain of her throbbing headache. The emanation rose around her, steadying her. She turned the pain into a knife and sent it against the Mystery Spot, tearing, ripping, rending. This time, the emanation was a tempest, and her mind was cold and empty, the taste of blood on her lips.

Chapter Twenty-Three

A Place Without Light

Kiar stood in a place without light and looked at the mist she could see anyhow. She knew, somehow, that there had never been light here. It was cold, but not freezing, and absent-mindedly she wondered where the warmth came from without light.

Stepping into the distortion had been a matter of instinct. As soon as she saw it, she knew that beyond the strangeness was the phantasmagory. What was there to be frightened of? She *recognized* what she was looking at. The distortion was a gateway into the phantasmagory, simple as that. A gateway to the place the eidolons came from. So she stepped forward and reached into the place inside herself where the magic came from, and twisted just a little—

She stepped in, and she thought of the eidolons in the plague. There was that to be frightened of. But it was too late.

When she went into the phantasmagory, she fell. But she

hadn't fallen here. She did not descend. She'd simply stepped *in* and there she was, standing in a place without light. It didn't feel very much like the phantasmagory, now that she was here. It felt... large. Wild. Alien. And it was full of far more mist than the phantasmagory usually was.

She blinked and remembered the world she'd glimpsed twice before: when she'd swallowed enemy eidolons and reached into the distortion within a sky fiend. *Ah.* This place was that place, and she was here for real. This was her body, not just her mind, in a world where eidolons lived. Perhaps it was a cousin to the phantasmagory.

She inhaled and something flowed into her lungs. It wasn't air, wasn't water. She wasn't drowning, but she could imagine she was. She could feel the thickness on her skin, seeping under her clothes, clogging her eyelashes.

She closed her eyes and reached inside. But that was no longer the road to the phantasmagory. She tasted the thick air in her mouth, like winter water. Was she without magic, as well? Fear flared, and instinct reacted. She held out her hand, and a flaming sword appeared. It was real, without the iridescent shimmer of an eidolon in the real world. She could feel its warmth and weight.

She turned in a circle, trying to find the way back. All she saw was grey mist, illuminated by her flaming sword. She whimpered. What if she couldn't leave? What if she was trapped here, in a place Twist couldn't reach?

She felt the sound on her skin, as if the mist reflected it back at her. Something else vibrated against her skin, and there was a cry, long and low. It undulated through registers lower than any human could achieve. Kiar froze, her sword still outstretched. Something moved through the thick greyness. She could feel its movement against her skin too, its slow, heavy tread on the ground and the flutter of motion higher than her head.

She was in the place where eidolons lived, and that had to be one of them. Unless it was something else? In the phantasmagory, did something exist below the dreams and memories the Blood layered onto the mists? She resisted trying to call up the Logos. That was likely a quick route to utter insanity. The flames of her sword burned slowly but did not illuminate the grey. The invisible creature groaned and trilled.

"What are you?" Kiar asked. Her voice sounded strange and distorted, like talking underwater. She walked forward, thinking about the eidolons she'd swallowed and the world she'd glimpsed through them. It had been mist-free, a vast, alien, monochromatic place.

As she walked, the gauzy curtain lifted, vanishing as if it had never existed. The world was deep black, but strands of colorless vegetation surrounded her, bright against the blackness. Moving through the stalks and leaves was a giant. It had six legs, thick and stumpy as tree trunks, and a straight, tall neck wound around with more vegetation. Where she would have expected a head, she instead found dozens of silvery birds, quite recognizable: two eyes, wings, tails. The birds fluttered and trilled, a hole opened in the flock and that deep groan emerged.

Kiar turned her head rapidly as she backed up, refusing to take her eyes off the giant for more than an eye blink. More of the vegetation surrounded her; it was a forest of vines and seaweed, growing in luxurious grey and white profusion.

"Time to reconsider," she said. "Do I really think this is like the phantasmagory? Are *you* in the phantasmagory, big guy?" The birds warbled in response, and several of them darted out to drag a length of vine back to their perch. She could just make out what appeared to be a spar of bone jutting out from whatever served as the base of the creature's head, before the birds obscured it again. The creature moaned again.

Kiar watched the creature until she decided it wasn't about to attack her. Then she spent more time examining her surroundings, letting her sword fade away. She crouched down to peer at the ground and discovered only a thickening mist that she could force her hand into, like very loose, very fine sand. The vegetation had root tendrils buried in the stuff. The giant had similar roots on its legs, though they waved and moved slowly.

She felt the noise of something else moving just out of sight and scuffed behind the thickest grouping of the vines, wondering if hiding was even meaningful in this place. Then she saw the black silhouette that padded up beside the giant, and her thoughts were swallowed by fear. She'd seen that shape before, clawing its way out of a sky fiend. These *were* eidolons.

She held her breath as the silhouette looked around alertly and pushed its head against the giant, who moaned in response. The silhouette was shaped like a human, but it moved like a deer, sudden and graceful, a black dancer cast upon a screen. *Andani* was the best name from the Catalog for it. It had four fingers on its hands and she could see movement like muscles beneath its skin.

The face was alien, save for the eyes, which were grey and disturbingly human. It had a dog's nose, an ugly, wide mouth, and it was totally hairless. It reached for the leaf on one of the vines twined around the giant and tore at it, shredding it with a sharpened bone plate in its mouth. Then it plucked another leaf and advanced on Kiar's hiding spot, holding the leaf out like an offering.

Warily, Kiar edged into visibility. She couldn't help thinking of flies caught by honey, but she couldn't hide behind vegetation, that was clear. Without conscious intent, a steel shield shimmered on her arm.

The black dancer sprang backwards, emitting a high whine. Then it fell to the ground and scuttled away, looking from side to side like a panicked animal. "Are you scared of me?" Kiar asked. "Or my magic?"

The andani made terrified clicking noises and hid behind one of the six legs of the giant. The giant had only moved a few steps since she'd first seen it, and it was unfazed by her magic. No—the birds were agitated. Several swooped down on the andani, their chirping rising in pitch. The giant stepped back, a surprisingly complicated maneuver. It was too much for the andani, which shrieked one final time and fled.

Kiar took a deep breath, wondering if anything else would come to investigate. She really needed to figure out how she was going to get out of here. That was the smart thing to do. This was a place where eidolons acted like people and animals, like living things, and it was the place enemies came from, a cousin to the phantasmagory but vaster and wilder. She had to share the mysteries with someone.

But surely more information couldn't make things any worse? There was no research in any book to help her. She edged around the giant and pushed her way out of the vine thicket, passing under a smear of buzzing she hoped was insects. Beyond was a shallow incline leading up to a cliff, then down in a wide, gently curving path. What passed for the sky beyond the drop was the stark black of a night without stars. Cautiously, Kiar dropped to her knees as she approached the edge of the cliff and then down to her belly, unwilling to let whatever might look up notice her.

The landscape below the cliff was just as monochromatic as the jungle: light grey for the land and dark grey pooling like water, here and there. The vines flowed down the cliff, though not in the profusion she'd encountered at her point of origin. She could see other giants moving through other tangles of vegetation directly below her. Further away, thin dark strips divided the areas of vegetation and giants into irregular, polygonal fields. To her left and right were other plateaus, precisely placed at equidistant points on a circle; each had a beard of vines. Beyond those plateaus was only darkness.

In the heart of the vast circle indicated by the plateaus was a teeming throng of creatures. There were many more black dancers—andani—, tightly packed into precise squares and other creatures as well: grotesque parodies of humans and giant birds and—Lord of Winter—the nemesis beast.

She stared at it for a long time, observing her own reaction. But what Tiana had done seemed to have worked. It was disgusting, but it didn't take up residence in her brain. It was just a thing. An eidolon nemesis beast, far more familiar than the six-legged giant. Perhaps the nemesis beast inoculated the Logos against these other strange monsters too, so that she could look and say, *Oh, how strange,* instead of screaming.

She remembered too, what Tiana had whispered to her. *Jinriki thinks it was engineered to hurt us.*

Then she methodically continued her inspection. Whoever had engineered an eidolon designed to destroy minds had been very, very busy. The mass of monsters in the distance crowded around a monolithic pile of stone, charcoal against the black sky. From the energetic movement of individuals within the army, she determined that they were very excited. About what, she couldn't imagine.

The giant moaned somewhere behind her. She looked around, saw an andani crouching near her, and rolled to her feet, stumbling back down the slope towards the vegetation tangle. Once she was a good distance away, she paused to study the creature again. It hadn't followed her, and it hadn't run. It was just sitting there... watching.

Kiar shivered. "I have to get out of here." Her voice was comforting, even distorted as it was. "Intelligence gathered. Time to wake up...." And she tried to wake herself from the phantasmagory, instinctively. But there was no indication there *was* a phantasmagory here. It was a cousin to the phantasmagory, but the two were not connected.

"This isn't the phantasmagory. There must be some other way," she told her observer. "It feels *real*. It's cold here. I can taste the air, I can feel the ground. Well, what passes for the ground. But how do you step out of a *world*?"

She fumbled her way back into the tangle, hoping she didn't get stepped on by the giant. But it had moved only one giant-sized step from where it was previously. She stopped next to the third pair of legs and pressed her fingers against one.

She could feel it, too. It was cool and pebbled, and she thought she could feel movement under the surface. Then the leg she was touching lifted and a trilling flock of birds flew down from the creature's head to perch on the leg. She backed away, hands raised to fend them off, but they didn't attack her. Instead all of them looked at her, moving their heads in unison. Then one of them trilled, and a second one picked up the sound, and a third, each one in at a different pitch. The beast itself moaned as well, creating an extraordinary harmony. She froze, staring up at it. The beauty seemed out of place.

Then she shook herself. "Oops. I was just curious." Kiar backed up, pulling some of the foliage between her and the giant. Another three birds trilled at her. Suddenly she was worried that she'd hurt it, that what she interpreted as beauty was actually pain. She covered her ears with her hands and turned her back, pushing her way deeper into the monochrome jungle. After only a moment, the vegetation was too thick to climb through.

That was unexpected. "And ridiculous," she whispered. "I didn't do any wading through a forest when I got here. I couldn't even see." But she conjured up her sword again and slashed at the vines. The cut vegetation shriveled where the sword touched it.

Her sword clanged off something. A set of four strands ran parallel to the ground, one above the other, starting at her knees and ending over her head. The vines twined around it, but after they shriveled and crumbled, the sword against the strands made only black sparks. They were very thin and hard to see; at first she'd thought they were just lateral vines. But they were smaller, dull black, and very taut.

Kiar hesitated. Something felt wrong. The thought almost made her laugh. Standing in a colorless world of monsters and something felt wrong? But she carefully cleaned all the vines off several feet of the strands and then stepped back, squinting. They weren't *quite* parallel. They were wider at the thinner side of the tangle, narrower at the thicker side. She held up her hand sideways, spread her fingers, looked through them. Yes. The strands were like thin, long fingers, like the strings on a violin. Presumably, somewhere in the deepest part of the thicket, was the place that they met the palm.

She needed to find out. She felt more cheerful as soon as she admitted that to herself. It was better to have a direction and an achievable goal, than to fumble around blindly, after all. And a guide, as strange as it was. But she'd only taken a few steps along the path indicated by the strands before she stopped and looked at them again. The third one was close to her eye level. It looked like thick wire, pulled taut. She wondered if it would make music when she touched it.

She brushed her fingers over it.

Vision exploded around her. Concepts without words flashed in her head: a great hive, a machine, pulling. Puppets full of needles, wire piercing her flesh. What happened to a world turned inside out? A team of horses could pull a man apart.

She was running through the vegetation again, swords whirling around her, running towards the iris, eye, valve, *gate* she was certain the strands led to. There it was. A flap of eidolon stuff, thick and organic, pulled aside by four wires on the near side and four wires on the far side. They reached through the flap to whatever was on the other side. Her world. Her world with hooks in it.

Almost imperceptibly, the wires tightened.

CHAPTER TWENTY-FOUR

THE TIME FOR BEER

Mousame's local beer was wretched, and Tiana hated every swallow she made herself take. After only two mugs, it stopped tasting so bad, and she wondered if adding salt would bring back the misery. They'd tried to convince her to relocate to the tavern when she'd run herself down beating on the Mystery Spot. She'd demanded they relocate the tavern to her, instead. It was liberating to stop caring if they were frightened of her.

They'd brought her a table and a chair, and bread and salt. And a bottle of wine, to start with, but that was too good for her. Beer. With salt in. Kiar was gone. Yithiere would cut her to pieces.

Lisette snatched the salt crock out from under Tiana's fingers. "Oh, stop it."

Tiana slouched in her chair. "I can do what I want."

Lisette, sitting to Tiana's left, handed the salt crock to the nervous tavern boy hovering nearby. "You don't want the salt. You don't even want the beer."

Berrin, sitting to Tiana's right, sniffed at the untouched mug in front of him. "It's not that bad."

Tiana narrowed her eyes at Berrin and gulped at the salty beer. It made her thirsty, so she drank more. Her tongue began to hurt, and Berrin pushed his mug over to her, eyes crinkling. Scraping her tongue against her teeth, she poured the untainted beer down her throat.

"You're quaffing," Lisette pointed out, wrinkling her nose.

Tiana turned so fast she almost knocked her chair over. "Why haven't you sent one of them back to tell everyone what's happened?" she demanded. "Tell Jerya all about it. Bring back people who know what they're doing. I can't believe I thought my insane father had a good idea."

Lisette's eyes shadowed. "I won't betray you. We'll go back when you say so."

Tiana tilted her chair back. "Yithiere or Twist or even Jant could find Kiar. Even Gisen."

"Kiar's either gone or she's not. Rushing around won't change that." Her eyebrows drew together. "First you attacked the Mystery Spot and now you're attacking yourself. Stop it. Notice it."

Tiana looked away, towards the Mystery Spot across the street. It was more than just a fuzzy round blur now; her ministrations with the emanations had warped it into the rough outline of a human. It made no difference, though; she still couldn't force it to respond to her as it had to Kiar. The horrible blankness of it felt imprinted on her eyes; she no longer had to search for it. She had the awful feeling that rather than molding it into the shape of a human, she'd uncovered a shape that was already there, a shape that was all that remained of Kiar.

She gulped at her beer and then coughed as she swallowed too fast. Then she swallowed more, until the ache in her throat subsided. Dammit, she'd just saved Kiar. She'd unleashed some kind of monster and for what? Kiar to be eaten by a tourist attraction?

Lord of Winter, she wanted to tear this town down, looking for her. It was a dismal place, though the gawkers mostly stayed on the other side of town. The villagers did something or other with cotton when they didn't have so many tourists. Kiar would have known. There were strange little huts scattered between the houses. She had no idea what was in them. What if there was another Mystery Spot? What if Kiar was trapped?

There was shouting from the road behind her. Slater moved away to investigate and Tiana tipped her chair forward again. Jinriki was on the table between her and Lisette, shining in the afternoon sunlight. She traced her fingers over the engravings, felt the rough texture of the red-stained lower blade, the stone that had once been black and was now clear. All that power, spent. He hadn't spoken to her since she'd hurled him away. She wondered if he'd like it if she started tearing down the mysterious buildings. Wouldn't he like that?

But Jerya wouldn't approve. Her stomach tightened painfully. Jerya never approved of anything she did. Jerya certainly wouldn't approve of this. It would be about as far from approval as Jerya could get. Kiar would never have come here if Tiana hadn't suggested it. Everyone would be at home and safe.

Tiana lowered her head until her forehead was resting on Jinriki's cool handle. She wished she could make the ground open up and swallow her or wrap herself in an untouchable shield like Kiar. If only she'd had Kiar's powers and Kiar had hers. Responsible Kiar with the emanations and empty-headed Tiana, locked in a cage out of everyone's way. Jerya would never miss her.

Her eyes felt gritty and dry. She knew what she should do. She needed to rise, take up Jinriki and order everybody back to the city. She ought to end this foolish misadventure and let people who knew what they were doing try to rescue Kiar. If she could even be rescued, if she wasn't already just a smear of emptiness. *Life isn't a drama.* In her mind's eye, Jerya turned away.

She pushed herself to her feet and went to investigate one of the smallest buildings, which was exactly what Kiar would have predicted and completely undramatic. When she returned a few minutes later, Jinriki wasn't shining any longer. The sky had clouded over. There was more shouting behind her, and she realized that Berrin had gone as well. Lisette was standing a few feet away.

Tiana's head hurt again, an ongoing dull pain rather than the throbbing ache of before. "What's going on?" She picked Jinriki up.

Lisette had cleaned the dust of the street from her face and hands, and smoothed her hair back. "The people on the hill saw something exciting. Berrin's gone to see for himself." She was troubled, though she kept it from her face.

Tiana stood on her toes, shading her eyes with her free hand. People were running. Some of the tents and stalls were packing up without any care for organization, while other campers were talking animatedly. Four riders galloped north, scattering chickens and children. She saw Berrin and Slater galloping back towards them.

"What is it?" she called.

"Raiders," said Slater as they drew up. "Enemy raiders, on a line to the town."

"Oh, Rann's balls." Lisette's eyes widened at Tiana's vulgarity. Tiana stomped her feet. "Keldera's cunt!" Liberating. She tightened her hand on Jinriki's hilt and took a deep breath, inspecting that place inside that brought forth the magic. She was still recovering from her earlier exertions, an hour after a hard race and she didn't know how long her second wind would last. Adrenalin made her breath quicken.

Lisette and the guards were watching her. A horse stomped, and a young man scrambled past, calling to someone. Then Lisette said, "My horse is lame, and I'm not leaving." She turned away.

Tiana said, "I'm staying. Lisette, you should leave, get someplace safe—" She blinked and paid attention to what Lisette had just said.

"Of course you're staying. Figure out a good plan, Princess, because I'm not leaving." Lisette's voice was hard.

"You can't stay. What if you got hurt?" Tiana protested, but Lisette just walked away. "I'll be distracted," she called after. "I've got to do this! Lisette!"

Slater said, "We'll protect her, Princess. What are *you* going to do?"

She wished—but she was here now, and that was that. The burst of adrenalin fell under the shadow of a darker feeling. More of the merchants packed up their wares. A door slammed and rattled. She could hear the fear, high and shrill, in the murmur of voices. *Jerya. Oh, Kiar.*

She felt the phantasmagory below her, like cool water just touching bare toes. She slipped in, no splash, with a sigh. There was nothing around her. The phantasmagory was empty and calm. The biters were gone, and the black silhouettes, and the ghost. All the ancestral memories and the personal strongholds were gone, too. Everything was gone, like it had been purged, or made new again. She felt a peculiar chord of grief for what was lost, for all that she could conjure up her own special place whenever she wanted.

Then she inhaled and let the emptiness fill her up.

There she goes, said the tall one. Look at her face.

We should get her and the other one out of here, said the strong one.

If she doesn't—Princess?

She moved past them, forcing words through forgotten lips. *There's nobody here to tell. Nobody will know. I'm sorry.* The hill loomed ahead, glaring bright, distorted by the lens of the phantasmagory.

A black cloud with a crimson core and argent eyes walked beside her. "Is that fear, little one? Such an odd taste."

In two worlds, she said, *I'm not afraid. Don't worry about that. There's no room.*

The tall one turned away and said, *Hell. This—*

She stopped and looked back at him.

He lowered his head, raised it, said, *All right. You're doing your job, Princess. I don't understand how, but—we'll do ours. We'll take Lady Lisette to the tavern. It looked defensible.* He walked to Lisette.

The strong one caught her hand and brought it to his lips. She saw her own shadowy feelings reflected in the twist of his mouth, until the black cloud moved across her and the sword in her other hand raised to point at him. He dropped her hand, swung back onto his horse. *Good luck, Princess.*

She walked past him, down the long road and up the high hill. They stopped as she passed and watched her go, with her long sword in her hand. Faces peered out of shutters.

Children cried. A rider charged past and another horse reared, rather than go around her. Beyond the voices, there was a sound like thunder.

From the top of the hill, she saw the invaders. They moved like a flock of birds, dark shapes on monstrous mounts and creatures that looked like mount and rider in one. They moved quickly; they were not exploring, not watching their flanks. They were very close. Soon, they would sweep past the east slope of the hill and into the town.

Soon. Not yet. Tiana stepped off the steep side of the hill, spreading her arms.

When her grandfather had walked off Reader Tower, his eidolons had soared to the tower's peak, but he had not. He fell to the flagstones far below, and nobody ever knew if that was what he intended, or just… one of his little confusions.

No one will know.

"Little girl, I know."

She drifted gently on an emanation. It was easier than she remembered. She must have recovered more than she thought. "You aren't supposed to call me that."

The black cloud beside her shifted, glinted red. "Sometimes it is all that is speakable."

The troop of invaders was so near now. The riders were slender and armored all in black, from helm to boot. Their mounts were more wolf than horse, though they ran on heavy hooves and bore three horns. They were the color of deep water. The other creatures—they had the hands and heads of men, and twice the legs, but the clawed feet of beasts.

Tiana looked at the sword in her hand. "I don't know how to use you."

The black cloud said, "Do what you always do. Do what you did before."

She flexed her hand around his handle. "I might drop you."

"No. You won't."

She paused, watching the movement of the invaders. They grouped together as they swerved around the hill and slowed as they noticed her drifting above them. Then she said, "When I fall, they'll take you from me. Your revenge will be lost. I'm sorry."

The black cloud's voice turned cold. "Let's kill them all, then."

She sighed. Then she swept her hands forward, Jinriki in one hand, the other hand straight like a knife. The emanation scythed away from her, rippling down to the leading edge of the invaders.

The mounts screamed, a high whine interspersed with hiccuping thuds. Three reared, stumbled backwards, fell. Two more failed to swerve around them. Then rising dust screened the details.

"Three?" Tiana said. "Three at once? Did I hit all three? I just meant to trip the leader." The phantasmagory vanished from her perception as she strained to make out what was happening below.

Well done. Jinriki's voice was saturnine.

"You just make my magic stronger? Why didn't you help me before, at the Mystery Spot?" Tiana shook the blade in aggravation, her quiet dispassion chased off by her surprise.

Pay attention! Something dark and thin flicked by her face and then her knee, and the emanation supporting her vanished for a plummeting heartbeat as she flinched away.

"Ah! What—do they have bows?" She tried to focus on the dust and riders below. *But he should have helped me earlier!* Another dart skimmed past her cheek and she flung out her hands again, frustration propelling another emanation down to the riders, untargeted. It sliced through the dust and more creatures screamed. She saw one of the mounts snap its tail forward, and Jinriki twisted in her hand. A dart spanged off the blade.

Bewildered, Tiana pushed her free hand forward, fingers spread, sending the emanation rushing forward like the wind. A black spike pinwheeled. She crooked a tendril of force to bring it to her.

It was as long as her forearm, a thin, dark, mottled horn. She scowled and hurled it away from her, back at the riders. Then she sank into the phantasmagory again, where Jinriki was a black cloud beside her, not a sword in her hand.

My hand is a sword. She sliced. The screaming of the mounts was joined by the deeper, guttural cries of the four-legged creatures. She saw one of the slim riders standing at the edge of the wreckage of mounts and riders, looking up at her. Then more darts flew at her.

My hand is a shield. She held it up. But it was Jinriki who cut one out of the air and her flinch-and-drop that saved her from another. Infuriated, she sliced and sliced and sliced again, cutting blindly at dust and screams and darts. She realized part of the enemy had continued on, into the town.

"You have no idea how to defend yourself," Jinriki observed.

Shut up! Why didn't you help me before? I could have saved Kiar—

"That rider is still watching you. Don't let it live to report what it's observing."

Black specks flying—she reached out with the emanation and the sword and cut them out of the sky, one, two, three. The fourth one cut through her clothing, grazing her arm even as she jerked and fell another few feet. Its path against her skin burned.

Her emanation stuttered around her as she caught herself. Jinriki made her stronger, but she was still worn out and getting wearier. *Damn you, if you'd helped earlier, I wouldn't be so tired now.* She blew and the emanation parted the dust long enough for her to take in what was happening beneath her.

A shape moved at the heart of the black cloud and Jinriki's sudden rage was a palpable force against her mind. "You were having a tantrum, accomplishing nothing. Are you having another one? Will you get yourself killed to punish me for not indulging such a childish urge in one who could be so much more? I promise you, that's all that would kill you today." His voice turned acrid as he said, "I regret that I was ever placed in your hands."

She stared blindly as the dust parted and swirled together again: a mass of dark shapes, some moving, some not. Some of the shapes were limbs, parted from their bodies. The lone watching figure had not moved. White and grey eyes, real and living, scrutinized her.

She startled out of the phantasmagory and focused on the watcher. "That's not a helm," she muttered. "That's its face?"

Apparently. Kill it now, and examine it later. His voice was cold and dispassionate again, and she wondered if the rage was gone or merely hidden. Jerya's disappointment slipped out like that sometimes. She flinched away from the thought, dropped a few inches. Then she curved one hand into talons and clawed at the watcher. It stepped nimbly to one side, never moving its gaze from her. One of its hands twitched. A mount moved behind it, tail cracking violently. A spike flew.

Tiana bit her lip hard and pushed herself into the phantasmagory again, curving both hands around into claws. She thrust her hands out and then jerked them apart, tearing the watcher apart as easily as she tore apart the eidolon at Tomas's funeral. The black spike filled her vision, moving, true. Then it shattered against Jinriki's blade.

In a voice nobody but she could hear, she whispered, *I'm sorry.*

The black cloud said, "Do you wish to pursue those who continued into the town? You and I have quite an advantage over them, but they will be formidable opponents for your so-called bodyguards."

Tiana looked at the seething mess below. *Maybe they'll go back.* She flexed the emanation supporting her and she began to rise to the top of the hill.

"Or maybe the people of this village will clean up." She caught a hint of displeasure in his voice.

At the top of the hill, she stepped onto the ground again and darted down the slope. It seemed like the larger portion of the invaders had spread out through the town. A four-legged man was rocking a covered cart back and forth. Begging and squeaks emerged from the cart. Tiana skidded to a stop. Then she lashed out, slicing the one of the four legs from the creature's torso. It coughed explosively and fell, twitching.

Oh. No blood? She started running again.

"They ooze," said the black cloud.

Belongings had been scattered all over the street from overturned wagons and abandoned packs. She slapped a rider and its mount away from a fallen woman and hoped the woman's friends would return for her. Ahead, in the town's intersection, a handful of mounts were digging in gardens, and crashing into buildings. The road beyond, leading to the Mystery Spot, was clogged with riders. Tiana could just see her table, overturned and broken, before the curve of the road eclipsed her view.

What are they doing to the Mystery Spot? She skipped into the intersection and sent an emanation out to tangle among the legs of the monsters there. *Is that why they're here?* Absently, she pushed a volley of tail spikes away and slashed. *How could they know?* Something roared at her and she ducked, pushed. *Hey, Jinriki, how did Twist know I was doing something with the Logos earlier?* She tilted her head, thinking about spider webs.

"No! Pay atten*tion!*" Something hard and heavy smacked Tiana from the left. Pain exploded on her side and shoulder, and she staggered and fell, unable to catch herself. The light phantasmagory trance slipped through her fingers, but her mind was still full of spider webs.

She rolled. A four-legged man stood over her, holding a maul. He reared, those clawed feet flashing over her head. She stared at him and thought, *Is this how I die? Now?* Panic shook her away from spider web distractions. She flailed for an emanation but they were deep and distant, a spool almost emptied and hard to reach in her terror—and the sword Jinriki was in her hand.

Up, up, she forced herself to her knees, her shoulder screaming, and surrendered herself to the sword. Then, an observer in her own body, she watched and winced as she threw herself to one side, the sword slicing out. It was just like when she used emanations, except she felt the shock all through her arm and spine as the sword sliced into the monster's torso. And afterwards, pulling it out, it stuck. Not much, just a little, but it was slow to come out and the emanations never were.

Blood is richer than this stuff. Go on, let us go to your wretched Mystery Spot, if it is so compelling that it blinds you.** Once again, the sword's voice was cold.

"I told you I didn't want a sword! But you insisted," she muttered as she ran down the road.

Alas for both of us, then, that my caretaker didn't ask first.

She lashed out angrily at another four-legged man and dodged a mounted rider. Something scraped across the back of her leg and she threw herself down to the ground, crying out at the pain in her ribs and arm. She fumbled, trying to find the shallow phantasmagory trance that made everything flow, but she was teetering on the edge of the deep end. She pushed the emanation out from her, slamming it into another mount and scrambled to her feet again, dodging over to a building, where at least she'd have her back against a wall.

There were a handful of riders standing around the Mystery Spot. One of them had its hand pushed right up to the Mystery Spot, closer than Tiana had been able to come with her own hand. The strange sick feeling Tiana had felt right before Kiar vanished resurfaced. She fought for breath and reached down deep for more power. "What are they doing? I don't care what it is, it's bad!"

Even with Jinriki's amplification, she was running out of energy. But she wasn't dead yet. She was hardly even hurt. There was still a lot more damage she could do, with emanation, sword, teeth. She dragged in another breath, batted a mount out of the way.

The rider touching the Mystery Spot pushed his hand into it and wrenched. It felt like he'd reached inside Tiana herself. Nausea overwhelmed her and she vomited up all the earlier alcohol. Her magic blinked out of existence for just a moment, and then the rider pulled his hand back out of the

Mystery Spot, holding onto an arm attached to the struggling figure of Kiar.

Two other riders raised weapons but Kiar was shrieking at them, twisting and kicking. Six flaming swords orbited around her and then flew out of the circle of riders to slash at the air around the Mystery Spot.

Tiana realized she was shouting too, that Jinriki was urging her onwards. She sent everything she had left rushing across the street, clawing and rending as her hands twitched and blurred. Then there was nobody left standing around Kiar.

The hand holding Kiar's arm opened and fell away. Kiar's swords dissolved and she looked around, puzzled. Then she met Tiana's gaze. "That was really hard," she said, almost accusingly, and dropped to her knees.

There was a scream from back at the intersection. It sounded like Lisette. She was in pain. Tiana pushed herself—

The edge that kept Tiana from the deep phantasmagory eroded to nothing. She fell, and Lisette was left to the monsters.

Chapter Twenty-five

Where Bad Girls Go

Even in the deep place where Tiana hid herself, time passed. Outside the phantasmagory, things happened. Within, she made for herself a room, filled with her favorite stories and a dozen dresses, but not a single mirror. There was one very small window that she could not close, and outside it a thousand nightmares played out. She did her best to ignore them.

Time passed, but she could not say how much. An hour or a day or a week—it was all the same. She didn't care. She didn't want to wake up, to look out the window, to find out what had become of the screaming and her own weakness. She didn't want to understand why her dream had not finished in an endless brightness of pain. Sometimes, she wondered if it had. Perhaps she was the first new ancestral memory of the cleansed phantasmagory.

After a while, she heard Kiar calling for her, outside the room, elsewhere in the phantasmagory. This concerned her more than all the nightmares beyond her window, so she took The Book of Splendid Tales and stuffed it into the high, small window. Kiar's calling stopped.

Then the black cloud appeared in her room. She threw The Wedding of Princess Annath at it and cursed it for finding her. But her book sailed through the cloud, and it did not seem affected by her curses. It spoke to her in a man's voice.

"You've hidden long enough, foolish princess. Your ladies and guards are discussing tying you to your horse in order to take you home."

"I fell apart," Tiana explained. "I heard Lisette screaming. She could be dead now." And then she clapped her hands over her ears and watched the red flashes in the black cloud. Coins rained down around her, heads and tails, so she shut her eyes too.

It was no use. The room flowered around her. What did closed eyes mean in the phantasmagory, and how could she close her ears? The black cloud drifted through the space between the room and her closed eyes. It said, "Both ladies are hale. Your guardsmen are not totally incompetent and neither is your lady-in-waiting."

Tiana hesitated and then shook her head. "It doesn't matter. She *could* have died. That's just luck. I can't trust luck. I can't thank luck. She screamed and I was empty, I failed her." The window in this room was an octagon and outside the nightmares resumed.

The black cloud was silent. Tiana sighed and arranged pieces from The Bridge of Sherata in front of her. Then the black cloud said, "Is this your choice?" It drifted closer.

"The phantasmagory was empty but now it's full again and everything is bad. All my bad dreams. Even this one."

The black cloud obscured The Bridge of Sherata. "My master was not fond of children, though he was credited with the spark that begins life." She worried at his nearness and closed her eyes.

A new room flowered around her. The window was almost perfectly round, though very high. But the black cloud seeped through the space between rooms, even closer than she remembered.

"He said that it was wrong to bind a mature soul to an immature understanding. But it was done and the world is full of children looking at a world they do not understand, judging the world and themselves."

As politely as she could, Tiana said, "I'm afraid I don't understand."

The silver eyed cloud regarded her. "Why do you hide in this quiet space instead of surrounding yourself with your nightmares?"

Tiana scrambled away, into a corner of the room. A bookshelf fell over, spilling a mountain of books between her and the cloud. From the safety of the corner, she shrieked, "This, this is my worst nightmare! I can't let them in! I can't stop!" She began to stack the books into a useless wall. "I can't look."

He began that slow steady drift over to her again. "I am but a voice here. I can feel your manipulation of this place, though I cannot influence it. But I can always find you. Would you like my nightmare? I promise, your denial cannot keep it away."

Her eyes filled with tears. "How could you stand it?"

"I had no choice." The cloud enveloped her.

She lay in state in a sacred place, her father's deepest and most powerful servant. She was his hand, his eye, his symbol. She waited to be called or sent out. The least of her father's servants attended her, slaking her thirst, keeping the mundane elements of the fleshy world from tarnishing her shine.

Then, through the bond she shared with her father, she felt his interest in something new, then his amusement, and finally, his fear and the gathering of his strength. That included her; there was a calling, but before she could jump out of the world to his hand, everything shattered. The universe died.

But she did not. Her roots were so deep, so strong, that she could not lose herself in the wave that swept everything else away. When the last of the wave had passed, there was a universe again. It was a poor shadow of what once had been, a corpse that hadn't the grace to die when its heart was destroyed.

Of her father's other servants, only the weakest and smallest had survived unbroken: his human worshippers. She was drained and her mind cloudy, but she cried out to them and they whispered to her of revenge. There was nothing else worthwhile left.

The black cloud moved away and she was Tiana again. "Now you know what might have been," he said.

The universe died, she thought. *Yes.* Outside the window, the nightmares were gone. *It's like a story.* "But I don't need revenge, if she lives. I don't want to reach that point. I don't."

"Then next time you must be faster and stronger. Open your eyes."

She did so, emerging cleanly and instantly from the phantasmagory. She found herself in a sun-drenched room, lying in an uncomfortable, narrow bed. A new pain stabbed at her head, and her entire body ached. She sat up, shading her eyes from the dazzling morning sunshine. Jinriki had been placed on a small chest at the foot of the bed, but otherwise the room was empty.

She stood up and mumbled, "What am I wearing?" It was scratchy and too big, a woolen shift of some kind. There was a full mug by the head of the bed, and she picked it up and sipped cautiously at the water before downing the whole thing.

Lisette hurried in and then stopped. "Oh! You're awake. That's good! Kiar said you were hiding from her." One of Lisette's hands was bandaged, but she seemed well otherwise. She'd had time to arrange her hair into a pair of complicated braids.

Tiana dropped her gaze to the mug. "It's morning. I'm sorry."

Lisette took the mug with her uninjured hand. "You saved the town. Don't apologize."

"You were injured. I heard you scream."

Lisette glanced at her hand. "You were covered in your own blood when we found you. Those spikes cut you up. Even your face. This is nothing."

Tiana frowned and touched her face. There was a scab running horizontally along her right cheekbone. It burned when she pressed her fingers against it, and she drew them away hastily. "Oh, well, that's just wonderful. Do you think it will leave a scar? I've hardly healed from last time."

Lisette hesitated. "I don't know. Here, I'll go find some clothes for you. Are you ready to go back?"

"I guess so. Jerya's going to flay me. It didn't seem like a problem yesterday...."

Lisette's smile was absent-minded and worried. "At least

she'll have the chance." Then she hurried off.

Sooner than Tiana expected, she'd been bundled onto her horse. Lisette was riding some merchant's palfrey while Berrin led her mare, because apparently her mare really had hurt her foot. Kiar slouched in her saddle. Tiana felt a rush of pleasure at seeing all of her party healthy and mobile.

And when she saw the townsfolk cleaning up from the day before, *Maybe it's good that I snuck out here....*

She asked Kiar, "So what happened to you yesterday?"

Kiar said, "I said I'd explain it once we got home. I need to tell Jerya. But I have to think about it some more." She grumbled, "Pity we couldn't get out of there without attracting attention."

Tiana's black mood rose, but she bit her tongue and kept it inside. Kiar didn't exaggerate. But she hoped it might distract Jerya, all the same.

CHAPTER TWENTY-SIX

POLITICS ARE CRAZY

Twist found them on the road, appearing just long enough to confirm that they were all alive and relatively uninjured.

"Tales from yesterday have preceded you," he said. "And Jerya thought she had enough to worry about."

Fingers of cold tickled Tiana's spine. "Good tales?"

"Some good, some bad. You're getting quite a reputation for violence, Princess," he replied. "But everyone will be glad to see she didn't do something terrible to you, Kiar." The blonde girl scowled and looked away.

Tiana thought, *Of course. Blood tells.* She felt like crying.

Who cares what they think? asked Jinriki.

Of course you'd say that. You're a sword. I've always tried so hard—but she sealed that thought away and pulled the black mood over her head again.

A full dozen guards joined them outside the city, escorting them for the remainder of their journey. It was an even mix of Regency and Justiciar guards, Tiana noticed, but she didn't know what that meant. But they responded to Slater and Berrin with the same careful, uninformative courtesy that her own greeting garnered, so she took some comfort in the idea that she wasn't the only one in trouble.

After they entered the Palace proper, the commander of the Regency Guard pulled Berrin and Slater aside and waved the rest of them onward.

"Can't I even go and change?" Tiana protested. Berrin grimaced sympathetically at her.

Lieutenant Thadden bowed and said, "Your Highness, the Crown Princess and your father the King are waiting for you in the Blood's Hall."

Kiar said, "Oh, good. I won't have to repeat myself." Tiana rolled her eyes at her cousin and sighed. Kiar added, "Trust me, Ti. This will distract her too much to be angry at us."

Tiana followed along. She was still apprehensive about the location: why not have a little chat about responsibility in the safety of her own rooms, or Jerya's rooms? Why so official? Well, she didn't have to put up with it; Jerya was her sister, not her Queen, Blight or no Blight.

The Blood's Hall was nearly as full as it was a few days ago, though this time there were more guards and less of the Family. Jerya and the King sat together at the head of the table. Seven of the King's shadows clustered around them. The King's face was calm and simple, and he smiled as they entered.

Jerya didn't smile. She looked at each of them carefully and then said, "I'm happy to see that you're all still alive. But there are those who won't be nearly as pleased."

Kiar shook her head and said, "Jerya, I have news that shouldn't wait."

Jerya's face was like a marble sculpture. She inclined her head. "What do you have to say, then?"

The King said, "Oh, a story?" and Jerya touched his arm.

Kiar said, "I don't know what you've heard already, about the fortress and the town. But what I found, you won't have heard about. I don't have answers, just new questions. But we all need to know about them. Everyone will be facing the Blight."

She took a deep breath and then continued, "In Mousame, there's an anomaly. A space that isn't there. When we approached it, it felt familiar. I realized it was an entrance. I went inside." She glanced at Tiana and Tiana frowned ferociously at her. "I didn't think about it until it was too late.

"It felt like entering the phantasmagory, except it was real. It was a place, a world. There was no light and yet I could see. Can you understand that? I hardly can. It was like the place spoke to me and my family magic listened. It made me realize we don't know anything about the phantasmagory, not really. We studied the dreams there, but the phantasmagory itself we simply accept as our birthright."

Jant nodded vigorously as Kiar went on. "How are we connected to it? Why? What is it? Those are my first questions, and if that place is as like the phantasmagory as it felt, they may be important ones." There was a murmur around the room, and Kiar moved a hand. "There's more."

"Things lived there that do not exist in our phantasmagory. Monsters." She hesitated and corrected herself. "Creatures. And the stronghold was there. The invader's stronghold, we saw it from the hill in Mousame, and then I saw it again inside this other place. And it was surrounded by creatures.

There is an army's army of creatures in there. Waiting." She raised her voice over more noise. "What is this enemy who comes from a place like the phantasmagory?"

Tiana shifted uncomfortably, thinking about the copy of the Royal Pendant and how she and Jinriki had theorized it was connected to the phantasmagory somehow. And she remembered a dream, in which somebody had said, *Will it hold? The first one cracked.* She wondered if she should mention the pendants, or if it even mattered anymore. After all, they were both cracked now.

She'd bring it up later, she decided. She couldn't do it now, with everyone here and with Jerya looking so forbidding.

One of the King's eidolons stepped into him, merging with him. His smile flickered.

Cathay said, "Maybe the similarity is simply that they are other places, secret places. You said it was more real."

Kiar shrugged. "Maybe that's all it is. But it *felt* like our place. Making an eidolon was like creating a phantasmagory dream. And there's more. That's not the most pressing question. When I was trying to find my way out, I found lines that connected that world to our own, through the anomaly. They were... pulling." She stopped and swallowed.

Cathay raised his eyebrows. "Pulling." Tiana realized he was angry, angry at Kiar, and wondered why. Jerya moved a hand to quiet him.

"Like I might tune a violin," Kiar snapped. "It was bad. The world isn't meant to be pulled on. Not like that. I couldn't dislodge them, and I did try." She glanced at Tiana again. "Some of the creatures tried to stop me, though. So maybe I didn't try hard enough."

Another of the King's shadows stepped into him, and his smile vanished entirely. He sighed. "Like hooks in fish.

Things haven't been the same since the dying started."

Everyone looked at the King. He looked down at his hands. Finally, Jerya said, "Somebody's always been dying. Kiar, is there more?"

Kiar shook her head. "No. I was able to get out with a little help from the other side. I came back and found myself in the middle of a battlefield. I think they tried to stop me from both sides." Another tiny glance at Tiana. "I believe it's a serious threat, maybe one the big fortress and the bands of monsters are supposed to distract us from. So we should focus our defense there."

"Thank you," said Jerya gently. "The scouts who have returned tell us that your anomaly is not the only one, however."

Kiar said, "No! That's more—" and then stopped, falling into a brooding silence.

Jerya said, "Additionally, you skipped an exciting scene at the Justiciar's Court. Aren't you pleased?"

Tiana forgot everything else and said, "What? They ratified the Blight!"

Jerya said, "Yes. And claimed day-to-day management as their own. Then they brought a representative from Vassay out. They discussed all the disruptions caused by this Blight, in day-to-day management. They're not sending an army in, no, they're sending in troops of engineers instead. And an honor guard for their official ambassador. They told me to tend to the Blight." Jerya was angry again, but this time she wasn't crying.

Tiana frowned. She didn't know what to think. "They could be helpful, right? I mean, I saw the river."

Jerya hesitated. "They could. If they trusted us. If they could be convinced we weren't a danger to Ceria ourselves.

But you *heard* them in the catacombs, Tiana. You told me about it yourself. They want us out of the way."

The King looked up. "Send the girls to the Citadel." Another eidolon drifted into him and he grimaced.

Jerya looked at him sharply. Then she said, "That would be convenient." She looked up, meeting Tiana's eyes.

Tiana said, "What? Shouldn't the Citadel be coming here?" She tried to remember when Antecession was. Four days? The Magister would arrive tomorrow.

"Yes, you missed that, too, yesterday." Tiana winced. This was worse than a lecture on responsibility. "The Magister isn't coming this year. He wants representatives of the Blood to celebrate Antecession at the Citadel." Jerya was thoughtful.

"But the Magister *always* comes here. Why would he do this now? Because of the Blight? But that's more reason for us to stay here."

Jerya sighed. "The pretty tale is that the Firstborn gave Ceria to our ancestor. The political reality is that our eidolons and emanations defend the Citadel from those who would work the Logos against it. I think he knows we can't afford to weaken our relationship with the Citadel right now. And I expect Vassay's been pressuring them to increase plepanin production. We won't really know until someone goes and finds out." She looked more cheerful. "Besides, the library there is even older than ours. It might have insights into this particular Blight. You and Kiar will go."

Tiana said, "What? Why me?"

Rather than answering, Jerya stared at her for a while. Then she shook her head and said, "Because the King asked you to go."

Wild anger bubbled through Tiana. "You can't seriously be suggesting I go off to a fortress at the top of a mountain to celebrate Antecession for some goatherds and monks."

For a moment, Tiana thought she saw entreaty in her sister's eyes, but—no, she must have been mistaken. Jerya's mouth tightened and she said, "You will go and take our part in Antecession. Kiar will go to research the Blight. And you will take Lisette's political advice, if she provides it."

Tiana demanded, "And how will this be 'convenient?' How will this be useful? I'm more useful fighting these monsters! Send Gisen! Send Shanasee! We don't have time for a holiday, no matter what some old monks think. Didn't you *listen* to Kiar?"

Jerya's words were clipped. "It will take you away from the Court and all the whispers of your temper. It will slow your undermining of our family's position with your rash actions. It will strengthen the court's sense of my authority. Do I need to go on?"

Tiana thought she might be dying inside. She'd thought she was used to failing her sister, thought she was prepared for her sister's annoyance. She was wrong.

"No. No, please don't." She swallowed tears and felt bitterness rise to replace them. "I'm sure you'll make a fine Queen, big sister." She blinked away wetness and realized the others in the room were looking anywhere but her. "I'm going to go and pack for this journey, then. Right now. We can leave right away. Come on, Lisette." Not looking to see Lisette's expression, she fled the Hall.

CHAPTER TWENTY-SEVEN

ALONE

Later, Kiar paused outside her own door, looking at Tiana's door further down the hall. She thought she should stop by and see if the princess really insisted on departing at dawn. She thought she should stop by and see if she could understand what rift existed between Tiana and Jerya. She thought she should argue with one of them, both of them. How could any of this be right? There was a mistake somewhere, some confusion, they hadn't understood what she saw. They were unfocused. She was always in favor of research, but how could research help this?

She pushed her door open and closed it behind her, standing just inside, staring unseeing at the carpet. Her father had been in the Hall, leaning against the wall behind Jerya and the King, and he'd spent more time examining Lisette than herself. She knew it was just how he was, but with the shadow of the plague still on her brow, she'd hoped for something more. Foolish hope. She might as well still be in the other world.

"Are you unwell? You can come in, you know." Even Twist didn't sound very concerned.

She squeezed her eyes shut, then jerked her head up in surprise. "This is *my room*!" He was lounging on her couch, peeling an orange pilfered from a bowl of fruit someone had placed on the table. She wondered who. She didn't have a personal maid.

"I would never have imagined from the way you were waiting at the door. Would you like some fruit?" He broke his orange and proffered half to her. His words might have been mocking but his face was serious. She couldn't bring herself to meet his eyes.

"This is my room! Why are you in my room?" She took a deep breath, calmed herself. "What do you want?"

"I'm very pleased to see you're feeling well enough to be testy." He put both halves of the orange down on the table and stood up. "I thought I'd save you the trouble of coming up with an excuse not to talk to me. Was I fast enough?"

She stared at him in confusion.

He answered himself, "I suppose I must have been. Tell me about what you saw yesterday."

She scowled and walked past him to the cupboard where she stored her winter clothes. "Where were you earlier? I already said it once."

"Must you be so exasperating?" She flinched away from the amusement in his voice. "I was busy. Your cousin has kept me very busy today."

She hesitated and then told him about the other world, about the blindness and the creatures and the fortress and the lines. She sorted through her winter clothes as she spoke, shaking each item out, inspecting it, and refolding it. She was very aware of where Twist stood behind the couch.

When she was done, Twist said, "Do you think anybody other than the Blood would have any hope of survival there?"

"I don't know. I think they would be helpless, though." She rubbed the mouse-eaten edge of a skirt between her fingers. "This is why I don't understand why Jerya is sending both of us. If there are more holes—"

"There are," Twist said. "What is your opinion of the fiend?"

She looked up at him and then looked down again. "You mean Tiana's sword."

"I do."

She took a deep breath. "I saw the village after she fell over. I heard what some of the villagers said. It makes her powerful. As powerful as any of the stories I've heard about Benjen or even ancient Tyanth."

Mildly, Twist said, "Not positive comparisons."

Kiar considered, "I suppose the bad ones seem more powerful because they don't scruple. That's interesting."

Twist asked, "Do you think it's dangerous to her?"

Kiar scowled. "Everything I know about fiends I learned from you. What do *you* think?" She looked up, meeting his eyes. He wasn't smiling, but he wasn't angry, either.

He waited. She realized, belatedly, that she'd been staring too long. She ripped her gaze away, her cheeks warm, and folded a sweater. From the corner of her eye, she could see Twist regarding her with a pleasant, bemused curiosity.

She bit the inside of her cheek. "It encourages her. She's wilder, more aggressive, more careless. It wants her to do something, though I haven't worked out what. She doesn't like to talk about it. But I don't know how to interfere with it; it's got hooks that reach her even when the sword is out of her grasp."

"A conundrum," said Twist cheerfully. "I'm sure the Citadel will sort it out. Antecession is a purification ritual, after all. And of course, there are a great many Logos initiates there." He tossed an apple at her. "Enjoy your packing." He vanished.

Kiar caught the apple in one hand, staring at the spot where he'd been sitting. Then, savagely, she bit into it.

Chapter Twenty-Eight

Deep and Away

Lor Seleni was usually described as nestling at the base of Sel Sevanth, the sacred mountain, but even in ancient times, access to trade and moving water had been more important than access to the Firstborn. This meant the city was actually sprawled across the bend of the Mise River where it curved toward the mountain, thirty miles away. A sufficiently motivated traveler could make it to the Citadel of the Sky in two days, with most of that spent on the ascent.

Tiana was anything but motivated, but she was still startled and irritated to discover they were less than five miles away from the city when Lisette called a halt for lunch in a pleasant grove nestled in the valley of two shallow hills. Sixteen mounted nobles and guards, three servants on ponies, and five mules didn't move nearly as fast as five skilled riders. She'd wanted five skilled riders, but Lisette and Jerya had objected strenuously.

She curled her legs under her on the picnic blanket and nibbled on an apple. The guards were staying a discreet distance away from the ladies, and the groom was inspecting the horses, but Misa the maid and Dennys the cook were both crouched nearby. Tiana frowned at them until Dennys drew Misa away, offering to show her some interesting weeds.

Lisette saw Tiana's expression and asked, exasperated, "What is it?"

Tiana pulled the skin off her apple with her thumbnail. "I can't do this. We're going the wrong way. The little girls should be doing this. There are people out there who need me. Us." She turned her most appealing look on Kiar.

Both other girls were silent, and then Lisette said, "No." She shook her head and her voice trembled. "No. We need to do what we were told to do."

Tiana was first taken aback and then hurt. "Why are you always on Jerya's side? Fine! You and Kiar want to go perform a stupid ceremony? Go, go ahead. I'll just go by myself." It was a threat and she felt stupid making it, but the hurt and the desperate desire to be out fighting, doing *something*, pushed the words out of her mouth.

Kiar scowled, her lips thin. "Actually, I'm on your side." Surprise tempered the hurt until Kiar continued. "But... I also agree with Lisette. The Citadel wants us up there for a reason. They have secrets and histories there that the rest of the world has forgotten. And Vassay does want the plepanin. I think maybe Tiana shouldn't go, though." She was talking to Lisette now, earnest as only Kiar could be.

Lisette frowned. "Why?"

"Yeah, why?" Tiana asked.

Kiar rolled her eyes toward Tiana. "You don't want to go, remember?" To Lisette, she said, "She's a troublemaker.

Better she makes trouble for the enemy than our allies, right? If she loses her temper up there, it could be scary."

Lisette's eyes were shadowed. "You're volunteering to perform Antecession instead? While Tiana goes off—no, that's ridiculous. What are you thinking?"

Kiar looked uncertain. "I just think we don't both need to be there. And she's stronger. She saved that town!" She clasped her hands behind her back, fidgeting.

Lisette said, "You're lying about something." She stared at Kiar, her lips white and her eyes drawn with worry.

Tiana said loudly, "It doesn't matter if either of you approve. I said I'll go on my own." She curled her fingers around Jinriki's scabbard on the blanket beside her. Unfocused anger bubbled inside her and she rose to her feet, dropping her apple.

"Go where?" Slater moved up behind her.

"Away!" she snapped. "Someplace useful. Someplace my temper won't ruin anything." Lisette and Kiar were both staring at her.

Slater said, "I don't think you should do that, Your Highness." His voice was careful and controlled, but his words infuriated her just the same.

"Why? Did Jerya tell you to say that? To try and stop me? Dammit, she isn't the Queen! She hasn't seen this thing!" She looked around for her horse and slung Jinriki over her shoulder.

Slater spread his hands placatingly. "No, it's not that. But, if we let you go off by yourself, we'd be neglecting our responsibilities. No matter how powerful you are, even with that sword, there are times when you sleep. And there are too many enemies abroad for you to sleep unguarded. However, if we split the company to accompany you, that leaves Lady

Lisette less defended." He kept his voice calm and steady, like he was soothing a horse. Tiana wanted to kick him. She wanted to scream. She wanted to flee into the hills.

She settled for stomping over to the horses. The groom fled at her approach, but she ignored him and wrapped her arms around Moon's neck.

Your failure to protect Lisette previously caused you great concern. Jinriki sounded almost regretful. ***You should insist she accompany us.***

"Oh, shut up." Tiana watched as Kiar stalked away from Lisette and dropped her gaze as Lisette looked at her.

Then Lisette was standing beside her. She said, "You don't see how you've changed, do you."

Tiana said, "Yes! It's the Blight. It's awful!"

Lisette took a deep breath. "Ceria has seen Blights before. And some of them came from within."

Tiana sucked in her breath, staring at Lisette.

Earnestly, Lisette said, "You alone would never do that. Not if you knew. But you aren't seeing yourself, and I can't let that go on. For your sake. You're getting more and more aggressive, ever since you picked up that sword. I know you're angry. I know the sword is a burden—"

Loudly, Tiana said, "No, I'm fine." She squeezed her eyes shut and when she opened them, she softened her voice. "Thank you, for your thoughts. I'll take them into consideration. But really, I'm fine. Let's just keep moving."

Princess of pretty lies. But she kept the fear buried so deep inside that she couldn't think about it at all.

Interlude

Blighter

Shonathan was cursed to never forget, but he possessed seven shadows. One was for his father, and legacies. One was for Math and his son, and fire. One was for Pell, and the future. One was for Rinta, and the past. One was for Shanasee, and betrayal. And one was for sweet Annis, and love.

The seventh wasn't for anyone at all. It had made itself at home among the others, many months ago. For a time, he'd thought himself very cunning to create a seventh shadow that was empty of any of his memories and required no maintenance. It was a vessel he could pour himself into when six were no longer enough. He'd tried to tell Tomas about it, but words were hard when he had six shadows. Thinking was hard.

On good days, when he didn't need all six shadows, the seventh shadow frightened him. It moved like the others, whispered like the others, but he thought when he closed his eyes, it looked at him. It saw him. It lived.

One day, Tomas noticed the seventh shadow. Shonathan tried to explain how it was a vessel outside him, how it had eyes, how it did not ever return to the place inside him where all memories lived. He had tried to explain how it frightened him, though it shamed him to admit that. He always still felt shame. No matter how many memories he sent outside himself, the shame remained. Tomas understood. Tomas and his music, so gentle. Such a dreamer.

Tomas understood, but he could find no answers. He wanted to tell Yithiere. Yithiere always knew what might be happening, unseen. He made things safe, he understood, even though he could forget in the usual way.

After Tomas, the seventh shadow returned to him. He sent out the six, but he kept Tomas's memory close to him, and he filled his vision with his daughters. What could he tell them? How could he save them from his own nightmare? The seventh shadow stood beside him as they played their little games, watching them with his eyes.

He kept the memory of Tomas close, and he listened. Sometimes he took the memory of Math back, or his father. Once, he took the memory of Pell back. For his daughters, he took back the memory of Annis. They brought him the mind and awareness he'd invested in them. He looked at the seventh shadow, and then he looked around him. He watched as, once again, the world fell apart.

He took almost all of them back, left only two of the true shadows outside. Two, so he could think without weeping. Two, so he could plan.

He and the seventh shadow walked together.

"I know what you are," he told it.

"I know what you are," it mocked him.

"You're part of that dark place Kiar found. You are the

Blight. Is it Ceria's shadow, as you are mine?" He went to his chambers.

"You're part of Ceria. You are the Blight. Tired, used-up, nothing left to offer," the shadow whispered.

"I know," he sighed. He removed the pendant from his neck and stared at it. The horror and fear he felt when he first saw the crack flooded through him again. He dropped it on a table.

The shadow whispered, "No, take it up again. Take it out into the countryside. All things must come together."

The King's hand closed around the pendant again. "That doesn't really seem like a good idea," he admitted.

"And yet, you shall. You wish to protect your daughters. It is understood." The shadow flowed around him.

Shonathan shuddered. "I do. But what will this serve? I cannot—" Another shadow stepped out of him, and his expression grew confused.

Gently, the seventh shadow said, "You want to see the enemy's devastation for yourself. You are the King. Who could stop you?"

"My daughters…."

"They will be safe, of course. We will take care of them as well. But that is for later."

"Oh…." Shonathan looked even more bewildered. "Yes." He put the pendant down again and gathered up a cloak.

The seventh shadow chided him, "Take the pendant, son of Shin."

He frowned at the pendant. "Oh, yes. I would have forgotten."

"Yes, but I didn't. I never would." The shadow's voice was smooth and sweet.

"Oh," said Shonathan. "You make it so easy."

"Yes. Come now. Your people are waiting for you."

CHAPTER TWENTY-NINE

BLOOD SPEAKS LOUDER THAN WORDS

It was just restlessness, Tiana told herself. She was just tired of trying to be something she wasn't. She tried to think of the heroes. But even that failed, for wasn't a Benjen a hero between his Blights? Math had named his son for his great-uncle, and everybody grieved for it.

She visited the phantasmagory for a while, but it was no longer comfortable there. Too empty, too eager to be populated by her own negative thoughts. Her own memories of violence drifted around her and changed for the worse. And when she went exploring, everything she found made her squirm, because she knew it had grown very recently, that those silken sheets and that tumbled statue, the charred roses and the corpses of children all came from minds she knew and loved. It was too intimate, too soon.

She remembered the strange dance between the ghostly woman and the biters, and how the woman had burned both the motes and the scenery away in one tiny flash. Done enough, that might have cleansed the phantasmagory. But it was troubling: how had a ghost done that? And had the biters really infected *everything*? Those weren't questions she was prepared to think about.

She touched the copy of the Royal Pendant that rested under her cloak. The phantasmagory pendant, she supposed. The dreams were cleared away but the pendant was still cracked and she didn't want to think about that, either.

Instead, she spoke to Lisette and Kiar gaily about court gossip, and lost the thread of the conversation as soon as she'd unspooled it, staring off into the distance hopefully, or looking at the phantasmagory before skittering away again. It was a long ride.

That evening, after they were camped, there was a thunder of hooves on the road from Lor Seleni. Slater listened and then waved his men back to their relaxations. "Just one rider."

The black horse came around the bend, a dark rider on his back. "Cathay," Tiana muttered, and stood up from her dinner. "What are you doing here?" she called. "Did Jerya come to her senses?"

Cathay reined his horse in and slid off. The animal was lathered from a long run. The groom came to take his lead, giving Cathay an angry look that he ignored. "I doubt it," he said cheerfully. "Your father's left the city, though. I'm glad I don't have to see her face when she finds out I'm gone as well." He gave Tiana a lazy smile.

Tiana's thoughts scattered. "What? Where did Father go? Why are you here?"

He shrugged and stretched. "I've no idea where he went. Perhaps the same place you did a few days ago. He ordered some guardsmen to accompany him, had his horse saddled, and left. Has the camp dined yet? I'm starving."

"The cook can make more." She tilted her head, staring at him thoughtfully. "We don't *all* need to celebrate Antecession. At the Citadel, I mean. It's just a holiday, just tradition."

Lisette, behind Tiana, interjected, "Cathay, thank you for the news, but you should go back." Tiana barely stopped herself from saying *No!*

Cathay laughed. "Maybe I should, but I'm not going to. I think events at the Citadel are going to be far more to my taste than waiting for Jerya to make a decision about what to do. And Antecession in Lor Seleni won't be any fun this year." He gave Tiana another intimate smile, which she tried to ignore.

Lisette seemed truly angry. "This isn't the time for games, Cathay! There's a Blight! Jerya needs you."

Cathay brushed past Tiana and kissed the Regent on the cheek. "Jerya has plenty of support from Seandri and Yithiere, and she knows how to find me. Don't be jealous, Your Ladyship. It doesn't suit you." He looked past her, at the cook. "I'd love a plate of that, if there's any left over."

Tiana said, "No, we can make it work out, Lisette. He can go to the Citadel, and I'll go deal with the fortress."

Good girl, Jinriki said.

Cathay looked delighted. "That's a lovely idea. But Kiar would be sufficient for a small Antecession ceremony, and you and I could go deal with the Blighter. We could stop the invasion from spreading." He seemed entirely earnest.

"No!" she said, before she could stop herself. "No, that's not what I want!" She met Kiar's concerned gaze.

Lisette said, "Antecession is a public performance. Kiar doesn't do those." She gave Tiana a familiar half-smile, and for a moment Tiana's irritation was replaced by warmth.

But Cathay's cheerfulness flickered and then vanished. "Yes, but there is no chance I'm going to let you wander around a Blight alone. I've already lost enough people dear to me. It's not going to happen again." He nodded soberly to them, his humor gone, and went to eat some roast duck, settling himself against a tree where he could watch the camp.

Flustered, Tiana went back to her own meal on the picnic blanket with the other women. She ate absently, unable to stop herself from stealing a glance at Cathay every so often. He finished his plate and put it aside, staring off into the gathering darkness, his arms around one knee.

Kiar said, "I really can't tell if you're interested in him or not."

Lisette said, "She's not. They want different things."

Kiar said, "Then why does she keep looking at him? Look, see?"

Tiana thought wistfully about sneaking away in the middle of the night. If only she could come up with to leave without being followed by… well, by almost everybody, she wouldn't hesitate. "I miss the time when Cathay was just my cousin."

Lisette patted her shoulder. "It's good to resist him, even if he makes a dashingly tragic hero. He'll get over you, eventually. Whether or not you give in."

"Maybe I could trust him. Maybe he'd change. The stories are full of dashing lords with wandering eyes who are tamed by true love." She'd seen Lisette push the hair from his eyes, laughing, and imagined doing it herself.

"They're just stories, Tiana." Lisette's voice was gentle.

Kiar was less patient. "Try it, then. Better than both of you moping the entire holiday."

Tiana turned an astonished gaze on Kiar. "*You're* complaining about *me* moping?"

Kiar shrugged. "It's just irritating sometimes. And it might be amusing at home, but it'll make the Citadel awful, since neither of you will have anything else to do"

Lisette said lightly, "It has all the makings of a grand and tragic ballad, the two of them together."

Tiana was still marveling at Kiar's words. "*You* think *I'm* irritating and mopey?"

Kiar said impatiently, "Yes, I do. Why are you going on about it?"

Tiana shrugged with forced casualness. "It's just astonishing to hear you describe somebody else as 'mopey.' *You* mope about everything: lessons, magic, boys."

Kiar snapped, "I do *not* mope about boys!"

"You don't even notice! That's just— No wonder you're not sympathetic. I should have seen it. You don't even *realize* you're moping over—"

"Tiana, do you want him to hear you?" Lisette tilted her head towards Cathay's position. Tiana hadn't meant Cathay, and Lisette knew that. But Lisette probably had a point to her misdirected interruption.

Kiar looked pained. "Please. There are more important things to think about than romances and theater."

Tiana rose to her feet, her face flushed. "Like a Blight? Like this stupid celebration? Let's hurry up and wait some more. You do too much thinking, too much waiting, and not enough action! Look what happened with the plague!"

Kiar looked up at Tiana. "Yes, you and that fiend created a monster. And who knows what it'll…." She trailed off, looking past Tiana into the twilight sky. "Oh, Holy Mother."

Tiana looked up. There was a charcoal smudge against the deep cobalt dusk. She squinted and realized it was moving. It was an enormous winged creature, bigger than any bird had any right to be. Nothing that big should fly. It dropped closer and the sky showed through a strange slit in each of the massive, scalloped wings. It drifted like a kite, or a bird of prey, but it was something far more alien.

Lisette whispered, "Do you think it's one of them?"

Kiar said breathlessly, "In the Catalog, that's a dragon."

Tiana was filled by a wild, violent joy. She unleashed an emanation to billow around her and hoist her up, stretching her hands up towards the enemy above.

Jinriki whispered, **Yes. More.**

Then Kiar had her arms wrapped around Tiana's legs, and she was pulling Tiana away from the sky, twisting against the emanation. Tiana squirmed and wriggled. "Hey, get off!" She let Jinriki's strength take her higher despite Kiar's assault. "You'll fall."

Kiar grunted as Tiana's knee hit her chin and gasped, "Lisette, the sword…." A moment later there was a sharp tug and a twist from behind, and more weight. Then something snapped, and the weight fell away.

"Kiar, get off," snapped Tiana. "It's *right there*. We can take it. We have to protect—" She reached over her shoulder, but Jinriki was gone, though the baldric remained. She pushed part of her emanation downward, twisting around Kiar like a maelstrom, until the other girl let go and fell a couple feet to the ground. Then she turned.

Lisette was behind her, sitting awkwardly on the ground where she'd fallen, the scabbard in her hands. "Tiana, come down."

Tiana was bemused. "I'm just going to go deal with

that creature. Why did you take Jinriki?" She paused in her upward drifting.

Kiar said, "Tiana, this is not you! You're not normally this stupid!"

Stung, Tiana said, "How do you know? I was too young to fight before! Now I'm here and I'm doing something, and you know what? Even if you take the damn sword away, it still makes me stronger. See?" The emanation raked the campsite, snuffing the campfire. "Look, Benjen wanted the crown, wanted Lor Seleni, wanted the mountain. I don't! I just want to *do* something!" Everybody was staring at her—the cook, Slater, Cathay. Cathay had a certain look in his eyes, and she smiled at him, suddenly certain he understood.

Lisette looked down at the sword, and the color faded from her face. Moving slowly, like she was sleepwalking, she rotated the scabbard and put her other hand on the hilt, pulling Jinriki free. The blade caught the heart of the twilight, drinking in the crimson flame of the setting sun and the deep blue of the calling dark.

Tiana's emanation weakened abruptly. Somehow, Lisette drawing the sword disrupted the magnification effect that Jinriki generated. She could feel Jinriki's distraction. Below, Lisette whimpered. Red leaked between her fingers as the sword fought her touch.

Cathay sprinted over and put his hands over Lisette's ears, as if to block out noise. He rested his forehead against the back of her head. The sword jerked and jumped and her other hand moved inexorably to grip the hilt as well. Jinriki jumped again and Lisette writhed away from Cathay, swerving to face him. With a sick feeling, Tiana realized the sword was trying to get to Cathay. One of Kiar's shields interposed itself between them. Slater approached, a blanket wrapped around his hand.

Tiana's feet touched the ground. She shrieked, "Stop it!"

Lisette relaxed her grip. There was a soft, wet sound as the hilt slid out of her hands. Tiana knelt in front of her and shoved Jinriki back into his scabbard. "What were you thinking?" she demanded.

She was quite aware of what she was doing. She was interfering, said Jinriki, his voice acid.

Lisette said, "Please don't go. Please, see yourself." Tears spilled from her eyes, and Tiana ducked her head to look at Lisette's hands. Her left was nearly uninjured, her right, pierced and torn in half a dozen places. She looked up again, this time at Cathay standing behind Lisette. His own bandages, over Jinriki's slow-healing bites, were hidden by gloves, and his eyes were downcast.

"Fine," Tiana muttered. "If it's going to make you crazy, I won't go anywhere. But if it comes down here...."

"You won't be alone and your feet will be on the ground." Kiar pulled some bandages out of her luggage. Tiana looked up at the sky again, but it was nearly dark now and any charcoal shapes were lost against the deepening night.

Berrin said, "It didn't approach. If it saw us, it was no more eager for an engagement than we were. Well, than I was."

Tiana leaned forward to kiss Lisette's cheek. "Don't ever do that again, Lisette. Not ever." Then Kiar shooed her out of the way so she could clean the injuries.

Miserably, Tiana said, "I wish I didn't feel this way. But it can't be Jinriki. Jinriki's not subtle."

Cathay interjected, "That, I can vouch for."

Tiana went on. "It must be me. I'll be strong for you, Lisette. You may have to put me down in the end, but for now, I can be strong." She felt so sad and scared.

"Plucky," said Lisette, staring at her fixedly.

Kiar said, "I'm not sure thinking she's a Blighter in the making is any better."

Suddenly she was face to face with Cathay. He met her gaze and said soberly, "It *is* a monster, Tiana." His forehead wrinkled. "It talks inside my head when I'm near you, and it's so evil. I don't know whether to feel glad or bothered that it doesn't seem to treat you the same way."

Startled, Tiana looked down at Jinriki. "Right now? Stop that." She shook the sword. "What is he saying?" she asked Cathay.

Cathay lifted his head, looking past Tiana, into the distance. "Nasty, cruel words. Things I don't want to think about. I hope you'll forgive me." He offered a crooked, tired smile.

Tiana scowled. *Don't tempt me to throw you into the river*, she thought fiercely.

But I'm so useful.

You heard Kiar. I'm rash, I'm a fool, don't you think I wouldn't. And in her mind, she pushed against him firmly, as if she could shove herself between the sword and Cathay.

As you wish, then. Jinriki sounded regretful.

Cathay released his breath in a long, low sigh.

"Did he stop?" Tiana asked. "If he bothers you again, just let me know." And she gave another mental shove, just to be sure.

Cathay chuckled thinly. "I suppose I shouldn't have worried about you." His gaze roved over her face and intensified. "You're extraordinary, do you know that?"

Tiana swallowed and shuffled backwards. She managed to conjure a light tone, though, as she said, "You think that now, but just you wait. You'll change your tune."

CHAPTER THIRTY

THE CITADEL OF THE SKY

They saw the dragon twice more the next day, but it never came closer than the initial sighting. And no one would listen to Tiana's arguments that they needed to deal with it before it did something awful. It was a monster, part of the enemy forces invading their land, and just letting it roam freely was almost intolerable. Almost. But she'd promised Lisette. They could go on all they wanted about managing engagements and how the whole invasion force was close enough to the mountain that they had to focus and even make sacrifices, but all Tiana really held onto was that she'd promised Lisette. Nothing else made sense.

The road switched back and forth up the mountain, and several times their guide suggested they dismount to lead the horses through the more dangerous portions. Tiana led Moon along a path with a wall to the left and a sheer drop to the treetops hundreds of feet below to the right, and wondered if she'd catch herself if she fell. Her grandfather hadn't, after all.

It was mid-afternoon when they came around a spur of rock and Tiana saw the Citadel of the Sky for the first time. At first, it seemed unreachable, an impossibly large tower rising like a secondary peak from a mass of green and grey. But as they climbed closer, somehow it seemed smaller, less fantastic and more real. Tiana couldn't help but compare it to the true heights of the mountain, where no trees grew and it was always white.

It was late afternoon when they finally reached the entrance to the Citadel, circling around from the south on a relatively flat portion of land. The sun was hidden behind the mountain, and it was colder than Tiana expected. She huddled under her cloak, trying to avoid exposing any skin and let her horse follow the other horses while she stared at the Citadel through her eyelashes.

It was a round tower built of a rose-colored stone and surrounded by a wall that incorporated the surrounding rock outcroppings. There were the traditional conical blue roofs spaced around the wall, with robed figures sitting on platforms under them. A pair flanked the enormous red wooden door in the wall.

Their guide waved and called out, "Hail the doorman!" as they approached. Neither of the fellows on the platforms responded, but a third person appeared over the door.

The newcomer responded, "Hail the traveler," and then paused, looking over the rest of the party. He was younger than their ancient guide, but Tiana thought he was still quite elderly, with tufts of white hair and huge, frog-like eyes.

She wondered what the wall was for. With the big, bright door and the peculiar towers, it didn't look useful for defense.

Perhaps it was inscribed on the inside. Would any of that matter if an attack came from above? She looked up to see if the dragon had reappeared.

Cathay said, "What's going on?" and Tiana glanced back at the door, wondering what the delay was. She realized then that the doorman was staring directly at her, as were both the men on the platforms.

Brother Timothy, their guide, looked puzzled. "I'm not sure," he whispered back and then raised his voice. "Guests of the Magister, come at his command."

The doorman said, "Yes. Just a moment." He vanished behind the door, and there was a long, uncomfortable silence. Tiana huddled under her cloak and wondered if they were staring at Jinriki or at the phantasmagory pendant she wore under her cloak. It had to be Jinriki; they'd seen the Royal Pendant plenty of times when visiting Lor Seleni and they'd never had any comments on it. And the two were identical. It had to be Jinriki. It wasn't *her*, was it?

The two remaining monks were still staring even now. She didn't like it.

Don't hide, Jinriki said. **You are a princess. You have me. Did you hear the monk? Have you indeed come at the Magister's command?** The sword sounded irritated.

"I wasn't hiding, I'm cold," she whispered, but she shook back the cloak and lowered the hood. Loudly, she said, "If the doorman's having trouble with such a heavy door, I'd be happy to help him." She slid off Moon and led him towards the gate, gathering her emanations into a whirlwind that moved before her.

Lisette said, "Tiana!" and slid off her own horse. Tiana studied the door, noticing that it was actually two doors and that one was a much smaller door, sized for individual people, built into the larger one.

Lisette skittered over and took Tiana's hand. "I'm aware," Tiana said. "I'm not looking to fight." She flexed the fingers on her other hand, raising them to point at the door.

"Nobody will believe it."

Tiana dropped her hand and looked at Lisette. "Why should we have to wait out here, Lisette? I'm cold and I want something warm to drink, and we're not petitioners. We're not servants. We're not disciples. They invited us and they're being rude."

Lisette looked at her, with a familiar calculating expression and then said, "You're right. Sometimes there're fights and sometimes there's finesse."

"I'm just making a point," Tiana said, grumpy.

There came the sonorous boom of a gong, at first muffled behind the wall and then sounding clearly as the red doors cracked open. The doorman stood between the doors as the space between them widened and bowed to Tiana and Lisette. "Hail to the pilgrims. Be welcome within, yourself and your beasts. There is sustenance for the body and soul here."

Tiana sighed and let the whirlwind dissolve, making a face at Lisette as she did so. Then they were parted by the rest of the party surging forward through the doors. Even Moon was eager to get inside to the smells of straw and grain and shelter, practically stepping on Tiana's feet as he pushed forward.

The courtyard inside the wall was paved in a dozen shades of blue tile flowing in symmetric waves. The interior door was painted blue as well and the wall was covered in murals in white and blue. Tiana scarcely had time to stare at them before a young man was taking Moon's reins from her hand

and Brother Timothy was beckoning her to the great white door of the tower itself. She glanced around and saw Slater communicating with another man in a cerulean coat. The rest of the staff had vanished into the jumble of people.

Oh, well. It would all be worked out. She followed Brother Timothy through the white door. Immediately on the other side was a small, square room, paneled in golden wood. Hooks with cloaks hanging on them were spaced between severe stone benches on each of the walls perpendicular to the great door and the floor was simple stone.

Kiar followed her in and paused, staring around the room. "Wow. This is really… wow." Tiana assumed it was a Logos thing.

The Magister hurried through a door in the opposite wall, followed by two men and a woman. He was the oldest man Tiana knew, maybe even the oldest man in the world, thanks to the preservative effect of plepanin. Every year she could remember, he had traveled to Lor Seleni to oversee the celebrations of Antecession and Fallendre.

She studied him critically. He looked healthy and, while he was definitely ancient, she didn't think he was any less mobile than Brother Timothy was. So why had he violated precedent and demanded that they travel to him this year? The Royal celebrations of Antecession and Fallendre were popular public events. Was it really just politics?

"Welcome, my children," he said, spreading his arms benevolently. "I'm so pleased that you agreed to come."

"We'll see. Dire creatures are afoot. And in the air, too," Tiana informed him. "There's a dragon from the Blight over the mountain."

The Magister's eyebrows rose and he closed his hands together. "Is that what it is?" he murmured. "Well, well."

"Perhaps you should have come to Lor Seleni after all."
Tiana gave him a hard smile.

He smiled back, his eyes crinkling. "I know that the
people of Lor Seleni will miss you during Antecession.

Tiana demanded, "Why are we here? What is going on?"
The door opened again and Cathay and Lisette entered.

"Why does autumn follow summer? Ah, my dears,
welcome to the Citadel." He spread his hands in greeting to
the newcomers. "Did the elder Princess remain behind?"

"Father has run off, and Iriss is very ill," Tiana said,
barely controlling her voice. "And Vassay is trying to invade.
I don't imagine she's in the mood to celebrate."

"Did she say that?" The Magister sounded concerned.
"I'd heard about Lady Iriss, but I'd hoped to see Jerya here."

"No," Tiana admitted. "But she wanted me out of the
way, so I wouldn't blow up any diplomacy."

The Magister hesitated and then said, "We have
representatives from Vassay attending. They come as pilgrims.
But you must be tired from your journey. I recall how tired I
am each time I must climb up the mountain after the holidays.
My assistants have aired out chambers for you."

Kiar said, "As pilgrims. They want more plepanin."

Cathay asked, "Are they threatening you?"

The Magister said, "Goodness, no. They're here to
persuade, not threaten. They hadn't mentioned an invasion,
though."

Lisette said, "Technically, they're offering us aid against
the Blight and uninclined to take no for an answer."

"I see," said the Magister. "How thoughtful of them."
He looked at Tiana. "Your family has always been a potent
obstacle between Sel Sevanth and those who wish to claim
its power."

Tiana said, "Well, yes. It's our duty…." But the Magister was staring off into space.

Abruptly he said, "I'm glad you came. It shows that the Blood may still be flexible. Come, we will talk of Vassay and the future after Antecession, but until that blessed day is past, let us keep our minds tranquil." And he gave Tiana the same keen look the monks outside had.

CHAPTER THIRTY-ONE

MEET VASSAY

Tiana tried to keep her thoughts tranquil the next day. She had a flurry of meetings with excited monastery specialists to discuss the music, the clothing, the distribution of treasures. Whatever politics had pulled her here, the ordinary monks and students of the Citadel were thrilled to have the Blood present at their local celebration of Antecession.

They weren't the only ones; by early afternoon, many mountain folk had arrived. When Kiar and Cathay wandered off to tour some of the ancient inscriptories, Tiana and Lisette went down to the side entrance of the Citadel, where a large open courtyard sheltered the gathered mountain folk.

The atmosphere was similar to Mousame before the attack. But this time there were many fewer merchants and many more children running and playing. And here, everybody stared at her. They weren't hostile stares, but she was used to moving through an environment that saw both the Blood and nobility regularly. It was clear these goatherds and hunters and subsistence farmers looked to the Citadel as their broadest horizon.

However, the Blood wasn't the only novelty to gawk at; on the other side of the courtyard, seven figures in black and white striped cloaks were consulting and making measurements. Nearly a dozen monks and apprentices clustered nearby.

Lisette said, "The Vassay delegation. I don't know what they're doing."

After a few minutes, the seven figures spread out in a line, a few arm spans apart. The center figure spoke, projecting his voice to carry across the yard.

"Good afternoon! I am Master Camerind of Vassay." Adults and children stopped what they were doing. "In my home province of Sayer, Antecession is celebrated as a children's holiday. Every little one receives a gift. I have asked, and received, permission to bring a little of my land's celebration of Antecession here, to you. Tomorrow night is a solemn celebration, but today I would be happy to help the children play." He spread his arms.

As one, the six figures flanking him started murmuring, and the air began to sparkle. People looked around, puzzled. Tiny colored crystals coalesced and began drifting to the cobbled ground. A small girl caught one on her finger and licked it. "It's snow," she said. "Rainbow snow!"

Tiana held out her hand and watched tiny blue and green flakes of snow melt. One of the Vassay Logos-workers was directly across from her. He frowned when he met her gaze, and his murmuring skipped, but the colored snowfall didn't lessen.

The snow was falling across the courtyard, but in four

tints, evenly spaced. It was a blizzard without wind, and the children were already running hither and yon, tracking colors from one band to the next. She tapped her fingers together and then called to a small boy already packing a blue snowball, "Would you like a castle?"

He said, "Oh yeah!" and then looked up, staring at her. She smiled at him and looked at the band of blue through her eyelashes. Then she swept her arms together, and blue snow across the courtyard swept itself together, packing into a curved wall. She patted it with another emanation, making crenellations as she walked along. She noticed the leader of the Vassay smiling at her.

The boy cheered, flung his snowball at a dark-haired little girl and scrambled behind the wall. The other children raised their voices in admiration and jealousy. Tiana smiled at Lisette walking beside her and called, "I'll make one on the orange side as well." And she did it again.

When she was done, she arranged to be on the side of the courtyard where the Vassay delegation was. Most of them were maintaining the snowfall, but their leader, Master Camerind, was still watching her. She walked towards him, behind the line of Logos-workers, observing the monks and apprentices who monitored the demonstration. Some of them were interested and some disapproving. She wondered if what the Vassay delegates were doing was hard.

She stopped in front of Master Camerind, and he merely said, "Good afternoon, Your Highness." He was tall, with pale skin and dark hair. His beard was a mix of white and black hairs.

"Good afternoon, sir. What a striking cloak that is. I'd thought it dyed, but I see now that it's all of one skin. Is it also Logos-worked?"

Master Camerind chuckled. "No, merely the product of animal husbandry. Are you enjoying playing in the snow?"

She tilted her head. "Should I be? I thought it was for the children." He only laughed again, and she said, "What is it you want, Master Camerind?"

He spread his hands. "To make the world a better place. The Collegium teaches that as the highest goal." She raised her eyebrows and he said, "The Collegium guides many people and many people guide the Collegium."

"How nice for you," Tiana observed.

"We have achieved great things, Your Highness."

"Some of them have even reached our ears." She let out her breath. "Perhaps I should have been more clever. What is it you want *here?*"

He retained his little smile. "I understood you. The study of the Logos is the backbone of the Collegium."

Tiana glanced at Lisette, who seemed calm and attentive. Then she said, "My sister tells me an army of engineers will be aiding us. How are you different from any Blighter? Engineers seem like a subtle form of the usual invasion."

He was unfazed by her question. "One could ask the same of you, Your Highness. Who's to say Shin's lineage isn't just a Blight that's lasted?" She blinked. He was more than unfazed; he was prepared, and he continued. "Why is it Shin's bloodline is gatekeeper to the source of plepanin? I can see only one reason: because we cannot stop you. But are you guardians or jailers?"

Tiana's breath hissed between her teeth, and she remembered the dungeon beneath the Palace, the empty room, the box, the pendant.

He studied her, and she fumbled for words. "I suppose you should ask the person on the other side of the gate."

Master Camerind swept her a bow. "And thus you see why we are here. I wish you a good evening, Your Highness. I eagerly anticipate your performance tomorrow night." He waved his hand, and the snowfall and chanting stopped.

CHAPTER THIRTY-TWO

THE DISSOLUTION TESTAMENT

While Cathay and Tiana met with the music master for a final rehearsal before the Antecession pre-ceremony, Kiar and Lisette explored the library. The librarian was a plump, middle-aged monk with oversized bushy eyebrows named Hammad. They'd made an appointment for his assistance that morning, but when they arrived, he was arguing with Twist.

"It's not very kind of you to keep me out," Twist said.

Hammad said, "You're just like all the other scholars now, and I'm glad of it. You've been such a thorn in my foot, young man."

Lisette cleared her throat, and Hammad spun. "Ah, the young ladies."

Twist complained, "Kiar, he's found a way to disrupt my skipping. And they're supposed to be my allies."

Hammad snorted. "He's a book thief. Don't learn his bad habits."

Kiar stared at Twist in horror. "You *steal books?*"

"Of course not," said Twist. "I bring them back. In any case, I didn't come to face Hammad's cruel betrayal. I wanted to speak with you." And he crooked a finger at Kiar.

Kiar dropped her gaze. "Um, we were going to do research on the Blight."

He said, "Yes. I won't take up too much of your time." He sounded sad, which was so alarming that she found herself following him into the stacks.

Once they were out of sight of the others, he said, "Are you enjoying it here?"

"It's amazing. I mean… it's… all the inscriptions! I never imagined—" She stopped before she could embarrass herself by babbling.

"Would you like to learn inscriptions yourself?"

Caught! She said, "Um, yes, eventually, I suppose. But—"

"But not next Tuesday, right?" He sighed. She lifted her gaze to his face, but he was looking at his hands. "I never had the knack, myself. Not immediate enough." He stuck his hands in his pockets and looked up, his blue eyes shadowed. "I'm turning you loose, Kiar. Easier to tame a tiger than teach you."

Distantly, she wondered why her chest suddenly hurt so much, why her vision was blurry. She said, "Oh." Then, in a small voice, she added, "I tried to tell you."

He shook a hand out of his pocket, brushed his thumb across her cheek. "You're such a fool." Then he stepped back. "I'd like you to look around here for someone you'd be happy learning from. We'll make it happen, somehow. All right?"

Numbly, she nodded.

"All right, then. Go dig up what there is to dig up. I've got my own reading to do." He flicked his fingers at her, and obediently she turned and walked back to Lisette and Hammad.

Lisette said, "Kiar, what's wrong?" She came close, looking up at Kiar's face and then embracing her.

But Kiar pushed her away. "Nothing. Everything's finally the way I want it. Except that Blight. So let's see what this library has to say." She met Hammad's gaze.

"Yes. The history section begins here and extends to there." He pointed. "I've been doing my own research on the Blighter, but I don't have the benefit of your, ah, hands-on experience."

Kiar nodded absently and moved over to the bookshelf, while Lisette smiled encouragingly at Hammad. "What have you found?"

He went over to a long, low table built into one of the library walls. "There're a few more books over here. Collections, mostly, documenting the dominant characteristics of the various Blights and their creators. The internal ones are a grim business. They usually start out smaller, very localized. A corrupted village, not a lost county."

Kiar said, "The farmer's plague," not looking up from the book she'd buried her nose in.

Hammad nodded thoughtfully. "Plague has come from Blights before, though I can't recall anyone discovering a Blight that way. Here, I've made a list of some of the more common early manifestations. Back in my childhood, these were the kinds of things the town militia would drill on. I've circled the ones that I've identified in the current Blight."

Lisette glanced over the list. "Nightmares, geography changes, presence of an army, swells in fiend activity…

nightmares?"

"No nightmares? The pilgrims from Vassay said the same thing. I suppose it's just limited to the Niyhani, then." Hammad sighed and stacked some papers.

Lisette inquired, "What are your nightmares about?"

Hammad lowered his head. "I'd rather not say, if it's all the same. But they're very... troubling." He turned away and began to shuffle some papers around, keeping his expression hidden. Lisette ducked her head and began to compare the list he'd given her to her own notes on recent kingdom events.

Some time later, Kiar closed her book, frustrated. "This is almost all the work of fiends. Sir, what about humans? What about members of the Blood who have turned Blighter?"

Hammad turned around again. "I have those volumes under the table. Lots has been written about Benjen, of course. A biography of Black Siten and a collection of anecdotes of the Venom Queen. And an anthology of folktales about earlier Blighters but, honestly, I don't know how true they are. And none of them were subtle."

"The Blood rarely is," Kiar observed. She ran a finger down the spine of a book and pulled it out. "And Logos-workers?"

"Those books aren't out in the general collection. It's not the sort of thing considered safe for apprentices and students."

"Is it? Maybe we should take a look at those. Since at least half of all Blighters have been wizards." Kiar lifted her head from her book and gave the librarian a flat, assessing stare.

Hammad smiled. "We document what we can of the specific gifts there. That kind of information is dangerous for apprentices. Which, I note, would include you, Your Ladyship.

But Twist believes you're wiser than most apprentices." Kiar clasped her hands tightly behind her back.

He beckoned the ladies to follow him. Unlocking the door, he said, "I suppose it could be a rogue talent. For example, Twist could definitely be causing more trouble than he does. And did, once upon a time."

Kiar muttered, "I can imagine." She could smell the books in the room beyond Hammad even before he picked up the lamp: glue and paper and the heady scent of ink. There was a small reading table holding a sheaf of paper, an inkwell, and several new books, and partially-filled bookcases lined three walls.

"I'll fetch books that might be interesting. Why don't you sit down and go through them?" Hammad directed Kiar to the chair and began piling books on the table. She opened up the first one and started skimming.

When the onslaught of books had slowed down to a trickle, Lisette said, "This book's got Tiana's sword on the cover. What's in it?"

"There's nothing you need to see on that shelf, girl," said Hammad. "Put that back!"

"It won't open!"

Kiar looked up to see Lisette struggling with a heavy book bound in old, red leather and Hammad waving his hands as if he were uncertain he should actually interfere or not.

"Of course not," he said. "Those are the Shrouded Books, what this room was actually built to protect. You think they'd open for any handmaid that managed to sneak in here?"

Lisette dodged around him and brought the book to Kiar. "See?" She pointed at a stylized sword over a circle on the cover.

Kiar was dubious. "How do you know that's the fiendish sword?"

Lisette tilted her head towards the outside room. "One of the books out there mentioned it by name, alongside the same image. 'Jinriki the Darkener.' A note on banishing superior sky fiends. But there wasn't anything else about it."

Kiar considered this. "Huh. That's more interesting than what I've found so far." Lisette tilted the book into her lap, and she studied it. In the Logos view, there was a complex knot of Logos modifications bound around it, forming a magical lock. Something about the workings of the lock made her uneasy. "What's inside?" she asked Hammad.

She realized he was sweating. He stared at the cover for a long moment. "I have no idea."

Lisette was surprised. "You've never read it?" Kiar wondered how a librarian managed to never read his own books.

He said slowly, "I've never gotten 'round to opening it. It never seemed… interesting." He gave the volume a puzzled look.

Kiar realized she could see what he meant. There was something dreadfully dull about the plain red volume. Then Lisette said, "Is there a working on it to make it seem boring?"

She blinked and studied the knot around it closer, resisting the desire to yawn. Something was buried in the structure of the book itself, defining it as both something that did not open and something that was not interesting. And something else….

Kiar glanced up at the walls of the room, and beyond, at the Logos modifications marking every inch of the Citadel of the Sky. "It's like the whole structure is pressing down on it," she said wonderingly, and then looked at Hammad. He was still staring fixedly at the book. "I'm going to open it," she said.

He tore his gaze away from the book. "Why?" he said, and then, "Don't." His face was pale and shiny.

Lisette looked between them and said, in a light, even voice, "I'd like to know more about what has its hooks in Tiana."

Kiar nodded, as if agreeing, but what she found herself saying was, "Books are meant to be read."

"Books are meant to preserve knowledge," he protested. "So people don't have to. Especially the books in here." But he didn't move.

Lisette said, "I always thought things were written down so they'd be useful someday."

Hammad gave Lisette a blank, uncomprehending look, and then returned his attention to Kiar and the book. Kiar waited for him to command her to put the book away, but he simply stared at it, breathing shallowly. Finally, he said, "I had a dream that in the foundation of the Citadel there was a sin, and clouds obscured it from view. We were digging for a garden and the acolytes turned over a skeleton. Then eyes opened in the sky, but it wasn't Niyhan's blue sky. It was orange and grey and terrible. Under it, every shadow had scissors, and they cut paper dolls from the book of each acolyte's soul." His voice was low and trembling, his words dropping into the silence.

Lisette said bit her lip. "It's just a book." Again, Hammad looked at her like she spoke another language. Kiar understood. She lifted her hands away from the leather cover.

"Books are words, and words are the Logos, Lisette. It never hurts to be careful." Lisette drew her brow together and Kiar added, "Why don't we do some research on the book before opening it, if you're sure you want to know what's inside? It must be catalogued somewhere." She made herself laugh. "We have enough problems as it is; we don't need to invoke a fiend or something."

Lisette snapped, "We already *have* a fiend, Kiar. But fine. If you don't want to open it, I bet I know somebody who will." She snatched the book out of Kiar's lap and started for the door.

"What? Who?" Kiar asked, and then realized she meant Twist. "Oh, no, he wouldn't. Would he? Lisette, wait! No! I'll do it." She stumbled hurriedly after the other girl. Lisette paused at the door and half-turned, keeping the book on her far side.

"What is wrong with you? You don't want to do it but you'd rather do it than let him do it?"

Kiar reached for the book, feeling hot and stupid, and knowing she'd feel worse if Twist unlocked the book. "I don't know. Here, give it to me. He's busy and I'm here."

Lisette sighed and passed the book over. "You'll be careful. I know you're always careful."

Kiar mumbled, "Not careful enough," and carried the book back to the worktable. Hammad was leaning against the wall, his arms wrapped around himself, still pale and distracted. As gently as she could, she said, "Sir, I'm going to unlock the book. You could leave, if you wanted."

Hammad hesitated and then shook his head. "I want to know why."

Lisette said, irritated, "Of course you do. Information nobody knows is useless, and books aren't people."

Kiar took a deep breath and began to unwind the Logos knot around the book. It was tricky; she had to restore the book back to its natural state without telling the book to be something else. It would be all too easy to restore the book too far and make all the pages blank, and there were little traps along the way to encourage just that. She avoided them, but she was constantly aware of the sensation that the book was connected to everything around it. That, she didn't know how to solve. At last, the knot was untied and she knew she could open the book and read the contents.

It took a long time, and her throat was dry and scratchy. She coughed, resting her hands on the cover. Then she glanced up. Lisette had curled her legs under herself on the floor and Hammad had his eyes closed. Twist was standing in the doorframe, watching her somberly.

Kiar lowered her gaze again and opened the book, flipping through the first few pages. "It's a religious text," she said. "Very old." The book was hand-written, just as most of the volumes in the Shrouded Room were. But it was illuminated as well, with flowing illustrations of fiends in the margins every so often, and the occasional colored drawing of a piece of religious paraphernalia. The language itself was archaic and strange. "Worshipping someone called Innis."

"Look for the parts about the sword," Lisette directed, rising to her knees to peer at the book. "Is it in another language?"

"No, it's just very old." She turned back and forth through the pages, searching for some kind of context.

Lisette poked at an illustration of a sword, stopping just shy of touching it. "What's it say here?"

Kiar pushed Lisette's hand away. "It says leave me alone and let me read the book." She flipped slowly through the book, scanning whole pages. "This claims he's the Eldest of the Firstborn."

Lisette said, "Niyhan is the Eldest. Right?" She looked at Hammad for confirmation, but he had his eyes closed.

"That's what we learned, yes," Kiar answered, still skimming. "This is ancient, from the time when the Firstborn still walked the earth. They didn't seem to like Niyhan very much. These are warnings against being led astray by his teachings. This guy, Innis, seemed to emphasize family and hard work over study. Praises the innocent and righteous. Describes the fiends as his messengers."

"That's creepy," said Lisette.

"Yeah." She flipped more pages. "These are some fables. The sword is in them. I guess it was his, and believe me, that's troubling. I think these are multiple texts collected into one volume, by a single set of scribes."

She turned to the end of the book. The last paragraph read *The insane yet call for him, but all that was once dhember is now black and his messengers are as mad dogs, and I think this book is all that is left of the Lord of Falling Stars, Innis. But if there is something left that carries his essence, whether in the shattered hearts of his followers, or on the tongues of fiends, or in the very wind that touches the Earth, may He have mercy on us all.*

She read the passage again, then began reading backwards up the page, saying, "I think he was... destroyed? Can that happen?" She turned back a page and saw something that left her fingers nerveless. The book slipped out of her hands, but Lisette caught it before it could hit the floor.

"What?" She turned the book around and peered at the ancient script.

Kiar swallowed. "Shin Savanyel." She pointed at the place on the page, but Lisette only shook her head and handed the book back.

"I can't read it. What does it say?"

Kiar scanned the page again. "'On the day the god died, the dhember and gold yevins that nest above the great house twisted and died on the wing. When they fell to the ground, they were black and rotting. The sun put on a mourning veil and the aravis blossoms turned to ash and dust. The messenger in the second temple went mad and slew the priests and attendants. The efey lost their voices and became as horses, and the shepherds of the dreys devoured their charges. By these signs and more, we knew the Eldest had been murdered.' And then, later, 'For those shattered, the vengeance of the Firstborn provided no solace, for what was lost could not be regained. And the surviving Firstborn withdrew from the Holy Land, leaving it in the care of the architect of their vengeance, for he was a hero in the eyes of the people.'"

Lisette said, "I've never heard that story of Shin Savanyel before. What *is* this book?" She craned her head to look at the cover again.

"This part's called the Dissolution Testament. But I don't know. Something hidden. Something nobody was ever supposed to read." She ran her fingers over the neat calligraphy and then flipped backwards until she found an illustration of the sword. "The sword talks to Tiana, doesn't it?" Lisette didn't answer, and Kiar looked up to see that she was staring blankly at her bandaged hand. "Lisette?"

Lisette jerked her gaze up. "It talks. It spoke to me when I held it. It told me I was proving my worthlessness. And that I didn't deserve Tiana's affection. That I was useless meat—" She stopped as Kiar put her fingers over Lisette's mouth.

"Stop it! Don't remember."

Lisette whispered, "It wanted to kill Cathay. It wanted me to do it."

Kiar curled her fingers into her palm. "It's a monster. This Firstborn was served by monsters. We're probably all better off that he's gone." She flipped back to the doctrinal section. "Look at this. Innocence. Ignorance. He forbade the study of the Logos." She clapped the book shut. "This is rubbish."

Hammad's voice was thin. "How do you kill a Firstborn?"

Kiar hesitated. Lisette was staring at her hand again. "It didn't say. Maybe he wasn't a Firstborn. Maybe he just claimed to be. Maybe he was just a powerful fiend."

Lisette bit her lip. "You said the other Firstborn rewarded Shin for avenging him." She shivered and wrapped her arms around herself.

Reluctantly, Kiar opened the book again to the Dissolution Testament. "Twist, you're so quiet."

But even as she said it, she realized the fourth person in the room was not Twist, but a woman of the Blood. Her skin prickled and she froze, staring at the corner where the woman stood quietly. She was gazing at the ground, with a distant look that made her seem blind.

"I'll go get him." Lisette stood up, but Kiar shook her head.

"No... I thought he was here already." She darted a look at Hammad and Lisette, but they seemed oblivious to the stranger.

"It's a good idea, though." Lisette pushed the door open and stepped outside the room.

Kiar turned her Logos-vision on the woman in the corner and then sighed. She wasn't there at all; it was the phantasmagory leaking. It was strange, though. The phantasmagory had been scoured clean. What did the woman represent? She had the features of the Blood, but she was completely unfamiliar.

The woman fell out of focus as Lisette returned with Twist, explaining the story of Innis. "And we're confused because, well, it doesn't make sense." Kiar looked down at the page she had her finger on, away from Twist.

"The Firstborn created the world, according to the maker's marks," Twist observed, in his wry, smiling voice. "They are more powerful than any fiend. They not only use the Logos, but shape the raw substance of the universe: the vessel as well as what it contains. If any one of them were to… stop existing, I imagine part of the universe would simply cease existing as well." He paused and Kiar looked up, unable to fathom why he was smiling. It was a grim expression. "But how was it done?"

Kiar said, "It just says he was betrayed." But she forced herself to slow down, read every word. "The murderer's name was Ohedreton. Oh, no. No." Her stomach dropped away at what she read. "They must be confused. It says Ohedreton had powers that were resistant to the Logos, resistant to, um, the lux. He was able to do many things and created many adversaries, but to the forces of the world, his minions were as phantoms. But that can't be right. Shin Savanyel had that magic. They must have misinterpreted how he triumphed over this traitor, this Firstborn murderer." She glanced up, hoping for reassurance. "Right?"

Lisette had her fingers stuffed in her mouth. She shook her head, pulled them out, and whispered, "The Blighter has that magic too."

Kiar stared at her. Then, accusingly, she said, "I don't understand. This doesn't make any sense. How could they all have the same magic?"

Twist said carelessly, "So Shin Savanyel learned his magic from the Firstborn slayer, who was the first Blighter. And our current Blighter uses identical magic to the first Blighter and has quite a grudge against Shin's descendants. It seems very straightforward to me." Kiar lowered her head again, resisting the desire to throw the book at him.

Lisette shook her head. "Is that what the Regents died for? To punish the Blood for something that happened generations ago?" She sighed. "And the dead Firstborn's sword has found Tiana." The half-hour bell tolled and Hammad animated, looking around as if waking from a sleep. Lisette sighed. "Almost time for Antecession. We should tell Tiana about this afterwards."

CHAPTER THIRTY-THREE

PURIFICATION

At midnight, a host of tiny stars rose to fill the galleries of the atrium at the heart of the Citadel, and the inhabitants of the Citadel gathered to celebrate Antecession. The cold light sparkled on the water falling from an eagle's claws in the great round fountain dedicated to the holiday. The monks and students gathered in the cloisters and spilled out onto the pavement around the fountain.

Tiana stood in the shadow of a statue of a former Magister, wishing for the warm, traditional lamps in Lor Seleni. Lisette had pinned her hair back, and the Citadel had provided her with a simple white gown. It was ancient and lovely, but she was cold. There were windows open somewhere high up.

Cathay and the Magister stood with her, while Kiar, Lisette, and Twist stood in the front row of the watchers. Cathay was bare-chested, wearing white pants that matched her gown. He smiled at her, and she noticed resentfully he didn't have goose bumps at all. "How can you not be cold?" she whispered.

"Come here and I'll show you," he whispered back and then laughed at her. "The fountain's snow-melt."

Tiana sucked in her breath. "That can't be true!" She turned to the Magister. "He's teasing me, right?"

The Magister had a benevolent smile. "Nothing is more pure than the snows of Sel Sevanth, Your Highness."

"Cruel," she whimpered.

Cathay fits right in here, I see, observed Jinriki.

The Magister patted her arm. "The bravery of your family is legendary. Now, I must begin the ceremony." He adjusted his thick robes and walked to the center of the atrium. "Antecession!" he began, his voice becoming large. "The time of purification! Their Royal Highnesses are here to lead us through the ritual, but first, I would like everyone to look inside themselves. This is the time to remember the actions that have shamed you, the decisions you regret, the failures…."

The Magister was an excellent speaker, but Tiana was familiar with the Antecession sermon and she didn't want to pay attention to the cold. She wasn't supposed to dip into the phantasmagory during the ritual, but her part hadn't technically started. She lowered her gaze and then startled as Cathay's hand touched hers. He was very warm.

"Don't go," he murmured. "Nothing you regret?" Before she had a chance to react, he continued, "I do." His hold on her hand remained light and she looked at him sidelong. His face was calm, his eyes closed. "I wish I were less of a capricious fool. I'd temper my heart into something worthwhile, if I could. Flame and water." He squeezed her hand and stepped forward as the Magister beckoned, towing her with him.

At the curve of the fountain, she couldn't bring herself to pull away first .The smile he gave her was sweet and sleepy. He bowed and kissed the back of her fingers before he released her. She watched him follow the arc of the fountain to the north side, only remembering her own role when he pulled out his flute. Then she hurried to the south side of the fountain, wondering if having regrets was better than not, after all.

Cathay's flute started softly. Tiana had picked the music; her favorite of the Antecession hymns. Usually she sang without musical accompaniment, and she hadn't watched another member of the Blood in their Antecession performance since she was ten. In Lor Seleni, the Blood spread out through the city to lead neighborhoods in the ceremony, since tradition dictated that the family magic be involved if at all possible.

Cathay's eyes were closed again, and Tiana wondered how seriously he took the purification part of the ceremony. She'd always looked forward to the collecting of the treasures more, but now she felt a twinge of guilt. In this holy place, perhaps she'd better consider more important things.

She sang the first verse of Edge of Twilight and remembered the young men who had attacked her. Did she regret her decision? That she had to make it, yes, but—*You'd better run, because I'm not going to.*

She regretted her recent aggression. She regretted embarrassing herself. And she regretted that her mother had left. But those were uncomfortable thoughts. Those went in directions she didn't want to go and besides, the verse was almost done, and with the second verse came the wading into the fountain. Snow-melt. That was something to regret.

She regretted it already, as she ascended to the rim of the basin.

The water was mind-numbingly cold, shocking the air out of her even though she'd tried to expect it. She heard a curse from across the water as she drew in a ragged breath and looked up to see Cathay squeezing his eyes tight. He'd already advanced up to his knees.

Tiana looked at her barely-wet feet and then took a big step forward into the cold, her gown clinging to her. She took another deep breath, and then Cathay picked up the flute's song again and it was time for the second of four verses. By the end of the verse, she'd waded in as deep as the pool got, to her chest. Beyond the fall of water from the eagle's claws, she could see that Cathay definitely had goose bumps now, and she suppressed a giggle. She thought she was probably freezing under the surface of the water, but she couldn't tell at all. She brought her hands together under the surface, wondering if they were numb. But she could feel her own warmth and a gentle tingling. Then she noticed the sparkles at the bottom of the pool. Laughing, she submerged herself entirely.

The water closing over her head felt pleasant rather than icy, and she lifted her feet to float in a ball as she studied the scattered treasures. There was a golden ball, a battered silver mug, a little pile of fabric, a crystal sculpture of a fish, a bronze platter, a glass rose, the glitter of jewelry. Richer treasures than she expected; in Lor Seleni, she distributed toys and small tools of more functional materials.

Quick as a snake, she snatched the fabric and surfaced again. It was a red silk scarf patterned with yellow flowers, and it unrolled like a ribbon as she drew it out of the water. She caught the eye of one of the monks and, smiling, tossed it to him. It spiraled like a leaf into his hands, guided by her magic. Cathay crooked his finger at a young female student, and an emanation carried the bell he'd chosen to her. The audience was very appreciative; outside Lor Seleni, attendants had to distribute the treasures of the celebrants and most of these people had probably never seen the Royal magic before.

It was time for the third verse. This time they both sang, and it was surprisingly delightful to wind her voice around his. The water under the starry night was so peaceful that she had to resist the inclination to float on her back. She wasn't sure where her sensitivity to the cold had gone but she'd never felt so clean and free before. More than just free, she was calm and relaxed; the biting irritation was almost gone. Oh, yes. She regretted how irritable she'd been. She felt amazing. If she could only hold this all year long, she'd never need to flee to the phantasmagory.

As she dunked herself a second time, languorously picking up the glass rose, the skin of her forehead burned. She brushed her fingers across it and the burning intensified. Shaking her head, wondering if she'd cut herself somehow, she surfaced again and looked around for someone to give the rose to.

Lisette was standing by the edge of the pool, Kiar holding her upper arm. She stood awkwardly, like something was wrong, and her face was a mask of horror. Tiana frowned and waded over to offer Lisette the rose. She raised her eyebrows as she presented the treasure, wondering at the cause of Lisette's distress. Kiar seemed confused, too.

Instead of taking the glass rose, Lisette clasped Tiana's hand in both of her own. Her voice was strange and rough as she said, "You must stop this." She moved her grip to Tiana's wrist and yanked hard enough to pull Tiana off her feet. But she wasn't strong enough to lift Tiana bodily from the water. Tiana kicked, trying to regain her feet and not snap the stem of the glass rose. But Lisette didn't let go, and only Kiar's grip on her shoulder prevented her from tumbling into the fountain as well.

"Hey!" Kiar whispered. "What's going on? Why—"

But Lisette paid no attention to her. Her eyes were wide and dilated, and she was breathing in short, jerky gasps, staring at Tiana.

"I'm enjoying myself, Lisette! You're right, I've been a menace lately. I can't believe I made such a fuss." The burning on her forehead was growing more intense, but somehow she knew a third dunk would wash away whatever was hurting her. "Here, have this rose. My wonderful Lisette." She smiled up at her Regent. "I'm sorry I was jealous, too." And she was, she was so sorry, and she knew the final dunk would wash away that as well.

"No," Lisette said. Her voice was creaky. "No. Please. No. Don't do this. Don't wash me away."

Lisette's desperation finally started to penetrate Tiana's pleasant peacefulness. She put the rose on the edge of the fountain and looked around. The audience was staring, murmuring, and Cathay was moving across the pool. Lisette tugged on her again, pulling hard.

Kiar stared at Lisette and then released her shoulder like it was hot. "Oh, no. The fiend has her." Lisette teetered on the edge, twisting like a cat to regain her balance. But she wouldn't release her tight grip on Tiana's hand and it was too much. She splashed into the fountain, the water closing over her head. Tiana kept her own head above water and wrested her hand free, backing away, watching cautiously.

When Lisette surfaced again, she screamed, "No!" She blinked through the water streaming out of her hair and then surged forward, clutching at Tiana again. "No. You've already washed so much away." Lisette's fingers, always so gentle, pressed against Tiana's face.

"Jinriki?" said Tiana, feeling for his presence in her mind. There was only that pleasant peacefulness, like silk had replaced sandpaper. And the burning on her forehead, so like the burning when Jinriki's caretaker had painted a glyph on her skin.

"Yes!" Lisette cried. "Please."

Tiana put her hands over Lisette's on her cheeks. "What did you do to Lisette? Where is she?"

Lisette pressed her forehead against Tiana's, whispering, "She is here. She is watching." Her eyes widened and she said, "But if you wash me away, she will be mine eternally. I will have nothing else left to me for my revenge, yes, nothing else but to wear the skins I take, no other recourse!"

Panic surged in Tiana and she writhed backwards, trying to escape Lisette's grip. But Lisette clutched at her, grabbing anew each time she freed herself. Then Cathay surfaced behind her, a wooden rod in one hand. He wrapped his arms around Lisette, holding her away from Tiana.

"No!" Lisette shrieked, turning on Cathay. In the blink of an eye, she'd kicked him twice and hit him with her forearm, making him stagger back. "You! I'll kill you—" He pulled both of them under the surface of the water and she emerged, shrieking again.

"Your Highness," said the Magister. He was standing at the edge of the pool behind Tiana. "Best finish the ritual quickly, before anybody gets hurt." He looked contemplative.

"But what if he—it—he said he'd just do what he's

doing. Steal people's bodies." She imagined Jinriki's thirst for revenge pointed at her and her family, and felt sick.

The Magister focused on Tiana and said calmly, "I believe we will be able to bind the fiend and prevent it from doing more harm. But you must be free of its taint before that can happen."

She brushed her fingers over her forehead. Lisette had escaped from Cathay and scrambled out of the pool again. She crawled closer to Tiana along the edge of the water, stopping just out of reach of the Magister. There was something inhuman about the way she moved and her gaze was bestial. "Please," she breathed.

"Your Highness, you must finish the ritual. Submerge yourself a final time and take up a treasure." The Magister's gentle voice was even and unconcerned. "Why do you pause?"

"My mind is so quiet now. I feel so peaceful. I never noticed what I had until I lost it," she said to Lisette.

"You washed me away," Lisette said, her broken voice creaking with sorrow.

"You wanted to fight, all the time."

"I am a weapon. I am a *sword*!"

"That's true," she murmured and looked away from Lisette's contorted shape, toward the passage that led to her chamber, where she'd left Jinriki's true form. It was just as fair to blame a baby for crying or a member of the Blood for being eccentric.

Cathay said, "Tiana, it's a monster. Look what it's done to your best friend." He was nursing a cut across one cheek. "You don't understand how evil it is. You can't stand here and discuss it! You owe it to Lisette!"

"Lisette," Tiana whispered and remembered the feeling

of being confined to her big toe, remembered rising like a wildfire to overpower the wind.

Then she remembered sobbing when her mother left her. She remembered a silver-eyed cloud finding her among her nightmares and giving her a reason to come out again.

Kiar was looking around the atrium anxiously, but now she called, "Tiana, there's more you should know—" Tiana held up her hand and Kiar stopped.

She addressed Lisette again. "I feel so nice now. I bet this is going to hurt." Lisette moved her head warily, and Tiana could see Cathay sloshing closer to her from the corner of her eye. She held out her hand to Lisette. "Jinriki the Darkener, leave my friend and come to me." The burning on her head intensified.

Then everything happened at once. Cathay pushed on her shoulders as the Magister said, "Oh dear," and Kiar said, "Oh, no!" Lisette relaxed into a huddled pile, blinking rapidly. An awful tearing sound filled the atrium.

Tiana had a dim sense of something invisible happening around her, but that was swiftly overwhelmed by the pain in her head. It felt like somebody was applying a brand and at the same time, Cathay was pushing her down, trying to immerse her.

"No, stop it, Cathay...," she panted, but he wasn't listening, and he was too strong. Her emanations flickered around her. She *pushed* with them and flung Cathay away. She tried to aim him at some water; he was just trying to help her, after all. He thought she didn't understand, but he was the one who didn't understand. The sword was a lens and a channel and they would need him to fight the Blight. But he was also a soul, and she could *not* leave him alone in the dark, more alone than she had ever been.

The light in the atrium flickered and dimmed. In the air above the fountain, a huge, ghostly geometric shape was unfolding. It swallowed the light around it and all its twisting planes were in shadow. The atrium was full of people shouting, babbling to the Logos, moving their hands as they worked, and she realized they were all focused on the unreal geometric shape. She looked to Kiar. Her cousin's gaze was riveted on the shape, but she was silent.

Tiana put her hand over her forehead and blinked up at the image. "I thought you were a sword." She reached out to the shape. "Jinriki." It surged and rippled, as complicated as a flower. There was a flare—

All the remaining sources of light went out as one, and all the babbling Logos voices cut off. There was a heavy, familiar weight in Tiana's outstretched hand. Her forehead no longer burned.

Jinriki was laughing in her head. **These fools could never have bound me.** Sandpaper had become silk, but the silk had not turned to sandpaper again. She could feel him bound to her, his pattern overlaying hers, but the fit was better, steel instead of grit.

"What happened?" she whispered. She couldn't see anything, but she was still in the water, and suddenly it was shockingly cold. She hefted herself out of the pool and tilted her head, listening to the sounds of breathing around her. Even the fountain had stopped flowing.

I made the Logos stop listening to them. My master despised the Niyhani. He sounded very pleased with himself. **It's only temporary, unfortunately.**

Kiar's voice came out of the darkness. "It's all crumbling, Tiana. You can't see it but… the Logos was built into the Citadel. There are ancient workings here… so many inscriptions… but it cut through them all." Kiar sounded as if this had physically injured her.

So I did. Excellent. But she thought he sounded surprised.

"Magister?" Tiana called, and then when there was no answer, "Lisette?"

"Here," came Lisette's faint voice, a few feet away. "I'm fine. Tired. I knew what he was doing. I saw him… it was the right thing to do."

Tiana moved carefully in that direction. "You didn't hurt them, did you, Jinriki?"

They're still alive. She thought he seemed rather unconcerned for someone who almost got washed away. **They're standing still. I have no idea why. You can hear them breathing.**

Lisette asked, "Is it dangerous, Kiar? Were the workings holding up the Citadel?"

Kiar said helplessly, "I don't know! I don't think so." There was a pause. "Everything that was pressing down is releasing pressure. It's all going back to its natural form." She laughed, sounding hysterical. "Lord of Winter! He really is the Darkener. We found out about your sword's previous owner, Tiana! A murdered Firstborn—"

An distant unfamiliar voice said, "I had a dream that a darkness lay over the city and a voice declared, 'Bring The Darkness To Me.'"

A different voice, closer, said, "I had a dream that the betrayer was punished, but the shadow sustains him yet."

Another voice called, "I had a dream that inside a soul was a universe."

Then there was a clamor of voices describing their dreams, all at once. Tiana looked around wildly, unable to see, unable to identify individual voices. "What's going on? Why doesn't someone make a light?" She moved restlessly, her dress wet and heavy against her legs.

I didn't do this. I don't know what's going on. They're all mad.

The susurration of voices was strange. She could only make out individual words here and there, but the ones she heard almost made a complete thought. Then she didn't have to try; there were whole sentences drifting out of the noise, and a second shape was glimmering in the darkness overhead.

The corpse of the Eldest cast a shadow between in and out
Bring a descendent of the shadow to my throne.
Bring a gate into shadow to the light.
Bring the light to a gate into the shadow
Bring light to the shadow realm
Turn the shadow to light
Free night from the shadow
In between twilight and night is the shadow
In between is the shadow
Between is shadow
We are light
Gather what we have given
Bring our light to dark places
Gate into shadow
Walk the road to the place furthest from heaven
Follow the path laid down by your ancestor
Between two halves of your soul is the shadow
Seal the cracks as Savanyel did
Seal the break
Make what is broken whole, as Savanyel could not

He gave her eternity
Seal the break
Create the light
Take this

The darkness streaked with midnight blue and azure and cerulean and cyan and more shades of blue, twisting together to form the image of a great throne. It shimmered like a jewel, simple and tall and radiant.

"What is it, Jinriki?" asked Tiana nervously. There was no answer, no words but the murmur of the susurration. "Kiar? Lisette?" Tiana raised her voice over the noise. Jinriki was still in her hand, and she tried to lift the sword over her head. She couldn't move. She tried to conjure up the emanations again, but all she could see was the great throne lowering towards her.

The chant of the susurration started anew, and Tiana wanted to cover her ears, wanted to scream, anything to interrupt the cadence of the voices. She could do nothing. When the chant finished a second time, the throne of brightness shivered over her head. Then, with a sharp, clear chime, it shattered, and blue light rained down on her. Where it touched her skin, it vanished, sinking inside of her, carrying the words of the susurration inside her.

The droplets of blue light brought with them awareness, as well. She could feel the stone of the Citadel around her and the mountain sleeping beneath her, could identify the individual breaths of each person within the Citadel. She felt the wind that caressed the earth, she could smell the winter yet to come, and all around her were words: prayers and oaths and lessons, the foundations of civilization. The light of Niyhan was blue, and it soaked into her.

A timeless moment passed away. She realized there were three other lights to gather before the true light could be created and the shadow banished. She could feel them. They called her, pulled on her. A yearning welled up inside her, a deep desire to attend to them all at once. But she could only go in one direction at a time! The vast need was discouraging and tears spilled out of her eyes. "Please," she begged.

That's enough of that. Jinriki spoke and snuffed out the extraordinary longing, dousing it to only the smallest awareness of *something* she needed to get. And now she was aware of her body again. And she was aware of the ground shaking, and people shouting and scrambling around her. There were flickers of firelight here and there, and Lisette and Kiar were holding her up by her arms.

"What's going on?" she gasped.

"Earthquake," Kiar said. "That… it came out of the words. The Throne. The power. We saw it. Into you. The Throne kept the mountain calm. The Logos is still ignoring us."

Tiana blinked and tried to swallow; her throat was dry. The wet dress was slimy against her skin and she reflexively tried to push water out of it with her free hand. "It's not stopping."

"No," agreed Kiar, her face grim. The statue of the Magister that Tiana had waited beside crashed over.

Tiana fumbled for an awareness of the mountain again, reaching into that unreal space inside, where the blue light shimmered. She found a faint sense of the mountain, and she could see the surging core of fire and the great masses of earth and stone that groaned and scraped against each other. Unless the mountain was soothed back to sleep again, the core of fire would leak past the barrier of stone. That, she felt, would be bad.

"Are you going to help me this time?" she asked Jinriki.

I *like to fight.*

She slipped into the phantasmagory, just a little. Just enough that she was no longer sensible of her slimy dress, just enough that she could pretend that she was big, huge, mountain-sized. The emanations, magnified by Jinriki, were as her hands. She awkwardly pressed them against the places where the stone was rotten and weak, trying to still the tremors. They weakened and slowed as her pressure increased, but when she slackened, the rumbling began again.

Kiar was in the phantasmagory with her, studying the manifestation of the mountain that Tiana projected. "Here," she gestured at a point low on the other side, where three masses of stone leaned against each other. "Push that one a little lower, if you can."

Tiana nodded and released her hold on the upper mountain. She could feel the renewed shaking even through the phantasmagory. She tried to focus on keeping the emanation coherent, moving them around the mountain and—there! She pushed as hard as she could. There was a terrifying creaking sound and a final sharp jolt, and then the vibrations of the mountain subsided into mere grumbles.

Tiana could hear Lisette calmly talking Kiar and herself away from debris, and she reached up out of the phantasmagory to hug her. Or at least, she tried to. She was caught on something. She looked down.

The ghost woman was holding onto her heel.

CHAPTER THIRTY-FOUR

ALL A MAN CAN DO

In the distance, Lisette asked, "*Is it over?*" Kiar struggled to shake her head. The ghost woman was holding both she and Tiana by the feet. She had a queer, blind smile and somehow her grip prevented them from leaving the phantasmagory. It was changing around them.

"Hey, stop it," Tiana cried, waving her hands. "Jinriki!" An amorphous black and red mist swirling next to her darted over to the ghost.

"There's nothing," the mist said, in a gravel-toned, masculine voice.

"Who is she?" Kiar asked.

"I don't know! She's been around for a while. Since Tomas's funeral."

"I saw her in the library earlier. There's something familiar about her...."

Tiana gave her a grateful look. "At least you're here this time."

Kiar looked away and noticed other members of the Blood fading in, Cathay and Jerya and the others. "She's bringing us all. Wherever we are. That's a good trick."

The mists rolled away, and the family was standing in a large solar, with a giant window dominating the west wall. The King gazed out of it, his back to the others. The phantom woman touched his shoulder, and he looked up and smiled. "She brought you." The woman curtseyed and stood quietly.

Tiana demanded, "Daddy, who is this?" just before questions burst out of everyone else. But Kiar went to look out the window. It was a view onto the broken lands, the Glooming, with the Blighter's stronghold squatting in the center. The body of the King sat on a horse at the edge, a single eidolon trailing him.

The King in the solar said, "I've no idea, my darling, but she's been such comforting company in the phantasmagory the last day that I asked her if she might look about and see if any of you were present before I went. I tried to wait as long past Antecession-midnight as I could."

Jerya said, "She dragged us all down, Daddy." Her voice sharpened. "What do you mean, went? Where did you go?"

"Oh," he said, looking embarrassed. "You can see." He waved a hand and windows opened around the solar, showing a different view in each direction. Kiar looked at the image of the King on his horse, far below. The eidolon holding the stirrup of his horse looked up, as if it could feel her gaze. Kiar shivered and looked at the King in the solar. He nodded at her, a strange, sympathetic look on his face.

She ducked her head and moved to peer through another window. It looked onto a village. Several of the Regency Guards loitered on the high wooden porch of a villager's home. One of the King's eidolons stood on the porch as well, unmoving. Kiar stared hard at the scene and realized there was an empty blurring behind the eidolon, like the one in Mousame. The guards were aware it was there; they moved around it as they paced the porch.

Kiar squeezed her eyes shut against a rush of anxiety and stared at the scene. At another window, Tiana called, "This is Mousame. Where we were the other day. Did you go to see the view, Daddy? Oh, but why is your eidolon standing next to the place where we lost Kiar. Isn't that—"

Kiar returned to the main window as Tiana thudded up, Jerya taking long steps behind her. "He's got a great view," she said bleakly.

"Daddy, what are you doing? You're confused, Daddy, you must have half a dozen eidolons out there and so far apart. I never knew you could have them so far apart. It must be so hard. Please come home." Tiana wrapped her arms around her father. Kiar looked at Yithiere, wondering distantly if she'd hug him if he were in Shonathan's place. He met her gaze and sighed, and she looked out the window again.

The eidolon was tugging on the King's leg, urging him forward. It spoke to him. Kiar wanted to know what it was saying and dreaded knowing what it was saying. In the solar, the King tilted his head towards his daughters. "I wanted to see you before I went. To let you know I was sorry. I've been a terrible father."

Jerya said urgently, "Daddy, do you know what you're doing?"

"Yes, my dear one. It's for the best." He chuckled. "Even the Other thinks so. He doesn't know everything, though. I have my tricks." He winked. "He thinks they're watchers."

Jerya bit her lip, and Tiana looked horrified. She buried her head against his chest. "Don't leave me, Daddy. I can't bear it."

"Why does the Other want you?" Kiar asked.

"He hates me." The King sighed, stroking Tiana's hair. "For something Shin Savanyel did. His hate has lasted a long time. He spent years coming up with inventive punishments. He's been telling me about them. I've tried not to listen, but— oh dear."

Down below, the eidolon dragged the King off his horse and pulled him into the blasted land. Once he was entirely inside the shadowed land, it yanked the Royal Pendant off his neck. It spoke again, and this time the flat copy of the King's voice echoed through the phantasmagory. "My prison. It was you who handed it to the wizard who cracked it open. Hook, he was called. Hooks are useful."

Shanasee, looking out one of the other windows, cried, "The King's eidolons are going inside the holes! And they're changing. I've never…." She trailed off.

The Other continued to speak. "Thank you for bringing it to me. Such a petulant little man." It kicked him. The King below twitched and jerked in response, and the King in the solar averted his face.

"Oh, I don't want to watch. I think this will be unpleasant."

"Shin grounded it in the earth, in the land. He thought that would make it inescapable. But he made it too strong. The connection goes both ways. A crack in this prison becomes a crack in your world. Shin was so clever, he had so much promise… and look at his descendants."

The King in the phantasmagory sighed, his gaze still on the floor. "He grounded us in the land, too. All those holiday rituals, every year, binding and rebinding us. So we'd never lose track of what our purpose was."

Again, Kiar had the sense that the Other was aware of them, before its attention was jerked away. "This isn't my prison! What did you do? Where is it?" It kicked him again, and stepped on his hand. One by one, monsters were appearing around them. "This is a replica. Ah, no, I see. The prototype." It held the pendant to its eye.

Malevolence swept through the phantasmagory, a pure, sticky evil, and Kiar *knew* beyond a shadow of a doubt that it was aware of them now. The black mist near Tiana was muttering something over and over again: "That's him, that's it, that's him…." The ghost woman looked alarmed and vanished.

But the King glanced up, and Kiar saw a flash of the man he once was as he said, "You'd been trying to get it from me for ages. And you really thought I'd let that happen?" The flash of the old King faded and Shonathan lowered his gaze again. "Silly Blighter."

The Other ignored him and laughed. "Ah, I've been here before. Your playground. Were you hoping to cage me a second time? With such an obvious trick? But this one is flawed. It's been flawed since the beginning. Too bad. I'd had plans… but no." The monsters paced around the cringing King and the Other. "Enough. Let the land die slowly instead of quickly, then. The hooks are in. And I have you. A consolation prize, but I will *enjoy* it." It tossed the copy of the Royal Pendant into the air, where it remained, spinning gently. The King's face contorted and he screamed.

"Oh dear, oh dear," mumbled the King in the solar. "Let's close the curtains. Let's not watch. Let's please not watch." He hid his face.

Kiar felt sick. Tiana pawed weakly at her chest, where what was apparently the real Royal Pendant hung. "This is really you, right? You're here with us?"

Shanasee's voice was distant and cold as she reported, "The King's eidolons are still changing. I can't describe it. And they're calling the hooks."

"I can see them," Kiar whispered. The true eidolons of the King rippled, changing into a shadow on their surroundings, and the hooks moved from the world to themselves. But they were always connected to their source. The hooks rode the conduit from eidolon to creator.

The King whispered, "Now I am Ceria." One after another, six hooks attached to vanishing lines pierced the King's flesh.

The Other looked bored. "My goodness, how self-sacrificing. How inventive." It crouched down beside the quivering King. "My friend, I will be happy to pull each member of your cursed bloodline apart before I finally get to the land itself. It would be a pleasure." It brought its hand out in a sharp, commanding gesture. The lines tightened. The King below screamed.

The King above staggered away from the window, his daughters supporting him. Tiana said, "Daddy, stay here, stay. I know you can. Please, please don't go. The phantasmagory can keep you. Lisette said there were ghosts here, like your friend, see? Daddy? See? You're so brave, Daddy. I love you."

The King grunted and said, "I'd hoped it would end quickly… I don't want to go."

Kiar stared out the window, stared at the Other, her heart raw and aching. Then a shout tore out of her. "Ohedreton!" Her voice filled the phantasmagory. "Ohedreton! I recognize you! I know you! Betrayer!"

The Other looked up at the high window and snatched the phantasmagory pendant out of the air. "I've had just about enough of you," it said.

She had never felt such rage. "Come and do something about it, then. I know you! Vengeance waits for you!" And she laughed, hysterical, thinking about Tiana's sword, Jinriki.

The Other's face twisted. "Revenge is *mine*, innocent. Flee, for I am coming." It spread its hands and the hooks flew apart, ending the King's pain. Then it clapped its hands together and crushed the phantasmagory pendant between them.

The phantasmagory disintegrated.

CHAPTER THIRTY-FIVE

OHEDRETON

First, Kiar realized that she was still alive. That probably meant the worst was yet to come.

Then she realized that the Logos was still inattentive, merrily taking its natural course. That was frightening.

Finally, she realized that her head was in somebody's lap. That was *dreadful*.

She sat up as she opened her eyes. Twist said, "Feeling better?"

Kiar scowled and tried to clear her head. A part of her mind had always been connected to the phantasmagory, she realized. And she only realized it because now that conduit led only to a hard wall trapping her inside her own skull. The phantasmagory was *gone*.

Tiana had her head in Lisette's lap, and she was crying through closed eyes. Kiar remembered the King. She remembered the Other. Ohedreton. Her fury. She looked up.

Lamps lit the atrium, and groups of people were assessing the damage done by the earthquake. The Citadel still seemed to be standing. Jinriki was lying beside Tiana.

Twist said, "What happened?"

"The King is dead. The Blighter killed him. We were all pulled into the phantasmagory, and then the Blighter destroyed it. Somehow." She shook her head. "It's not over. It was angry. I said things." She clenched her fists, remembering what she'd shouted. She must have been mad, losing her temper like that.

Twist laughed, and she glared at him. "Poor girl," he said fondly. "What can he do, send a dragon?" She stared at him. Was he joking? It was a really bad joke.

Something crashed into the top of the atrium, raining dust and rubble down. "Laugh at that," she snapped and ran over to Tiana and Lisette. "Tiana, make your sword fix the Logos. Something's here." Something roared outside.

Tiana's eyes popped open. She stared up at Kiar, her face streaked with tear stains. "How do I get out there?" She pushed herself up and looked at Lisette as she picked up the sword. "The aggression before was the sword's. This time, it's mine. I'm going to fight the damn monster now."

Twist gestured at the wall. "There's a staircase up to the roof of the west wing there." Tiana gave him the same flat stare and then ran over to the stairs. Lisette followed her silently. Twist considered the two figures and then observed, "They're going to freeze in those wet dresses." He strolled after them.

There was another crash on the roof and Kiar shouted, "Fix the Logos, fiend!"

Tiana paused at the top of the stairs and shouted back, "He says he can't. He says it's temporary. He says shout loud enough!" Then she was gone. Twist sent a sardonic smile in Kiar's direction and wandered out after her.

Debris clattered around Kiar and she snapped an eidolon shield over her head, looking around for the Magister. The groups of monks surveying the damage had scattered to the cloisters along the sides of the atrium. Now some were venturing back out to tend to those who were injured in the first fall of rubble. Others were fleeing. Human misery surrounded her. Somebody cried out, "Niyhan has abandoned us!" She scowled, and put up as many shields over other people as she could. Then she found the Magister, under the shelter of a cloister.

She stumbled over to him, her vision wavering. "'Shout loud enough,' she said."

The Magister put a hand on her arm. "We heard. We're doing what we can."

Master Camerind was there. He said, "We are as well." He smiled and managed to look both worried and smug at the same time.

Kiar paused. "Do you know what's going on?"

The Magister smiled faintly. "Your cousin was given a very precious gift to fight the Blighter with, and I imagine he's not very happy about that."

Kiar shook her head. "No, he's not. His name is Ohedreton. You have a book in the library. He came once before. Shin banished him." She paused. "Do you think Niyhan has abandoned you?"

"My dear, the Firstborn left us to fend for ourselves hundreds of years ago. They left us tools and help, they left us words and the still voice in our hearts. And they left us guardians." He smiled strangely. "You should know that, Lady Kiar. They left us in your care."

Kiar stared at him. Then one of the Magister's assistants yelped, "There was a response, Magister! It's waking up." The whispering babble of Logos invocations became louder as everybody nearby started talking to it.

"Well done, my children." The Magister gave Kiar a knowing look and waved his crook at her. "This is not your place. Go on, Your Ladyship. Defend us from monsters. We'll bring the Logos back."

She turned and ran, her eyes stinging. Dust, she told herself. Stone. They were the scholars and masters. She was just a failed apprentice, a bastard of the Blood. She climbed the stairs to the roof, reaching instinctively for the emotional blanket of the phantasmagory. But it was gone. She was alone, cut off, just like always.

She paused at the top of the stairs, at the door to the roof, looking down at the people below. She felt so isolated, perched above the stone, below the sky. But she could feel part of herself down there. Four strangers scurried from victim to victim with an eidolon shield over their heads, sheltering them from falling rubble. They wouldn't break. They couldn't break. She was notorious for that. It was the one thing she did well. Hysteria bubbled up again and she laughed, wiping the dust from her eyes. Then she turned and ran out to the roof.

There was a veranda and beyond it the peaked wooden roof of the hall below. Tiana was standing near the edge of the roof, legs braced against a chimney. Lisette stood close behind her, pressed against her back. Tiana had her chin jutting out aggressively, and she was holding Jinriki against her shoulder like a club. Cathay was halfway across the roof, kneeling down for stability as he stared at the sky. And Twist was standing on the veranda, arms akimbo. There was no sign of the enemy.

"Is it over?" Kiar called.

"Nope," said Twist. Something enormous soared up from below the roof and Tiana swung wildly. The shape shuddered and kept rising. Kiar stared at it. It was the dragon they'd seen before, one of the shadow creatures—but at its heart was a corrupted fiend, like she found in the mulberry grove.

Cathay said, "If you're going to use a sword, use the *edge*, Tiana! Cut with it!" He edged further along the roof.

"Shut up! I'm trying! It's hard!" Tiana shouted back. Other, smaller creatures surged over the edge of the roof and Tiana fell backwards, catching herself against Lisette. "Where—?" The andani scrabbled towards her.

Emanations flickered around Cathay and then three big cats surged out of him, leaping onto the graceful black forms. Cathay fell to his knees and began crawling. He was muttering something, but Kiar couldn't make out his words.

She shouted, "It's spawning them! There's a fiend at its heart—" she shook her head. It was too complicated to explain and only Twist would understand.

Lisette said something, her words whipped away by the wind. Tiana straightened, ignoring the fighting around her and pointed Jinriki at the shape soaring higher into the sky. There was a horrible wrenching sensation and once again, Kiar saw shadows of Jinriki's deeper nature unfolding. Once had been enough. She looked away, and realized she was paused in the process of climbing over the veranda railing. Twist was holding her arm.

An inhuman, sepulchral voice from all around spoke the Logos: *Izeneeea, release yourself. Take the beyond. Banishment comes. Go!* The dragon writhed and clawed at the air, and Kiar could see the fiend at its heart screaming defiance. It was resisting.

Beside her, Twist said brightly, "I can do that," and began to mutter. He was right. The Logos was attentive again. Kiar swallowed and squeezed Twist's hand hard. Four shields. Every little bit. She joined in, encouraging the Logos to reject the fiend, force it out. It was sheltered by the alien flesh around it but she guided the Logos through it as best she could.

Another shadow squeezed itself out of the dragon's heart: another andani, this one with bat-like wings. It soared gracefully down to land on the roof between Tiana and Lisette, and Cathay. Kiar frowned at it and continued wrestling the Logos against the dragon fiend. Her mouth burned.

Twist's voice strengthened, and she raised her voice as well, unable to stop herself. There were other voices she didn't know. Then, with a swallowing sound, the fiend at the heart of the dragon vanished. The dragon itself remained, soaring up into the darkness.

Cathay's cats charged the winged andani. But when they leapt, a frighteningly wide smile stretched the andani's face, and the cats vanished. Kiar thought they'd been sucked into the andani. She swallowed. She remembered doing that.

It spread its arms and she shouted, "Ohedreton!" Inhuman eyes turned on her.

"Innocent." It looked around. "You are all innocent. To send eidolons against me!" It laughed. It no longer had the King's voice, but something strange and only distantly human.

"We know how to kill Blighters without eidolons, too," said Cathay, rising to his feet and drawing his sword.

It bowed mockingly to him, and then crooked a finger. An emanation swirled around Cathay, lifting him high into the sky. He struggled, suspended. Panic swept across his face and he seemed unable to do anything to save himself.

Kiar licked dry lips, staring at the andani. She untangled her hand from Twist's, kicked off her shoes, and climbed over the veranda again. Carefully, she walked along the point of the roof. The andani smiled at her again and looked at Tiana. "My, what a big sword you have. I think that belongs to me." It closed its fist. "Part of an estate I claimed long ago."

"Come and take it," Tiana snapped. Lisette was sprawled on the roof at her feet, unwilling to get closer to the edge. The andani spread its wings and an emanation rushed at Tiana. Her own emanation met it, slowed it, and then fell back. The andani's emanation surged forward and then parted around Jinriki's gleaming point.

The andani tilted its head. "What's this? Hmmm." Emanations streamed from it, an endless river that continued to part around Jinriki. Kiar held her breath as she walked gingerly up behind it. Cathay was high over her head. He'd fall. It couldn't be helped. Tiana could be a hero. Her feet gripped the point of the roof, her warmth melting icy patches. Stealthily, she reached out. Her head was spinning, but she was afraid to even breathe.

Tiana was advancing from the other direction, Jinriki still held before her. She called, "He knows what to do to you. He's been studying us. You've got bad timing, what was your name? Ohedreton? Bad timing. You're in for it now. We're going to take you apart."

Smiling faintly at Tiana's bluster, Kiar pushed her hand into the eidolon stuff of the andani's wings. Then she grabbed everything available and pulled, opening her own eidolon source as wide as she could.

An abyss yawned inside her and suddenly she was back in the eidolon world, with its strange creatures and its vines and cliffs. It filled her, and she filled it, and painted against the sky, she could see Tiana's silhouette, glowing with blue light.

She was on the roof, and she was choking, trying to swallow something much larger than she expected. The andani was face to face with her, half inside her.

It tilted its head again and whispered, "This is more like what I was expecting." Then the mind animating it fled, and there was no resistance to absorbing the eidolon stuff left behind. It crumpled into her.

Cathay fell, and Tiana was a hero. She lowered him gently to the veranda. Then Twist called, "The dragon!" It was still there, drifting high above, blocking out the stars. It flapped once and then dived—not at the Citadel, but at the mountain itself. Kiar struggled to catch her breath and hoped that it was fleeing as well. For a moment, there was silence. Then she heard a member of the Vassay delegation say, "That was amazing."

"Hush," she snapped. She strained her ears, but when it happened, she didn't need to work to hear it. A dull boom echoed across the Citadel, and the ground began to shake again. There was a flare of reddish light high on the mountain.

Tiana shouted in frustration. "It woke the mountain again! Is there no respite? The rotten rock—the lava—oh, no!" There was a low, distant roar. "Kiar! Make a shield! There's a river—it'll be a river of mud—the snows and the fire and the steam, it's coming!"

Kiar was aghast. "I can't make a shield big enough to stop a landslide I can't even see! I can't! Nobody could, not with eidolons, not with the Logos!"

"We can," said Master Camerind. "We know how to work together to do such things." He paused, his eyes glittering.

"Then do it!" Tiana snapped, hanging onto Lisette as they were both bumped around. She hefted the two of them into the air and began to drift over to the veranda. "Kiar?"

Kiar crouched on the peak, closing her eyes, holding up her hand to forestall Tiana's rescue. She imagined the mountain as she'd seen it before and let the rumbling flow through her. Then she bit her lip. "No," she whispered. Then she stood up and flung herself at the veranda. "Go," she shouted at Twist. "Go! It won't touch us! He didn't aim it at us. He's targeting Lor Seleni! GO!"

CHAPTER THIRTY-SIX

DARKNESS

They'd gathered together after the phantasmagory disintegrated, into the Hall. Jerya sat in the big chair, wondering why she couldn't cry. Gisen was sobbing on Yevonne's shoulder. She was too young to see some things, really. Uncle Jant was blowing his nose. But he was an old man. He was allowed to grieve.

Seandri's eyes were red, and she smiled at him. She loved him for his sensitivity. He would capture her father's death in poetry later and maybe then she could let herself go, let herself sob against his chest. Maybe later. Now, everyone had to be shepherded through this. There was a Blighter to fight. There was a coronation to arrange and Vassay to face. There was so much to decide. But right now everybody grieved. It was what they needed. It was what it was time for. But she couldn't cry.

When the second earthquake came, stronger and longer than the one that had ended Antecession, she became afraid for her sister on the mountain. The bells in

Lor Seleni wouldn't stop ringing.

Then Twist appeared. He swallowed and said, "You have to cross the river." His voice was hoarse, as it was when he spent too much time with the Logos. "The mountain is erupting. A mudslide is going to cover the north side of the city, but the river might stop it. You have to go! Or get someplace very high and very strong!" He coughed. "There's maybe an hour."

Energy flooded Jerya's leaden limbs. She wasn't crying, and that was *good*. She understood the situation immediately. "Your skipping. Have you worked out how to carry others yet?" she asked Twist. He looked stricken and shook his head. "Not even the little girls? No? Then go, tell others. Do what you have to." He vanished.

Jerya clapped her hands. "It's time to go to Northbridge now."

Yithiere and the little girls were already leaving. Yithiere said, "I'll keep Iriss safe."

The others were slower. Jant was horrified. "I won't go! I can't leave the Palace. I'll stay in my rooms, thank you very much."

Quietly, Shanasee said, "Father."

"I'm too old to hurry!" Jant snapped.

Jerya studied Shanasee. Then she said, "Shan... an hour isn't enough time. I know what you did before. Against Benjen. How you held him down. Nobody but you had the strength."

The older woman met her gaze. She was trembling all over. "No! Didn't I do enough? Haven't I given enough?"

Jerya bit her lip until she tasted blood. Then, with exquisite, painful care, she said, "Darkness is coming. It will swallow the city. We will all be lost within it."

Shanasee twitched. Then she said, "No." She clutched at Cara beside her and then pushed her away. "Go."

Jerya turned her gaze onto Jant. "Seandri, take Jant and go. Carry him." She loved him because he didn't argue. Jant did, but when Seandri scooped him up, he only turned his dark eyes to Shanasee.

"Come with us, Shan, my darling."

In a liquid voice, Shanasee said, "How can he tell everybody? How can the bridges hold enough people? I have held a nightmare inside me for so long, Father. Cara! Take my painting."

Cara's expression was frustrated, bitter. She appealed silently to Jerya, who said, "We won't fail. Go. Don't make her worry for you." Something flared in Cara's eyes and then she fled.

Seandri bent to kiss Jerya on the cheek, over Jant. "I will worry. Leave soon. We need you."

He carried Jant away, the old man feebly pounding his shoulder, calling, "Dammit, leave me! I'm old!" Then it was just Shanasee and Jerya in the Hall. They faced each other. Shanasee's eyes were wide and frightened.

Jerya said, "It's our place to protect them." She almost hated herself.

Shanasee drew in a ragged breath. "I know."

Gingerly, Jerya took Shanasee's arm in her own, and together they walked to Starset Tower. She set a lamp on the table at the base of the stairs. "Darkness is coming, Shanasee," she repeated.

"I know!" Shanasee snapped. Then she gasped, "Please, stay with me, help me, I can't do this. Don't make me. Let the sleeping ones die. I can paint! Isn't that enough?"

And now, when it was least useful, tears welled up in Jerya's eyes. "I love you, Shan. Pell built this tower. You'll survive here. You can save so many and the darkness won't take you."

"But it will," she whispered. "I'll be lost in it. Stay with me."

Jerya hesitated, wondering if this terrible pain in her heart was why her father had eidolon twins. They *needed* her on the other side of the bridge. There would be chaos without a firm hand to restore order. Somebody had to keep Yithiere and Jant, without their Regents, stable. Somebody had to keep everybody calm.

"You don't know what it's like," Shanasee whispered.

The tears overflowed. Surely this was why her father had split himself. "Show me," she said and picked up the lamp again.

When the night turned to grey dawn, it broke on panicked people in the streets, fleeing to the south side of the river. Jerya and Shanasee sat in the tower, looking out the window. Beyond the city was a wall of darkness, held at bay by five flames. Each one was the size of Starset and danced like a candle flame. Was it five eidolons or one? Jerya couldn't tell. It'd only taken one to trap Benjen....

She held Shanasee's hand and hoped. She wondered if her sister was alive. As the grey turned to golden dawn, Shanasee said clearly, "I never thought it'd feel like this. Like mud." An eidolon flame flickered out. Another one died and another. The final two flared and bent towards each other, as the ooze crept around them. Then Shanasee slumped, the flames blinked out, and the flowing darkness swallowed the city.

Jerya sat in the silence after the roaring of rocks and

mud faded away and wondered what happened to her tears again. She sent a bird into the dawn to find her uncles. Then she wiped drool away from Shanasee's mouth and she waited.

Here ends Citadel of the Sky, *Book 1 of* The Thrones of the Firstborn *pentalogy*

DRAMATIS PERSONAE

The main of our story takes place in **LOR SELENI**, the heart of Ceria from which all strength springs forth.

THE ROYAL FAMILY

The following is an incomplete listing of The Scions of the Royal Blood, Protectors of Ceria and Wardens of the Holy Mount, in order of succession:

HIS ROYAL MAJESTY, KING SHONATHAN II, blessed with a perfect memory. Represented by a mirror.

HER ROYAL HIGHNESS, THE CROWN PRINCESS JERYA, his eldest daughter. Represented by a hawk.

HER SERENE HIGHNESS, THE PRINCESS TIANA, his younger daughter. Represented by lightning.

HIS HIGHNESS, PRINCE YITHIERE, younger brother of the King. Represented by a wolf.

HIS HIGHNESS, PRINCE CATHAY, the King's nephew. Represented by a hunting cat.

HER HIGHNESS, PRINCESS GISEN, the King's niece. Represented by a white horse.

HIS HIGHNESS, PRINCE JANT, uncle to the King. Represented by a fox.

HER HIGHNESS, PRINCESS SHANASEE, the King's cousin. Represented by a candleflame.

HIS HIGHNESS, PRINCE SEANDRI, the King's cousin. Represented by a red stag.

LADY KIAR SUAN, a natural daughter of the Royal Blood. Represented by a sword and shield.

THE REGENCY COURT

ANTECEDENTS AND COUNSELORS

The Regency Court manages the day to day life of the Royal Blood, among many other tasks.

HIS EXCELLENCY, CHANCELLOR BRYN HALE

HER LADYSHIP, IRISS BASCOMB, Regent to Princess Jerya

HER LADYSHIP, LISETTE CONRA, Regent to the Princess Tiana

LADY YEVONNE HUAR, Regent to Princess Gisen

HER LADYSHIP, CARA MISTONTE, Regent to Princess Shanasee

HIS LORDSHIP, HARTHEN BYERRES, Regent to Prince Seandri

HER HIGHNESS LADY JULINE INGAE, wife of Prince Jant and mother of Princess Shanasee

HIS HIGHNESS LORD JAIME EIRCEDE, widower of Princess Rinta and father of Princess Gisen

HER HIGHNESS LADY SIANA CALAIN, widow of Prince Pell and mother of Prince Cathay

HER MAJESTY, QUEEN ANNIS, dwelling at the Hypana Ducal Court

THE JUSTICIAR'S COURT

LAWMAKERS FROM THE SIX DUCHIES

THE JUSTICIAR'S COUNCIL

LORD TERRENCE AUBIN OF BORZEE, land of tumbled hills and crashing cliffs, along the western coast

LORD DONATIEN WICHARD OF KANURA, mountain land rising from the Telamic Sea

Lady Rosalyn Scott of Ardoza, fair southern land of wine and silk

Lord Millard Bellamont of Ingae, the richest farmland in all of Ceria

Lord Warrane Dunstan of Dalein, the northern orchards

Lord Jasper Gueran of Hypana, the forestlands farthest north

Keepers of the Flame of Faith

His Grace, Dorian III, Magister of the Citadel of the Sky

Gone But Not Forgotten

The Blood bastard, Benjen Black, great-uncle to the current King, who twice brought a Blight to Ceria and once saved it.

The first King, Shin Savanyel, given dominion over Ceria by the Firstborn

King Math III, Shonathan's elder brother, who died fighting Benjen

Prince Benjin, his infant son, kidnapped and murdered by Benjen Black at the start of his second Blight

Prince Pell, Shonathan's younger brother, an architect

Princess Rinta, Shonathan's younger sister, a librarian

Princess Viani, aunt of the current King, a famous beauty, and well-favored with the Royal magic.

Lord Tomas Ferya, the Crown Regent, recently departed in an upsetting way

Lord Zavien Eircede, a Regent for Prince Yithiere

Lord Geoseph Yarzee, a Regent for Prince Jant

Lord Sennic Ardoza, a Regent for Prince Cathay

Natina Suan, mother of Lady Kiar

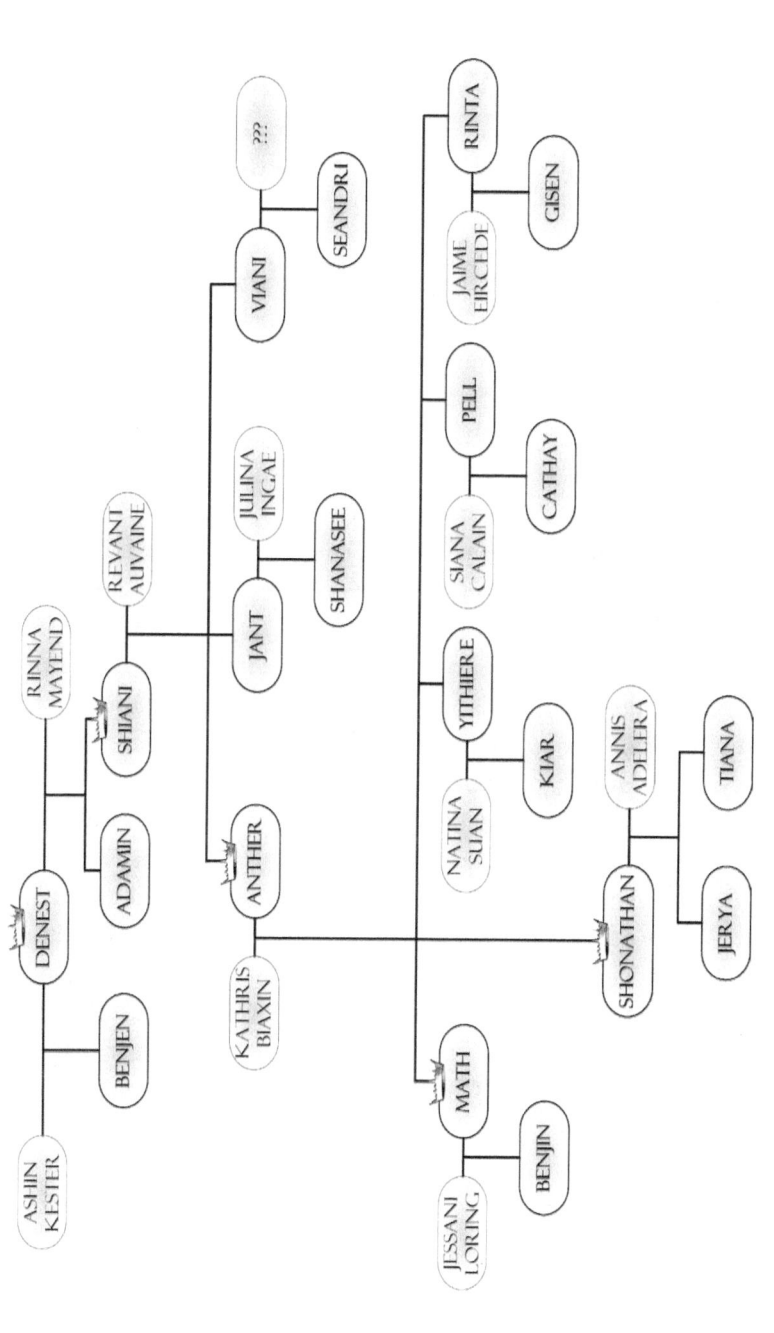

Acknowledgements

This book would not exist without the efforts and contributions of many, many people:

My wonderful editor who said "you don't need to list me" yet did most of the heavy lifting, and my husband, who did the rest. My cover artist, Ravven Kitsune.

As well: Cathy Maginn, Stacy and Neil Laughlin, Michelle Curtis, my little brother Nathan Fall, the marvelous Jason Rogers (phantom reviewer extraordinaire), Carl Rigney, Rachel Cotterill, Robin D. Owens, Leah Weaver, Robert Maughan, Karen, Sara Harville, Althea Clark, Catherine Sharp, Max Kaehn, Lori Lum, Kayla I.,Trip Space-Parasite, Dina S Willner, Christine Chen, Michael Brewer, Deborah Donoghue, Rick Saada, Ted Butler, Brian Fried, Don, Beth & Meghan Ferris, Beth aka Scifibookcat, Holly Tidd, TRS, Gunnar Högberg, Christopher Sarnowski, SwordFire, Noel Thingvall, Gretchen, Catie Murphy, Candice Bailey, Mikaela Lind, Patrick Reitz, Sarah Brown, April Steenburgh, Tom Ladegard, Angie Mathues, Camille R Lofters, Michael Stevens, Suzanne or Zanne, Helene Wecker, Franklin Nacobo Krause, Christie V. Howard, Kristina Zimmermann, Kalen "Zuki" Boley, Rachel Gollub, Jeff Jensen, Mayer Turkin, Robert Early, Tasha Turner Lennhoff, Paul Knappenberger, Sarah B, Katherine Malloy, Chad Bowden, Cesar Cesarotti, Kisha Delain, Kathleen T Hanrahan, along with other friends, Hadites, word warriors and anonymous supporters. And then there's Kay Perry who's in it for the fudge.

THRONES OF THE FIRSTBORN
CONTINUES IN

GREEN WILD